going on nine

A Novel

praise for going on nine

"Going on Nine chronicles a time of great change in America, as seen through the eyes of a young girl trying to make sense of her corner of the world. Charming, engaging, and bursting with colorful characters, this vivid novel will keep you reading long past your bedtime."

—Kelly O'Connor McNees, author of *The Lost Summer of Louisa May Alcott*, *In Need of a Good Wife*, and *The Island of Doves*

"Catherine paints a wonderful picture of the 1950s through the charm of Grace Mitchell's childhood. The wonder of this little girl is that she learns empathy for others through hard lessons. The language, attitudes, and news of the times speckled throughout the story make the era come alive."

—Genny Zak Kieley, author of
Green Stamps to Hot Pants: Growing up in the 50s & 60s

"Fitzpatrick's high-concept treatment of revisited childhood uses multiple neighborhood households and parallel voices, past and present, sending readers to a community of mid-20th century, Midwestern, middle-class life. It is both intimate as told though the eyes of an almost-nine-year-old girl in the Wise Child tradition of Scout in To Kill a Mockingbird, but also universal as its reach and powerful insights extend far beyond the confines of these neighbors homes. The humor, pathos, and genuinely interesting folks down the street make this an engaging read throughout."

—Whitney Scott, Publisher, Outrider Press

"I want my parents to come back to life and read Catherine Fitzpatrick's novel, Going on Nine. Better yet, I want them to have read it before I turned eight and knew for sure that all the other kids' families were nicer and less embarrassing. If my folks read through to the end, and I can't imagine anyone putting it down, they would know that I, like Grace Mitchell and a kabillion other kids, learned my lesson after all."

—Judy Bridges, founder of Redbird Studio,
A Writer's Place, and author of *Shut Up & Write!*

"A sweet coming of age story whose heroine confronts life's deepest mysteries with plenty of heart and not a small dose of pluck. Baby boomers will be enthralled, as I was, by Catherine Fitzpatrick's exquisite attention to detail that makes the summer of '56 come alive in the form of an eight-year-old adventuress named Grace Mitchell."

—Marcy Darin, editor,
Prisms of the Soul: Writings from a Sisterhood of Faith

"Only an incredible writer could have created such a heart-warming story, and unforgettable little heroine."

—Shellie Blumenfield,
Middle School teacher, Whitefish Bay (WI) School District

"In more than a decade as a licensed clinical psychologist specializing in relationship issues, women's and adolescent girls' issues, I've witnessed the devastating effects when socially aggressive school girls maintain their status by playing spiteful tricks. In a single powerful, authentic chapter, Catherine Underhill Fitzpatrick's coming-of-age novel shows how the cold-blooded games of a supposed 'friend' up the ante on cruelty, until a tragic twist of fate turns the aggressor into a victim."

—Dr. Erika Holiday, Psy.D, co-author of *Mean Girls, Mean Women*

"Going on Nine brings back those days of freedom for youngsters and the restrictions related to class and ethnicity. Not much diversity here on the surface . . . but in reality, tremendous differences among families, differences actually much deeper than race and class. I like the way (the author) illustrate(s) these differences."

—Jeanne Warren Lindsay,
author of *Sunflower Days: Growing Up In Kansas 1929*

"Grace's journey leads to the inevitable truth that things are not always as they seem. Reading Going on Nine, I found myself yearning for a simpler time when children played outside with abandon, and terrorism wasn't part of our vocabulary. Congratulations to Catherine Fitzpatrick on a precise portrayal of Grace and a tightly written remembrance (that) makes you want to click your heels and say, 'There's no place like home.'"

—Kathleen McElligott,
author of *Mommy Machine*, 2009 National Best Books Awards finalist

"Going on Nine brings out all that was special about Brentwood in those days. Every family had their own story, their own hardships, and they helped each other through joys and sorrows. In a lot of ways Brentwood is still that way, still has the cozy feel of a 'Mayberry' type atmosphere, where families have remained over the years, and stay active in the community. . . . It was a time when kids used their imaginations, played outside, and valued the friendships in the neighborhood."

—Dan Fitzgerald, president of the Brentwood (MO) Historical Society

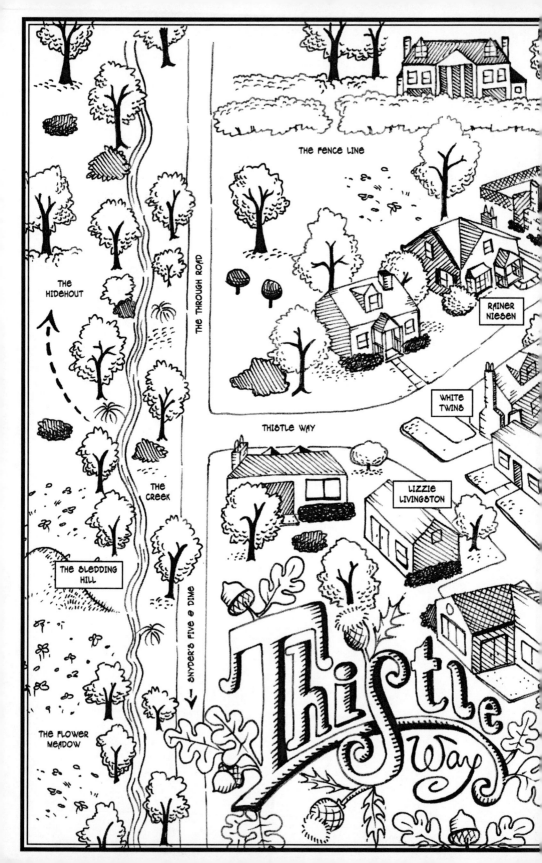

Published by Familius LLC, www.familius.com

Familius books are available at special discounts for bulk purchases for sales promotions, family or corporate use. Special editions, including personalized covers, excerpts of existing books, or books with corporate logos, can be created in large quantities for special needs. For more information, contact Premium Sales at 559-876-2170 or email specialmarkets@familius.com

Library of Congress Catalog-in-Publication Data

2013954817

pISBN 978-1-939629-12-8
eISBN 978-1-939629-14-2

Printed in the United States of America

Edited by Maggie Wickes
Cover design by David Miles
Book design by Maggie Wickes
Map illustration by David Miles

10 9 8 7 6 5 4 3 2 1

First Edition

table of contents

prologue xv

Grace: the deal 1

Davey: the tunnel 14

Dezso: the truck 32

Melinda: the popular girl 45

Carolyn: the catastrophe 57

Cherry: the cabin 59

the Blairs: the newcomers 71

Missy: sunshine time 74

Mrs. Pearson: the secrets 83

Charlie: the fever 97

Patsy: the show 105

Meegan: the white box 120

Benny: the bugle 127

the Zaldoni Boys: the trattoria 130

Rainer: the hideout 140

the Haverkamps: the planets 152

Cate: the queen 168

Mark and Sissy Eagan: the names 180

the Dailys: the shank end 183

Theresa: the dream 193

the Neighbors: the party 204

Odetta: the heat 215

the Mitchells: the end and the beginning 230

epilogue 238

discussion guide 256

For Dennis, again, always
and Claire and Meg, my best work

"Remembrance of things past is not necessarily the remembrance of things as they were."

—Marcel Proust

prologue

I am grieved to the bone.

Charlie's gone. My sweet little brother—a gentle, mellow soul dispatched to the hereafter one week ago by the ragings of a madman.

When a death is so shocking that every tick of the clock is a shiv plunged into living hearts left behind, when the here and now is unthinkable and the prospect of moving on buckles you, the past can bring a measure of comfort. And so I've been thinking about my childhood, trying to put into writing how it was during one extraordinary summer.

In June of 1956, I was eight years old, and aside from steering clear of the notorious Zaldoni brothers, I had not a care in the world. School vacation had just begun. Everyone I knew and loved drew breath, and the world held nothing but promise. That was more than fifty years ago, and yet everything that happened is clear as a bell, as if it were yesterday.

So. Where to begin? With the bells, I think. Even after half a century, I hear them still.

Among the obligations for which I was held accountable as a child was the ability to discern between the sounds of all the bells I could ignore and the one bell I must heed. Early on, I calculated how long I could safely ignore the bell I was to never ignore. The algorithm was simple. After I heard Mom ring her old bell and before I dawdled home for dinner, I could flip six more baseball cards against a wall with Davey Lofton or pop eight more tar bubbles with Melinda Potter. I could shore up the wall of a plundered fort with Janice Haverkamp, add three flowers to a clover-chain necklace with my sister, or scoop two tadpoles into a mayonnaise jar with Rainer Niesen.

Our family lived in a white brick house in suburban St. Louis, in a neighborhood filled to overflowing with children. My friends and I had a thousand ways to fill a summer day. Released from the obligations and rote recitations of school, we entertained ourselves for long stretches of time with rudimentary equipment and minimal supervision. We nailed boards to fissured oak trees, constructing ramshackle platforms that accorded us bird's-eye views. We spread blankets in the shade and brought out cookies and jugs of iced lemonade. We knelt on bald dirt by the fence lines, shoveling Missouri clay into mountains, valleys, and winding canals. We played tag and hide-and-seek across eight back yards, hopscotch on driveways, and kickball in the street. We crawled through garage windows and helped ourselves to Popsicles out of chest freezers humming in musty darkness. We made pilgrimages to Snyder's Five & Dime to swipe root beer barrels from open boxes Mr. Snyder situated conveniently near the door so our petty thievery would not disrupt the paying customers. We were scabby and sweaty, chigger-bit at the waist, and mosquito-bit everywhere else. We didn't care. It was summer.

In the late afternoon, parents stood on front stoops and rang, clanged, chimed, and whistled us home for dinner. Each child recognized his or her distinct summons—the sound that meant a meatloaf was nicely brown and crusty or a tuna noodle casserole was bubbling under a topping of crumbled chips.

Mrs. Pearson rang the earliest bell. At 5 o'clock on the dot, she clanged an old school bell until her wattled arm trembled, which wasn't long. She had never been blessed with children of her own, but having taught school for forty years, she knew that children require ample time to stop doing what they want to do and start doing what they have to do. She rang her bell as fair warning that other bells would soon follow.

The Lofton's bell was next. Lieutenant Lofton lowered a pristine American flag from a pole in his front yard and then rang a nautical bell— ting-ting, ting-ting—as if marking a sailor's watch at sea. The lieutenant kept a shine on the brass so the words he'd had engraved there were clear:

In Memory of the USS Indianapolis

Mr. and Mrs. Daily carried out two TV tray tables on which they had arranged a set of graduated hand bells. After slipping their fingers into white cotton gloves, they each picked up two bells and held them upright. Then Mr. Daily stretched his arm forward and made a single, circular motion, producing the first note in a crystalline pealing that resonated across the neighborhood.

Mrs. Potter jingled a thick leather strap studded with sleigh bells, which sounded as merry in July as they did in December.

Our bell was a square-shaped cowbell with a rusty clapper. Every time Luca and Antony Zaldoni heard it, they fell down laughing. I was mortified, but I could see their point. The bell broadcast a dull, hollow clanking that sounded as if a heifer were plodding through a pasture gate. Mom didn't give a thought to my humiliations; she'd found that cowbell when she was a girl, and it remained one of her prized possessions.

Not all the bells of Thistle Way were bells.

Mrs. Finnegan played "Danny Boy" on a tin whistle. She was a fun-loving woman, and sometimes she danced a little jig.

Mrs. Warfield dreamed of studying at the Julliard School in New York City, but life sometimes interferes with dreams, and so she wound up in the suburbs of St. Louis with a husband and a baby, and she was not at all unhappy. Each evening at suppertime, Mrs. Warfield waited on her porch for the neighbors' dissonant chimings and clankings to fall silent. Then, with a bit of fanfare, she raised a metal triangle and struck it with a slender rod, sending out a score of staccato plinks. It was her nightly concerto.

Mrs. Zaldoni lumbered out from her kitchen with a rolling gait, whacked the bottom of a pasta pot with a wooden spoon, and lumbered back again. The aroma of Bolognese sauce accompanied her at all times.

Detective Greeley blew a long, earsplitting note on a policeman's whistle that sent Bullet, his dog, into paroxysms of misery.

Up at Snyder's Five & Dime, Mr. Snyder always rang the final bell of the day. Fifteen minutes before closing time, the balding little man pulled the chains of a shopkeeper bell mounted just outside his store. Mr. Snyder believed that children who might wish a late-day candy purchase—a ribbon of dots or a Baby Ruth bar—had a right to know they must hurry.

From the morning of my eighth birthday, I regarded myself as going on nine. By then, I had long since melded into the loose confederation of children who were essentially feral from apricot dawn to lavender dusk. Our world was Thistle Way, a neighborhood of twenty-eight modest houses that faced one another in a circle. There were forty-seven kids in the circle that summer, counting the babies. I could name every single one. I knew every member of every family.

Or so I thought.

Grace

the deal

Each child is a dazzling universe unto itself, unique, bursting with promise. Yet within a given year, most girls and boys fulfill a predictable set of expectations meticulously calibrated by people who devote themselves to analyzing childhood development.

According to the experts, a girl who is eight years old knows what she likes and what she doesn't like. She speaks her mind, if only to try out how it sounds. Paradoxically, she's beginning to recognize the benefit of concealing her emotions. She wants to know the "why" of things. She takes pride in solving her own problems, sometimes creatively. She makes up elaborate fantasy games.

More and more influenced by peer pressure, she needs to feel as if she's part of a group. She is emerging as either a leader or a follower. She is short on patience and long on melodrama. One minute she's cheerful and eager to please, the next minute she's rude, bossy, or pouty. She has an urgent and abiding need for love, especially from her mother. Above all, she's trying to figure out exactly who she is and how she fits into the world.

As I recall, at eight, going on nine, I conformed to the paradigm quite well. Here, let me show you. . . .

———————————— ᛞᛞᛞ ————————————

I wish I was Sally Daily.

Sally's got the best mom and dad in the whole world. She's got her own bedroom too, and plastic palomino horse statues, and a humongous collection of dolls that takes up half the basement, which her mom and dad don't even mind.

The next best thing to being Sally Daily is playing at her house, which I do lots. Mrs. Daily says, "Grace, I think I'm your second mother." I like that.

This morning, Sally and me are spreading out a kabillion dolls on a blanket in her yard. One doll has long blonde hair that you can make into different hairdos. We play a long time and then, right when my stomach is starving, Mrs. Daily calls out, "Girls, are you hungry for lunch?"

Mrs. Daily doesn't just hand you a dumb old apple. She cuts it into slices and sprinkles cinnamon on it. She calls it a dusting of happiness. And she doesn't just slap together a peanut butter sandwich and give it to you whole. She cuts off the crusts.

Sally carries the tray out to the blanket, and I carry the Thermos bottle. "Is it milk?"

"Nope, lemonade!"

For the kabillionth time, I wish Mrs. Daily was my mom.

"Look what else my mom gave us," Sally says.

She opens a small sack and pulls out tiny silk flower bouquets, bobby pins with diamondy things stuck on them, and a bunch of lace scraps. Sally goes right to work; she says she's making a bride veil. I wash down one of the sandwiches with a glug of lemonade and start on a veil too.

I'm almost finished when I hear Mom clanging her danged cow bell. For some reason, Mom's started taking naps in the afternoon with Charlie, my little brother, and I have to trudge home cuz Mom doesn't want me gallivanting all over Thistle Way while she sleeps, which is stupid cuz I gallivant all over Thistle Way while she's awake.

The whole way, I scuff the toes of my Keds on purpose. By the time I get to our house, Mom and Charlie are conked out on the sofa. My sister Jane's out back, flopped on the hammock, reading. That's Jane's favorite thing. She says reading gives one a scintillating vocabulary, and one can enjoy a good book even in the stupefying inertia caused by ninety-three degrees of heat and ninety-three percent humidity. Jane's always using big words.

A week ago, right after school let out for the summer, Jane checked out three books at the library, and already she's down to the last one, *The*

Ghost in the Gallery. Jane's nutso about mystery stories, especially the Dana Girls.

I pick some dandelions and stick them in a Welch's grape jelly jar and put it on the kitchen windowsill. Then I go back out and look for acorns the squirrels missed last fall. There's no good ones though, ones that still have their caps so they look cute when you paint faces on them. I tiptoe over to the hammock and start to tip it, but Jane sees me and thwaps me in the face with her stupid book, and I get a gol-durn bloody nose.

"You'll be sorry!" I shout.

"No, you'll be sorry! You started it so you should be the penitent one."

The penny tent one? What the heck does that mean?

Back in the house, I press a wet towel to my nose. I wish Mom would wake up and feel sorry for me and get mad at stupid Jane, but she doesn't. I think about how maybe I can play bride doll at my house. I don't have half the dolls Sally does, and most of mine are kinda wrecked. I lost the key to Wanda the Walking Wonder Doll so I can't wind her up and make her walk anymore. Also, her eyes don't open unless you pry them with your fingernail. And Charlie ripped the hair off my Mary Jane doll and got teeth marks all over her nose, so she's no good as a bride. Last Christmas, I asked for the new Hollywood Bride doll. Hollywood Bride would have been perfect, but Santa brought Cuddle Bun instead.

Shazaam! I know who can be the bride—me!

I dredge out my First Holy Communion dress from the closet under the stairs. The dress is white and fluffy like a bride dress, but it's gotten sorta dinky. Maybe it shrank in the wash. I step into the dress like Mom showed me, but the dang dress won't go up all the way, so I try putting it on over my head. I get part of my arm poked through, and then I'm stuck. Stuck and suffocating and buried in fluffy flounces of First Holy Communion dress. I yank off the dress real fast, which makes some sharp, ripping sounds, but that's okay.

I'm disappointed about not having a good bride dress. Then I remember Jane's got a new nightgown, and it's white and lacy and kinda bride-y. I tiptoe upstairs, hopping over the third and fourth step from the bottom cuz they creak. I sneak into the bedroom Jane and me share with Charlie, and I get the nightgown.

Great! Now all I need is a groom and a wedding ring.

The groom part's gonna be a problem. I could ask Davey Lofton— he lives next door. Davey's usually working on one of his contraptions, though. I could ask Benny Herman. Nah, Benny's fat. The Zaldoni boys would laugh me off the face of the earth, and Rainer Niesen's always swimming at his dumb country club. Rainer's the only kid on Thistle Way that gets to go swimming this summer. He says the lifeguards told him that polio doesn't get into country club swimming pools, just the public pools.

If I can't have a groom then I'm gonna have a ring. I know just where to get one too.

Mom keeps her good jewelry in a velvet pouch on a high shelf in her closet. The bedroom door's open. I go to the stair landing and peek down into the living room. Mom's still conked out on the sofa, and Charlie's curled up next to her. His wispy hair's all sweaty. A trickle of drool is leaking out the side of his mouth. Charlie's pretty darn cute, I'll tell you that. His cheeks are always pink and soft as flower petals. Anyways, Odetta—she's our maid—taught Mom a good trick. She told Mom to tie one end of a ribbon around Charlie's ankle and the other end around Mom's wrist. That way, if Charlie wakes up and tries to crawl away, Mom'll know.

Back in Mom and Dad's bedroom, I stand on tiptoes and pull down the velvet pouch. There's a bunch of jewelry in it, but I only want Mom's engagement ring. I slip it on my finger, but it's so big that the diamond part slides around to the bottom. I twirl the diamond back to the top and make a fist so it stays that way.

When I reach up to put the pouch back, some jewelry stuff falls out. That's okay, I'll put it back later, after I finish playing bride.

Outside, I decide the patio will be my wedding chapel. And I pretend the aisle I have to walk down goes all the way around the whole back-yard. I start at the mock orange bushes back by the lot line. Then I walk slowly around Charlie's wading pool and around the swing set. I hop across Charlie's sandbox, duck through sheets on the clothes line, and tightrope-walk along the flat bricks outlining Mom's flower bed. While I'm there, I pick a few zinnias for a bouquet.

I'm almost to Dad's chimney barbecue pit when I notice Davey Lofton's outside too. I toss the flowers away and climb on the crossed-board fence between our backyard and the Loftons'.

"Whatcha doin'?"

Davey looks up and squints one eye. "What the heck are you wearin'?"

"Shut up. I'm a bride."

"Well, c'mon over."

I throw one leg over the top of the fence and snag Jane's nightgown on a splinter. That's okay, I can fix it later. Wow, I see Davey's built a bridge over one of the basement window wells, and now he's filling the window well with hose water. I'm kneeling right next to him, watching the window well fill up, when Mom clangs her cowbell again. She's standing at the back door, holding Charlie on her hip. Charlie's squalling like he does when Jane or me puts on a clean diaper and accidentally sticks him with the pin, and Jane's back there too, screaming her lungs out.

What the heck?

"Grace Mitchell, you get back here right now!" Mom sounds mad.

I slink around to the front door. My plan is to get Jane's nightgown back in the bedroom chiffarobe before she sees me, but I forget to hop over the stupid third and fourth stair steps, so they creak. Mom and Jane come running.

Caught!

Mom marches me into the living room. I turn around once to see if there's smoke coming out of her ears. She plops Charlie down on the floor, which usually is okay cuz his diaper is kinda like a pillow, but this time he falls over sideways right when Jane is tramping into the living room like a raging bull. Jane stumbles over Charlie and goes kerplop onto the rug, with Charlie kinda wedged between her knee and her elbow. Right about then, a garbage truck rumbles up the driveway, the Vegetable Man rings the back doorbell, the telephone in the hall niche jangles, Mom starts yelling, Jane bursts into tears, and Charlie goes into orbit.

There's different kinds of spankings, every kid knows that. There's the kind a mom gives, which is a swat on the behind with her hand. It catches you by surprise, even when you know it's coming, but it doesn't hurt much. There's the kind a dad gives, which is you bend over, and he swats your behind with a rolled up *Saturday Evening Post* or *National Geographic*. It hurts more than Mom's swats. There's something called a stropping, which Sister Josephina told us about. She said orphans who lived in orphanages back in England a long time ago got spankings with a strop if they asked for more oatmeal, and it really hurt cuz the orphans only had thin rags to wear, and they were always starving and had no parents to love them.

The worst spankings are called a strapping. That's what Davey Lofton gets when his inventions and projects don't turn out so well. Lt. Lofton unbuckles his belt and whips it out of the belt loops. He makes Davey kneel down in front of a chair or couch and pull down his pants. While Davey's waiting for his punishment, Lt. Lofton folds the belt in two and snaps it together, and the sound is really scary. Lt. Lofton gives Davey six hard whacks on his bare bottom with the belt, and he makes Davey count. Sometimes the metal buckle gets in the way, and that part hits Davey too.

One time, Davey lifted up his shirt and lowered his shorts a little bit to show me the red marks and bruises. We were both quiet for a minute, and then I told him, "Holy cow, Davey, you sure are brave."

It was all I could think of to say.

The first words out of Mom's mouth are about what I'm expecting.

"Where is my ring, Grace?"

Uh-oh.

"I found my good brooch on the closet floor. My earrings were in my shoes. And my diamond ring, the ring your father gave me the day we got engaged, the ring is missing."

Yep, there's practically smoke coming out of Mom's ears.

I hold out my hand and spread the fingers. The ring's gone! I must've dropped it. That ring could be anywhere. Somewhere out on the patio, slipped in between the bricks. Or way out by the bushes. It could be buried in the sandbox or lost in the flower garden. Heck, it could be over at Davey's, maybe even in the window well with all the spiders and mucky leaves and icky hose water.

I think I'm gonna throw up.

"—and don't try telling me you have to throw up, Grace. You've used that once too often, young lady."

"I was just playing bride, like Sally and me do at her house," I say, kinda sniffling. "I didn't have a gown or a ring so—"

"Don't say another word. Just tell me where you hid the ring."

Jane's giving me her you're-gonna-get-killed look. I've gotta tell Mom the worst part, which is I didn't hide her diamond ring. I lost it. I go all blubbery and snotty, and Mom gets the drift.

"Go to your room and stay there until your father gets home."

Jane clomps up the stairs, right up behind me.

"Mom's gonna wash my nightgown and sew the hole you made in it," she says. "But you're in the biggest trouble of your life about that ring. I wouldn't doubt it if you get a hundred spankings and no allowance for a year. How could you do such an imbecilic thing?"

"I don't know." I rub my eyes with my fists. "I just wanted to play bride."

Jane flounces off. She makes sure to close the door quietly behind her, which means she feels sorry for me, which means I'm gonna get killed when Dad gets home.

I always get blamed for everything, even when the thing isn't my fault. Like last Christmas when Charlie batted the green pickle ornament off the Christmas tree and it fell on the floor and broke and Mom thought I did it, and she sent me to my room for the whole afternoon. And the time Jane and me traded dishwashing days and then Jane just waltzed off and didn't do the dishes, and Mom and Dad made me do the dishes all by myself for a whole week. And last year at school when Marty Throckmorten poured a whole bottle of bubble bath down the drinking fountain drain, and each time a kid took a drink, bubbles poured up like crazy and spilled out onto the hall floor. Marty told Sister Josephina it was me who played the trick, and Sister Josephina said she was as sad as can be, and then she took me to the principal's office, and Sister Eustace made me stay a whole extra fifteen minutes after the last bell and stand in the hall, facing the drinking fountain and silently meditating on something she called the evils of school sandalism, which didn't make sense cuz sandals aren't evil.

Heck, it's not my fault the stupid ring wouldn't stay on my finger. It's the ring's fault. I hate Mom. I hate Dad, and Jane too. I hate Charlie's poopy wet diapers and stinky diaper pail stinking up our bathroom all the time. I hate our whole family, and I hate living here. I'm gonna run away from home. I'm gonna go way far away and never come back. Then they'll be sorry.

I dig around in the back of my closet and haul out the plaid suitcase I use when Jane and me spend the night with Grandma and Grandpa. I think hard about what to pack cuz the suitcase won't hold all my stuff.

Besides, I hate most of my stuff. Just about everything I wear is a hand-me-down. The minute Jane outgrows her school uniform or her feet get too big for her shoes, they go down to me. Even if the uniform blouse has stains on the pits or the shoes have stretched-out buckle holes. Jane's the oldest and Charlie's a boy; they get everything new.

I have the meanest parents in the world. Mom doesn't even buy good vitamins. No-o-o. Every morning, we have to take stupid old vitamin drops that taste like rusty swing set chains. And we never have Kleenex. If we blow our nose, we have to use two squares of toilet paper. And we never got suntan lotion, even back before polio when we could go to real swimming pools. Every other kid at the pool smelled good, like Coppertone, but me and Jane smelled like nothing.

I don't get it. Grandma and Grandpa Reinhardt are rich, so why can't they give Mom some of their money?

I asked Dad about that once.

"Your mother and I are frugal by choice," he says. "Your mother had lots of money when she was a little girl, lots of pretty dresses and toys and dolls. She even had a pony that she kept at a stable out in the country, which is where she found that old cowbell she loves so much. But what she really wanted was brothers and sisters, and she didn't get any. When she grew up, she wanted a house filled with children, and so did I."

"Our house is filled with children."

"Your mother and I love you and Jane and Charlie so much, we'd like some more."

"More?"

"Let me explain something to you, Grace. I think you're old enough to understand. When I married your mom, I was working at Monsanto, just like I do now. I like it there, and when Grandpa Reinhardt offered me a big job at his department store, I turned it down. That hurt your grandpa's pride, and he never forgot it. And I never forgot that he quietly held it against me. So your mom and I and you and Jane and Charlie get by on my salary from Monsanto without handouts from your grandpa. And we get by pretty darn well, I'd say."

I decided to not ask Dad any more questions about stuff we can't afford.

I toss some clean socks and underwear and shorts and tops into the suitcase. Also my coloring book and crayons. And Cuddle Bun, a towel, and the medal Sister Josephina gave me at the end of third grade for exemplary behavior in the cafeteria line. At the last minute, I toss in Arf-Arf, my little china dog.

Dad won't be home for another hour. Mom and Jane and Charlie are crawling around the backyard, looking for Mom's ring. Well, I'm pretty sure Charlie's just crawling for the heck of it.

I start out running lickety split, but by the time I get to the entrance of Thistle Way, I'm out of breath, plus I've got a stitch in my side. I could go to the hideout me and Rainer Niesen found. It's down the creek and surrounded by cattails and weeping willow branches. It'd be a perfect place to live, except Rainer knows where it is. He might tell. Probably not, but you never know.

Instead, I jump across the creek and lug my suitcase up the sledding hill, which is not as hard in summer as lugging a sled up in winter and dodging Zaldoni boys whizzing down, aiming straight at you. At the top is a big field with lots of Queen Anne's lace. Beyond that is a neighborhood, but I've never gone that far.

I spread my towel on the grass behind one of the trees in the field and sit cross-legged.

It's quiet here.

I wonder if there's snakes around.

It's really hot.

I wish I'd brought a book.

A mosquito lands on my arm, and I swat it to death and wipe off the mosquito guts with a corner of the towel. I wonder if Mom knows I'm gone.

I open my suitcase and take out my coloring book and color a picture of a castle. I go really slow, and it's the best picture I've ever colored. Jane's probably telling Mom right now that I'm not in the bedroom.

Coloring's boring. I wish I'd brought my paper dolls.

I lay on my back and watch the clouds. I wish I'd brought a Thermos of lemonade.

I take Arf-Arf out and pretend he's a firehouse dog and there's a big fire in that far neighborhood and none of the firemen can get in the house so they send Arf-Arf in, and he comes out holding the baby in his teeth. The baby's not hurt cuz Arf-Arf just holds the baby's undershirt.

Mom's probably bawling her eyes out right now. I'll bet she's sorry about yelling at me so hard.

Why the heck didn't I bring water? And I'm starving to death. Maybe this field's got nuts and berries. In a little while, I'm gonna go gathering. Then I'm gonna build a house so it blends in perfectly with the field. Nobody's ever gonna find me.

I lay down on the towel next to Cuddle Bun. Nobody'll see if I suck my thumb, so I do.

Dad's probably home by now. I'll bet he's mad at Mom and Jane that they made me run away from home.

It's hot. I'm just gonna close my eyes and . . .

Holy cow! I must've fallen asleep. It's almost dark out. Where am I? Mom should've rung the cowbell for dinner by now. I'm starved.

Wait, who's that? Cripes, it's a policeman! He's coming across the field!

"Grace? It's time to go home. Are you all right?" He bends over with his hands on his knees. "Did anybody hurt you today?"

I'm scared the policeman's gonna put me in jail for stealing my mom's ring, so I just make a high whiny sound, like when you blow up a balloon and pinch the top and the air goes out real slow. The policeman takes off his cap and wipes around the inside with a handkerchief. I hear the walkie-talkie radio crackling in his police car.

"Let's pack up your things and get you home again," he says. "There's some folks on Thistle Way worried about you."

By the time we get to my house, I'm feeling better cuz I don't have to go to jail.

The policeman comes around to my side of the car. He leans over and crosses his arms on the window opening. "I won't lie to you, Grace. You're in big trouble. Just tough it out, kiddo. You've got a swell family in there. They love you more than you know. Next time there's some sort of brouhaha, don't run away from it. That's no solution."

Mom's running down the driveway with her arms stretched wide. Dad's right behind her. Jane's on the front porch, holding Charlie. They're all smiling. Hey, maybe I'm not in trouble after all.

Mom hugs me so hard my legs are dangling. We twirl and twirl and then Dad picks me up like a baby and carries me up to the house. Behind me, I hear Mom crying and thanking the policeman and crying some more.

Me and Dad sit at the kitchen table while Mom makes me two peanut butter and jelly sandwiches and a glass of milk.

"There's pie, too," Mom says.

Jane's standing in the doorway, just waiting for Mom and Dad to stop being all relieved and lovey and get to the punishment part. I stick out my tongue at her, which makes Mom and Dad notice she's there.

"Jane, take Charlie up to bed," Dad says. "The fireworks are over for tonight."

The whole time I'm eating my sandwiches, Mom and Dad are asking me a ton of questions. Did anybody come near me? Did I go into a stranger's house? Did I go any farther than the field where the policeman found me?

Finally, Dad says, "Honey, what were you thinking? Did you intend to come back?"

"I don't know."

Mom butts in. "Well I do—"

Dad shoots Mom a look, and she turns to the sink. I keep scraping the pie plate with the edge of my fork. Dad takes hold of my hand, and I stop.

"Do you have anything to say to your mother?"

"I don't know."

"Grace, you need to apologize to your mother."

I say "sorry" real fast, cuz I'm not sorry. Mom's the one who clanged her stupid cow bell and made me come home from Sally's. All I did was borrow a stupid ring so I could play bride. Mom's the one with the big fingers, not me. It's not my fault, none of it, not even Jane's stupid nightgown getting ripped. That's the stupid fence's fault.

Mom gives me a sour look. "It doesn't sound like you're one bit sorry."

I'm the poor kid who had to spend the whole dang afternoon sweltering in the middle of a poison ivy snake field. I'm the kid who almost died of hunger and thirst and mosquito bites out there. I'm the kid who almost got kidnapped by strangers.

"I'm not sorry! You're the ones who should be saying sorry, not me. I hate you! You're the worst family in the whole world! There's lots of ones much, much better. Why'd I have to get stuck with this family?"

Mom goes all white. Dad leans back in his chair. It's so quiet I hear the clock on the kitchen stove ticking and the tube light above the sink humming and June bugs batting at the screen, trying to get in.

Mom looks like she's gonna holler. Instead, her eyes get all teary. Dad puts his arm around her waist.

"Your mother and I are going to take a little walk outside," he says. "Grace, you stay at this table. We won't be long."

They take forever. Finally, I hear them walking up the drive.

Dad starts. "There's no excuse for taking your mother's ring without her permission, Grace. Jane found it, by the way. It was in the sandbox."

Whew. I was afraid it was at the bottom of Davey's flooded window well.

"There's also no excuse for taking your sister's nightgown, is there?"

Yeah, I needed it to play bride. "I guess not."

"You guess right," Mom says. She's still kinda scowling. "For the next month, one-half of your allowance will go to Jane. Is that clear?"

Dad folds his arms across his chest. "Grace, your mother and I have discussed your opinion of our family. Although we don't agree, not one iota, we think you have a right to your own viewpoint."

I do?

"Your behavior and your attitude are hurtful to all of us, but mostly to your mother. That's why I left your punishment up to Mom."

Great. Now I'm gonna get it ten times worse.

"Stop scowling, Grace," Mom says. "You're going to get exactly what you want."

Huh?

"You think you got stuck with a terrible family? You think there are plenty of families better than ours? Fine, Grace. Fine. We'll put your theory to the test."

I'm not sure where this is going.

"Here's the deal: for the next three months, you can stay with any family on Thistle Way—or all of them, if they'll have you. Do you understand?"

"I think so."

"You can choose the families, but only a night or two at each house."

"Okay."

So, I'm not getting a spanking?

"It's a test, Grace. An experiment. At the end of the summer, you'll know what other families are like, what they're really like on the inside. We've got great neighbors, but I think you're going to find out that the place you want to be is right here at home."

A whole summer of sleepovers with my pals! My stomach's getting shivery just thinking about it. I don't want Mom and Dad to think I'm too happy, though. They might change their mind.

You could say I grew up in heaven, and you wouldn't be far wrong.

I was born in a time of peace and burgeoning prosperity, carried home to a small brick house planted in solid Missouri soil, a middle child united with siblings by genetic similarity, common experience, and the fact that no alternative to being united was readily apparent. My mother and father loved one another, and they loved us.

Our yard was shaded by fifty-year-old oak trees skirted in English ivy. In spring, my friends and I made bouquets out of forsythia sprigs. In fall, we raked leaves into great, rustling piles and then ran up and jumped in them again and again until somebody's dad reassembled the tatters. The piquant scent of burning leaves perfumed the autumns of my childhood.

Up the street was a candy store. Off a ways was a creek that froze in winter, ran swift in spring, and trickled along in summer, speckled with tadpoles. On any given day, at any given hour, I had somebody to play with.

The setting was idyllic, the times golden. You could say that, and you wouldn't be far wrong.

You wouldn't be absolutely correct either.

It was more than fifty years ago, the afternoon I ran away from home, fell asleep in a flowered meadow, and returned in a squad car to face the music. That night, I slept in my own bed, slept like a baby on linens infused with the familiar scent of home, on a pillow that conformed to the planes and knobs of my head. I closed my eyes alongside my older sister in a room with chenille coverlets and pastel wallpaper, with deep closets for games of hide and seek, and with Venetian blinds our parents angled for skyline views so that we, their beloveds, drifted off with stars in our eyes.

I went to sleep happy and expectant for all the wrong reasons.

Davey

the tunnel

By the summer of 1956, Davey Lofton had dredged, drained, and diverted just about every waterway within roaming distance of Thistle Way, including one or two downspouts. I think the kid was part North American beaver. When he wasn't digging for China, Davey was repurposing boring objects into fantastic gizmos, some of which actually worked.

I was certain Davey Lofton would grow up to be famous, like the Wright Brothers or Thomas Edison, a brilliant inventor who, despite countless failures and mishaps, would finally dream up something that changed the world.

There were so many things I was sure of, back then.

My dumb mom just loves to dole out chores. Every Saturday I have to wash all the breakfast dishes for the whole dang family. I used to not rinse the juice glasses and just dry them soapy and put them away, but one time Charlie threw up his whole breakfast, so now I rinse Charlie's glass.

In summer, I like to look out the window while I'm scrubbing the pancake skillet. I like to remember what it was like when it isn't so gol-durn hot. This morning I'm remembering the day last winter when Davey Lofton built the world's first North Pole Electrified and Illuminated Sleigh Machine. It was right before Christmas. The wind was blowing crackly leaves around in circles and the air smelled dry, like any minute it was gonna snow.

After I finished my arithmetic homework, I blew on the dining room window and wrote my name on the fogged glass. That's when I saw Davey. He lives next door. His garage door was open, and I could see he was decorating his Hopalong Cassidy bike with Christmas lights in there. I pulled on my galoshes and coat. By the time I got to Davey's garage, he'd wrapped strands of colored lights around the handlebars, wheel spokes and fenders—even the basket.

"Whatcha doin'?"

Davey didn't look up. He just crinkled his eyebrows and pushed his bangs out of the way, which never works cuz they always flop right back down over his eyes.

I'd left my mittens back at home, and my fingers were already numb. I was thinking about going home in a huff to teach Davey a lesson, when he looked up.

"Just about done, Grace. Wait till you see it. This thing's gonna be super duper!"

Davey plugged the last strand of lights into a black extension cord. Then he lugged the other end of the extension cord to an electrical outlet box on the garage wall.

"Observe, one and all," he shouted, "the world's first North Pole Electrified and Illuminated Sleigh Machine!"

I backed up. Davey Lofton combined with electricity was pretty goldurn scary.

As soon as Davey plugged the extension cord into the outlet, all the holiday lights switched on. Oh, it was beee-u-tee-ful! Davey's bike was so bright I had to squint to look at it. The whole inside of the garage was bright as day. Even the zipper on Davey's jacket flashed like when you wave a mirror at the sun. Everything was a new color. The blade of Lt. Lofton's snow shovel was half silver, half blue. The hammers and screwdrivers on the work bench were rosy red, and Mrs. Lofton's watering can was the same color as the lilacs out back by the Lofton's fence line.

"Shazaam!" Davey cried.

"Holy cow, Davey!"

Davey got on his bike. Pretty soon he was pedaling slow circles around the inside of the garage.

I jumped up and down, clapping and shouting, "Ho, ho, ho!" Every "ho" sent a little puff of white breath out into the air.

By then it was getting dark, and sleet was falling. It felt like ice needles were prickling my cheeks. I shuffled my feet to test whether the driveway was slick, and it was, so I pretended to be an ice skater, sliding in circles. Davey stopped to watch. I think he figured it was funny, an ice skater wearing red rubber boots. A few other kids were watching by then, but staying off a ways. Everybody knows Davey's contraptions sometimes don't work out too good.

Davey pushed off again, hard this time. I ran in front of the bike and sang "Rudolph the Red-Nosed Reindeer" at the top of my lungs. Davey belted out "Jingle Bells." We were the happiest kids ever. I was sure that if we shouted Christmas carols loud enough, none of us would hear the bells I knew would be ringing any minute—not me or Davey or the kids watching from the street. First, Mrs. Pearson's school bell. Then, Mrs. Finnegan's tin whistle. Mrs. Warfield's triangle and, later, Lt. Lofton's boat bell and Mom's stupid cow bell. If we just sang loud enough, I figured, nobody'd have to go home for dinner.

Davey got real excited, which he always does, and he made a huge-o-mongous mistake: he started to zoom down the driveway. That made the extension cord stretch to its limit. And back in the garage, that made the plug twist sideways in the socket. I backed up even more. When the kids in the street saw me, they ran home, even the kids whose bells hadn't rung yet.

Davey was halfway to the street when the cord snapped. All of a sudden, his bike stopped, but Davey kept going forward, headfirst over the han-dlebars. After he splatted down onto the icy driveway, he rolled on his back and slid all the way to the street. He looked pretty funny with his legs and arms swishing around in the air, kinda like when Melinda Potter's little pet turtle with the palm tree painted on its shell accidentally flipped itself upside-down. That was before Melinda's turtle mysteriously died. Anyways, Davey's bike skidded down the driveway too, and lots of the Christmas lights snagged on cracks in the concrete and broke to pieces.

I stumbled down the drive in case Davey needed me to save his life or anything.

"You okay?" I cried.

Davey just curled in a ball and waved me away.

The sleet was coming down harder, and it was getting kinda dark. I scrabbled up the drive on my hands and knees, climbed over the fence, and skedaddled home. Jane was right at the back door; she told me she'd watched the whole thing from our living room window and that the front tire of Davey's bike was crumpled, and the seat broke clean off. She said when Davey walked the bike back up his driveway, it was dragging strands of Christmas lights that clacketed like Jacob Marley's chains. Jane's always saying stuff like that.

I took one last look over to the Loftons' before I sat back down at the dining room table and pretended to do my arithmetic problems, which I'd already done. I noticed Mrs. Lofton running through her breezeway toward the garage. When I squinted my eyes and looked real hard, I saw the electric box had pulled way out from the wall, the plug and part of the extension cord still in it. Also, a bunch of yellow and blue flashes were coming out of the socket. Also, a little part of the Lofton's garage was pretty much on fire.

All that happened last winter, but it's kinda fun to think about now when it's summer and bloody hot, and I'm stuck doing the dumb dishes. The window over our kitchen sink has a good view of Davey's yard. If I look way out, I can see part of the stone house on the far side of Davey's and my back fences. That house is in Warwick Knoll, not Thistle Way. Warwick Knoll houses are bigger and fancier than Thistle Way houses.

I'm washing Mom's coffee cup when I notice Davey's outside. He's sitting smack in the middle of his yard, on grass still wet with dew. I smile, thinking about his wet pants. I keep watching, and pretty soon he takes a bunch of stuff out of a cardboard box and lays it on the grass. There's a clothesline, pieces of wood, a broom, a paper cup, some of his dad's tools, and a . . . potato? This looks promising. I stash a skillet crusted with pancake batter at the back of a cabinet and run over to the Loftons.

"Hey, whatcha doin'?"

"Makin' a catapult."

"A what-a-pult?"

Davey cuts through the last threads of the clothesline. Thwack! The arm of a three-foot catapult flips up, sending the potato sailing over the fence between the Lofton's yard and ours. Mom is bending to plunk Charlie in his sandbox. The potato whistles over her head and lands in her zinnia bed.

For once, I wish I'd stayed inside and finished the dishes.

The next morning I go over to the Loftons' to find out what Davey's punishment was. Grounded. He can't even go outside to his yard, so we sit on the linoleum floor in his bedroom, and I watch while he cuts up one of his mom's pillowcases. After a little while, I kinda figure out what he's making.

"Wings!"

"Yep," he says, "the first and only Human Flight Machine."

Davey makes some curlicue shapes around the edges, sort of like angel wings. After that, he makes a flour-and-water mixture in the bathroom and pastes the edges of the two wings around two wire coat hangers. Then he pokes the curved ends of each coat hanger through holes in his father's spare belt.

"Okay, Grace, go play with my sister a while."

"Why? Mary's not that much fun."

First off, Mary's never invented a gol-durn thing. Second of all, she barely talks cuz she's so shy. Third of all, ever since she got polio, if she even gets the sniffles, her mom and dad don't let her go outside. And fourth of all, she can't play Tag or Swinging Statue or even Hop Scotch cuz of her leg braces.

"The glue's gonna take a while to dry." Davey sounds exasperated. "Meet me out back after lunch. You can help me get the wings on."

Oh, the glory! To be the assistant of the first boy on Earth to invent a Human Flight Machine!

I have to wait a kabillion years for lunchtime, but finally Mom gets out the peanut butter and Wonder Bread. I wolf down a sandwich, except for the crusts. Before I run over to Davey's, I stick a couple of tangerine wedges in my pocket.

"Yoo-hoo, Davey!"

"I'm up here!"

I squint into the sun and see that Davey's lugged a ladder to the back of his house and climbed up on the roof. There's no upstairs to Davey's house, and the roof isn't too slanty, but still, he's high off the ground. I see he figured out a way to buckle the harness around his chest and shoulders, cuz he's sure as shootin' wearing those wings. A sudden breeze sends his bangs flopping across his forehead and flutters the edges of the wings.

"Look at this, Grace," he calls down. Davey's attached a string to the upper tip of each wing. When he yanks on the string, the wings flap like real wings. Davey's a genius at inventing.

I wave my arms like mad, doing the airport runway signals Davey taught me before lunch.

"Ready in the air?" I call.

"Ready."

"Proceed at will!"

Davey flaps the wings once, twice, three times, and jumps.

On the drive home from the hospital, Mrs. Lofton murmurs lovey words to Davey, who's sprawled across the back seat with his head in his mom's lap. His left leg is wrapped up in a flesh-colored elastic bandage. The doctor said his ankle's just sprained, not broke.

I'm squished in the front seat between Lt. Lofton and Mary Lofton. The Belvedere's a big car, but I'm still closer to Lt. Lofton than any kid wants to be. The whole way home, Lt. Lofton glares into the rearview mirror and yells at Davey about how he displayed the common sense of a jackass and behaved like a damn fool, and how could his son possess the sheer stupidity to try to fly off a roof with pillowcase wings.

I glance real quick over my shoulder to see how Davey's doing. He looks okay. In fact, he's smiling. Mrs. Lofton is opening her alligator handbag and taking out a Tootsie Roll Pop. It's purple, and grape is Davey's favorite flavor.

Davey's ankle heals in no time. Two days after the Human Flight Machine disaster, I ask Davey if it's all right for me to stay over for two nights. Davey asks his mom, and Mrs. Lofton picks up the telephone and dials our number. Mom says she's just pouring a glass of iced coffee, would Marjorie Lofton like to join her on the patio? Davey and me and Mary watch from the Loftons' breezeway while our moms yakkety-yak. Finally, Mrs. Lofton says she has a casserole to make and Mom says she has a meatloaf to make and Mrs. Lofton says she and Lt. Lofton would be happy to have little Grace for two nights and Mom says thank you I hope she won't be too much trouble and Mrs. Lofton tsks and says of course not, and that's that. Personally, I do not think Lt. Lofton will be all that happy to have me under foot, but by the time he gets home from the Brown Shoe Company, I'll be sitting at his dinner table with a paper napkin tucked into the waistband of my shorts.

The Loftons are the first family I'm gonna stay over with, which makes sense. They're right next door, so I don't have to lug my red plaid suitcase very far. Also, Davey's my best friend who's not a girl. And best of all, the Lofton's whole house is air-conditioned. Believe you me, I'm looking forward to seeing what it's like to live with the Loftons.

I think Mom and Dad would rather I latched on to Davey's sister.

Mary's a year older than Davey and me. She has the same straight brown hair as Davey and the same brown eyes. She's nice, but playing with Mary is dull. Davey's always doing interesting stuff. There's something exciting about palling around with a kid like Davey, cuz you never know what's gonna happen.

On the first day of my staying over with Davey, he's all busy working on a new contraption. He tells me it's gonna start with toilet paper and end with mass destruction.

"Neat-o. Can I help?"

"Nah. You can watch later, though. Go get your suitcase unpacked."

I dump my suitcase in Mary's room and then me and Mary go outside to play. She sits on an old canvas chair, and I squat on the driveway next to her. One by one, she hands me fat sticks of colored chalk from a brand new box, and I turn the Loftons' driveway into a big picture of flowers. I'm doing a white daisy with a yellow middle when Davey trounces right across my picture. He's carrying a box and holds it low so that Mary and me can see what's inside—a bunch of Popsicle sticks, some marbles, a whole lot of toy soldiers, and a cardboard toilet paper tube.

"Looks like you're gonna make something good," I say.

"Again," Mary sighs.

Davey takes the box over to Mrs. Lofton's new Belvedere and cuts us a look that means "don't follow." After a while, he sails a paper airplane that lands right in Mary's lap. She opens the folds and reads aloud the secret message Davey wrote inside.

Meet me at the Belvedere in five minutes!

Mary picks up her leg braces and stands up. It takes her a second or two to get her balance and then she clunk-clunks back a ways. I guess she's not going to meet Davey at the Belvedere.

Back when Mary was five, she had to spend a whole winter in bed; first she got scarlet fever and then pneumonia. Two summers ago, in the fall, Mary got polio. The doctors told Lt. Lofton and Mrs. Lofton that Mary was one of the lucky ones because she wouldn't die, but they said she'd never walk right again. At first, Mary got stuck in a part of the hospital where visitors can't go. She had to stay there for weeks and weeks, and she could only talk to her mom and dad and Davey through glass, using hand signals. I went to see her when she got home, and her bedroom looked kinda hospital-ish. If she wanted to stand up, her mom or dad had to strap metal braces on her legs. Mary told me the braces weighed seven pounds, but just being able to get out of a wheelchair was worth it. She told me her mom gave her leg rubs every morning and afternoon, which felt good. Davey said it took their mom forever to give Mary her bath, which kinda blocked up the bathroom.

Mary missed school all that fall, but after Christmas, she got to go back. Mary and Davey don't go to Immaculate Heart of Mary because they're Protestant. Davey told me the other kids at their school kinda stay away from Mary. He says they're worried if they get too close, they'll catch polio. Recess is the hardest for her, he says, cuz she can't play games on the playground with the other girls. Davey says he's Mary's only friend now. Him and me.

I wish Mary had more friends. Being her only not-family friend is kinda a burden.

I gather up the stubs of chalk and shove them back in the box. Then I run to meet Davey at the Belvedere. Mrs. Lofton's new car is beautiful—turquoise and white with big tail fins.

I watch Davey open the passenger-side door and stand on the running board. He takes a big wad of bubble gum out of his mouth and uses it to stick the empty toilet paper roll to the roof of the car. One end of the tube faces the back of the car, and the other end faces the front.

"See this tube, Grace?" he says. "It's the barrel of the most powerful cannon in the whole world."

I'm sorta worried about that gum sticking Davey's toilet paper tube cannon to his Mom's brand new car, being as it's sunny today. And hot.

"Ready?" he yells over his shoulder.

"Ready."

"Bombs away!"

"Bombs away over Tokyo!"

Davey puts a marble on the roof of the car and twangs it with his finger. The marble rolls into the back of the tube, straight through, and out the front. By the time it gets to the front windshield, it's going really fast. It bumps over one of the windshield wipers and falls on the hood and keeps rolling. Finally, it drops down the front grill and lands like a bomb on the toy soldier camp Davey set up below the fender.

"Wowzer! It worked perfect!" I shout.

Davey smiles and then rolls three more marbles to polish off the rest of the toy soldiers.

After the bombardment, Mrs. Lofton starts to come outside with a plate of sugar cookies. Mary manages to get in front of her mom and steer her away from the Belvedere. Mary's good like that. Mrs. Lofton says, "Why don't you kids sit somewhere in the shade and play Twenty Questions while you eat your snack?" I'm pretty sure she doesn't know there's a toilet paper roll stuck with gum to the roof of her brand new car.

Davey takes the plate of cookies and carries it to the back fence, and we all sit under the lilac bushes. After Twenty Questions gets boring, I ask Davey and Mary why everybody calls their dad Lieutenant. Davey says his dad was on a boat called a destroyer escort during the war, and the boat was in a big battle called the Battle of Samar.

"Dad told us the whole story, how his little boat decided to attack a much bigger Japanese cruiser. And how his boat fired three torpedoes that blew big holes in the cruiser, but a bunch of enemy ships were firing back, and one of them sank Dad's boat, and ninety guys drowned."

"But not your dad?"

"Nope. Dad and a whole bunch of other guys got onto life rafts and floated around a long time, but finally got rescued."

"Is that why he likes to be called Lieutenant?"

Mary answers, "When my dad was in college, his best friend was named David. Right after college, they both decided to go into the Navy together. Dad got on a destroyer escort, and David got on a much bigger boat called the *Indianapolis*. That boat got blown up, but right before it sank, lots of guys jumped into the water. The guys in the water didn't get rescued for five days, and by then, most of them had gotten eaten alive by sharks."

"Or had their legs chewed off," Davey adds.

I don't say anything for a long time. Then, "Did your dad's friend get rescued?"

"Nope," Davey says. "When I was born, Dad gave me his buddy's name, to honor him. Mom told me Dad went to war and did his patriotic duty, and he was just as much a hero as David was. She says my dad feels bad about his friend dying and him not dying. She says Dad still thinks a lot about that battle of Samar, cuz guys on his ship got their intestines blown all over the place and stuff, and that's why he doesn't joke around like other dads or play ball."

Mary adds, "Mom says the whole world changed because of our dropping the bomb on Hiroshima, and even though that was horrible, it stopped the war. She says now we're in the Atomic Age, but Dad's still the master and commander of our ship. That's why he likes everything orderly and in its place, just like when he was in the Navy. We have dinner every night at 6:15, and if it's late, he gets mad at Mom. A few weeks ago, Mom had one of her bad headaches and didn't make dinner, and when Dad came home, he got so mad he gave her a black eye. A week later, she got her new car."

"That's good," I say, although it doesn't sound that good to me.

"Sometimes Dad spanks Davey too hard," Mary says, "but Mom says Dad really loves us."

"I wish he'd joke around like other dads, though," Davey says under his breath. "I wish he'd work on some inventions with me."

I feel bad about Mrs. Lofton getting a black eye. She's a little chunky, but she's a real nice lady. She never gets mad at Davey, and she gives both kids hugs a kabillion times a day. She buys them the best toys, too. Mary has an Easy-Bake oven and tons of little cake mixes. She's got Play-Doh in every color, a watercolor paint set, and a box of forty-eight Crayola crayons. She's got books of paper doll clothes that aren't even cut out yet, and a whole shelf in her room crammed with china-face dolls. Davey's got a tropical fish tank and a terrarium with a tiny chameleon living in it. He's got Uncle Milton's Ant Farm and a model train set, Tonka trucks, and cap guns, too. And more games than a toy store! There's Candyland, Chutes and Ladders, Parcheesi, Yahtzee, Monopoly, and Stratego, all lined up in the basement rec room. And none of the corners on the boxes are ripped, either.

My favorite thing to do at the Loftons' is play with their Block City sets. Me and Davey and Mary open the fat cardboard tubes and dump out tons of little white brick-shaped tiles onto Davey's bedroom floor. There's clear blocks for windows and green blocks for doors and roofs. You can build skyscrapers and mansions and schools, oh, just anything. Once, we built every house on Thistle Way, and it took up most of Davey's floor. Even Lt. Lofton said we'd done a fine job.

By suppertime, Mrs. Lofton still hasn't seen that gum on top of her car. After we finish our meatloaf and mashed potatoes, she slices the peach pie she made that afternoon, but before I even get the first bite in my mouth, Lt. Lofton starts pointing his finger across the table at Davey, telling him he's not living up to his namesake.

"My friend David gave his life for America. That's what being a true patriot is about. You hear me, son?"

Davey tucks his head and doesn't answer.

Lt. Lofton stares all squinty-eyed, aiming somewhere over Davey's head. "And we need patriots right now, what with all the lefties in Washington sitting on their haunches. I swear, the Soviets are infiltrating our government."

I nod my head. It's always a good idea to agree with Lt. Lofton.

"Every day, some Red operative is passing our critical defense secrets to Moscow." The Lieutenant stops to think a second and then turns to Mrs. Lofton. "Did you join the Minute Women yet?"

She waggles a knife till it cuts through the pie crust. "I will, dear. I'll get to it first thing in the morning."

Lt. Lofton frowns and looks off again. "McCarthy's the only levelheaded one in the bunch, I tell you. If somebody doesn't stop the Reds, it won't be long before they change our whole way of life." He pounds his fist on the table.

I look over at Davey; his eyes are blazing like stars.

Last summer, Davey watched Captain Midnight every Saturday morning. He even sent away for a Captain Midnight Secret Squadron membership card and decoder. But Captain Midnight isn't on TV this summer, so Davey's got all interested in G-Men, secret agents, and spy stuff. After dinner, he takes me into the bathroom and closes the door, which is kinda weird. He turns on the faucet, so nobody outside can hear.

"Shhh!" he hisses, glancing around to see if anybody's listening, which is dumb considering we're in a bathroom. "He made contact."

"Who?"

Davey glares at me. "A special agent of the United States government."

I get the impression Davey's cooking up a project, one that will make his dad proud of him. That would be something. I can't remember a single time Lt. Lofton acted really proud of Davey.

"I've been contacted by the government," he whispers.

"What?"

Davey's talking so low, and he's running the water so durn fast that I can't hear a thing.

"The federal government needs me to investigate a suspected spy ring."

A spy ring? On Thistle Way? Holy cow!

I go through all the neighbors in my mind, trying to figure out which one is a secret Commie spy. Nobody seems quite right.

"Who are we investigating?"

"Mrs. Krieger," Davey says. Then he makes his voice all official sounding and adds, "As you know, Dr. Krieger's whereabouts have been unclear for some time."

"Wait, Dr. Krieger died, didn't he?"

Last winter, I heard my mom tell my dad that Dr. Krieger had died of a heart attack in Grandpa Reinhardt's department store. Dad said Dr. Krieger was buying a pair of garters for his socks, and he keeled over dead in the menswear department.

"No. That's what the Commies want everybody to think. Dr. Krieger defected and is now living in Moscow. Mrs. Krieger is mailing him top-secret formulas about how to make poison, enough poison to kill everybody in St. Louis."

"Holy smokes!"

"Shhh!" Davey hisses. "Come with me. We're going to do our patriotic duty, even if we have to die doing it!"

There's still a bit of daylight. The sky's all pale and peachy. Somebody's mowing their lawn, and the air smells grassy. We walk out to the back fence without talking. Davey puts his finger to his lips and points to the Krieger house. I can barely see it, though, cuz there's lilac bushes on Davey's side of the fence and big pine trees on Mrs. Krieger's side. The Kriegers' house is twice as big as any house on Thistle Way. There's two twisty chimneys and all the windows have little diamond-shaped glass in them.

I've seen Mrs. Krieger a few times. She kinda looks like the wicked witch who tried to fatten up Hansel and make Gretel her cleaning girl. She's got whitish hair, and she always wears a black dress and black shoes. She walks bending forward with a cane, and she's got this big hump on her back between her shoulder blades. She doesn't go out of her house, except once a week, she just goes out to her flagstone patio and gives a white envelope to a guy who mows her lawn.

I'm wondering how we're gonna spy on Mrs. Krieger when Davey runs to his garage and comes back with a cardboard shoebox. Inside the box is a pencil, a pad of lined paper, two empty soup cans, a ball of twine, and Lt. Lofton's Navy binoculars, which I know for a fact Davey's not ever supposed to touch.

Davey and me crouch under the lilac bushes and make a walkie-talkie out of the soup cans and string. I twist the viewer on the binoculars till it isn't all fuzzy and start surveilling Mrs. Krieger's yard. All I see is pine trees, squirrels, the yard guy, and a cat. Just when I'm about ready to give up, Mrs. Krieger comes out to her patio. She's leaning on her wood cane cuz the flagstones aren't too smooth. Davey and I crouch lower, waiting, but all that happens is the lawn guy slips the white envelope into the back pocket of his jeans and rolls the push mower to the far side of Mrs. Krieger's house. I've been kneeling so long my feet are all prickly, and I'm getting bored.

"Davey!" I whisper into the chicken noodle soup can, "did you hear anything?"

"Nah."

Davey forgot to talk into his soup can, but I hear him loud and clear. We're crouched only about five feet from one another.

"Wait!" he hisses.

"What?"

"She's back inside, see? Up in the top window. She's looking out!"

I peer through the binoculars and find the window. Mrs. Krieger's staring straight at us!

Davey and me run like mad back to the breezeway. We hide behind some stacked up old lawn chairs, breathing hard and staring bug-eyed at each other.

The next morning, Davey comes up with a plan to spy on Mrs. Krieger. He tells me we're gonna dig a tunnel that starts at the lilacs, goes under the fence, and keeps going all the way to Mrs. Krieger's house. Then we'll bash through to the basement, creep upstairs, gather evidence, crawl back through the tunnel, and report Mrs. Krieger to the CIA.

I think that sounds nuts, but I don't say so. Davey gets pouty if you pooh-pooh his ideas and then he tells you to go on home. I can't go home yet cuz I told Mom I'd be at the Loftons' two nights, and I still have one night to go. This is my first test to see if another family is better than mine, so I'm sure as shootin' not gonna risk having Davey tell me to go home.

"We'll start the tunnel under the biggest lilac," he says, "so the entrance is almost completely hidden. And Grace, don't you dare tell anybody. Not even Mary or Jane. This mission is top-secret."

After lunch, Mary asks me if I'd like to go to her piano recital. "It's in a hotel ballroom in Clayton. I get to play a baby grand piano."

Mary's face is all bright and smiley, and she's got on a pretty blue dress with a white collar. Seeing Mary play a big piano in a hotel ballroom sounds neat-o, but I promised to help Davey with his secret mission, so

I say sorry and kinda stare at my toes. Mary says it's okay cuz her mom and dad will be there.

As soon as the Belvedere backs down the drive, Davey and me run to the fence line with shovels, trowels, and a garden claw.

After a couple of hours, the mound of dug up dirt is pretty dang big. I'm worried somebody's gonna notice it. Davey must be thinking the same thing, cuz he goes into the house and comes back with a pink blanket, which looks exactly like the ones on the twin beds in Mary's room. He lays the blanket on the ground near the lilacs and starts digging again. I pile the extra dirt on the blanket, drag the bundle across the grass to the house, and dump the dirt down one of the basement window wells.

After Mary's recital, she and her mom and dad are gonna see *The Searchers* at the Hi-Pointe movie theater. Lt. Lofton's a big John Wayne fan. By the time they get back, the cicadas are raising a racket, and Mrs. Finnegan's playing "Danny Boy" on her tin whistle. Any minute now the Dailys are gonna be ringing their hand bells, and after that, Mom's gonna be clanking her old cow bell for Jane to come home from Lizzie's house. Lizzie is my sister's best friend on Thistle Way. By the time Lt. Lofton pings his ship's bell, the tunnel is almost as long as Davey.

The next morning, Lt. Lofton goes to work at the Brown Shoe Company like always, and Mrs. Lofton takes Mary to get a haircut.

"Grace and me are gonna play checkers in the breezeway," Davey tells his mom. He puts on his dopey angel-boy smile, which anybody except Mrs. Lofton can see is fake.

It's another blistering day. Soon, brown streaks of sweat are trickling down our cheeks. I spit on my pointing finger and rub a line of dirt off the inside of my elbow. When we hear the Belvedere coming up the drive, Davey and me dash to the breezeway and hunker over the checkerboard.

After my two nights at the Loftons are done, Davey and me continue digging like crazy every chance we get. I'm afraid we're gonna tunnel right under Mrs. Krieger's house and accidentally come out the other side, but Davey says we haven't gone nearly far enough. By now there's barely enough room for Davey in there, even laying flat. He's having a hard time reaching around with the little pail to send dirt back to me at the entrance. I think I might go spend a night with somebody else, maybe Susan and Sharon White, but Davey says he needs me to work on the tunnel, so I don't, which is good cuz Susan and Sharon White kinda drive me nuts.

Our fourth afternoon of digging gets interrupted when Mom calls out the back door, "Yoo-hoo, Grace!"

I have to babysit Charlie while Mom takes Jane into Clayton to get her eyes tested for glasses. For a whole hour, Davey keeps on digging. He's all alone out there, which I'm thinking isn't such a good idea. When I finally get back to the tunnel, it's almost dinnertime. I can hardly see Davey cuz he's so deep in the tunnel. I'm thinking he must have been scraping lots of dirt while I was gone cuz there's tons of mud, roots, and pebbles piled up behind him. I crawl into the tunnel and lay on my stomach and push the stuff behind me as fast as I can. All three basement window wells got filled up pretty fast, so now I'm dumping the spare dirt along the fence line. It's sorta hidden by the lilacs.

When I get back to the tunnel again from dumping off a load, I scrooch in as far as I can. The stupid tunnel is getting skinnier as it goes deeper. This morning, I could see Davey's legs all the way from his shoes up to his knees, and as he passed dirt behind him, I could clear the passageway pretty well. Now, even when I scrooch as very far as I can, I can only see Davey's feet, and the air gives me a headache. I crawl back to the tunnel entrance.

"Come out, Davey, it's gonna be dinnertime."

I hear him say something. It sounds like, "Just a few more scoops."

I wait a few minutes, but Davey doesn't scrooch backwards. I crawl in again and go as far as I can. It's really hard to breathe, and much more dirt is piled up behind Davey. I can barely see the bottoms of his sneakers.

"C'mon Davey, come out."

No answer.

I work my way forward as far as I can and shove dirt backwards. Pretty soon, though, I start to choke cuz I can hardly breathe. I'm scared. There's tons more dirt between me and Davey.

"Davey?"

No answer.

I grab one of his shoes and shake it, hard, but it just flops back down. I squiggle backwards, fast. At the tunnel entrance, I stand up and yell for help. I don't see anybody, and nobody comes.

The Loftons are running their air conditioners—they've got one in every window. At my house, there's a kabillion fans going. Mrs. Henry's probably playing her Frank Sinatra records. The Niesens are probably at their country club, and the Mooneys always go to Michigan for two weeks in June. Nobody can hear me.

I pace back and forth. My hands are balled into fists. I don't know what to do. I scream for help again, scream bloody murder.

I hear somebody behind me. It's the yard guy! The yard guy's running across Mrs. Krieger's lawn, slapping pine tree branches out of the way.

"What's wrong?"

I point to the entrance to the tunnel. "Davey's in there." I'm starting to cry.

The yard guy jumps the fence and drops to his knees at the tunnel entrance. He crawls in up to his shoulders, then in all the way to his waist, scooping out dirt as he goes. Big globs of mud sail past where I'm sitting on the grass, bawling my eyes out.

Now Lt. Lofton's running out of the house. He gets to the tunnel entrance and falls to his knees, pawing at the dirt, frantic.

The sound is muffled, but I can hear the yard guy shouting, "Kid, hey, kid!"

Me and Lt. Lofton are shouting, too. "Davey! Davey!"

I stand up and lean against the fence. Zigzags of light dazzle across my eyesight. Right when everything starts to go swoozy, I feel arms reach over the fence and take hold of my shoulders. I smell nice perfume. The eyeball dazzles start to go away. I notice a cane on the ground, and I turn around to see who's holding me. It's old Mrs. Krieger, and she looks worried.

The yard guy backs out of the tunnel, pulling Davey out by the ankles. He lays Davey face-up on the grass. Davey's eyes are closed. His lips are blue-ish. Every place there's not dirt, his skin looks way too white.

Davey's dad pushes the yard guy out of the way. Lt. Lofton sticks two fingers into Davey's mouth and pulls out gobs of dirt. He cups his hand under Davey's chin and blows air into Davey's mouth. He puts his ear to Davey's mouth and waits. Nothing. He blows again, harder.

Nothing.

Mrs. Lofton is running across the lawn, screaming Davey's name. Mrs. Krieger's smoothing down my hair, like you'd pet a cat. She's telling me to be brave, telling me not to worry, calling me "dear." It feels good, but I'm still worried.

Lt. Lofton pinches Davey's nose. He pulls Davey's head backwards and blows into his mouth again, but still nothing happens.

Lt. Lofton sags back on his heels. Mrs. Lofton starts to screech. I clap my hands over my ears and cry harder.

This time, the yard guy pushes Lt. Lofton out of the way. He grabs Davey by his armpits and sits him up. Davey's slumpy, but the yard guy keeps him sitting long enough to give him two good thwacks on the back.

Davey gags.

We all stare at Davey and hold our breath. The yard guy gives him another thwack. Davey takes a huge gulp of air. Mrs. Lofton stops screeching. Lt. Lofton squeezes his hand over his mouth so hard his knuckles go all white. I think he's crying.

"C'mon, boy," the yard guy says, and he gives Davey another whap. "You can do it. Get it out."

Davey throws up.

I've never been so happy to see a kid throw up, I'll tell you that.

Lt. Lofton gathers Davey in his arms and carries him toward the house. Mrs. Lofton clings to both of them. Mary holds the breezeway door open.

I stop crying. It's gonna be okay.

And you know what? Mrs. Krieger doesn't look witchy when you see her up close. She smiles at me and runs her fingers across my forehead. Her fingertips are dry as feathers. I stand on my tiptoes and kiss her cheek. It's wet; she was crying too.

Mom was vacuuming, that's why she didn't hear the ruckus. When I tell her what happened, she holds me really, really tight and makes me go over all the details six times. She gives me a glass of milk and a Hostess Twinkie, which I didn't know we even had cuz Mom hides stuff like that so Jane and me don't eat them all on the first day. I don't want the Twinkie, which makes Mom worried. Upstairs, I fall asleep like a log.

The next day, Mrs. Lofton asks Mom if I can come over. Mom says, "Are you sure, Marjorie?" Mrs. Lofton says she thinks I would be a good diversion for Davey and Mary.

Me and Davey and Mary play with their Block City sets. I stay for dinner too. Mrs. Lofton makes tuna casserole and Bisquick biscuits and cherry Jell-O with marshmallows, which is just about my favorite dinner. I don't think I'm being a good diversion for Davey, though, cuz after dinner, we get in a fight.

I keep trying to convince Davey that it was really Mrs. Krieger who saved him. She stood at her diamondy window watching us. When I screamed, she got her yard guy to go help us. And she hugged me the whole time he was unconscienced.

Davey keeps shaking his head no. No, he's sure Dr. Krieger is a spy for

Moscow, and Mrs. Krieger is a traitor. He's still determined to catch them and report them to the government. I'm pretty sure Davey thinks that if he does this, his dad will be proud of him and love him more.

After dinner, Mary and me play Monopoly in the breezeway. I'm passing GO when Davey barges out, all excited. He cups his hand around my ear and whispers, "Grappling hook."

I jump up and knock over the table. Monopoly money flutters to the floor. While I pick up the money, Davey crawls under the fence and creeps toward Mrs. Krieger's house. I see he's got one end of a long rope tied to the handle of a steel gardening claw. He swings the rope like a big lasso and slowly lets out the length of it. Then he flings the claw end up. It catches on the rim of the gutter, high near the roof shingles. He tugs the rope, and it holds. Moving hand-over-hand, he hoists himself up the side of the house.

Mary squeezes my arm.

Davey is almost up to the highest window when the gutter starts to bend. He tries to get his toes on the windowsill, but he can't. The gutter makes a crinkly noise. Davey looks across the yard at Mary and me. It's getting dark, but I could swear his eyes look sad.

The gutter gives way.

Davey remained in a coma for a month. When he awoke, and when he had sufficiently recovered, he was transferred to a rehab center in South St. Louis. Eventually he learned how to walk and talk again.

I have scant tolerance for risk. I will not parasail, hang glide, wind surf, jet ski, swim with the sharks, swim with the whales, swim with the dolphins, swim with the sting rays, parachute jump, base jump, bungee jump, deep-sea dive, zip-line, try out a black diamond run, or ride out a hurricane on the front porch.

I could not have put it into words back then, but as I watched Davey swing that homemade grappling hook, I realized my brilliant, impulsive, paranoid, obsessive childhood pal was motivated only in part by a longing to earn his father's respect. Primarily, I think he sought the heady thrill of danger—loved it, craved it to a fault, and shunned the tempering hand of caution.

In the ounce of wisdom that age confers, I know this:

The line between brilliance and madness is illusory.

Dezso

the truck

I can't imagine why the odd little man crossed my mind after so many years. Curiosity, I guess. I took a stab at the spelling of his name and came up with Dezso. With a quick Internet search, I discovered Dezso is a Hungarian name. It means "longing."

I wonder what Dezso might have longed for, if anything. Maybe the old country; maybe he remembered how his grandmother set out steaming bowls of halaszle, trout with sweet dumplings, and feather-light Dobos cake. Or, he longed to hear an uncle named Janos play Liszt again on a shawl-draped piano. Maybe he yearned for a house of his own, a wife, children.

Children, surely.

Dezso was a man of reserve, disinclined to share the longings of his heart with kids who every Saturday afternoon listened for his truck to putter onto Thistle Way as he made his rounds. He did not linger to converse with us, and we did not think to engage him. Even his name was unimportant to us kids. We never spoke it. We didn't even know it.

To us, he was simply the Vegetable Man.

It's no use sneaking into that truck until school lets out for the summer. That's the soonest he's got anything good, like strawberries. Before school lets out, all he's got is dumb old lettuce and radishes and stuff—which aren't worth the trouble, I'll tell you that.

The Vegetable Man's face is kind of orangey-yellowish-brownish, and his skin's all wrinkled like a raisin. He always wears the same white shirt, and he's so short and skinny that he has to buckle his belt on the farthest hole so his trousers don't fall down. His hair is black and wavy, but you can hardly see it because he wears a droopy hat attached to a droopy brim with a little snap. The main thing, though, is his teeth. Some of them are missing, and one is made out of gold!

The Vegetable Man's truck isn't like any other truck I've seen. It's a really old blue-ish Studebaker, all roundy at the edges. Dad says it's seen better days. At the dinner table one night, Dad said the corn and tomatoes were especially fresh and that got him on the subject of the Vegetable Man. Dad said that one time, he was out watering the front lawn when the Vegetable Man came around, and he asked the man about his truck. Dad said it was the only time the Vegetable Man talked his arm off.

Dezso told Dad that the truck's first owner was my Grandpa Reinhardt's department store. He said the store bought the truck new in 1937 for $735 and used it as a delivery truck.

"I was just a kid when the '37 Studebakers came out," Dad said. "But I know they were beauties. Black and shiny, with whitewall tires and fancy chrome trim. They came with a heater and a little clock built into the dashboard."

Dezso told Dad that after a few years, the department store wanted a brand new truck, three of them, so they sold the Studebaker to a hauler. I thought Dad said a heller, which I didn't get.

"No, Grace, a *hauler*, a man who gets paid to haul things away," Dad explained. "The hauler painted the truck bright blue, but he nearly drove it into the ground hauling loads of lumber and steel pipe all over the city. Then, about five years ago, Dezso bought the truck from a farmer who'd been using it like a packhorse to take loads of feed corn to a grain elevator over in Caruthersville. The finish had lost its shine by that time, and the engine had lost its spunk, but Dezso claims the thing is powerful enough to pull a cargo plane into a hangar."

Dezso? Who's Dezso?

Anyways, the Vegetable Man's truck isn't sleek or shiny anymore. The whole back part is a compartment that somebody added on. The compartment sticks out a ways from the back wheels, and it's got a roof and walls high enough for kids to stand up inside and not clunk our heads on the ceiling. Two little steps hooked onto the back of the truck lead up to a door that gets you into the compartment. Inside, it smells like spinach and grapes and apples. Also, like garden dirt after it rains. It's dark in there when the door's closed, so you have to feel your way along, but usually you can see pretty good with the door open. On both sides of the skinny aisle are wood shelves, and on the shelves are all kinds of fruit and vegetables in little boxes about the size of a cereal bowl, only square. The stuff in the compartment's always changing. After the asparagus, lettuce, strawberries, and parsley are gone, there's corn, tomatoes, cucumbers, peaches, and carrots. Oh, and zucchini. In fall, there's not much good stuff, just Brussels sprouts, beets, and cauliflower—and squash, which I hate.

At the far end of the compartment is a round metal pan attached to a scale that hangs from a hook in the ceiling. The Vegetable Man puts carrots and turnips and rutabaga and stuff with leafy stems on a little chopping table and cuts off the raggedy tops with a folding knife before he weighs the vegetables on the scale. Mom says that's a good deal cuz the regular stores weigh carrots before they chop off the part you don't eat. The Vegetable Man puts apples and pears and plums and bananas in little brown paper sacks and folds over the top edges all neat and tidy.

On Saturday afternoons when we kids hear Veg-tibuls! Vehj-tuh-buls! we know it's the Vegetable Man cuz he's calling out the window while he drives his truck around the circle, real slow. Also, we know he's gonna leave the motor running and the compartment door at the back of the truck wide open while he writes down orders at the houses. We crouch in the bushes, and when we hear the ratchety sound of the truck's hand brake, we get ready. The Vegetable Man's gonna have to stand at each kitchen door awhile cuz every mom takes a year to make up her mind about how much celery and how many potatoes she'll need. As soon as he walks up a driveway, kids can sneak into his truck and gorge on free fruit.

It's a whole week since I stayed over at Davey's house, and since the day he fell all the way down to Mrs. Krieger's stone patio. I forgot to dump my dirty clothes out of my suitcase till today, and they're kinda smelly. I stuff them in the washing machine and dump in some Oxydol. Then I add more Oxydol till the water gets real bubbly. Then it gets too bubbly, and it bubbles over the top. I slam down the lid, but the gol-durn bubbles keep squishing out from the edges of the lid, so I run up to my room.

I have to figure out a couple more houses to stay at. Jane's talking on the upstairs hall phone, making plans to sneak out with a friend and see Tab Hunter and Natalie Wood in *The Burning Hills*. I'm in no hurry to spend the night with Katie Greeley and her killer dog, or stupid Jean Marie and June Marie Walsh. First of all, they're not my good friends. Second of all, other people's beds are either too hard or too soft or the pillow's too smushy or too spongy, and the sheets don't smell like the sheets at my house. Third of all, I might have to eat a bolagna sandwich slathered with ketchup. Everybody knows you put mustard on bologna, but, oh no, not Mrs. Finnegan. And Davey Lofton's house is so spick-and-span, I was afraid to leave my wet toothbrush on the sink, so I had to stick it back in my suitcase on top of Cuddle Bun and now she's got a dried-up toothpaste splotch on her forehead.

When I hear the Vegetable Man's truck coming, I get up off my bed and go hang around right outside the kitchen door. Mom's inside, balancing Charlie on her hip while she decides which vegetables she wants. Mom always changes her mind a kabillion times. The Vegetable Man has to write things down on his order pad with a stubby yellow pencil and then scratch them out again and again. I stand on tiptoes and peek over his shoulder, trying to see what we'll be eating this week, but his writing makes no sense. The Vegetable Man gives me a sort of half-smile.

"I make it simple," he says, turning the pad toward me. "See, girl?"

I shrug my shoulders up and down.

He lowers the order pad so I can see better. "Your *anya* want a pound of lima beans, so I write *1lb lima*. See, girl? She want a quart of strawberries, I write *1qt straw*. She want a quart of snap peas, I write *1qt snap*."

"Ahh," I say. I beam at him with my best adorable kid smile. "I get it. Thanks."

Mom shoots me one of her squinty sideways looks, the ones she gives when she knows a kid is up to something but she doesn't quite know what. I figure she wants to get on with her order.

One day last fall, I overheard Mom and Mrs. Henry talking about the Vegetable Man, only they didn't call him that, they called him Dezso. Mrs. Henry said she gets her fruit and vegetables at Kroger's. She said Dezso is a Gypsy, a dirty Gypsy who probably lives in a tent or a wagon. She said his wife probably wraps her head in a turban like a swami and has bangle bracelets jangling up her arm and charcoal eye shadow and huge hoop earrings.

"I'll bet you a nickel to a donut his wife is one of those fortune-tellers who dupe people out of their quarters reading palms or tea leaves or staring at a crystal ball," Mrs. Henry said. "They're all alike, petty thieves and pickpockets. I'll bet if I called the police, and they searched that truck, they'd find stolen wallets and cocktail rings and who knows what-all."

Mom said she doubted that, but it sounded to me like Mom was thinking about believing Mrs. Henry.

Anyways, today, Mom's yakking extra long with the Vegetable Man.

"Your peaches, are they Missouri peaches or from somewhere else?"

"Yes, ma'am, Missouri peaches."

I roll my eyes at the Vegetable Man, but he doesn't seem to see so I walk down to his truck.

"And the bananas," I hear Mom saying, "are they ripe?"

"Yes ma'am."

"—because last week, they were too green to eat for days."

While the Vegetable Man is telling Mom how the bananas and peaches and nectarines are all okay this week, I join some kids in the back of the blue truck. Pretty soon, there's so many kids in the truck I have a hard time getting through to the raspberries. It's dark in the compartment, and everybody's trying to squeeze past each other. Benny Herman goes for the blueberries. Then he bites into a tomato, thinking it's a plum, and spits it out. Joey and Pete Haverkamp are fighting over a glob of red grapes. I weasel my way to the back of the compartment and find a spot next to Mason Mooney, who's stuffing cherries in his mouth. Mason got head lice a few weeks ago, and now his and his sister Molly's heads are shaved clean as cue balls. Mrs. Mooney didn't want the older boys to get lice too, so they're spending a week at their grandma's house in Webster Groves.

"Remember to stick the seeds in your pocket," somebody whispers. It sounds like either Joey or Pete Haverkamp.

Benny likes to be the lookout. Every so often, he leans across the shelf and peers through a crack in the plywood walls. Suddenly, he bolts up. "He's coming!"

We don't have to rush. The Vegetable Man always starts down a driveway and then pauses about halfway to the truck. Then he takes a homemade cigarette out of his shirt pocket and gives the papery ends a quick twist. After that, he flicks a wood match with the nail of his thumb and lights the cigarette. And then he turns his back to the truck and stands there puffing on the cigarette, taking his time, blowing streams of smoke out his nose. I always think he must be looking at a tree or a cloud or something, but I don't know why he'd do that cuz it gives us kids plenty of time to get out of the truck and run like the blazes.

Today is different. First of all, the Vegetable Man didn't get to Thistle Way until it was almost dinnertime, hours later than usual. Second of all, Mom had a small order. And third of all, the Vegetable Man must have been out of cigarettes.

Benny sounds the warning. Joey and Pete Haverkamp, the Mooneys, Jane and her best friend Lizzie, me, Patsy Warfield, Tommy Stieger, Susan and Sharon White, along with a couple of Finnegans race down the aisle. I'm at the back of the line. The Haverkamp boys start bickering again and clog up the doorway. Way at the back, I slip on a slimy apricot seed, clunk into Lizzie, and fall down on my butt. Through all the legs of the other kids, I see the Haverkamps on the floor too, still wrestling.

Benny was first out of the truck. He's long gone.

I shove the Haverkamps toward the door. Joey falls out of the truck, lands on the street, and scrambles away. Pete has the sense to use the stair step, but as soon as he's out of the truck, he turns around and slams the door and latches it from the outside. I'm stuck inside the truck!

"Lemme out," I scream, but not too loud cuz I don't want the Vegetable Man to hear me. My mind is racing, going over escape plans in the dark. *Maybe I can get the door open from the inside.* I slide my hands along the door. There's no handle. *Shoot. Maybe I can run out real fast when the Vegetable Man opens the door to get Mom's order together. He'd see me for sure, but I can run at least as fast as him. What if Mom winds up not ordering anything this week? Our house is always the last stop on Thistle Way, and the next subdivision is probably far away.*

I hear a click. The Vegetable Man is opening the driver's side door. He's releasing the brake. He's pressing down on the accelerator. The engine is chugging. The truck's moving!

Any minute, any minute, any minute, I tell myself. *Any minute we'll stop.*

The truck rounds a corner, and I tumble onto a carton of string beans. I scrabble around in the dark, picking up stray beans. *We've gone a ways, when is he gonna stop?*

The truck makes another sharp turn that sends me tumbling head over heels down the aisle. After that, we drive in a straight line for a long time.

It's warm in the compartment with no windows to open. The scale and pan sway on their chains. I pop a couple of cherries in my mouth and spit the seeds upward, trying to get them in the pan. One lands with a ping. Ha! I can't exactly see the pan, but I must've hit it. I pull a plum off a shelf and bite into it, but the skin tastes bitter so I put it back. I curl up on the floor and stick some paper bags under my head for a pillow. I can feel the engine purring. The compartment is rocking gently. I'm sorta sleepy. . . .

Holy cow! Slashes of blinding light are hitting me smack in my eyes. It's a flashlight. I sit up fast and turn my head away.

"Who's that?"

It's the Vegetable Man. He's standing in the open doorway. "Who's in there?"

I fight back hot tears. "It's Grace Mitchell from Thistle Way. I got stuck in here."

He clicks off the flashlight. "Come out so I see you."

I crawl out of the compartment and look around. It's nighttime almost. Wherever I am, it's a place I've never been to before. On both sides of the street, there's a bunch of red brick houses, and they're attached at the sides. The front yards are dinky, and there's hardly any trees or bushes.

Little veiny bulges are popping out on the Vegetable Man's neck, and he's sorta gulping like when a person drinks fizzy soda too fast and it won't go all the way down. He pulls off his cap and swats it against his leg. I look away and concentrate on working out a plan, and I come up with a good one. I'm gonna ask to spend the night with the Vegetable Man! I'll get to stay in his gypsy wagon and get my fortune told. Heck, Mom and Dad said I could spend up to two nights with any family on Thistle Way that would have me. Well, the Vegetable Man's part of Thistle Way. Kinda.

I ask the Vegetable Man if I can spend the night at his house, which I'm not even sure is on this street. I mean, maybe these are more customer houses or something. Anyways, he just turns away, puffs out his cheeks, and lets out a long sigh. I'm pretty sure I should not talk in case he's thinking over my plan, but when he throws his cap to the ground and starts raking his hands through his hair, I figure he's not gonna let me sleep over in his gypsy wagon. In fact, it's looking like he's good and mad about the fix we're in. Right about now, I get the feeling there's no gypsy tent or wagon.

"You live here?" I stare at the row of red brick houses on one side of the street. They look ordinary, except for all being attached. I'm thinking stupid Mrs. Henry was wrong.

"You know your telephone number, girl?" the Vegetable Man says.

"Sure." I've known my phone number for a kabillion years.

"Good," he says, looking relieved. He hands me his stubby pencil, and I write my telephone number on his order pad.

"Now, you stay here, understand?" He waggles a finger in front of my nose and walks up to one of the front doors. A fat lady with a long apron is there, waiting for him. They talk a little. The Vegetable Man glances over his shoulder to make sure I'm still standing beside his truck, and then he and the fat lady go inside.

I count to ten. I count to twenty. Thirty. I thought counting would keep me from thinking, but it doesn't. *How long was I asleep in the truck? How far from Thistle Way is this place?* Way at the end of the block is a street sign. *Okay, I'm on Hickory Street.*

Where the heck is Hickory Street?

To get the butterflies out of my stomach, I start singing "One Hundred Bottles of Beer on the Wall." A boy wearing a striped T-shirt turns onto the block and starts walking toward me. He's about Jane's age, and he has cowlicky hair and pimples. He's tossing a baseball in the air and catching it in the pocket of a glove while he walks. The baseball glove is soft and folds completely around the ball. It's a rule of mine to stay out of the way of twelve-year-old boys at night on a street where I've never been to before. But the Vegetable Man told me to stand right by his truck, so I do. I look at the boy as he passes by me, and he looks at me, but we don't say hi or anything.

The sun is all reddish and almost behind the row of houses. Shadows are spreading all the way across the street to the other side. The cicadas are starting up too. Pretty soon, the lightning bugs will be out and then it will be really late for me to be way far away from Brentwood, standing all by myself next to a vegetable truck. I'm hot and sweaty and starving to death, and I'm thinking maybe Hickory Street isn't even in St. Louis. Maybe the Vegetable Man won't ever come out of that house.

How the heck am I gonna get home?

I'm down to sixty-seven bottles of beer, and my singing is sounding kinda wavery-scared when a screen door creaks open. It's not the

Vegetable Man's door, though. Two old men drag a pair of kitchen chairs out to the front porch. Pretty soon, they're talking real loud . . . talking in a foreign language!

I've been kidnapped to a foreign country!

I lean against the truck even though it's hot as a skillet, and bury my face in the crook of my elbow and cry. The Vegetable Man comes running out of the house and scoops me up and carries me to the porch. I'm snot-out-the-nose blubbering.

He sets me down and bends over with his hands on his knees. "I call your house," he says. "I talk to your *apa*, tell him you hide in truck but you safe now, and I bring you right home. He want to come get you, but I insist and hang up. I bring you right home."

The Vegetable Man breaks into a smile so big I can see his gold tooth and both of the holes where there should be a tooth but there isn't. I stop blubbering. There's something I want before we go back to Thistle Way.

"Can I see your gypsy wagon? Please? And can your wife tell my fortune?"

The Vegetable Man takes a step back. He stands up tall and puts his hands on his hips. "My what?"

"Mrs. Henry says you're a Gypsy and you live in a tent or a wagon and your wife wears a turban like a swami and she can see my future in her crystal ball. Can she tell my fortune? Please?"

He looks away for a long time. When he turns back to me, his eyes are soft.

"I am Lovari, little one," he says. "My name is Dezso, and I am Lovari."

I shrug my shoulders up and down. Wagon or no wagon, I'm not going home until I see the inside of a gypsy house and get my fortune told by a lady in a turban and big hoopy earrings. Also, I'm starving. I figure Dezso must have a kabillion bowls of fruit in his house. Corn on the cob and tomatoes too. I beg to go inside, and then I start to whine.

"Only in front room," Dezso says. "And we keep the door wide open. Come. Meet my anya."

Dezso doesn't live in a gypsy wagon. He lives in one of the no-side-yard houses with his mother and his uncle. He doesn't have a wife who wears a swami turban and gold hoopy earrings and charcoal eye shadow, either. And there's no big bowls of fruit on the tables.

"Where are all the cherries and raspberries and grapes and stuff?" I ask. "Don't you get them for free?"

Dezso gives a little laugh. It's not a ha-ha laugh, though. It's more like a sorry chuckle.

"Fruit is for customers," he says quietly.

Dezso's mother goes into one of the other rooms and comes back with two jelly cookies wrapped in waxed paper.

"Kiffles," she says, handing me the treats. Then she says something to Dezso in the foreign language.

"My aunt's birthday yesterday," Dezso explains to me. "Anya want you to have a treat from the party."

The kiffles are the best thing I've eaten the whole summer, except for Mom's Frost on Fire dessert. I thank Dezso's anya, and she gives me a kiss on my forehead. Her lips are soft and dry; it feels like being kissed by butterfly wings.

On the way back to the truck, I wolf down the cookies. Dezso gives me a dinged up apple, and I polish that off too. All up and down Hickory Street kids are playing in front yards and on the sidewalk. Lots of men and ladies are sitting on their porches. Some are just watching the kids; others are playing checkers and chess or reading the evening newspaper.

The street lamps come on, and a little breeze picks up. I like Hickory Street.

Dezso opens the truck door and bows like a chauffeur, and we both laugh. On the way home, he tells me he used to love history class when he was in school.

"I come from Solymar, a village in Hungary," he says. He pauses a long time, like he's thinking about growing up in a hungry village. Then he shakes his head and changes the subject. "I tell you about people who used to live here—on Hickory Street. Good people. Working people. Germans and Irish and Hungarians. Everybody got along fine."

I roll down the window and stick my head out. A cool breeze blows my hair back and dries my sweaty scalp.

"All this," Dezso says, pointing at the houses on both sides of Hickory Street, "all this built long time ago, but built strong."

We go real slow along Hickory Street, and Dezso tells me about some of the people who came to America before him and wound up living on his block. I tear out some pages of his order book and write them down. I want to remember.

"Go slow," I tell him, and he does.

"There were school teachers and streetcar conductors on Hickory

Street," he begins. "Shoemakers, carpenters, and masons. Tailors from Dublin. Butchers from Düsseldorf—"

"Wait! How do you spell Düsseldorf?"

"Any way you want, girl," Dezso says, laughing. "There was an organ builder from my country, Hungary. A bedspring maker. Brewery workers. Men who worked in a tobacco factory and a stove factory. An axle turner. An inspector for the City Street Department. Stenographers, telephone operators, post office clerks, railroad switchmen, firemen, leather workers. They worked in slaughterhouses and sausage factories, in a glove factory, a stone cutting yard, a metal foundry, a lumber yard."

I stopped writing way back at the bedspring guy. I can't keep up.

I look out the truck window. We're on Brentwood Boulevard now, so places look familiar. I see St. Mary Magdalene Church and the Brentwood movie theater. I ask Dezso how old he was when he left the hungry village and moved to Hickory Street.

"I was little boy in Solymár," he says, kinda laughing. "I grew up there. I was in my last year at Eötvös Loránd University in Budapest when Soviet tanks roll into my country. They say they come to liberate Hungary from Nazis. Ha! I wake up in the middle of night and see my father, my mother, my older brother listening to the radio. Their faces are pale, frightened. My father, somehow he get all of us to Austria, but then he have heart attack and die. My brother decide to go back to Hungary and work against the Nazis. My anya and I, we come to the United States of America in March of 1948. Other people on the boat tell us to go to St. Louis, find a place to live near St. Stephen's. Go live on Hickory Street. Now I go to St. Stephen's every Sunday for Mass, sometimes St. Mary's, mostly St. Stephen's. They got a real thorn from the crown of Jesus. They got part of the sponge that was lifted to Jesus' lips on the cross. They keep these precious things in gold cases."

"Wow," I say. "I'd like to see that."

I think I'm gonna lean against the door and close my eyes, just for a minute or two. Just till we turn onto Thistle Way. Just till I get home. . . .

I wake up the next morning in my own bed. Bacon. I smell bacon! Mom makes pancakes and bacon every Sunday, right after church.

I stay in bed a few minutes, trying to remember everything. The sweet taste of cherries. The sickening feeling of being locked in the truck compartment. Being disappointed cuz there was no gypsy wagon or fortune-teller. The boy in the striped T-shirt. Anya's delicious kiffles. Thorns in golden cases. Slaughterhouse butchers. Gloves and bedsprings. It's all sorta scrambled up in my mind.

There's a few things I'm clear on, though: Mrs. Henry was wrong about Dezso. He isn't a Gypsy, he's Lovari. He doesn't live in a wagon either. He lives in a red brick house on Hickory Street. He doesn't have a wife who charges a quarter to tell your fortune. He lives with his anya, and they don't get free fruit. And that little bit of dirt under Dezso's fingernails? It's from scraping the last bits of dust off vegetables so they'll be clean when he brings them to our kitchen door.

I don't care if Mrs. Henry goes to Kroger's to buy onions and bananas, but they won't be any better than Dezso's.

I sit up in bed. Right then and there, I make a new rule. I'm never gonna sneak into the back of Dezso's truck again. He needs all the grapes and cherries and oranges to sell to his customers.

Besides, half the fun was playing a trick on the Vegetable Man, sneaking in and out of the compartment before he caught us. But we didn't have to run.

I'm pretty sure I know why Dezso always stops to smoke a cigarette and look the other way, and why he never catches us.

In 1950, St. Louis was the eighth largest city in America. Of the 856,796 men, women, and children who lived within the city limits, almost 2,300 were born in Hungary.

The median annual income for city residents was just under $3,000. The median value of a single-family home was about $9,000. One in nine households kept food cold the old-fashioned way—with ice. A total of 800 households had no central heating, and 25,000 households had no running water.

Those were the statistics for the city of St. Louis, where Dezso lived. The suburban numbers were different.

In the census tract where I lived, the median value of homes was $20,000. Each and every one had central heating. One out of every three had a television.

And as far as I know, the only person born in Hungary to spend any time in my census tract eked out a living selling fruits and vegetables to suburban housewives—Dezso.

He was a wary man, weighing each order to the ounce, counting the change to the penny. At a woman's kitchen door, he confined his comments to the matter at hand, and did not linger.

And he never, ever, accused a child of stealing cherries off his truck. Had he done so, even once, he risked losing every customer on Thistle Way.

A man like Dezso—a man from Hungary and, thus, automatically of suspicious origin and intent, a man who weighed orders to the ounce and made change to the penny, who had survived a holocaust and had built a life out of nothing—such a man does not take risks.

Melinda

the popular girl

Melinda was a "mean girl" long before the term leapt from the psychology of adolescence to the filmography of Lindsay Lohan. As third graders at Immaculate Heart of Mary Parish School, we could distinguish diphthongs from cardinal vowels. We could add $4.15 to $2.62, and we could recite the Ten Commandments by heart. We even wrote in cursive.

Melinda had mastered several other subjects as well: the power of random ostracism, the art of the malicious rumor, and the efficacy of prank phone calls. She was omnipotent, as well as resented and revered by every girl in Sister Josephina's classroom. We lived on a razor's edge, ever vying for Melinda's affection, ever avoiding her wrath.

For the entire school year, Melinda Potter had been the epicenter of a universe around which we orbited, held fast by the centrifugal forces of adulation and fear. In early June, as I left sweet Sister Josephina for a summer of boundless diversions and serial encampments, I had no reason to expect an impending change in the social order. No reason at all.

There were sixty-three kids in my class last year at Immaculate Heart of Mary. The rows of desks went from the blackboard to the cloakroom doors. We were stuffed in there to the gills, but Sister Josephina never yelled or made anybody hold out their hand so she could smack it with a ruler. She never hauled boys out to the hall by their ear, even though Freddy Langley deserved it, I'll tell you that.

Every morning, Sister Josephina walked into the classroom with a smile. The minute we saw her we all scrambled up from our desks and said, "Good morning, Sister Josephina." Then we made the sign of the cross and recited Sister Josephina's favorite prayer:

> *"Angel of God,*
> *My guardian dear,*
> *To whom God's love commits me here;*
> *Ever this night be at my side,*
> *To light and guard, to rule and guide.*
> *Amen."*

Third grade was a lot of reading, spelling, phonics, arithmetic, penmanship, and a whole lot of religion. Twice a week, we had science. On Friday afternoons, we got art or music. And about a kabillion times a day, Sister Josephina reminded us to wash our hands with soap before leaving the lavatory.

Last fall, on the first day of school, she gave us our seats. I didn't get too good of a spot—halfway back in row four, right behind Marty Throckmorten and right in front of Melinda Potter.

Melinda started pestering me right off the bat.

"Psst, Grace! What color do you think Sister Josephina's hair is?"

Daryl O'Meara was at the front of the room, reciting a chapter of *The Tale of Tommy Fox* from our reading workbook. Tommy Fox was giving Roger trouble.

"I don't know what color it is," I whispered. "I can't see her hair."

Sister Josephina's face bulged out from these crisp white cardboard things that went around her forehead, her chin, and her neck. A black veil went all the way down her back to where I supposed her knees would be. She had a crucifix necklace and a rosary for a belt.

Melinda poked me in the shoulder. "Go up and ask her, Grace. If you go up and ask her, you can be my best friend all year."

A chance to be Melinda Potter's best friend? What an opportunity!

Daryl O'Meara was stalled over a hard word. Sister Josephina thanked him and asked him to return to his seat. "Class," she said, "please re-read the entire chapter silently to yourselves." Daryl trudged down aisle five to his desk.

"Look," Melinda whispered a moment later. "He's moving his lips in the shape of every word."

I sorta chuckled cuz Melinda was chuckling. When Melinda makes a joke, it's best to laugh.

"If you have any questions," Sister Josephina told the class, "come up to see me one at a time."

I made my way up aisle four and stood beside her desk. When she looked up, I said, "Sister, what color is your hair?"

Sister Josephina wrinkled her eyebrows, like she was trying to remember. It got me thinking maybe nuns sleep with their veils on, and that got me thinking it might have been ages since Sister Josephine saw her own hair. Holy cow!

At last, she said, "Purple with yellow polka dots."

I bolted back to desk seven in aisle four. As soon as I sat down, Melinda hissed, "What'd she say?"

I squirmed around sideways and held my reading workbook in front of my face. "Purple with yellow polka dots."

"Gee," Melinda said with a little laugh, "with a name like that and purple hair, it's no wonder she became a nun."

Melinda was as good as her word. All last year, for the whole of third grade, I was her best friend. It felt pretty gol-darn good too, I'll tell you that, except when she played tricks on girls just to see what they'd do. Like the time Connie Wertz was late getting to the cafeteria.

Eight of us had rushed to find a seat at the popular table—that's what Melinda called the table nearest the windows, where she always sat. There was one empty place left, Connie's.

"When Connie gets here, everybody start laughing," Melinda said.

"Why?" a girl named Chrissy asked.

Melinda glared at Chrissy. "Because I said so, that's why. And when you see me raise my pinky finger, laugh again."

As soon as Connie Wertz put her lunch box on the table, Melinda's finger shot up, and we all started laughing.

"What's funny?" Connie asked.

Melinda raised her pinky finger again. We all laughed again. Connie looked from one of us to another. "What?" She was starting to look miserable.

"You can't sit here today," Melinda snapped.

I could see why Connie was confused. For the past two weeks, Melinda had been telling the whole world that Connie Wertz was her best-best friend. I didn't mind so much cuz I was still Melinda's best friend.

"Because you have buck teeth," Melinda said. "That's why."

Connie's front teeth do stick out pretty bad. Melinda's tricks always work because there's some little thing about them that's true that makes a kid embarrassed.

"Buck teeth, buck teeth," Melinda chanted, taking care to keep her voice low so the cafeteria monitors wouldn't hear.

At the far end of the popular table, Chrissy and another girl chimed in too. So did I. We were all nice girls, but we went along with Melinda cuz we know she'll pick on one of us next if we don't. Melinda whispered something to Sharon White, and Sharon opened Connie Wertz's Tinkerbell lunch box and dumped out all the food. Melinda sat back and watched, smiling, as Connie gathered up her sandwich and potato chips and went to an empty table. I felt bad for Connie, but I was sure glad it wasn't me.

Melinda Potter's got pretty greenish-grayish eyes and pretty hair that's yellowish and silky. She wears barrettes that are little satin bows, a different color for every day of the week. Her uniform blouses look brand new cuz they're whiter than anybody else's, and there are perfect creases at the top of the sleeve. Her saddle shoes never have scuff marks. Every girl at Immaculate Heart of Mary has to wear the exact same uniform, so we notice.

None of the teachers had any idea Melinda was picking a best-best friend one day and kicking the girl out of the group the next. Teachers just loved Melinda. In kindergarten, she got to pass out the Friday Treats, which was a pretty big honor. In first grade, she got to lead the May Day procession around the playground. When the procession got into church, Melinda didn't have to go into a pew like the rest of us. She got to walk right through an opening in the communion rail and up to the altar. Then two of the most popular eighth grade boys helped her onto a step stool, like she was a princess or something, while the rest of us suffered to death on hard old wood kneelers while we sang Virgin Mary songs.

"*O Mary we crown thee with blossoms today! Queen of the Angels and Queen of the May. . . .* "

Melinda Potter took her sweet time placing the gol-dang crown of roses on the statue of Our Lady that day, and the whole afternoon she got to flounce around in her First Holy Communion dress while the rest of us had to wear our same dumb old uniforms.

Even chubby, sweaty Sister Agatha in the cafeteria got all gushy when Melinda went through the lunch line. Melinda Potter was the only kid who got to pass by the boiled spinach without taking a scoopful on her tray. And lots of times I saw Sister Agatha give Melinda an extra cookie or a carton of chocolate milk instead of white.

Melinda is the luckiest kid in the world. First of all, she's the most popular kid ever. Second of all, she's the prettiest kid ever. And third of all, she's an only child. She never has to share anything with anybody.

It's my first summer of being best friends with Melinda. We've been out of school for three weeks, but I haven't seen her much. In fact, I haven't played with Melinda since school let out. I have already asked her if I can sleep over, and she didn't say no, so I pack my red plaid suitcase and walk over to her house. I make sure to include my cutest pajamas—the ones with the little French poodles on them—so Melinda will be impressed. When she answers the door, I expect her to be scruffy like all the other kids on Thistle Way, but she isn't. She's standing back a couple of feet from the doorway cuz it's raining and also cuz she's all dressed up in a fancy pink dress and a pink velvet headband and white patent leather Mary Jane shoes. Her socks have little pink ruffles on the edges.

"Hi, Grace."

She doesn't sound too thrilled to see me.

"Hi, Melinda. Wow, you look pretty, like you're going to a birthday party or something."

"Yeah, Connie Wertz's party is this afternoon."

Wait. What? Connie Wertz is having a birthday party and Melinda is invited and I'm not? I start to get a sick feeling in my stomach. Melinda is watching me with sharp eyes.

"Connie brought over her invitation a week ago. I told her you were the one who thought up the bucktooth joke in the cafeteria that time, so you probably wouldn't want to go to her party."

I've seen Melinda play this kind of trick on other girls, so I have to think fast.

"Well," I say, shrugging my shoulders up and down, like I don't much care, "I really don't want to waste an afternoon on Connie Wertz's birthday. She's boring."

Melinda looks surprised. "Well-l-l, in that case, Grace, want to play cards on the back porch? The stupid party doesn't start for an hour."

Close call.

I've never been inside Melinda's house before. It's the smallest one on Thistle Way, so it only takes two seconds to show me around. I especially like the bathroom cuz it's got pretty pink and black tiles on the wall. I expect Melinda's room to be beautiful, but it isn't. I don't see any stuffed animals or dolls or toys, and when I put my suitcase away in Melinda's closet, I notice the only things hanging there are her Brownie uniform, her navy blue school uniform, and two uniform blouses. The window doesn't even have curtains, just a pull-down shade.

Out in the hall, Melinda grabs the telephone from a little shelf on the wall. She stretches the cord around the corner to the living room. We sit on the sofa cuz the only other place to sit is a folding chair. Next to the sofa is a table with a bunch of pictures on it.

Melinda puts the phone down on the couch, so she can show me each picture. There's one of her dad during the war. Him and some other soldiers are in front of a gigantic airplane. Mr. Potter is pointing to the spot on the side of the plane where somebody painted a lady in a skimpy swimsuit. In another picture, Mr. Potter is pushing Melinda in a stroller. Melinda looks happy, but Mr. Potter looks sorta tired.

Melinda gives her dad's picture a kiss and puts it back on the table. Then she hands me the phone and a piece of paper.

"Dial this number," she says.

"What for?"

"It's Jimmy Huebner's number. Go ahead, dial."

"What do I say if somebody answers?"

"You say, 'Hello, is your refrigerator running?' And when they say yes, you say, 'Then you better go catch it!'"

"You do it," I say, shoving the phone at Melinda.

Melinda knows the phone number for just about every kid in our class. She also knows how to do lots of different prank calls. She calls up Craig Bolinger, and when he answers, she starts belting out "Jingle Bells" and then hangs up real fast. She calls up three more boys and tells them Connie Wertz has a crush on them. That one's really funny, but the next one's the best.

Jean Marie and June Marie Walsh are twins, just like Susan and Sharon White. Jean Marie and June Marie are a year older than us, but they got held back a grade cuz they're so gol-darned dumb.

Anyways, there's at least eight Walsh kids that I know of. So Melinda calls up Jean Marie and June Marie's house, and when their mother answers, Melinda says, "Mrs. Walsh, where do babies come from?" Then she hangs up real quick, and we laugh our eyeballs out.

When the telephone tricks get boring, Melinda changes into a pair of shorts and a top, and we go out to the Potters' screened porch to play cards. I tell her Bridget Finnegan has been trying to teach me and Jane how to play Canasta when she babysits us. I thought Melinda would be impressed about me learning Canasta, but she just says Canasta's boring, and she's gonna show me how to build houses and towers out of cards. We're sitting on old bath towels cuz it's been raining like crazy all day again. Most of the porch floor is kinda wet. There's a bunch of dead worms in a corner—fat, pasty-looking ones.

The summer started out blazing hot and sunny. Our climbing roses drooped on the trellises and even the snapdragons wilted. They've perked up now, though. It's been raining for the last two days. Everything smells kinda swampy.

All of a sudden, Melinda stares at me real hard and pokes me a couple of times with her pointing finger.

"Grace," she says, "you're the best friend I ever had, so I'm gonna tell you a humongous secret. Do you want to be popular, like me?"

Do I want to be popular like Melinda? Heck, yeah, I do. I hardly dare breathe in case she changes her mind.

While Melinda builds a keen-o tower out of cards, she explains how she and me are gonna be the most popular girls in fourth grade.

"First of all," she says, "we whisper in front of the other girls."

"What do we whisper about?"

"It doesn't matter. The point is to make the other girls feel like we know something and we're not gonna tell them."

"Oh. Okay."

"Remember, it only works if you or me points to one of them and then we both laugh and whisper some more."

"Okay."

"Then we let another girl into our group, say, Betsey Bauer. We tell her she can only be part of the group if she plays a trick on one of the other girls."

"What kinda trick?"

"Well-l-l," Melinda says, "like in the girls' lavatory at school, when

Marlene Rowland goes into one of the stalls. We tell Betsey Bauer to go into the next stall and stand up on the toilet and look over the divider at stupid Marlene while she's peeing."

"Holy cow! That's so mean!"

Melinda has a smug-looking smile on her face, so I figure she doesn't much care how awful Marlene would feel.

"To make the trick even better, Betsey should make fart noises while she's spying on Marlene."

I don't say anything. I don't think Melinda notices cuz she's already telling me more secrets of popularity. The first one I've already seen her do, which was not letting Connie Wertz eat at our lunch table and dumping all the stuff out of her lunch box. The second one I would never have thought up in a kabillion years.

"You bring a rubber band to school," she says. "Out on the playground, you hold both ends and stretch it out as long as it will go and then twist the ends so the rubber band is all kinked up. Then you call over Betsey Bauer—she's good cuz she's got that long frizzy hair. You tell her to turn around with her back to you and cover her eyes. She'll do it, I know. Then you hold the twisty rubber band right next to her hair and pull the ends of it real far apart and let go! The rubber band will snap into Betsey's dumb frizzy hair and scrunch up in there, and her mother will have to cut out the huge tangle. Isn't that great?"

I'm thinking about my sister, Jane. She has curly hair. Not frizzy, but curly. I'd sure hate for anybody to do that to Jane. And besides, didn't Melinda just say we're gonna let Betsey Bauer be in our popular group?

Melinda is about to tell me another secret of popularity, when the phone rings. We look up, staring bug-eyed at each other. We're thinking the prank calls backfired, and now somebody's parents are calling to snitch. Mrs. Potter answers the phone, but she doesn't say anything for a long time. After a minute or two, we hear her say, "Oh, no . . . "

And then we hear a hollow thump.

Melinda jumps up and runs inside. I get up too. From the doorway, I see Melinda and her mom. The telephone receiver is dangling by its cord from the little shelf in the wall. Mrs. Potter's on the floor, fainted dead away.

I glance over my shoulder. The beautiful house Melinda made is wrecked, just a bunch of cards on a wrinkled old towel.

I wait on the porch a long time by myself, just worrying, cuz Mrs.

Potter and Melinda are in one of the bedrooms with the door closed. Mrs. Daley and Mrs. Lofton are in there too. I hear crying.

Somebody must've called my mom cuz she walks right in the Potters' front door and out to the porch and gives me a huge hug. The whole way home, she holds my hand, which she never did before, I'll tell you that. I'm so worried about my best friend that I don't much feel like eating dinner. Mom says it's okay, and she lets me go up to my room. A while later, Dad comes up and sits on my bed. He takes me onto his lap, which he hasn't done in a long time, and he sorta rocks back and forth a little, like he's thinking hard about what he's gonna say.

"Frank Potter had a hard time during the war, Grace."

"But Dad, they've got a picture and . . . "

"Don't interrupt, honey. Just try to listen, okay?"

Dad tells me that when the war was over, some men came home and they looked okay cuz they didn't have any cut-off legs or shark bites, but they weren't okay on the inside because they couldn't stop thinking about bad stuff that they'd seen during the fighting. Dad says he thinks Mr. Potter is one of those men who were hurt on the inside because of seeing really bad war things.

Dad thinks a minute and then goes on. "Those poor guys have a hard time adjusting, Grace. They just can't seem to forget certain things. The bad memories come up sometimes, even when they're at work, and they make mistakes."

I'm wondering why Dad's telling me all this bad stuff about Mr. Potter.

"Ever since the war ended, Frank's been hired and fired by three big plumbing contractors. I don't know what went wrong, but he's been taking any odd job that comes along, jobs the union men turn down because they were too small."

Dad gives me a look that says, you following?

I nod. When's he gonna tell me why Mrs. Potter fainted?

"A couple of days ago, the pipefitters walked off a big city sewer project. Mr. Potter and some other men took the work. They had to cross picket lines, but I suspect Mr. Potter's big concern was working on a nest of old, rusty pipes in a twenty-foot-deep storm sewer."

There's something I don't understand. "Dad, what's a union?"

"Shhh, Grace, it's maybe too complex for you to understand tonight. Go to sleep now. You can ask all the questions you want in the morning."

It's about a kabillion hours before I finally fall asleep.

The next morning, Dad brings the newspaper up to my bedroom, which he never does. He unfolds it and shows me the front page. There's a big picture of Mr. Potter! Then he reads the newspaper story to me:

After days of steady rain here, hundreds of thousands of gallons of water have turned parking lots and lawns into ponds. North St. Louis was particularly hard hit. Rainwater swept into storm sewers and down into underground channels built when the northern part of what is now St. Louis was far less populated. Over time, vacant lots that had soaked up rainwater were paved over and built on. Today, much more water pours into those old underground channels than they can handle.

According to the City Water Department, by this morning, huge quantities of water had backed up behind a weakened valve that had been diverting the surge away from the area where independent plumbing contractor Frank Potter, 51, of Brentwood, and four other men were working. At 3:47 p.m., the valve burst.

"What happened to Melinda's dad?"

"He drowned. The whole crew drowned. The searchers are still looking for them."

Almost everybody on Thistle Way is at Immaculate Heart of Mary for Mr. Potter's funeral Mass, even the Protestant families, even Benny Herman's family—Mom says the Hermans go to a temple to pray instead of a church. Anyways, Mrs. Potter and Melinda are in the first pew. Melinda is wearing the pink dress and velvet headband she had on for Connie Wertz's birthday party.

After church, I hear somebody say Mrs. Potter will have to hock her wedding ring to get out from under. Somebody else says that might not do it.

I don't know what hock means, but it doesn't sound good.

A few days later, I stop by to see Melinda. There's a "for sale" sign in her front yard. Melinda opens the door, but she says her mom won't let her have guests because she's home alone.

"Where's your mom?"

"Working. She got a job at Pope's Cafeteria."

"Well, she's a good cook," I say, trying to think of something positive.

"We're moving next week. I'm gonna go to a different school next year, and I won't have to study religion either."

Melinda starts to close the door, and then pauses.

"Just so you know, Grace Mitchell, you're not gonna be the most popular girl in fourth grade. I made up those secrets I told you. I told the real secrets to Connie Wertz."

Across the breadth of human experience, friendship is among the most common of all bonds.

And the most complex.

Its variations are legion, from workplace associates to true blue soul mates, from best friends to fair-weather friends. There's the golf buddy, the tennis partner, the gals in a bridge group. There's the college roommate who lets you borrow her anthropology notes, the two-de-grees-of-separation friend, the friend of a friend of a friend. There are fleeting friendships, lifelong friendships, and hibernating friendships that go dormant and then, years later, awaken. Somewhere not in my universe, there are friendships with benefits.

Although it would seem to be an oxymoron, there are toxic friendships.

Toxic. That would describe my relationship with Melinda. I realize that now, though I didn't then. Little Miss Potter was a user. A grade school Machiavelli whose intricately plotted games pitted friend against friend while an amused Melinda sat back, observing. There was only one winner, Melinda. Only one object of the game: to underscore her social supremacy. The shattered players were irrelevant to her.

I was no match for that cunning girl. Despite a few pangs of con-science, I was glad to serve as her loyal assistant, a role that, over time, would surely have left its mark on me. At eight, going on nine, a child's personal integrity is unformed and, as such, ever so vulnerable to outside influence. But for the drowning of a man in a sewer, who knows what damage my toxic "friendship" with his daughter might have done in the school year to come—to others, and to me.

I was stunned when I left Melinda's doorstep that day. Sucker-punched. I'd come within a hair's breadth of becoming the second most popular girl in the fourth grade, an appellation swept away by the brown rush of rain-water through a municipal sewer. Focused on my own emotions, I was too self-absorbed to think much about her pain. And I was too young to understand the anxiety she must have felt, facing a future in which some other girl doubtless already reigned as the most popular of all.

Friendships are a blessing, an obligation, and, sometimes, a trial. But when they end, there is a palpable sense of loss.

For me, the void would be filled by a most unlikely new friend.

Carolyn

the catastrophe

I see her still.

Sometimes, in the muddled thoughts that swirl when I'm almost asleep or almost awake, I see my beautiful, doomed cousin, Carolyn Reinhardt. After all this time.

Caroline was my first cousin once removed, but who's parsing? Way past time for that, and time was what Carolyn didn't have. What she did have was beauty, wealth, a loving husband, and a baby boy on the way. Forever on the way, never to arrive.

Carolyn's unborn son was almost at term when, rashly, she climbed on a chair in her father's study to kill a bee clinging to the high arch of a Palladian window. She thought to keep her young husband out of danger, for he was—is—allergic to bee venom. In doing so, she employed both her most pronounced flaw, impulsiveness, and her greatest asset, selflessness.

Twice a year, my sister and I were invited to spend a couple of nights with our cousins at Blenheim, their magnificent estate in Huntleigh, on the outskirts of St. Louis County. We were there at Blenheim on that blazing afternoon when Carolyn swatted at a bee clinging to the arch of a Palladian window. It was high overhead, and she lost her balance, slipped from her chair, cracked her skull on the knife-edged window frame, and fell awkwardly through thin air.

She died the moment she hit the floor. Her unborn son died a few

moments after, still curled in his milky caul. Together, they took leave of this world and commenced singular, epic journeys into the next.

It broke our hearts.

It's late. I'm home from Blenheim, finally, but I can't get to sleep. My pillow's all wet from crying about Carolyn.

I get up and go over to Jane's bed and stand there in the dark. Jane holds up the sheet for me, and I crawl in. Her pillow's all wet too.

We hug each other, Jane and me, touching foreheads and crying.

That summer, for the second time in many weeks, I attended a funeral. This time, I gave myself over to grief. I did not wish to be consoled, and there was no one to do so anyway. Everyone was heartsick. That night, I pondered a novel and horrifying thought: some people die well before they should, before whatever or whoever takes them from us has any right to do so. It was a terrifying prospect—the idea that a bee could come along or a truck veer across a center line or a maniac get hold of a gun, and I could lose another loved one—snap—just like that.

I would have brooded far longer but for the immediacy of a child's world and a prior commitment that required me to pack up and leave home again.

Cherry

the cabin

A s a third grader at Immaculate Heart of Mary, I was taught how to write in cursive, read for comprehension, identify an ordinal number, locate the seven continents on a map, and genuflect without wobbling.

During a week at Camp Coureur des Bois, I acquired a far different set of skills: How to braid an eight-strand lanyard, how to fit the knock of an arrow into a bowstring, how to teepee my kindling, how to Allemande left on a square dance floor, and how to fold an American flag into a perfect triangle. The counselors had taught me skills that I regarded as critical in the summer of 1956 (and have not used in the half-century since).

However, it was a camper, a wiry hellion of a girl, who taught me the most durable lesson of all.

I've been waiting for this day forever.

I woke up at the crack of dawn, nutso excited to get to camp. Right after church, I changed into my new clam diggers and my new Keds (which weren't ever Jane's). Then I lugged Dad's old duffel bag and my bedroll out to the car.

I wanted to take my red plaid suitcase to camp, but when I laid out all the stuff on my bed that the Coureur des Bois brochure said I'd need, it wouldn't fit. I crammed and crammed, but there wasn't a smidge of room for my sweatshirt, my underpants, or Arf-Arf, my little china dog.

Jane sat on her bed the whole time, watching me. "If you want to bring your favorite suitcase to camp, why don't you just leave your underpants at home, Grace? That'd be real smart."

I put the plaid suitcase back in my closet and went to find Dad's old duffel bag from the war. It smelled kinda like our attic, but at least everything fit.

While I was packing, Mom poured sweet tea into a thermos, wrapped two bologna sandwiches and a bunch of grapes in waxed paper, and put the food on the car's front seat. Then I kissed Dad goodbye and stuck out my tongue at Charlie, who was sticking his tongue out at me. I stuck my thumbs in my ears and wiggled my fingers, and Charlie laughed like crazy. He's so cute.

Mom said the drive would take an hour, but it didn't. It took forever. We ate our sandwiches and counted the pumps at the filling stations we passed to make the time go faster.

We're here, finally! I shoot out of the car and run to a big open space where a kabillion girls are standing around, waiting for something to happen. The sun is frying the tops of our heads.

One of the campers turns to me and says, "The quad's always the hottest place at camp. No shade."

"The quad?"

"You're new, right? We're in the quadrangle, but nobody calls it that. Just say 'quad.'"

A man walks to the center, all important-like. Mr. Franklin, the camp director, is short and almost completely bald. When he blows his whistle, the sound makes everybody clamp their hands over their ears. He welcomes us all and explains that you pronounce the camp's name *coo-ree-yay day bwuh*. Then he says he'd like us to listen to a little "oration" he gives to all new campers.

First, he orations about what each face on the totem pole meant to Indians who lived in Missouri a long time ago. He tells us one tribe was called Chickasaw and another one was called Osage. He says they believed in wind spirits and sun spirits. Then he orations about how long ago nature felled a big tree on the campgrounds, and Chickasaws and Osages whittled the totem for Camp Coureur des Bois. He asks us to give a round of applause to those Indian artisans, so we clap, even though we're sweltering to death.

In summer, Dad and Mom have this thing they say to each other. Dad tells Mom the air is so thick, it's suffocating. Mom looks at him all lovey-dreamy and says no, it's sizzling. Then Dad says no, it's sultry. And Mom says no, it's scorching. Then Dad gives Mom a long, long kiss on the lips.

Me and Jane, we like that.

Anyways, Mr. Franklin finally stops talking about Indians and mops his forehead with a bandanna. I bend over to pick up my suitcase, but gol-danged Mr. Franklin starts orationing again, so I put it down and act all interested. Mr. Franklin tells us the name Coureur des Bois comes from a long time ago when French woodsmen went into the forest in America and learned lots of Indian ways to survive while they hunted beavers, which the white man liked to make into hats. . . .

When Mr. Franklin is finally done yammering, he invites all the parents to leave. One kid starts to cry. Another kid runs over to her father's car, climbs in, and refuses to come out. The counselors start singing "This Land is Your Land" at the top of their lungs to drown out the kid's bawling. I wave to Mom and watch our DeSoto until it's all the way down the gravel driveway and turning onto the paved road.

I'm feeling kinda queasy in my stomach and thinking I might be getting homesick, but right then a counselor calls my name. Miss Tina is the prettiest teenager girl I've ever seen, kind of like a cross between Princess on *Father Knows Best* and the littlest Lennon sister. She lifts the whistle attached to the end of her pink and blue lanyard and blows it, nice and soft. Me and some other girls pick up our duffel bags and bedrolls and follow her to a long row of grey-ish cabins. I stay up front, close to Miss Tina, so I can watch her ponytail swing back and forth.

At the cabins, Miss Tina turns around. "Grace, Mary Kay, Vickie, you're in a cabin with Cherry," she says.

Cherry? What kind of a name is that? I crack a smile, thinking about cherry-flavored Jell-O.

Cherry plants herself in front of me. "One thing y'all needs keep in mind, new girl," she says, poking my forehead so hard I tip backwards. "My name ain't funny."

Cherry looks to be about my age, but she's taller and way skinnier. Her elbows and knees are pointy. Even her shoulders are pointy. Her skin is so black that the places where she's scratched mosquito bites look like chalk lines. Her hair is a mess of tiny braids, and she's got on boy shoes—black high tops with knots in the laces.

Before I left for camp, Dad told me to stay sharp on my first day. "It might take a while until you learn the ropes," he said.

I thought he meant we'd be learning how to tie a bunch of ropes into knots, like the boys in my class did in Cub Scouts. But I'm thinking he might have meant steer clear of Cherry.

Last summer, me and Jane went to two weeks of day camp at the YMCA in Clayton. Jane wasn't nutty about it, I'll tell you that. She'd already polished off every Nancy Drew book they had at the library, and then the day before YMCA camp, she checked out three Dana Girls books. Jane and her friend Lizzie had a race to see who could finish reading all the Dana Girls books. Jane was worried camp would interfere with her reading time.

I was hashing my way through Beezus and Ramona, but I sure wanted to go to day camp at the YMCA. I loved weaving hot pads for Mom on a little red loom and playing Steal the Bacon and making the funny movements when we sang "Do Your Ears Hang Low." I would have loved swimming too, but hardly anybody got to go in a swimming pool last summer because of polio. Heck, my gol-durn mom still won't let me and Jane go swimming, even though we're supposed to get the new polio vaccine this summer.

"Listen up, girls," Miss Tina is saying. "We're Muskrat Unit. Got that?"

Vickie catches up to me and whispers, "Be glad we're not in Fox Unit. Miss Jean makes Fox Unit go on nature walks to gather trash. And last summer, Beaver Unit had to memorize the names of twelve kinds of trees just by looking at the leaves. We Muskrats have it best. Miss Tina gives out lemon drops, and during rest time, Miss Tina does up our hair in a French twist if it's long enough."

Dang, my hair's not long enough.

I whisper to Vickie, "The cabins are pretty dinky, aren't they?"

Vickie whispers back, "I think the houses in my Monopoly game are bigger!"

Inside, if one kid wants to walk to the back of the cabin and another kid wants to walk to the front, they have to turn sideways.

"We're gonna be on top of each other," Vickie says under her breath. We both look at the bunk beds and laugh.

Vickie and Mary Kay go to the same school. Right off the bat, they snag the bunk on the right side of the cabin. It looks like I'm gonna be bunkmates with Cherry. She flops down on the lower bunk and stretches out, watching me. I toss my bedroll up to the top bunk and plant my foot on the bed frame, careful to not touch Cherry. I take a quick hop to hike up, or I try to. Right then and there, Cherry shoots her foot out and knocks my foot off. I go down hard and land on my butt.

"What'd you do that for?" I say, trying not to cry.

"The upper's my bed," Cherry says. "Been mine since the start of summer. Get your shit off there!"

I grab my bedroll and shove it off the top bunk. Cherry's standing right behind me, so close I feel her breath on the back of my neck.

"C'mon," Cherry says. She reaches around and twangs my forehead. "Get this lower bed made up."

Across the aisle, Vickie and Mary Kay fluff their pillows.

I'm wondering how to get Cherry's stuff off the bottom bed without Cherry killing me, when she snaps her fingers in front of my face. "Stop lookin' at that bottom bed, new girl. Bottom bed's mine. Been mine all summer."

I hoist my bedroll to the top bunk again. I make sure to keep an eye on Cherry; I sure as heck don't want that girl to kick me down again. She's all interested in a mosquito bite on her shoulder, so I'm thinking it's safe to climb up.

Sheesh, it's even hotter up here. And the mattress smells like old pee.

It's the first hour of the first day of camp, and I want to go home.

"Hey Grace," Vickie says, "let's see if there's any wild daisies behind the cabin. I brought a jelly jar. We can make a bouquet and put it on our shelf."

When we're a ways from the cabin, Vickie gives me the lowdown about Cherry.

"A church group in St. Louis pays the money for her to spend all summer here," she says. "They probably figure camp will make Cherry turn out okay, but it isn't working. Last summer, she stuffed a whole pancake in her mouth and spitted it out, right onto the table. She even bragged about how she was gonna set Mr. Franklin's beagle on fire!"

Miss Tina blows her whistle. All twelve Muskrats line up on the side-walk in front of our cabins for our first activity—a tour of the camp. Cherry acts bored; she knows every inch of the place by now.

"This is the mess hall," Miss Tina says, pointing at a big log building. "The cooks specialize in ground beef like hamburgers, sloppy joes, chili, meat loaf, Swedish meatballs . . . but the pancakes are to die for, and they never run out of bug juice."

"Bug juice!" I cry. "Yuck!"

Miss Tina laughs and tells us bug juice is camp talk for Kool-Aid. "And if anybody invites you to go on a snipe hunt, don't do it! Snipe hunt is camp talk, too. It means they're playing a joke on you."

The latrine is down a short path from the mess hall, which Miss Tina says places a good degree of trust in a child's immune system.

At the far end of the quadrangle is the Great Lodge, a huge round building with no walls.

"Each night after supper, the whole camp assembles at the lodge," Miss Tina tells us. "Tomorrow night, we'll all meet here and then hike to the prairie field. There's a circle of logs to sit on, and a ton of wood stacked up in the center for a bonfire."

We pass the camp's swimming pool. The water is all clean and shining in the sun, but nobody's swimming. Miss Tina says Muskrat Unit won't be having swim time this week because most of the parents checked a box on the registration form saying they didn't want their kid to go in the pool.

That night, I climb up to my bunk bed and scrooch around until I get comfortable. My pillow smells like home, but I'm not homesick.

In a real perky voice, I say, "G'night, Cherry."

"G'night, your damn self."

I believe I've made headway with Cherry.

After dinner the next night, the whole camp assembles in the great lodge and hikes out to the flower meadow. We sit on big logs laid in a circle around a huge-o-mongous pile of twigs and branches. Mr. Franklin orations about Indians again and then lights a roll of newspaper and sets the lowest twigs on fire. Soon, a bonfire is sending smoke way up to the sky.

The counselors pass out song sheets with the words to "Kumbaya." Mr. Franklin leads the first verse, and we all join in, swaying along with the melody. Well, not all of us.

Cherry cracks a twig into little pieces and tosses them at the fire. She won't sing. She won't sway either, which botches up the sways in our whole section.

"Cherry, honey, it's much more fun if we all sing," Miss Tina says. "We'll do 'Greensleeves' next. How about you lead off?"

Cherry starts singing her lungs out, but the words are all wrong.

Alas, my glove, you doo-doo me wrong,
To piss me off discourteously,
For I have argued with you oh so long,
Delighting in your nudity.

The camp director rolls his eyes. Two girls in Beaver Unit burst out laughing. Miss Tina sighs. "Well, I'll sing it then," she says.

Alas, Cherry, you do me wrong,
To cast me off discourteously,
For I have loved you well and long,
Delighting in your company.

Muskrats are all my joy,
Oh, Muskrats are my delight,
Muskrats have a heart of gold,
Including my lady, Cherry.

I glance at Cherry. The fire has died down, so I can't be sure, but I think I saw her eyes had big tears in them. She doesn't cry, though. She just blinks real hard, and the tears go away.

The next morning, we have crafts during first period. The craft shack is at the edge of the prairie field. We sit at wood picnic tables in front of the shack and wait for something to happen.

My stomach isn't feeling too good. The cooks made the oatmeal so danged thick. Vickie stuck a spoon in hers, and it stayed straight up, and Cherry stomped up to the cook's window and demanded a knife and fork, but I was starving, so I ate the whole bowl, and now my stomach's sticking out like I swallowed a turtle.

A couple of girls try to guess whether the craft instructor, Miss Lynn, will bring out Popsicle sticks for jewelry boxes, material and yarn for sit-upons, paint and smooth rocks for paperweights, or strands of colored plastic for lanyards. At last she comes out.

Lanyards! Hurray! I'm gonna make one in every color and give them out as Christmas presents.

After lunch and quiet time, Miss Tina takes us to the stables. Horseback riding is the best thing about Camp Coureur des Bois.

The stable guy's name is Chip, and he looks exactly like Ricky Nelson.

Chip and Miss Tina make moony eyes while we stand around roasting in the sun. Finally, Chip shows us how to get on and off a horse without killing either ourselves or the horse. We get to pick our horses, and I pick a reddish-brownish one named Autumn Storm. Two stable guys give each horse a little push backwards to get it away from the barn. Right off, some kids kick their horses and yank on the reins and one girl slides over sideways, and pretty soon, all the horses are jumbled up.

Chip straightens out the mess, and when all our horses are in a line facing the same way, we clip-clop around the barn and go onto a trail. It's my first time riding a horse, except for the pony rides on Brentwood Boulevard across the street from St. Mary Magdalene Church. They have strands of white light bulbs over the corral, but the ponies are dinky, and you only get to ride around in the dinky corral, not on a real trail.

The camp trail winds through the flower meadow, crosses a shallow creek, and goes into the woods. Chip shifts sideways and calls back to us to watch out for low limbs.

I pat Autumn Storm's sweaty neck and tell her she's a good horse. Cherry's right in front of me. When we're deep in the woods, her horse lifts its tail and lets loose three huge-o-mongous plops of poo. The poo falls from its pillowy butt onto the trail, and Autumn Storm walks right through it.

"Cherry! Your gol-durned horse poo'd right in my horse's way!"

All the Muskrats start laughing. Two girls point at Cherry and hold their noses.

Cherry kicks her horse hard, and it gallops into the woods with Cherry bobbing up and down like she's riding a pogo stick. Miss Tina tells us to stop. She sounds scared. Chip gallops off to rescue Cherry. Our horses stamp their feet and make burbly noises; I'm pretty sure they're thinking about following Cherry's horse into the woods. I start to worry Cherry's horse rode off a cliff and Cherry died out in the forest, and then I start to cry cuz I'm the stupid person who made poor Cherry mad. Then I hear the sound of hooves thrashing through the brush. It's Chip and Cherry! And Cherry has a big smile, which I can't figure out. Chip nudges Cherry's horse into the line, and she turns around and laughs.

"Thanks, new girl."

"What for?"

"For the fine ride. They never let us gallop, but I saw my chance, and I took it. I got to gallop, and you ain't never gonna get to."

"Yee-haw!" Chip shouts. Right then, his horse takes off at a trot, and all the other horses follow. I hold onto the saddle horn for dear life. The breeze blows back my hair. My mighty horse speeds through the woods again. Leaves slap my face, but I don't care.

Camp Coureur des Bois is the funnest place ever.

Me, Cherry, Vickie, and Mary Kay are on our bunks, waiting for morning wake-up call. I'm sweating my brains out. Vickie gets up to open the door, but pretty soon a bunch of crackle-skinned June bugs are buzzing around the inside of the cabin, bonking their stupid June bug heads on the inside of the window that won't open. Every now and then, one of them buzzes close to Mary Kay, and she squeals like a pig, which is about the only thing that's funny about being in this bloody hot cabin. It's the middle of the camp week, and everybody's grungy. The showers in the latrine have slimy stuff on the floor and spiders on the ceiling. Nobody goes near the showers. Vickie says last year, they just counted the swimming lessons as taking a bath, but this year, hardly any of the counselors let their units go swimming.

Mr. Franklin sounds the morning whistle. Vickie and Mary Kay pick up their toothbrush cups and shuffle off. Cherry gets out of bed, too.

"Lord," she groans, "it's hot as Hades."

Cherry's shelf is bare. She takes what she needs from our shelves.

I sidestep along the aisle to the shelves. I'm almost past Cherry when my arm accidentally brushes against her. Quick as a wink, she shoves me, hard.

"Damn heat," she says. "Damn mess hall food. Double-damn June bugs."

I get up and start to pull on a sorta clean pair of shorts, trying not to listen, when she jumps up and plants her hands on her skinny hips.

"I done had enough o' your stink!"

My what? I smell?

Cherry snatches a tube of Ban Roll-On Deodorant from Mary Kay's shelf, yanks my arm above my head, and slathers my armpit with deodorant.

It's cool and wet and sticky, and I'm stunned.

Cherry and I stand face-to-face, glaring at each another. And then the strangest thing happens: Cherry bursts out laughing.

"Girl," she says, "you needed fumigat'n."

That strikes me as pretty gol-durn funny too. I wrap my arms around Cherry's bony shoulders, and we laugh until our stomachs hurt.

For the rest of the week, Cherry and me are best friends. When we do-si-do in the great lodge, I pick Cherry to be my partner. When we sing "If You're Happy and You Know it Clap Your Hands," Cherry smacks my knee to make the clapping sound. She gives me fourteen lemon drops, and I give her a green and blue lanyard.

The camp week is over way before I want it to be. I roll up my bedding and pack my craft projects and award badges. Me, Cherry, Mary Kay, and Vickie sign each other's autograph books. Then all the campers assemble in the quadrangle and sing "This Land is Your Land."

I see Mom in the parking lot with all the other parents. They're holding car doors open. I want to stay here and braid lanyards and ride horses and shoot arrows at targets. I want to sit on a log next to Cherry and sing "Kumbaya." Mom's waving. I've gotta go.

The whole time we're going down the gravel drive, I hang my head out the window. Cherry didn't even say goodbye. She's just sitting by herself near the flagpole. Mr. Franklin's beagle is curled in her lap. She's stroking its head.

I holler, but she won't look up.

That night in my bedroom, I write a letter.

> *Dear Cherry,*
> *I had a super-duper time at camp. Are you still a Muskrat? I hope so. Remember the trail ride when your horse plopped a big one (ha-ha-ha) and my horse trotted through it? I hope we can see each other soon. You will always be my friend.*
> *Love,*
> *Grace Mitchell*

Weeks and weeks later, a reply finally comes. I sprint out to the backyard. Mom's pinning towels to the line.

"I got a letter from Cherry, my camp friend," I say, handing her a clothespin. "Can I have Cherry for a sleepover? Can I?"

Mom looks at the note, and then at the return address.

> *PRUITT-IGOE*
> *2300 CASS AVENUE*
> *SAINT LOUIS, MISSOURI*

"No, and don't pester, Grace. One of the reasons your dad and I were happy to have you go to camp was because we knew you'd make new friends there, friends not just from Thistle Way or Immaculate Heart of Mary, but kids from all over."

"I did. I made lots of friends, but Cherry was my best friend." I'm starting to cry.

I rub away the tears and blaze my eyes at Mom. "I know why you don't want Cherry here—because she's colored!"

Mom doesn't answer.

I run to the patio, flop onto a wicker chair, and bury my face in my hands. I hear Mom flap a damp towel in the air. When I look up, she's pinning it to the line.

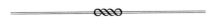

I view that afternoon now through the long lens of maturity, and I suspect my mother's decision was based on more than just what it seemed at the time.

Pruitt-Igoe was a huge public housing project on the fringes of downtown St. Louis in which misguided urban planners shoveled the poorest of the poor into a cluster of high-rise buildings. The apartments were purposefully small, lacked air-conditioning, and were accessed by elevators that stopped only on every other floor. The idea was that the occupants would congregate in a congenial, neighborly fashion outside the confines of their apartments. The reality was that they had to walk up or down dark stairwells to get home, to empty trash, do laundry, to go anywhere. And the stairwells of Pruitt-Igoe were perilous, home turf for rapists, slashers, thieves, and worse.

My mother had no idea whether Cherry's parents owned a car. If I invited her and then found out she had no transportation, we couldn't take back the invitation; that would have been cruel. My mother would have had to venture into one of the towers to get her, which wouldn't have been safe for her, or ask Cherry to wait outside for her, which wouldn't have been safe for Cherry.

I look back on my childhood—and I am not alone in this—and I remember the doctor who sat at the edge of my bed, the encyclopedia salesman who wore palm tree neckties, the nuns with men's names, the librarians with lavender hair, the movie ushers with flashlights, the filling station attendants with brimmed caps. To the last, they were white.

Aside from Odetta, our maid, I was unacquainted with a single person of color, except Cherry.

I never saw her again, but I thought of her over the years, and always with gratitude. That tough, skinny girl taught me a valuable lesson, one not found in schoolbooks: open your heart to a friendship that broaches fierce borders, and you open your heart to a color-blind world.

the Blairs

the newcomers

In the mid-1950s, in ways that have nothing to do with geography, Missouri was steeped in Midwestern moderation, as well as a smidge of old-fashioned Southern propriety. There were rules—unwritten, but understood: Ladies first through a doorway. Men's hats off in church. Hand over heart during the Pledge of Allegiance. In mixed company, children were seen but not heard unless directly addressed, and then we were to make eye contact, answer succinctly, and return at once to quiescence.

Everyone knew the rules. Everyone was expected to follow them.

Meanwhile, California, especially Southern California, was blissfully tossing off conventional codes of conduct like a tourist doffing woolens at the beach. Awash in sunshine, dotted with palms, studded with movie stars, Southern California lived fast, loose, and free, unfettered by the idea that conformity is necessary, or even desirable.

Or so it seemed to us back in Missouri.

Even as a child of eight, it was not particularly perceptive of me to suspect that a grown woman who wore cheetah print clamdiggers on moving day was probably not from Missouri. And I understood that a new neighbor who encouraged young children to use her first name was breaking one of our unbreakable codes of conduct. But never in a thousand years could I have predicted what a fast, free, and loose lifestyle Lou Blair and her husband had brought with them from Southern California.

I'm not doing much. Just sitting on our front porch sticking Silly Putty to the funny papers. The one I'm doing now is Prince Valiant. I peel off the Silly Putty and stretch it so Prince Valiant is short and fat. I'm just stretching it some more so Queen Aleta has a long nose when Rainer comes running across the lawn. Rainer Niesen, he's a pal of mine. Anyways, by the time Rainer gets here, he's almost out of breath.

"Somebody's moving in at Melinda Potter's," he shouts. "There's a big truck out front and furniture's getting unloaded. Let's go see."

Sounds good to me. My Silly Putty was getting kinda inky anyways.

Rainer and me run halfway around the circle and stand across the street from Melinda's house, looking at the new people's furniture. It doesn't look like the furniture at my house, I'll tell you that. First of all, the new people have a ton of palm trees growing in huge pots. And second of all, most everything is orange, yellow, or turquoise.

A lady totters down the Potters' driveway and crosses the street. She has to take baby steps cuz she's wearing the highest wedge-heeled sandals I ever saw, with crisscrossed ribbon straps.

"Hi kids, I'm Lou." she says, all peppy. "Lou Blair. And my husband back there, he's Ted."

Mr. Blair has the blondest hair and the tannest skin I ever saw, and he's carrying a surfboard into the garage, which is pretty stupid cuz the biggest watery thing around here is the Mississippi River, and I'm pretty sure you can't surfboard on the Mississippi River.

Rainer and me say, "Hello, Mrs. Blair" at the exact same time, and then right away we say, "Jinx, you owe me a Coke!"

Mrs. Blair's wearing cheetah print clamdiggers and a matching halter top that leaves her whole middle naked. Her sunglasses have sparkly diamonds at the pointy corners. Rainer's staring so hard at Mrs. Blair's naked belly button that I have to jab him in the ribs so he looks someplace else.

Mrs. Blair fishes two fingers into the pocket of her clamdiggers and waggles a skinny compact out. She opens it, runs her tongue along her top teeth, snaps the compact closed, and shoves it down into the pocket again. Then she gives Rainer and me one of those looks that means she thinks we're cute as the dickens.

"Call me Lou," she says. "I insist."

In due time, another new couple moved into our proper little community, a couple who shared Ted and Lou's zest for flouting Midwestern social conventions. None of them were constitutional scholars, but they sure knew how to test the limits of the First Amendment.

Six or so weeks from the day I first set eyes on Lou and Ted Blair, on a festive night in August, they and the new neighbors vaulted freedom of expression to a whole new level.

I know. I saw.

Missy

sunshine time

Each afternoon, from the day the first crocus popped up until the day the first snowflake drifted down, Missy Henry stood outside her house and wailed for her mother.

It was hopeless, all that crying and begging. It was the mother who locked the child out.

Our backyard was separated from the Henrys' by a chain-link fence. I spent a good deal of my childhood playing with my sister and brother in our yard, and how we managed to ignore the tribulations of Missy Henry, I don't know. But we did.

Everybody did.

Missy Henry's not a friend of mine or anything, but I do think it was kinda crummy when she turned six last week and didn't even get a birthday party. I knew it was Missy's birthday cuz her mom made a pound cake and stuck a couple of candles in it. She took the cake pan out to a table on the back porch and then yelled at Mr. Henry and Missy and Missy's older brother to come outside. As soon as they got there, Mrs. Henry told Missy to blow out the stupid candles quick, so they could eat the stupid cake before the ice cream melted and all her hard work was ruined.

I don't think Mrs. Henry worked that hard on the cake cuz I was playing in our yard at the time, and when I looked over the fence at the

Henrys standing around that little table, I could see the cake was flat and kinda burnt, and it didn't even have any frosting on it. Missy didn't seem to care, though. She gulped in air three times and whooshed it out before she got both candles blown out. I wondered if she'd done that on purpose, just to make the happiness last.

Missy didn't go to kindergarten, but I figure she'll start first grade at Thomas Hart Benton School in the fall. Thomas Hart Benton is where the kids in Thistle Way go if they don't go to Immaculate Heart of Mary. I'm worried the other first graders are gonna tease Missy cuz she looks kinda different. She's short and stocky with a big belly and a round face. Her nose is sort of pushed in, and her ears are a little too small for her head. Sometimes her tongue sticks partway out of her mouth, and she doesn't even seem to notice. And her hair is so straight and thin that her plastic barrette always dangles like a cockeyed earring.

I screw up my courage and knock on the Henrys' front door.

I've waited as long as I can before asking to stay over at the Henrys'. I want to spend a night with Missy and her family about as much as I want to get stung by a wasp. But at the beginning of the summer, when I ran away from home and got found, Mom said if I thought living with some other family was better than living with my own, then I could stay a night or two with any neighbors who'd have me. We made a deal, Mom and me, and I'm gol-darned if I'll let my end of the bargain just peter out.

Mrs. Henry answers the door and glares at me like I just dropped a bag of poo on her front porch or something.

"What do you want, Grace?" she says, in between sips of coffee.

It's after 9 o'clock in the morning. Mrs. Henry's still in her housecoat and floppy bedroom slippers. I'm thinking she's in the middle of another Toni Home Permanent cuz her hair's wound around teeny tiny pink curlers, and it stinks.

I ask in my most polite voice if I can stay over for a couple of nights.

Mrs. Henry sets her coffee cup on a little table just inside the front door and then she pulls out a pack of Tareytons from the pocket of her house-coat. She shakes out a cigarette and lights it. Two streams of grey-white smoke shoot out her nose and blow right through the screen door. Some of the smoke gets in my throat, and I cough. Mrs. Henry rolls her eyes, like my getting smothered by her Tareyton smoke is a big inconvenience.

She opens the screen door a crack, and I'm thinking she's gonna invite me inside, but she just sticks out her cigarette and flicks a good inch of ash into the bushes. When the door smacks shut again, she makes a big deal out of locking it.

"I don't care," she says.

I sorta wish she'd said no.

Jane plops down on my bed and bounces a couple of times, watching me pack my red plaid suitcase again.

"I know something you don't know," she says, giving me a sly smile, the one that means she knows something I don't know but I'd sure want to know.

"How much?"

Jane and I have this thing: if she has a secret, I pay her to tell, and if I have a secret, she pays me to tell. The better the secret, the more it costs.

"Well-l, let me see. It would have been a nickel, but since you're going to be living at the Henrys', it's a dime."

Cripes. A whole dime. I shake my piggy bank upside down until a dime drops from the slot.

Jane sticks the dime in her pocket. "Okay. I heard Mom and Mrs. Lofton talking about the Henrys this morning. Mom said she was kind of concerned about you staying with them, seeing as Mrs. Henry treats Missy so bad."

I glow. Mom's worried about me.

Jane goes on, "Then Mrs. Lofton said Mrs. Henry was no spring chicken when she got pregnant with Missy. And Mom said Missy must have been a surprise baby."

I want to ask Jane what a chicken surprise baby is, but she's talking a mile a minute.

"Mrs. Lofton went on and on about how hard it must be on Mr. and Mrs. Henry. On Jack too. And then they noticed I was listening, and they clammed up."

"I don't understand. What was hard for the Henrys? I want my dime back."

"You figure it out, Indian-giver." Jane flounces off with my dime.

I think about chicken surprise babies while I stuff clean underpants and socks in my suitcase. I still don't exactly get what Jane was talking about, but you'd have to be a spaz not to see that Missy is an aggravation. Heck, I don't like Missy much either. All those afternoons she spends cooped up in her backyard, and she never plays, just stands at the gate bawling her eyes out.

On Saturday morning, I walk over to the Henrys'. It's starting to drizzle, so I'm glad Missy answers the door right away. On the way up to her bedroom, we pass by Mr. Henry; he's sitting in a big easy chair, reading the morning paper. I'm halfway up the stairs when I hear a glassy rattling noise coming from the kitchen.

"Mom's taking out the trash," Missy says. "Daddy drinks lots of beer on Saturdays."

Missy stands there forever smiling at me with that goofy grin of hers. I've only been at the Henrys a few minutes, and the place is getting on my nerves already. This is gonna be the longest day of my life.

I play Go Fish with Missy in her bedroom until lunchtime. It's the only card game she knows. Mrs. Henry makes Missy and me peanut butter sandwiches and gives us a nectarine to share. She takes another sandwich and two bottles of beer to the living room. I peek around the corner and see Mr. Henry crouching over the television, fiddling with the antenna.

"Howard, what are you doing?" Mrs. Henry sounds exasperated.

"Trying to find the ball game."

"The Cards are playing here, Howard, at Busch Stadium. The game hasn't started yet. You can listen to it on the radio when it does."

Back in the kitchen, Mrs. Henry turns on a radio and stands with her back to the sink, leafing through an old *Movie Secrets* magazine. The KMOX weatherman is reading a special weather bulletin.

"*. . . damaging straight-line winds and golf ball sized hail are expected to hit the communities of Warrensburg and Sedalia hard this morning . . . *"

I ask Mrs. Henry if Missy and me can go over to my house and play Parcheesi when we finish lunch, though I don't think Missy is ever gonna finish her sandwich. She's poking holes in it and shouting, "Polka dot!"

The weatherman's still talking. "*. . . numerous reports of trees being down where wind and hail was most intense . . . *"

"That wouldn't be a good idea," Mrs. Henry says. She doesn't even look up from her gol-darn magazine. "It's almost Missy's Sunshine Time."

"Cool beans."

Sunshine Time! It sounds like we're going to a park. Or maybe Mrs. Henry's gonna take Missy and me to a swimming pool. Probably not a pool, though. The weatherman's sounding kinda worried.

"*Strong winds and a suspected tornado associated with this storm system caused power outages that affected seven hundred homes in Topeka overnight."*

I haven't been swimming since forever. Last week, Mom took me and Jane and Charlie up to Thomas Hart Benton School to get the new polio vaccine. A lady in a nurse uniform gave each of us a little paper cup with cherry syrup in it. Me and Jane drank ours, but Charlie spit his out and got red polio juice all over Mom's blouse. The nurse said Charlie might do better with an injection, which is a long word for a shot. I sincerely doubted Charlie would do better with a shot, but I kept my trap shut cuz Mom was looking very irked at Charlie.

Even after we got the vaccine, Mom was still worried we'd get polio at a real swimming pool, so Dad bought a three-ring wading pool and blew it up in the backyard. Charlie's diaper got so soaked, it fell right off, and he ran around naked, which was pretty cute. But after a while, the grass got all muddy, and the mud squished between our toes. We plunked Charlie back in the swimming pool, but he stood up and pee-wee'd in the water, and it wasn't nearly as much fun as going to a real swimming pool. . . .

There's that weatherman on the radio again.

"Lightning can strike as far as ten miles away from the rain area in a thunderstorm, but at that distance, it may even be difficult to tell a storm is coming."

If Mrs. Henry's gonna take us swimming, I'm thinking I'd better go home and get my bathing suit. Nobody's at my house right now—they're all at the baseball game, but Dad showed me how to use the house key he keeps under a flowerpot on the front stoop.

I'm watching Missy fiddle with her sandwich when Mrs. Henry suddenly stubs out her cigarette, grabs Missy by the upper arm, and drags her out the back door to the far end of the backyard where there's a big pen enclosed on all the sides with a chain-link fence.

Missy kicks and wheels her legs, but her mother's stronger. Mrs. Henry opens the gate with one hand and pushes Missy into the pen. Then she quickly backs out and locks the gate. On the way back to the house, Mrs. Henry rocks her head sideways, left, right, left again, and rolls her shoulders up and down, just like my mom does after she's peeled about a ka-billion potatoes and carrots.

Well, we're not going swimming. Missy's gonna be stuck in her pen a couple of hours. Funny, I live right next door, but I'm so used to Missy Henry wailing out there every afternoon that I hardly don't hear it

anymore. Missy's crying is just part of the regular sounds of the neighborhood, like cicadas whee-wheeing. Like the ice cream truck music and
the Vegetable Man calling, "Vegetables!"

Missy's Sunshine Time pen has a little play slide and a sand box with
some plastic bowls and spoons. There's a beach ball and a Mouseketeer
toy typewriter and a ratty stuffed animal out there too. The stuffed animal
is sitting in a doll stroller with a fringed sunshade. Missy just stays at the
gate screaming, "Mamma, no! Mamma, Mamma, no!"

I hear thunder rumbling, but it sounds kinda far. The radio man is
talking about hail and rain and wind and lightning. It's hard to hear him
cuz there's a ton of static. Back in the kitchen, Mrs. Henry opens the ice
box, and cold air billows out like fog. She closes her eyes and bends into it.
She takes out an ice tray and gives the handle a good crack, tosses a couple
of cubes into a glass, fills it with liquid from a bottle, and drinks it all down.

The radio man is still talking about the storm. He sounds real excited
now.

"Lightning can be fascinating, but it is extremely dangerous. It kills an
average of sixty-seven people per year in the United States."

Through the screen door, I see Missy leaning into the metal mesh gate.
Her fingers are curled around the padlock, and she's wailing, "Mamma,
no!" harder now.

I'll say this for Missy Henry, she doesn't give up.

I'm pretty sure Missy's dad is conked out in front of the television set.
Mrs. Henry pours more clear liquid in her glass. Then she goes upstairs.
I figure she won't mind if I stand at the back door and check on Missy.

The sky's a weird color, kinda greenish greyish, and there's a bunch
of black clouds moving fast. The wind's lots stronger too. Somebody's
trash can overturned, and pieces of newspaper are blowing all around,
getting all tangled in bushes. I watch an old sock slap against the chain-
link fence and stay there.

A bolt of lightning crackles, and I jump about two feet. Right after that
is a boom of thunder so loud, some glasses rattle in the sink. The leaves
on the tops of the oak trees are thrashing. It's starting to rain in slanty
splats that hit the grass and bounce up again. Out back, Missy's curled in
a ball on the ground with her hands over her ears. Her whole little body's
trembling.

Where's stupid Mrs. Henry? Why doesn't she unlock that gol-darn pen
and bring Missy inside?

" . . . a threat of organized severe thunderstorms over a larger area . . . "

I run upstairs looking for Mrs. Henry. Behind a closed door, I hear water splashing and Frank Sinatra singing "Jeepers Creepers." I guess Mrs. Henry's taking a bath. I guess she took a record player in the bathroom so she could listen to Frank Sinatra while she takes a bath.

I bang on the door. "Mrs. Henry!" I shout. The music's blaring.

"Go away, Grace! This is the one time all day that I have to myself."

I run downstairs and out the back door. It's raining hard. Lightning bolts are flickering in the clouds right over Missy's backyard. The thunder's closer too. I kneel outside the gate and stick my fingers through the mesh. I have to shout cuz the thunder and wind are so loud.

"I'll go get help!"

A huge gust of wind lifts the doll stroller into the air behind Missy and sends it flying.

"Duck!" I scream, but the stroller clunks the back of Missy's head. She starts crying again, but I think she's okay cuz there's no blood or anything.

At my house, I jam the key into the front door lock and twist it, but the stupid door won't open. It's starting to hail! I run to the garage and try to lift the overhead door. It won't budge, but the regular door at the back of the garage opens. The hail's hitting the garage roof hard. Inside, it sounds like a whole bunch of popcorn poppers all going at once. I look around for something I can use to open Missy's pen. I finally spot two things that might work: a stool and a rope.

Outside now, the hail's stopped, but the rain's blowing sideways. I drag the stool to the chain-link fence and tie the rope around one of the stool legs. Holding onto the other end of the rope, I climb on the stool, hop over the fence, and yank the rope till the stool jostles over the fence. Me, Missy, and the stool are all in the pen, like I planned.

It's blowing harder than ever. What if I wind up stuck in here with Missy? I take a deep breath and yank Missy up to her feet. She's all snotty and crying. She's shivering pretty bad too.

I haul the stool over to the gate, with Missy clinging to me for life. I'm eight, going on nine, and she's three years younger than me, but she's thick and sturdy. Somehow I get her on the stool. I give her a little push so she leans over the top of the gate. Then I give her a big push, and she flops over the top. I jump over too. We're free!

"C'mon, Missy, let's race for the house!" I shout.

Mr. Henry's still conked out in the living room. Upstairs, the bathroom door's still closed, and Frank Sinatra's singing, *"I'm gonna sit right down and write myself a letter . . . "*

I get Missy out of her wet clothes and find some clean shorts and a top for her. Then I change into dry clothes from my suitcase. Missy's hair is soaking wet, but she lets me comb it, and for once, the dang barrette stays in. Down in the kitchen, I give her a couple of Oreo cookies and pour her a glass of milk.

I'm gonna have my dad beat up Mr. Henry and send him to the hospital. I'm gonna have Mom bake a batch of poison brownies and watch stupid Mrs. Henry eat one and foam at the mouth and fall down dead on her kitchen floor. Then Missy won't have to suffer through any more Sunshine Times.

The rain finally stops. The radio man is saying the baseball game got delayed, but now it's starting.

"Jack Buck here for the St. Louis Cardinals. Top of the first. The skies have cleared and with a little luck, the stands here at Busch Stadium will be dry in no time. Dodgers' second baseman Jim Gilliam faces off against Cards' pitcher Murry Dickson. Ladies and gentlemen, it's going to be a beautiful day."

I knew Missy Henry was different. We all knew that. What I didn't know was that she had something no other child on Thistle Way had: an extra copy of chromosome 21.

It is likely that Missy also had a heart murmur, cataracts, hearing difficulties, persistent constipation, trouble sleeping and chewing food, poor judgment, a short attention span, mountains of frustration, and an IQ of about 50.

What Missy had was Down syndrome.

Back then, children like Missy were called Mongoloids, a term coined in the 1860s by John Langdon Down, the English doctor who published one of the first descriptions of the condition. Down likened the upward slanting shape of the children's eyes to those of people native to Mongolia, and the term stuck. Often, the children were hidden away, sent away, and denied life-saving treatment. According to one medical study, only forty-two percent of Down syndrome children born between 1940 and 1950 lived to their fifth birthday.

A syndrome. A condition. That's what Missy Henry had. What she lacked were two things that would have improved the quality of her life immeasurably, things Jane, Charlie, and I took for granted: a loving family and compassionate care.

Mrs. Pearson

the secrets

Sylvia Pearson lived in a small house on the other side of the circle. She had a long face and cloudy eyes under thick brows. Her bosom was full and low, her hair a sea of black waves reprocessed at a corner salon once a month on the dot, which was a conceit rendered hopeless, for one by one, the speeding years had wrinkled her powdery complexion and folded her neck so that it resembled the bellows of an accordion. Underneath a wardrobe of forgettable dresses, she was amply girdled. She did not indulge in cosmetics or perfume; I suppose there seemed little point.

Silvia Pearson must have been eighty the summer I was eight, going on nine. I think children shouldn't give a thought to the regrets of those near the finish line of life. I surely didn't, until the summer afternoon I went begging for candy at Mrs. Pearson's door and came away with her life in my hands.

"Wanna go begging?" Jane asks me.

She sounds kinda half-hearted. Begging's what Mom calls it when we walk over to see Mrs. Pearson.

I'm always in the mood to beg for candy at Mrs. Pearson's. Even when she's all out of candy, she gives you a banana, which is almost as good.

Me and Jane have a race to see who can get to Mrs. Pearson's the fastest. Jane wins, just like always. She's got longer legs; also, newer Keds.

"Good afternoon, girls," Mrs. Pearson says, holding wide the screen door. "It's Jane and Grace Mitchell, right? I think I have some Nonpareils. Do you like Nonpareils?"

I don't know. I never ate a non-parasol before. I'm thinking what the heck does an umbrella taste like and what the heck's gotten into Mrs. Pearson, making kids eat umbrellas instead of giving us candy. Is she going cuckoo or something? I look at Jane, but she just shrugs her shoulders up and down.

Mrs. Pearson's wrinkly face breaks into a smile. Some of her regular wrinkles smooth out, but she's smiling so hard, it makes a bunch of new ones.

"I'm sorry, girls," she says. "Nonpareil is a French word that means 'without equal.' Come now, into the kitchen. Jenkins and I will let you try one or two."

Jenkins is Mrs. Pearson's parakeet. She keeps him in a wire cage in a corner of her dining room. Jenkins has a swing and a little water dish in there. Last summer, Mrs. Pearson invited me and Davey Lofton in to see Jenkins, and I tried to reach in between the wires and pet him, but he nipped my finger hard. I'll never do that again. Mrs. Pearson told us that each afternoon when she's done reading the newspaper, she cuts up the front page into squares for the floor of Jenkins's cage, which is good cuz Jenkins poops a lot.

Jane and me stand around waiting for the non-parasol candy until Mrs. Pearson motions for us to sit at her dinette table. There's just enough room for Jane and me, even when we scrunch our chairs up so close to the table our stomachs touch the edge. We fold our hands in our lap cuz Mrs. Pearson was a teacher, and we figure she'll give more candy to kids with good table manners.

Jane and me watch Mrs. Pearson open a cupboard and take out a candy box, a red plate with little glass balls around the edge, and glasses with little yellow lemons painted on them. She fills the glasses with lemonade and puts the chocolate candies with white sprinkles on the pretty plate.

I don't know why Mrs. Pearson called the candy non-parasols. They're Sno-Caps, just like they've got at the Brentwood movie theater, only bigger.

Jane and me eat three non-parasols each and drink all the lemonade. Mrs. Pearson tells us the snapdragons she's got in a vase on her dinette table came from her garden. Jane says, "Aren't they pretty," and then she gets up to leave, which I think is kinda quick, being as Jane was the one to suggest we go begging in the first place. At the screen door, Mrs. Pearson thanks Jane for stopping by today, which is backwards from who should be thanking who, but at least Jane says "you're welcome" before she goes.

I tell Mrs. Pearson her non-parasols are quite tasty, and she laughs, which I don't know exactly why.

"Would you like to stay a while longer, Grace?" she says. "I have plenty of lemonade left, and one or two 'non-parasols.' Let's take our refreshments into the living room, shall we?"

I'm getting the feeling Mrs. Pearson thinks I'm gonna be at her house all afternoon, which I'm not too keen on. Sheesh, why didn't I go when Jane left?

"Excuse me a moment, will you, Grace?" Mrs. Pearson says.

The living room's got a saggy loveseat and two green chairs. All the little tables have white doilies on them and pictures of old people. I pick out a candied orange wedge from a crystal dish and pop it in my mouth. There's a card table in the corner, and it looks like Mrs. Pearson's trying to do one of those five-thousand-piece jigsaw puzzles. This one's really hard cuz it's just ocean and sky. When she comes back, her eyes are all red and watery. I'm pretty sure she was crying.

"Today's an anniversary," she says, "and I'm feeling a little bit lonely." She turns on a fan, which is good cuz I'm thinking I'm gonna be here a while.

"Would you like an orange wedge?" she says. "Have as many as you wish. I'm afraid the doctor has told me not to eat sweets anymore." She sighs and adds, "And I so loved them."

Sunbeams coming through the Venetian blinds are making stripes on the floor. The living room smells like violets mixed with mothballs. I eat three orange wedges and put the fourth one back in the crystal dish. I'm feeling kinda queasy.

Mrs. Pearson asks if I'd like to help her with the puzzle. She says she can't seem to concentrate today because she keeps remembering things. We both stay quiet, working on the puzzle. After a while, she asks if I'd like to hear about some of the things she's remembering.

"Sure. It's okay by me."

Mrs. Pearson tells me she has a tape recording machine from her days teaching in her classroom. She asks if I'd mind if she recorded her stories while she tells them to me.

I'm thinking that's kinda weird, but I say it's fine. We lug the big tape recording machine out of a closet and set it on the coffee table. I'm not too interested in old lady stories, so the whole time Mrs. Pearson is talking, I sing Camp Coureur des Bois songs silently in my head and work on the puzzle. I get lots done while Mrs. Pearson is remembering. Most of the time she looks kinda wavy-eyed, like she's seeing what she's remembering, and like she's talking more to herself than to me. Stuff about picking up the newspaper on a snowy morning and eating roast chicken and going out for a boat ride.

Today's the longest I've ever been inside Mrs. Pearson's house. It isn't so bad, except for the candied orange wedges. I'm never eating candied orange wedges again in my whole dang life.

After a way long time, an alarm clock jangles. Me and Mrs. Pearson sit up and look at each other, startled. "It's time to ring my school bell," she says.

So *that's* how Mrs. Pearson rings her bell at exactly five o'clock! I always wondered.

Mrs. Pearson looks a little rickety, so I follow her to the kitchen. You never know when somebody as old as Mrs. Pearson is gonna go all woozy and fall down, but she's okay. At the kitchen door, I thank her for the non-parasols and orange wedges I ate.

"Grace, would you wait a minute?" She goes to the living room and comes back with the reel of tape. "Would you keep this for me, dear? I don't need a tape recording to remember my stories, but I'd like to think they won't be forgotten. I don't have children, not even a niece or nephew that I know of."

Mrs. Pearson's eyes get watery again. Even though she's smiling, I'm thinking she's sad on the inside. I take the memory reel and reach up to give her a hug. At home, I stick the memory reel under my mattress. It's where I keep my most important things.

Jane walks in and gets all nosy. Before I know it, I tell her about Mrs. Pearson's memory recording.

"Pinky swear you won't tell, Jane."

"No way."

Jane's already running downstairs to tell Mom.

After dinner, Mom and Dad tell me to come into the living room. I'm trying to figure out what the heck I did wrong.

"You didn't do anything wrong, honey," Mom says.

Whew, that was close. Lots of times a kid does a wrong thing without knowing it.

There's a big tape recording machine on the top of the piano, which I'm curious about, but I think I know.

"Grace, we'd like to listen to Mrs. Pearson's tape recording so we can see if it's something you should be keeping."

"Sure," I say. Heck, I'm just glad I'm not in trouble.

At first, all we hear is scratchy noise, but then Mrs. Pearson starts her memories. . . .

From the very first day, I loved everything about teaching. I loved asking a lackluster student to read an excerpt from *Romeo and Juliet* or *Jane Eyre*, loved watching her face light up. I loved decorating my classroom with pictures of Byron, Keats, Shelley, and women writers like Elizabeth Barrett Browning and Edna St. Vincent Millay. I loved the tennis matches and football games and Friday afternoon assemblies. I loved the dusty smell of chalk. When I stayed late to grade papers, I loved the sound of the janitor's floor polisher whirring back and forth along the hallway.

For years, I willingly put my career before my private life. One morning, I woke up and realized I wasn't young anymore, but by then I had reconciled with the prospect of living in solitude, and I was not unhappy. Not at all.

In my late thirties, my first beau came along, and oh—the color he brought to my cheeks! He walked into the district office one afternoon while I was turning in my students' first quarter grades. He nodded to me, and I had just enough presence of mind to murmur "hello" before the school secretary ushered him into the superintendent's office. When the secretary sat down again, she told me that his name was Clifford Phillips and that he was applying for the position of school librarian.

"He looked interested in you, Silvia," she said, and I felt my face flush.

The secretary took an extraordinarily long while shuffling through my grade reports, and by the time she was finished, the superintendent was escorting Clifford past the frosted glass door of his inner office. Clifford did not appear to be in a hurry to leave, and after he adjusted his necktie and pretended to study a print of the Eades Bridge on the wall, he asked me if I would like to have dinner with him the next evening at Kemoll's. He was tall and sandy-haired with tortoiseshell glasses and boyish features. Quite impetuously, I accepted.

Cliff and I married in April and moved to a nice second-floor apartment on Kingsbury Boulevard near Central Avenue. By then my parents had passed away, and my only brother was living in England.

Oh, I was so happy to have someone with whom to share my life!

Each evening before we put away our reading and retired, Cliff would pat my hand and kiss me good night, first on the lips and then just here, above my cheekbone. Some nights I would wake up in a panic, thinking it had all been a dream. I would lie still and stare through the chiffon curtains, counting stars, listening to Cliff breathe, a sound so deep and rhythmic it reminded me of a bow drawn across the strings of a cello.

We quickly settled into a lovely routine. Our weekdays, of course, were filled with school matters. But on Saturday afternoons, we would go to a picture show, and on Sundays, we'd walk a bit in Forest Park. We loved the walk along the Grand Basin, looking up at the statue of Louis XIV and the façade of the art museum. On Sunday evenings, we'd talk about buying a little house somewhere in Brentwood, and we'd go through travel pamphlets and talk about all the places we'd visit once we retired.

We'd been married almost nine years when the unthinkable happened.

Each winter morning, Cliff wrapped himself in his flannel robe and padded down the winding back staircase of our apartment building. It was his custom to go down to the back stoop for the morning newspaper and the milk or cream the Pevely Dairy man left for us. Cliff was always concerned the milk would freeze in winter and go sour in summer.

I remember everything about that morning—every single thing. I puttered in the kitchen measuring coffee grounds and pouring them into the percolator's strainer basket. I sliced an orange in half and then loosened each tiny section in perfect wedges.

When it seemed to me Cliff was taking a long time, I called down the stairwell, "Cliff, breakfast is nearly ready. What's keeping you this morning?"

When he didn't answer, I ventured down a ways.

I saw his slippered feet first, turned at odd angles on the vestibule's terrazzo floor. I went down another step and saw shards of glass, a puddle of cream, and the hem of his robe. Freezing cold gusts of air were flapping the back door open and slapping it closed. Pages of the newspaper were sailing away with the wind. I stumbled down the last few steps and cradled Cliff in my arms. Flakes of dry snow swirled through the door and settled on us like dust. I called again and again for help, though I knew it was too late. Every ragged cry puffed into the cold air and vanished.

There was an autopsy. Cliff had seemed in such good health. The coroner said an aneurysm—a blood vessel in his brain—had ballooned out and then burst. No one could have predicted it.

We had found one another too late to have children, so I was alone again, more alone than ever. Cliff left me enough to buy a nice house, and this house on Thistle Way was for sale. It was just the right size and price for one.

A year or so later, I received a surprise telephone call from an older woman who had lived below Cliff and me in the apartment on Kingsbury. I didn't know her well, and I was curious about what prompted her to phone me out of the blue. She told me she had heard of Cliff's passing, and she wondered whether I might like to have dinner with her the following Sunday. She said the butcher had sent her home with a roasting chicken much larger than what she had ordered, and she could not let a perfectly fine bird to go to waste. After I reluctantly agreed to share her Sunday afternoon dinner, she told me her son, Lloyd, would be joining us.

I was not happy about being in the building where Cliff had died, and I was not happy about being bamboozled into what she clearly had cooked up to be a date with her bachelor son. So it was with a degree of surprise that I found both Violet Pearson and her son absolutely delightful.

Oh, Lloyd was not physically attractive, not like Cliff. Lloyd was about sixty at the time, on the short side, and quite round. His nose was bulbous, and he was bald except for a fringe of hair that cupped the back of his head from ear to ear. If one were inclined to make cruel comparisons, it could be said Lloyd Pearson was the very incarnation of Friar Tuck.

Mind you, I was not young anymore myself, and I had never been what fellows used to call "a looker." But Lloyd was so kind and caring, and his mother so down-to-earth, that I soon found myself happily joining them for Sunday afternoon dinners on a regular basis. In time, I came to love them both deeply, which must have been apparent, for Lloyd had taken to asking me to marry him practically on a weekly basis. Eventually he wore me down, and we married in March of 1951. Lloyd moved in with me here, on Thistle Way.

Lloyd was an only child. I never met his father—he died before I got to know Lloyd, though I understand the two were quite close.

Five years ago, shortly after Lloyd and I married, he saw an advertisement in the paper for a cabin in Wisconsin on Lake Winnebago. A small fishing boat with an outboard motor came with the property. Within the week, he bought the package, sight unseen. Before I knew it, we were packing up Lloyd's station wagon for the drive up to Lake Winnebago. Mother Pearson came with us, of course, and I was glad to have the female companionship. I envisioned Lloyd spending long hours out on the lake and then walking up the trail to the cabin with a string of fish for Mother and me to fry. But that was not to be. . . .

Lloyd was not a speedy driver, so we were a day and a night on the road up to the lake cottage. Along the way, Lloyd kept up a running patter about boats, fishing boats, mostly. I think he wanted Mother and me to feel comfortable when we were in the water, and he wanted us to be familiar with nautical terms like starboard and port, bow and stern, tiller and gunwale, and such. He talked endlessly about Wisconsin and its beautiful forests and lakes, especially Lake Winnebago. All of it was based on information in books he'd checked out at the library.

He told Violet and me the lake is large—twenty-eight miles long and eight miles wide—but it isn't deep. I was glad of that, for none of us knew how to swim. He said the average depth is about fifteen feet, but the water ranges from eight feet to twenty-one feet in places. On our side of the lake, Lloyd said, we must be careful to avoid the rock and gravel reefs.

What the books failed to say was that the shallow depth of the lake makes for hazardous boating conditions that can crop up suddenly, if the weather turns.

The cabin was charming, everything we'd hoped for. We arrived in the late morning, and before lunch, Lloyd went straight down to the water to take the boat out for a trial run. Violet and I stayed behind to scrub the place from stem to stern. When dear Lloyd returned, he looked pleased as punch about his first boat ride on the lake.

That afternoon, we dozed on Adirondack chairs on the porch. Sunlight speared through the pine boughs. Oh, it was heavenly. Lloyd spotted a red fox, but he couldn't get to his camera case fast enough to snap a picture. As yet we had no fish to fry, but Violet had brought a roasted chicken, fingerling potatoes, and a peach pie from home, all of which were nestled in a wicker hamper. We ate in the kitchen at a table covered with a gingham cloth. I was as contented as a woman could be.

Violet made a pan of soapy water and took care of our few dishes, spit-spat. Out on the porch, Lloyd scanned the cloudy sky and reported back, "No star-watching tonight, ladies."

I remember that. I do.

Violet asked if it were too late to go out on a little pleasure cruise, and Lloyd was only too happy to oblige. We all trekked down the path, holding hands to keep from stumbling. When we got to the dock we shared with our neighbor, Lloyd handed us into the open boat. The boat tipped precariously until we were seated, and it tipped again when Lloyd untied it and hopped down onto the plank seat at the rear. With a bit of coaxing, Lloyd brought the old outboard motor to life, and we puttered away from the dock. I trailed my hand in the water and was astonished at how cool it was. Later, I found out the water temperature in early June is never much above sixty degrees.

At first, Lloyd steered the boat along the shoreline. We did not try to talk over the noise of the motor. Violet peered through her opera glasses, searching for red-winged blackbirds and yellow finches. The evening grew dusky under low, dark clouds. We noticed other boats headed back to their landings, but we didn't turn back. Violet had spotted a great blue heron in the distance, and we all wanted to get a closer look.

A chilly wind picked up. I handed out the thick woolen sweaters I'd brought along. All of a sudden, a wave sent water splashing into the boat. I scrabbled around under my seat and pulled up a single life jacket, old and musty. I convinced Violet to put it on over her sweater.

Despite the worsening weather, we stayed out until almost nine o'clock. By then it was dark and raining, and we were a long way from our dock. I didn't understand Lloyd's decision to head out toward the middle of the lake, unless it was to avoid striking a shallow reef like the ones we'd seen closer to shore. Angry splats of rain began to strike us full-on, like flights of arrows. I pulled my sweater tight against the sharp wind and looked out across the water. There wasn't a boat in sight. Whitecaps rose up like tiger teeth and foamed away again. The lake was as black as the sky and wooded shoreline. I saw only a few dots of light. They came from cabin windows, I suppose, and seemed impossibly distant.

Lloyd struggled with the arm of the motor, trying to keep a heading that took the boat in a wide circle. He was afraid to go much farther out and afraid to go too close to shore. When the boat began to rock and pitch, I felt as if I might lose my dinner. I cried out to Violet to hang onto the sides of the boat; she was short and slight of build, and I was afraid she would be tossed out of the boat. From behind me, Lloyd called over the noise of the wind and drumming motor that he was going to turn the boat around. I knew then that he had lost his bearings. The next instant, the boat took a strong wave, and we were hurled overboard!

How cool the water was! I bobbed above the surface and gasped. I didn't know how to swim—none of us did. Soon I was sinking again. I flapped my arms and somehow breasted the surface. *Do not panic*, I told myself. *If you panic, you will swallow water.*

Lloyd was somewhere nearby. I heard him scream to me to hang onto the boat. I started to sink again, but this time I kicked hard. As soon as my head was above water, I took a deep, gasping breath and looked for the boat and saw it was upside-down. The white wood hull rocked madly in the churned water. I remember thinking how odd it was that the blades of the outboard motor were whirling in the air.

Lloyd was clinging by his fingertips to the shallow overhang of the thick plank of wood that ran along the upper edge of the boat's two sides, what Lloyd had told Mother and me was called the gunwale. He stretched out an arm and hauled me to him.

"Where's Mother!" I cried.

"Hang on. Don't move."

Lloyd had ripped off his heavy sweater. His arms were covered with goose bumps, and his teeth were chattering, but he managed to make his way around the front of the boat to the opposite side. I shrugged off my sweater too, and felt the lighter for it. Every few seconds, another cold wave splashed over my head, sending me into coughing jags so violent I nearly lost my hold on the gunwale. When the motor sputtered and then stopped altogether, I decided to inch around to the rear of the boat. My thoughts were a jumble; I was sure I could hang onto one of the propeller blades and stay well above the waves, but I soon discovered the blades were too high to reach and too thin and sharp.

"I have her!" Lloyd shouted. "She's got the life jacket on."

I nearly wept for joy. "Can you move her around to this side?"

Lloyd didn't answer. For long moments, all I could hear was the rumble of thunder and the splashing of waves against the boat. Finally he called out, "I think she's in shock—she won't budge."

I inched around to their side of the boat and embraced them awkwardly. The storm was roaring down on us, and the extra weight was causing the boat to dip. In seconds, the gunwale was a foot or more beneath the surface.

"Go back!" Lloyd shouted. Violet was pale as a sheet, shivering convulsively and taking quick, shallow breaths through her mouth. So was

Lloyd. So was I.

"I'll stay with her," I called out. "You go back. Reach under the boat on that side. There was a coil of rope under one of the seats. If you can find it, we can tie ourselves together somehow."

Lloyd disappeared around the back of the boat. Time seemed to stand still. Violet was too dazed to hang onto the gunwale, but the life jacket kept her afloat. I held on to the overhang and drew her close. The wind started to die down and with that, the waves did as well. My wristwatch had stopped, but I guessed we had been in the water twenty minutes or so. Violet's eyes were closed. Her mouth was set in a hard, straight line.

Lloyd appeared at the front of the boat. "I couldn't find the rope," he said. I heard real fear in his voice.

"Take my place," I said. "I'll go look."

I eased my way around the boat. On the far side, I tried ducking under the boat, and I panicked and flailed my way back. I was terribly tired, but I managed to grip the gunwale with both hands. I worked to stay calm and moderate my breathing. It was then that I experienced the strangest sensation of warmth. I wondered if the lake was heated, and I knew it was not. My condition was perilous.

For the next hour, Lloyd and I took turns on Violet's side of the boat. I tried to engage her, but she merely looked at me, dazed. I whispered prayers in her ear. It seemed to keep her calm.

The storm blew itself out. Heavy clouds were still clotted overhead, but the wind and whitecaps disappeared, and the water smoothed to ripples. Though my vision had become blurry, I saw dots of light in the distance. I called out to Lloyd, and we hollered for help, but it was hopeless; we were too far out to be seen or heard.

The evening dragged on. At one point, Lloyd called out in a panic, "Mother's thrashing! She's trying to get the life jacket off!"

Working my way around the boat had become excruciating. I was too lethargic to kick, and my fingers were growing too numb to grip the narrow gunwale. When I inched up next to Violet, Lloyd moved off without a word. There were a thousand things I wanted to say to him, but I simply smiled at him.

As soon as Lloyd was out of sight, Violet blinked, opened her eyes, and said, "He's not mine."

I thought I'd heard her wrong. With fierce determination, she glared at me and willed herself to speak again.

"He's not mine."

"Who, Mother?"

"Lloyd." She took a gasping breath and went on. "Harold and I, we couldn't have children. The girl next door was not married and very pregnant. Her father was a no-good drunk. Harold offered him fifty dollars for the child, boy or girl, it didn't matter to us. The father took the money. The baby was in my arms a week later."

They had *bought* Lloyd?

I told myself she was delirious. Her voice was strong, though, and for a moment longer, her eyes held mine with a piercing gaze. Then her body went slack, and she whispered, "Tell him the secret. He has a right to know."

I closed my eyes. Should I? He could panic, and if any of us panicked, we would drown.

"Give this to him," Mother said, the words almost unintelligible.

Something heavy and wet slapped against the hull of the boat. I jerked my head up, but I was so disoriented, I lost my grip on Violet and on the gunwale. I flailed about, kicking, bobbing, and gasping for air. By the time I got hold of the boat again, Violet had slipped below the surface and left the life jacket behind.

I screamed for Lloyd. Drawing close, he told me to stay where I was. "I'm going to find her."

It was insanity.

Lloyd grabbed the life vest and with swift, jerky movements forced my arms into it. I told him Mother wanted *him* to wear the vest, but he persisted. Then he kissed my forehead, took a ragged breath, and vanished beneath the surface.

Lloyd sank down into the lake and bobbed up again and again. Each time he stayed under until I thought his lungs would burst. How very brave he was. At last, when I was sure he had given up hope, I put a comforting arm around his shoulder, but he shrugged it off and bashed his forehead against the hull. When at last he grew quiet, he rested his cheek against the side of the boat and turned to me. Trickles of watery blood coursed down into his eyes.

"I heard her," he said, his breath cold in my ear. "I've known that secret for years. Dad told me. He heard a ruckus next door, in the neighbors' backyard. The girl's father was a two-bit thug, a stinking drunk waving a butcher knife at his daughter's belly. Dad had heard the guy threaten to kill the girl before, and it looked like he was going to do it right then and there. Dad went over, got the guy sobered up, and offered to pay him fifty bucks for the baby. The slob wanted the money, so after that he left the girl alone. Three days after I was born, Dad gave the girl a hundred dollar bill and a one-way train ticket to Los Angeles. He told me it was the best money he ever spent, and he made sure I knew it was our little secret—his and mine."

For long minutes, Lloyd said nothing, as if considering his parents' choice from an adult perspective. Then he said, "I love them all the more for it."

I started to sob, and I took in water and coughed and choked on it. The life jacket was soaked through, barely able to hold up my weight. Everything was an effort, and every effort seemed so pointless, and no single thought led to another. Did we catch any fish? Had we capsized? I loved our new cabin. I loved Lloyd, Cliff, Lloyd. Violet had drowned. Lloyd and I would drown too. Thoughts glided across my mind like schools of fish.

Lloyd was whispering something, pointing over my shoulder.

"Turn around. Watch that shore," he said. There was a firm tone to his voice I'd never heard before. He pointed over his own shoulder, behind him, and added, "I'll watch that way—the other way."

I faced the back of the boat. Time passed. I closed my eyes. For a long while, I heard only the lapping of water against the hull. My thoughts drifted awhile, until the moment I jerked awake and, with startling clarity and terrible understanding, knew he was gone.

I struggled free of the life vest, too weak to weep. Then I let go of the boat and watched it drift away. I floated a bit, almost horizontal, oddly relaxed. I wasn't cold, wasn't afraid. My back curved in a futile arc. *Almost there*, I thought, and I drew in a deep breath.

Almost there.

And then my feet touched bottom.

I had drifted onto a reef. I was standing chin-deep in calm water. For long minutes, I contemplated the irony, the tragic irony of Lloyd and Mother drowning so nearby. I stood there for an eternity, nodding off, jerking awake, and fumbling to regain my footing on the reef. I breathed in the scent of pine, the old-penny smell of dirt, the mineral tang of wet stones. I held out my hands and felt the water glide like silk between my fingers.

A sound! The high whine of a motor! A boat was zipping across the lake. The last clouds scudded off. A low, milky moon cast light on an open boat racing toward me. It slowed, sweeping a broad circle so the wake would not overcome me. With a kind of surreal detachment, I watched the foamy wake glitter in the moonlight, separate into a broad V, and melt away. A man reached out and hauled me on board.

It must have been the people next door, the middle-aged couple from Milwaukee. They must have seen lights blazing in our cabin long after midnight, must have tossed on sweatshirts over their night clothes and walked down the trail, found our boat was missing, and telephoned for help.

The driver of the rescue boat bent to me.

"Were you alone?" he asked, anxious.

"Two," I said, my voice flat. "Both gone."

I have buried the two loves of my life. A few weeks ago, the doctors told me that I'm near the end of my own life now. Cancer. I think it's time to pass along the secrets of that terrible night. I think it's a story worth telling, a testament to those I have loved and lost, and to the wonders of the human heart.

I still have the tape recording. I count it among my most precious things.

How courageous she was!

It's not for me to pass judgment on what Lloyd or his mother or Silvia Pearson did during that long, awful night in the water, what they failed to do, what they contemplated doing. I do, however, regard what Silvia Pearson did years later, during that long, sticky afternoon in her living room with me, as most courageous. Old and sick and terribly lonely, she made an unflinching account of her life and then made a sweeping leap of faith in passing her story on to a child.

The memories of past generations are intrinsically subjective. But whether written or spoken, sung or acted or painted on the wall of a cave, the stories of those who came before attest to the singular and collective experiences of the whole. They contribute to a repository that enriches the breadth of human knowledge. They transcend time.

Charlie

the fever

Throughout the early 1950s, polio was the dominant threat to a child's health, but there was something else just as threatening, and with reason: rheumatic fever. A complication of strep throat, rheumatic fever killed 22,000 Americans in 1950 and left many who survived with permanent heart defects.

I know a lot about rheumatic fever. I learned about it young from my mother and father, who kept vigil in a hospital ward and marked its ravages upon their son firsthand. To this day, I stay current about outbreaks and about diagnostic and treatment breakthroughs by searching the web for news every once in a while.

You would too.

Here's what you probably don't know about rheumatic fever: it's most common in children ages five to fifteen, but it can and does occur in younger patients. The first symptoms usually come a few weeks after an inadequately treated strep throat infection. ("Inadequately treated"—words my mother took in and carried for years, like a hard, dry knot at the pith of her.) The symptoms can include muscle and joint pain, vomiting, high fever, and a red rash on the chest, arms, and legs. Although the affliction has been identified since the late Middle Ages, it was not associated with a throat infection until the late 1800s, and it was not treated with any degree of success until the widespread use of penicillin in the late 1940s and early 1950s.

Charlie was born in the nick of time.

My little brother can't see very well. Nobody's too worried, though.

Charlie's three years old. He still has to wear a diaper, but only at night. Other than his poopy diaper wallowing in the toilet every morning, which is how Mom soaks out the stains, Charlie's the best little brother ever.

Mom's pretty proud of the way Charlie turned out. Heck, we all are. Charlie's more adorable than me and Jane combined. We just look kinda normal, Jane and me: brownish hair, normal-color eyes, nothing too cute, nothing too ugly. But Charlie, he's got beautiful hair, thick, long eye lashes, and huge-o-mongous blue eyes. Sky blue, Mom says. Oceanic blue, Jane says. Charlie's top lip is narrow and straight, but his bottom lip is pudgy, and it pooches out, which makes him look like he's pouting all the time, but he's not. Sometimes Jane and me tickle him, and when he laughs, we poke our pointing fingers in his dimples, which makes him laugh even more.

Charlie loves helping. Every night when I set the dinner table, Charlie reaches up into the silverware drawer and grabs out gobs of forks and spoons and toddles over to the table and plops them onto the plates. It makes kind of a mess, but I don't yell at him or anything cuz he looks so proud to be helping me with a chore. When Jane makes her bed, Charlie yanks the covers way up over her pillow, which Jane has to come back and secretly tuck in later. She usually waits till Charlie's taking a nap or eating Cheerios in his high chair, so he doesn't get his feelings hurt. And every time Mom carries a big load of clothes from the bathroom hamper down to the washing machine, Charlie picks up all the dirty socks and underpants that fall on the floor.

Sometimes when I break something, like a Christmas tree ornament or a juice glass, I blame it on Charlie, and he doesn't even mind. He just points at the broken pieces and looks at Mom with those big blue eyes, like he's saying, "Sorry. I might have done this. Can you fix it?"

Anyways, the reason Charlie can't see very well is cuz his hair's gotten so long it pretty much completely covers his eyes, which drives Dad nuts but doesn't bother Charlie much. A while back, he figured out how to get around without seeing. Usually, he claps a hand on the wall and follows the wall till he gets where he wants to go. Sometimes he grabs the hem of

Mom's skirt and walks around behind her. Every once in a while, he just drops down to his knees and crawls, which looks funny cuz Charlie's too old to be crawling.

The only time Charlie's hair is a problem is when I accidentally leave my set of Jacks on the floor, and he crawls over them, which makes him cry. That makes me feel pretty awful. But worse than Charlie having a couple of metal Jacks stuck in his pudgy little knees is when he mistakes Odetta for Mom and grabs onto the back of Odetta's blue uniform hem.

Odetta's our maid. Dad says Odetta's got a short fuse. Mom says short fuse or not, she needs Odetta this summer more than ever, so just steer clear of her on cleaning days. Odetta says the only thing worse than a houseful of kids getting in the way of her vacuum cleaner and string mop is a houseful of red ants, one-eyed snakes, inbred squirrels, and sun-burnt chickens. Jane says Odetta's got a way with words.

For the first two years of his life, Charlie had almost no hair. Dad called him Old Man Cue Ball, which Mom said she did not appreciate. About a year ago, though, Charlie sprouted a bumper crop of hair, and it's been growing like crazy ever since. Dad says Charlie's quite a towhead. Mom says, no, his hair is *silken blond*. Jane says nuh-uh, flaxen platinum.

This morning, Mom reluctantly admits Charlie needs a trim, and Dad looks at her and says, "I beg your pardon, our son doesn't need a trim. What he needs is a haircut!"

Jane and me aren't asked what we think, but everybody agrees it's time Charlie stops having to hang onto a wall or crawl to get any place.

Mom drapes an old bed sheet around Charlie and safety pins it at the nape of his neck so it won't slide off. Then she carries him to the back hall, plops him on top of the clothes dryer lid, and hands him a cherry sucker, which I didn't even know we had any of. Dad's right there, opening a bright red box.

"What's that?" Mom says, cutting Dad a look.

"Clippers." Dad tilts the box to show her. "Electric clippers. See? A ten-piece set. It's got everything I need to give the kids free haircuts. There's blade guards, blade oil, a barber comb, cleaning brush, mustache attachment. . . . "

Dad looks at Mom, and his smile melts away.

"Oh no you don't, mister," Mom says, clamping her hands on her hips. "You can go clip the hedges with those things if you want, but not my girls and certainly not my Charlie."

Dad smacks the box down on the clothes washer, which makes Charlie flap his eyes open wide behind all that hair. "Madeleine, this boy has looked like a girl for the past year. It's high time he got a good, close clipper cut."

"I suppose you think you're in the sheep-shearing business?" Mom responds. "Well, I'm not going to stand here and watch you buzz Charlie's beautiful hair down to the scalp."

Mom turns to go, then comes back and gives the clothes dryer knob a sharp twist. When Charlie was a real little baby, and Mom wanted to get him to take a nap, she'd put his wicker cradle on top of the clothes dryer and then turn it on. On the few days Charlie was fussy, it quieted him right down.

Mom hasn't done the dryer thing with Charlie in a couple of years, but it still works. The dryer starts to pulse. Charlie clamps his teeth down on the sucker and vibrates along with the dryer. I'm wondering if there's even any wet clothes in there cuz usually in summer, all our laundry gets hung outside on the line, but I can see Mom's in a royal huff and doesn't even care.

She marches through the kitchen and up the stairs to the bedrooms. Jane and me watch Dad start to rummage in the red box, taking account of all the clipper pieces. Meanwhile, Charlie's getting sweatier by the minute. His cheeks are real red and behind all that flaxen platinum hair he's got kind of a glassy-eyed look. I think it's because of being enswarmed by a bed sheet and getting plopped on a humming clothes dryer in the dead of summer.

When he gets almost down to the sucker's loopy rope handle, Jane and me make a quick bet on how long it's gonna take my brother to start crying. Charlie had a bad sore throat a couple of weeks ago, and he's been a little cranky ever since, which isn't like him at all. Usually Charlie only cries when there's a good reason to, like when Jacks get stuck in between his toes. Or like sitting on top of a clothes dryer with no sucker.

By the time Mom stomps back into the laundry room with her little sewing scissors, Dad's already clippered half of Charlie's head.

"Paul, what have you done?!"

Charlie opens his mouth in surprise. The sucker drops to his lap and sticks to the sheet.

Dad takes Charlie's chin in his hand and turns his little head this way and that, admiring the half of a haircut. He doesn't seem to notice

Charlie's platinum flaxen mustache and beard, which got made by hair clippings sticking to cherry sucker goo smeared around Charlie's mouth.

"Look at the boy, Maddy. There's absolutely nothing to get upset about. You'll see."

Mom lifts Charlie off the dryer, which is good cuz his cheeks are red and blotchy, not to mention hairy, and I think he's ready to keel over. Dad smacks down the electric clippers onto the dryer lid, but the clippers keep on buzzing and skitter across the dryer and clunk down to the floor and dance around while dangling by the cord.

In all that commotion, nobody notices Dad is stepping on a corner of the sheet, so when Mom marches off with Charlie, the sheet does not march off too, and Charlie's little neck gets yanked sideways. My brother does not know how stupid he looks with a mustache, a beard, and half his head shaved, but he sure does notice his neck getting yanked sideways. His little lower lip pooches out farther than ever, and he starts to whimper. Dad picks the sucker off the front of the sheet and sticks it back in Charlie's mouth, which only makes things worse cuz what little is left of that sucker is coated with clippered-off flaxen platinum hair. Charlie spits out the sucker, and it lands right smack dab on Dad's white shirt, and with that, Jane and me skedaddle.

In the middle of the night, I get up to go pee, and I hear Mom and Dad whispering in their bedroom. Pretty soon, they come out. Dad's holding Charlie in his arms. Mom's holding a cup of ice. All the way down the stairs, I see Mom try to feed ice chips to Charlie, but he just shakes his head away and whimpers.

"Wake up your sister," Dad says over his shoulder. "Your mother and I might be gone a while. We need to get Charlie to the hospital."

Odetta comes in the morning, which isn't even her cleaning day. She stays all day and doesn't go home until way after Jane and me have our baths, say our prayers, and get into bed. She only got mad and swatted us on the bottom twice, which is hardly any for Odetta. She did all the grocery shopping and cooking and cleaning and washing. She even got out Dad's push mower from the garage and cut the front lawn. The only thing Odetta didn't do was ring the cowbell. She didn't have to, though, cuz Jane and me never left the house.

"You girls stay close," Odetta said, that first morning. "Your Mamma and Daddy got a world of worry right now. They gonna be at that hospital from dawn to midnight, and it gonna be for a while, I reckon."

We begged Odetta to tell us what's wrong with Charlie, but she just pinched her lips and told us to scat.

Tonight, Jane sneaks out of her bed and crawls in bed with me. She cups my ear with her hands and whispers real low about how she heard Odetta talking to Mrs. Lofton and Mrs. Henry while they were all out hanging laundry. Jane says Odetta told them Charlie has romantic fever.

"Romantic fever—what's that?"

"Not romantic fever, you dope," Jane says. "It's rheumatic fever, and it's bad."

Jane starts bawling. I don't even mind getting my pillow all wet with my sister's tears cuz I'm pretty sure romantic fever is really, really bad.

"He won't die, will he? Will he? Jane?"

"I don't know. . . . He could."

Jane and me hug each other tight as we can. We both cry a long time, but softly cuz we don't want Odetta to come in and swat us. By the time I finally stop crying, Jane's asleep, and it's later than I've ever stayed up before. I keep thinking about how terrible it would be if Charlie died. Mom and Dad and me and Jane would be so sad that we would just cry all the time cuz there would be a big, empty hole in our family where Charlie was supposed to be. On birthdays and the Fourth of July and Christmas, when it's supposed to be happy, we wouldn't be nearly as happy as before, cuz there'd be just us—without Charlie. If Charlie dies, it's gonna leave a huge hole in our hearts.

You think everything will always be the same, but it won't. Melinda Potter's father died, and now Melinda has to live someplace else and go to another school. Things change, little things and way bigger things, and there's no way to stop them or even know they're gonna happen. A couple of weeks ago, Charlie got a bad sore throat. Mom didn't think it was bad enough to call the doctor, so she just kept him in bed and fed him ice chips and Jell-O and he got better. He's got something much worse now, some kinda horrible romantic fever, and he's maybe gonna die.

At dinner tonight, Odetta ate at the table with me and Jane, which should've seemed weird, but didn't. She told us we just have to accept what comes and pray Charlie makes it past the danger.

Me and Jane go upstairs right after dinner and get our pajamas on—which we never do. We don't even watch TV or play cards or read our books or anything. Just climb onto our beds and stay quiet. I lay on top of the covers for the longest time, but I can't fall asleep. Finally, I get out of bed and go stand at the window, watching for Dad's car.

Finally, I see it. When Mom comes in, she thanks Odetta and trudges up the stairs, slow, like she's really tired. I want Mom to come in and hug me and tell me Charlie's going to be okay, but she just goes right into her bedroom. Odetta waits at the bottom of the stairs till she hears Mom close the bedroom door. Then she goes outside. I look out the window again—Dad's in the car, waiting to take Odetta to the bus stop.

It's Tuesday. Charlie's still in the hospital. Mrs. Henry brings over an angel food cake for us. Mrs. Henry being nice is the worst possible thing, cuz now I'm pretty sure Charlie's gonna die. I feel sick to my stomach all day. Neither Jane or me take a bite of that stupid cake. Odetta cuts herself a small slice, but she just picks at it. Sally Daily calls on the telephone and asks if I want to come over and play dolls. I say no, thank you, I just want to be in our house.

Jane and me take all of Charlie's little clothes out of the drawers and put them in a pile. Then we fold them up again, all neat and tidy, and put them back in his little blue chiffarobe. Jane holds one of his little under-shirts up to her face and then hands it to me.

"Here," she says. "Smell. It smells like Charlie."

Wednesday. Grandpa Reinhardt sends over a bed and mattress and box spring and new sheets and a new pillow from his department store. The delivery men set up the bed in a corner of the living room. It's for Odetta, so she doesn't have to take the bus home every night and come all the way back again before breakfast. I guess Odetta's gonna be here a while.

Thursday. Odetta says Charlie took a turn for the worse overnight.

Friday. No news.

Saturday. Jane and me have hardly seen Mom and Dad all week. Odetta says they're exhausted and that we shouldn't forget how much they love us. I gotta say, Odetta being nice is almost as worrisome as Mrs. Henry bringing over that cake.

I can't stop thinking about Charlie in the hospital. Even when I'm doing something completely different, like playing Crazy Eights with Jane, even in the middle of a good hand—pow! I remember Charlie's got a terrible fever, and he might die. Even playing with Cuddle Bun or helping Odetta make mashed potatoes or taking a bubble bath or just brushing my teeth, suddenly the thought of Charlie lying there in the hospital, maybe dead already, floods into my mind, and I start to cry. Jane does that too. I've seen her.

If a kid has to get sick and die, why can't it be Luca Zaldoni? Why does it have to be Charlie? Charlie never hurt a flea. It isn't fair. It just isn't fair!

I'm thinking about going up to Immaculate Heart of Mary to see Sister Josephina, but Jane stops me. She says nobody can bother the nuns at the convent during summer because it's their only vacation from kids. Then she puts her arm around my shoulder and says, "If Charlie dies, at least he's gonna go right to heaven."

That makes me feel a little better, for about a minute.

Charlie did not die of rheumatic fever. Ten days after he was admitted to St. Mary's Hospital with a fever of 105 and a fluttery heart, he came home cool to the touch and was laid to sleep in his own bed.

A girl of eight, going on nine, is often self-absorbed, and has a perfect right to be. Within a day or two of Charlie's return, I had put the fearsome dread of his imminent death behind me and resumed my neighborhood search for a better family, oblivious to the fact that the disease had done lasting damage.

An autoimmune response to the strep infection had inflamed our Charlie's heart, cleaving its delicate valves with lesions that refused to close.

Patsy

the show

The visions of artists are among the special gifts granted to mankind. Painters, photographers, sculptors, dancers, writers, musicians. Designers of soaring skyscrapers and sweeping bridges; poets who compress keen observation into words and then compress words into the essence of human emotion; playwrights who create characters showcasing our public virtues and our secret voids; actors who portray us with uncanny, unflinching likeness; opera singers whose arias take us to the depths, raise us to the heavens, still our breaths, quiet our thrumming hearts, and, for a moment in time, soothe our discontented souls. In so doing, in striving to entertain, inspire, and impassion us, artists infuse our world with civility.

Although I now understand that, during the long, hot summer of 1956, artistic matters of a more temporal nature were on my mind.

Back then, Patsy's Players was the unofficial Thistle Way theater company. Each year, Patsy Warfield organized a show, and each show was an extravaganza.

As the company's founder, Patsy served willingly and ably as scriptwriter, talent scout, casting agent, producer, director, scenic advisor, lighting and sound coordinator, ticket-master, publicist, and MC. Patsy was twelve years old that summer—the summer she decided to shelve an epic Samurai romance in favor of a talent contest. In the end, that was a mistake, but who could have known? Patsy forged ahead, held auditions, presided over rehearsals, and stuffed broadsides into every Thistle Way mailbox. A week before the show, with funds from brisk advance ticket sales, she bought a silver-plated trophy to present to the performer whom she—and she alone—would proclaim the winner.

Patsy Warfield was prepared and capable. What could possibly go wrong?

Patsy's in a pickle. Nobody knows about it except Patsy and me, and I pinky swore not to blab.

I'm feeling bad about pinky swearing. I'm feeling like I should tell my mom or my dad or a policeman or somebody. Maybe they could stop the bad thing from happening. I'm not gonna, though. A kid can't go back on a pinky swear.

Today's the day of the big show. I'm spending the night at Patsy's tonight, which is good in a way cuz at least Patsy has somebody to talk to about the pickle she's in, but it's bad in a way cuz I don't exactly want to be that person.

Patsy's show is always the last Saturday afternoon in July. The Warfields' yard is the only one on Thistle Way with no trees, so the audience gets heatstroke even before Patsy starts things off by belting out "The Star Spangled Banner."

This morning, Mr. and Mrs. Warfield set up rows of folding chairs around the outside edge of their patio with a wide aisle going down the middle, just like at a movie theater. The show starts at three o'clock, but by half past two, most of those chairs are gonna be filled up with parents, grandparents, and kids too little to be in the show. They'll all be fanning themselves with Patsy's mimeographed program.

Two years ago, Patsy's Players put on a circus show called *Step Right Up*. Patsy was the ringleader, and she wore this shiny black jacket that looked like a tuxedo (only shorter and pointier) and black shorts and high heels. She had a top hat and a black whip too. Patsy's what my mom calls "a big girl" and what Mrs. Lofton calls "early to develop."

Pauly Finnegan was a circus clown. At the last minute, he took off his pointy clown hat and put on his winter hat with the earflaps and chin strap. A week before the show, Luca Zaldoni told Pauly that if an Irish kid doesn't wear a hat all the time then his brains are gonna leak out of his ears. That's when Pauly started to always wear a hat, which was a problem when Pauly's hair needed washing.

Cate Finnegan told me Pauly thrashed around in the bathtub on shampoo night, screaming like crazy, until their mom lifted him out of the tub and dried him off with soap bubbles still all over his head. One night, Mrs. Finnegan got so fed up she marched up to Snyder's Five & Dime and bought a pair of earplugs. Now that Pauly's got earplugs to wear on shampoo nights, his mom can rinse out the suds. So except for bath time, Pauly still wears a hat. Always.

For the circus Pauly rode his tricycle around Patsy's patio and threw candy into the audience. On the third loop, though, his trike wheel hit a bump, his little round eyeglasses fell off, and he rode right over them. Everybody in the audience moaned, but Pauly couldn't hear them because of his ear flaps, and he couldn't see anything because his glasses were wrecked, so he rode straight off the patio and landed in Mrs. Warfield's petunia bed.

Patsy gave me the part of the Bearded Lady, which I wasn't too crazy about. I told her I didn't have a beard and I thought that was that, but stupid Janice Haverkamp piped up and said she'd make me a beard.

Everybody knows the Haverkamps are artsy, but I couldn't see how Janice was gonna make a decent beard.

"Easy," Janice said. "I'll shave one of my brother's Chinese Foo dogs."

Janice brought the Foo dog beard to the first rehearsal, and it looked pretty darn realistic. I didn't like to think about what the Chinese Foo dog looked like.

Anyways, that was two summers ago.

This year's show is *The Stars of Tomorrow*. Fifteen minutes go by, and now all the kids are wondering where the heck is Patsy. I walk around to the front yard and see Luca Zaldoni running off. Patsy's sitting on a glider, going back and forth real slow. I plop down on a metal tulip chair and bounce it a little bit. Right off, the seat is frying the backs of my legs.

"I should've gone with my original idea."

"Huh?"

"I was gonna do an epic Japanese love story like the movie *Seven Samurai*."

I'm completely lost.

"Now everything's a mess. . . . Pinky swear you won't tell, Grace."

I can't figure out what's a mess. It's at least the third year Patsy's done a big summer show. She's had everything organized for ages.

In June, even before school let out, she stuck a note in each mailbox saying she was gonna hold auditions in her Florida room for *The Stars of Tomorrow* talent contest. My dad hates Florida rooms. He says they're a damn igloo in winter and a damn terrarium in summer, which is not me using curse words cuz I'm just saying what my dad says.

Anyways, on the day of the auditions, kids started lining up outside the glass door of Patsy's Florida room real early. We could see Patsy inside, sitting on a wood chair with a canvas seat and back.

At exactly three o'clock, Patsy waved the first two kids in. Susan and Sharon White's talent show act was called the "Yodeling White Sisters." They looked kinda cute cuz they had on matching red pinafore dresses with little white puffy-sleeved blouses and yellow-flowered aprons. Their hair was weird, though, cuz the ends of their braids were tied on top of their heads. By the time Susan and Sharon were done yodeling three verses of "Lovesick Blues," it sorta hurt my ears—I was not alone in that, I'll tell you that. Afterward, they took turns explaining that yodeling got started in the Alps when goat herders on different hills wanted to talk to each other.

Sheesh.

The next kid to audition was Jimmy Huebner. Jimmy's in my class in school. I'd seen him make balloon animals lots of times at kids' birthday parties, so I was pretty sure that was gonna be his talent, and it was. Jimmy worked fast. In about a minute, he'd blown up three balloons and made a balloon dog, a balloon giraffe, and a balloon mouse. Patsy was smiling, so I figured Jimmy had a chance to win the contest.

Next was Benny Herman. He handed Patsy a piece of paper with a list of all the bugle calls he had to learn for a Boy Scout bugling merit badge. While the rest of us kids sweltered in line out on the patio, we had to listen to Benny trying to play First Call, Reveille, Assembly, Mess, Drill, Fatigue, Officers, Recall, Church, Swimming, Fire, Retreat, To the Colors, Call to Quarters, and Taps. Benny announced the name of every one. Otherwise, nobody would have known.

One of the middle Finnegan boys did a short skit about Davey Crockett being king of the wild frontier, and then it was my turn.

Being as Patsy always opens her summer show by singing "The Star Spangled Banner," I figured I'd have a good chance at winning if I recited as much of the Declaration of Independence as I could memorize, which turned out to be the first chunk which starts out with, "When in the course of human events" and the last chunk that ends with "our Fortunes and our sacred Honor." I did okay, but Melinda Potter did better.

Melinda came all the way from her new neighborhood and brought along two shoeboxes. Everybody in the audition line was wondering what was in those boxes. When it was her turn, Melinda set the boxes on two TV tray tables. Then she did a little curtsey, opened the first box, and took out three chocolate cupcakes. Then she curtseyed again, opened the other box, and took out a bunch of squishy funnel things. She said she'd baked the cupcakes herself and filled the funnels with different colors of frosting. They each had different tips too. For her talent, Melinda made red roses with green leaves on the cupcakes and then outlined the edges with squiggles of blue frosting. Those cupcakes were beautiful! When Melinda did a final curtsey, everybody in the audition line applauded, me included.

The auditions didn't get over until Mrs. Pearson was ringing her school bell. By then, Marty Throckmorten had done bird calls, and Betsey Bauer had made a French twist hairdo on both the Walsh twins. Two other kids had done magic tricks, which weren't too good. Rainer Niesen had told funny jokes. One kid had tried to tap dance, but it didn't work so well on account of the flagstones. And the Walsh twins held up these easy paint-by-number pictures of woodland glens in autumn.

I wish Davey was here. He'd probably make some neat-o invention right before our very eyes, like a Slinky that glows in the dark, or a back-yard fountain that sprinkles kids with Kool-Aid, or maybe a little box you could stick on your dog's collar, right under their chin, so when they bark it comes out in real words! I sure wish my pal Davey hadn't fallen all the way down to Mrs. Krieger's patio and landed on his head. Some kids are saying Davey's never getting out of the hospital, but I don't believe them. Not one bit.

The whole time, all of us were trying to figure out who Patsy would pick. The winner gets to keep this beautiful silver trophy bowl, and everybody wanted that bowl.

Now it's only a half-hour till the show's supposed to start. Patsy and me should be in the Florida room helping kids get in their costumes. But Patsy's still sitting on the dumb old glider. I can hear the mothers and fathers and grandparents coming up the Warfields' driveway. I hear Mr. and Mrs. Warfield selling last-minute tickets and passing out programs.

What the heck could be the matter with Patsy, and what did I just pinky swear not to tell?

I figure Patsy's gonna tell me what's eating her, and she does.

"Last night, when I was putting reminder fliers in everybody's mailbox, Mark Mooney came out of his house. It was almost dark by then. And Grace, he kissed me on the lips. Right on the lips."

Holy cow! Mark Mooney kissed Patsy Warfield, in the dark, on the lips!

"He told me I'd done a great job picking out the silver trophy, and he'd sure like to be the one to win it."

"All the kids want the trophy," I said.

"I know. But Mark said he and his brother had a bet about which one was gonna go home with the trophy. He said if I named him the winner, I could wear his ID bracelet. I'd be his girlfriend."

"Wait. How do you know he'll be the best?"

"I don't, but it doesn't matter. If I name Mark the winner, everybody'll think I'm his real girlfriend, right? But Mark doesn't want me for a girl-friend. He just wants to win the bet. He'll break up with me in no time."

"So, are you gonna do it? Make him the winner?"

"No. It's not fair to the other kids, you know?"

Whew. I still had a chance.

"Then this morning, that little snip Susan White called," Patsy says. "I was afraid Susan was sick or something and she and Sharon couldn't do their act, but that's not why she called."

"I didn't see you talking on the phone. Where was I?"

"You were up in my bedroom. I guess you were unpacking your suitcase."

"What did Susan want?"

Patsy's biting the skin around her thumbnail. I've seen other kids do that, but never Patsy.

"Susan told me she and Sharon have been taking expensive acting lessons, and if they don't win the talent contest, their Dad's gonna make them stop. Then she told me her family's going to Disneyland next month, and she and Sharon each get to invite a friend to go along. She said if I picked the Yodeling White Sisters to win the talent show, she'd pick me to go to Disneyland."

"Holy cow. Are you gonna do it?"

"I've always wanted to go to Disneyland," Patsy sighed. "Who doesn't?

All I have to do is say Susan and Sharon win, and I get to go."

I feel like somebody just stepped on my stomach. Patsy's gonna decide the winner before the show even starts. "So you're gonna give the trophy to those stupid yodelers?"

Patsy wraps her arms around her waist and kinda hugs herself. I don't feel like looking at her anymore, so I just sorta kick the grass with the toe of my shoe.

"Susan and Sharon are not gonna win, Grace."

"No?"

"I probably wouldn't have that much fun seeing Disneyland with the Yodeling White Sisters."

"Great! Let's get the show on the road." I look at my Cinderella watch. "Fifteen minutes to go!"

Patsy isn't moving. "There's one more thing, and when I tell you, re-member, you pinky swore."

Cripes, what now?

"Did you see Luca Zaldoni when you came over?"

The Zaldonis are big trouble, everybody knows that. Last month when I was staying over with Davey, I heard Lt. Lofton say he knows for a fact that Mr. Zaldoni is in the Mafia, through and through. I asked my dad what "Mafia" means, and Dad said it means the mob, which didn't exactly clear it up for me.

A couple of weeks ago, I overheard Missy Henry's big brother talking to Missy's father about the Zaldoni boys.

"One of the guys I work with at the Shady Oak told me their grandpa's restaurant on the Hill is a front for laundering money," Missy's brother said. "The guy said the Zaldonis are hooked up with Tony Giordano, and it's just a matter of time before a triggerman from Chicago or Jersey pays them a little visit."

I asked Mom if Luca and Antony's dad is washing money and she said, "What?"

I told her a triggerman's coming to visit them, and that night, I heard Mom and Dad whispering.

Washing money didn't sound dangerous, but I've had a rule for a long time about staying as far away as possible from Luca and Antony Zaldoni. First of all, everybody knows their dad has a Tommy gun hidden in their basement, and he sleeps with a loaded barrette under his pillow, of which only the Tommy gun sounds dangerous to me. Second of all, Luca and

Antony like to sneak up behind me and Sally Daily when we're playing dolls in Sally's backyard and clunk our heads together hard. The Zaldoni boys are mean that way.

Back at the Warfields' side yard, I bounce the tulip chair a couple of times and kick the clump of grass again. I'm not sure I want to know what Luca said to Patsy.

"I wish I'd never bought that trophy!" Patsy cries, and she buries her face in her hands.

I get up and hold Patsy's hand. I feel kinda self-conscious, being as Patsy's a lot older than me, but I think she likes it.

"Luca said his mom's been bragging to all his aunts and uncles and cousins about how good his and Antony's skit is," Patsy tells me, between sobs. "He said all their relatives are coming from the Hill to see the show, and if he and Antony don't win, the family will be forever disgraced."

Patsy's in a mell-of-a-hess, I'll tell you that. That's what Grandma Reinhardt would say. My grandma never swears, even when there's something awful enough for a swear.

"Then he grabbed my ponytail and yanked it really hard. He didn't let go, though. He kept yanking my hair so my head went way back. He was right next to me, his face was right in front of me. Luca said he can get his dad's loaded Beretta any time he wants, so if I know what's good for me, I'll make him and Antony the winner."

I don't get it. Why's everybody afraid of a barrette? Even so, I've got goose pimples up and down my arms, which I haven't had since last winter when I went over to Davey's to watch his Electrified and Illuminated Sleigh Machine and I forgot my mittens.

"Grace, Luca said not to tell a soul. Nobody. You pinky swore, so if you blab . . . "

"I won't!"

I keep holding Patsy's hand, but thoughts are whizzing in my head. The show starts in ten minutes, and Patsy's gotta, just gotta give that trophy to the Zaldoni boys, which means Jimmy Huebner's gonna be doing balloon animals for nothing. It means Jane's gonna do her Swan Lake ballet dance and Benny's gonna do bugle calls for nothing. Rainer's gonna tell his jokes, and I'm gonna recite the first and last parts of the Declaration of Independence, and it's not gonna matter if we do great or if we mess up cuz Patsy's gotta make the Zaldonis win.

The inside of my mouth tastes like when you find a penny in the street, and you lick it to clean it off.

It's show time! Patsy marches out of the Florida room to the flagstone patio. Nobody'd ever know the terrible thing on her mind. She waits for the audience to stop talking and then she starts singing the "Star Spangled Banner."

Back in the Florida room, I peek out through the sheets. Most of the dads have their hands over their hearts. The moms too. I don't recognize any of the people in the third and fourth rows except Mr. and Mrs. Zaldoni; the rest must be relatives of the Zaldonis.

Patsy holds the home of the bra-a-a-ve a long time without taking a breath, which everybody loves. When the applause dies down, she thanks all the people who are here to see today's show. She says we all might be surprised when she announces the winner because Thistle Way has no shortage of talent, but this year, all the kids have really outdone themselves. All of them, she says again, louder. That's my signal to open the Florida Room door and hand her the trophy. Patsy holds the beautiful bowl high, turning it this way and that so everybody gets a good look. The sun sparkles off the silver, making the bowl look glittery.

"At the end of the contest," Patsy says, "this genuine silver-plated bowl will be awarded to the boy or girl who, in my humble opinion, has given the best performance of all, the performance of a lifetime."

She sets the trophy on a small table off to the side and waves her master of ceremonies baton.

"And now," she calls out, "on with the show!"

I open the Florida room door. The Yodeling White Sisters practically knock me over rushing out onto the patio.

The show lasts two whole hours. Patsy never leaves the stage. Each time she calls for another act, she steps to the side, next to the trophy bowl, and watches the performance. When one act finishes, she goes back to the middle of the patio again, joins the applause, and calls out the next act. She doesn't tremble or fidget or bite the skin around her fingernails. Not once.

Jimmy Huebner makes three balloon animals. Benny Herman does his gosh-awful Boy Scout bugle calls. Betsey Bauer makes a French twist in the Walsh twins' hair. Rainer pretends to use a microphone and tells some jokes. I say the beginning and ending of the Declaration of Independence and accidentally leave out the part about contracting alliances. Marty Throckmorten does bird calls. Melinda Potter decorates two chocolate cupcakes with frosting roses. When she finishes, Melinda walks down the aisle to the last row and gives the cupcakes to Mr. and Mrs. Warfield. Sheesh.

Next it's Jane's turn. My sister's wearing her white leotard and a fluffy pink tutu from our ballet class recital, so she looks like a real ballerina. I put a record album of *Swan Lake* on the Warfields' record player and turn up the sound, just like we practiced. Jane starts off with some quick movements on her toes and then a whole bunch of jetés and pliés. She looks like she's gonna flounce and leap back and forth forever, so Patsy raps her baton on the flagstones. Jane gets the hint and drops to the ground like a dying swan. I clap like crazy.

The Finnegan boys do their Davey Crockett skit. A couple of other kids sing songs and do magic tricks. By the time the Walsh twins show their paint-by-numbers pictures, their French twist hairdos are kinda falling apart. Lizzie O'Grady comes out wearing a flower crown and reads three poems she wrote herself.

When it's the Mooneys' turn, they surprise everybody cuz they're wearing their ice hockey skates with the guards on the blades. They do this really funny skit where they pretend to be playing ice hockey. I almost think the Mooneys should win, but then I remember what happened before the show, and I change my mind.

Antony and Luca Zaldoni are next. Nobody can figure out what their act is supposed to be cuz they just look like they're fighting with each other, which they do lots. Antony pounces on Luca and knocks him over. Luca punches Antony in the nose. Pretty soon the Zaldoni boys are scrambling around on the flagstones. When blood starts gushing out of Antony's nose, a few parents in the audience stand up and look kinda worried. One of Luca's shoes comes off, but he just kicks it out of the way and keeps fighting. He grabs Antony's shirt and rips it open, and all the buttons go flying.

Mrs. Zaldoni looks up to the sky and does the praying hands thing. Mr. Zaldoni leaps to his feet and shouts something in Italian at his kids, but I'm pretty sure they don't hear cuz they're not stopping. Mr. Zaldoni is tall and fat. Dad says that's why he wears suspenders cuz they don't make belts big enough to fit around Mr. Zaldoni's waist. Anyways, Mr. Zaldoni stomps up the aisle with his head about a mile in front of his big belly, grabs Luca and Antony by their shirt collars, and yanks them apart.

Then he hauls them by the scruffs of their necks down the aisle and over to their house, which is right next-door. Mrs. Zaldoni follows, dabbing her eyes with a corner of her apron. The Zaldoni relatives from the Hill down in the city file out too.

Holy cow! What a relief! Now Patsy won't have to make the stupid Zaldoni boys the winners.

The last act is the littlest kids—Missy Henry, Anna Haverkamp, and Pauly Finnegan. They're wearing white angel robes with feathery wings. Missy and Anna have fake halos over their heads. Pauly's wearing his halo over his beanie, which isn't working too good on account of the whirlybird part getting stuck on the halo part. Anyways, the little kids sing "Twinkle, Twinkle Little Star" in high, squeaky voices, and everybody's amazed when they don't botch up the words. Pauly even keeps his glasses on. When they finish, they keep taking bows until the audience is sorta laughing. Patsy takes Missy by the hand and leads her back to the Florida room, and Pauly and Anna follow.

Patsy ends the show like she always does, singing "Happy Trails to You." She's getting to the part about who cares about the clouds when a big commotion starts up at the rear of the audience. It's the Zaldonis!

Holy cow!

The Zaldonis from the Hill sit down in the exact places they had before, but Mr. and Mrs. Zaldoni march up to the stage with Luca and Antony between them. Patsy holds out her hands in welcome—wow, what an actress!

It's so quiet I can hear my heart beating, ka-thump, ka-thump. Nobody moves. Nobody says a word. Patsy's mom and dad get up and slowly walk toward the stage. I think they want to get close to Patsy, in case Mr. Zaldoni beats her up or something.

Mr. Zaldoni sticks out an elbow and nudges Antony forward, but Antony just balls his fists and stares at his shoes. Mrs. Zaldoni stops wringing the hem of her apron and gives Luca a good slap on the back of his head.

Luca says, "Sorry, Patsy. We're gonna do our act over and not mess up."
What?

Mr. and Mrs. Zaldoni take their seats next to the Hill Zaldonis. Mr. Zaldoni puffs out his chest so it's almost sticking out as far as his belly. He tucks his thumbs behind his suspenders, nods, and says something Italian. He looks proud.

Luca and Antony hurry through the boxing skit they were supposed to do, but it isn't too good. You can tell they're just pretend boxing, so it isn't even really a skit or act. When they finish, Antony goes into the Florida room with the rest of the kids, but Luca struts over to Patsy. Everybody waits to see what Luca's gonna do, but he makes sure to stand with his back to the audience, so they can't see his face. I'm behind Patsy, so I can. First, Luca gives her a crooked smile. Then he just stares kinda sleepy-eyed at her and slowly runs his finger around the edge of the silver bowl. I know it doesn't sound scary, but believe me, it was.

That night, Patsy and me get into our pajamas early cuz we're so tired. After the show was over, after Patsy announced who would get a trophy, after everybody applauded like crazy cuz it was such a surprise, after all that I had to help her stack folding chairs against the side of the house, drag the tulip chairs and glider back to the patio, and pick tickets stubs out of the lawn. Then we walked around the circle returning all the costume stuff that kids forgot to take home with them.

In that almost-conked-out time when I start to dream about a goat on ice skates shooting a loaded gun that looks like a bugle, Patsy sits up in her bed and says, "Grace, you still awake?"

"Mm-hmm."

"Did you count the money?"

"Mm-hmm."

"How much did we get?"

I push myself up on one elbow and look across the room at her. It's dark, and my eyes are swimmy. "About twenty-five dollars, I think."

"Good. That should be enough."

"Enough for what?"

"You'll see."

I try to go back to sleep, but I can't. I watch a breeze blow the curtains. I listen to the Greeley's dang dog barking his head off. I hear somebody's garage door roll down. A toilet flushes. Patsy's bed springs creak. I crack open my eyes. She's laying on her back with her hands clasped behind her head. I turn over too and clasp my hands behind my head. Now I'm really awake.

Patsy Warfield's got a lot on her mind.

It's Monday morning, two whole days since the talent show. Everybody's still talking about those Zaldonis. Anyways, just like we planned when I was staying over at Patsy's house, Mr. and Mrs. Warfield drive around the circle to our house and honk the horn. I slide into the back seat of their Pontiac next to Patsy, and we drive to Byron Cade, which is a ritzy store in Clayton. Byron Cade is so ritzy that Mom made me wear a dress today. On the way, Mr. Warfield says he's taking the whole day off, and maybe the whole week. I'm thinking he's not going to work so he can stay home and protect Patsy from the Zaldonis. When we get to Byron Cade, Mr. Warfield stands by the front door, looking out. Each time a car passes, he squints and goes up on his toes.

I wander around looking at all the expensive stuff they've got at Byron Cade. A little sign in a picture frame on one of the counters says, "Gifts of distinction create Treasured Moments."

I blow on the glass front of the display case to see if my breath will make fog so I can write my initials there, but it doesn't. A saleslady frowns at me, so I rub off the glass with my arm even though there's no fog.

Patsy brought along the silver trophy bowl from the talent show. She shows it to a saleslady and tells the lady she wants two more bowls just like the first one. The lady looks at Mrs. Warfield, who smiles and nods. Then Patsy hands a note to the saleslady and says, "Here's the names for the engraver."

The saleslady studies the note and then reads all three names out loud. Missy Henry. Anna Haverkamp. Pauly Finnegan.

Mr. Warfield hurries us out of the store and back to the car. Pretty soon we're all in the Warfields' kitchen eating peanut butter cookies with crossed fork marks on top. I would've thought we'd be out on their patio or in the Florida room, but Mr. Warfield says no, we'd better have our treat indoors. He put a baseball bat by the door.

I'm glad Mr. Warfield is protecting Patsy. Everybody knows Mr. Zaldoni has a Tommy gun in his basement and a dangerous loaded barrette under his pillow.

I'm kinda Patsy's friend now, I guess, cuz she asks me to stay at her house a while. We play three games of Clue. Then we watch *Guiding Light*, which I don't know what's going on cuz Mom never lets Jane and me watch soap operas.

When we hear Mrs. Pearson clanging her school bell, Mrs. Warfield fills an ice bucket and takes it out to a little cart in the living room. She fixes Patsy and me kiddie cocktails with two cherries each.

Mr. Warfield puts out bowls of Planters salted peanuts. "I'll have the usual, honey," he says. "No, make it a double."

We never have Planters salted peanuts at our house.

When Mom rings her danged cowbell, Patsy and me say goodbye. We're probably not gonna be real friends anymore cuz she's gonna go to high school in a couple of weeks. Even so, I think neither one of us is gonna forget these last few days.

That night, I dream Patsy gets shot to death by a goat. I wake up crying, but nobody hears me so I hug Cuddle Bun. The next morning, I pick the raisins out of my oatmeal and stick them on Charlie's high chair tray. I'm not too hungry. Dad goes out to get the morning paper and comes back with big news.

"You wouldn't believe what's going on out there," he says. "There's a crowd of gawkers in front of the Zaldonis.'"

Mom looks up. "Why? Is it on fire?"

"It's empty. The whole place has been cleaned out lock, stock, and barrel."

"Nice way to put it," Mom says, smiling a little. "Did they get robbed?"

Dad shakes his head. "Not that I can tell. Looks like they're gone, though."

Mom won't let Jane and me go see until we've all finished our oatmeal— even Charlie, and Charlie takes forever. He likes the raisin part, but he hates the oatmeal part. By the time Mom, Dad, Jane, me, and Charlie get there, just about everybody on Thistle Way is on the street in front of the Zaldonis' house. Mrs. Pearson has on a plastic shower cap. Mrs. Henry's got cold cream slathered all over her face. Detective Greeley's wearing his pajamas, which would be funny except nobody's laughing.

Lt. Lofton is talking to Mr. Daily, saying, " . . . either six feet under or on a slow boat to Sicily by now."

I look over at Patsy and smile. I don't know where Sicily is, but I'm sure glad the Zaldonis are gone for good. I've got my whole act planned for next year's talent show, and it's a doozy.

Most of us have a secret alter ego: prima ballerina, Broadway star, world-famous magician, gold medal skater, Nobel Prize-winning poet. It's the stuff of dreams. Then something like a neighborhood talent show comes along, a public, one-against-all slugfest that commences and concludes in the blinding immediacy of real time, and what little common sense we might have goes right out the window. The dream becomes a goal. The impossible becomes marginally probable, perhaps even achievable. The likelihood of failure slips from view, like a sailor flailing in the wake of an aircraft carrier.

When Patsy announced the winners, Susan and Sharon White ran home in tears. Lizzie O'Grady ripped up her poems and refused solid food for a week. Benny Herman quit his bugle lessons.

At the conclusion of the 1956 Patsy's Players Talent Show, Patsy Warfield bravely stood her ground. She rejected the ingenuous affections of a Mooney. She declined an all-expense-paid trip to Disneyland. And she stared down Luca Zaldoni until he finally turned on his heel and stomped home. Antony and the rest of the Zaldonis followed directly. The silence was thundering. When all Zaldonis had departed, Patsy cleared her throat and rapped her conductor's baton on the patio three times. Everyone in the audience who had turned sideways in their seats to observe the mortification of the Zaldoni's turned around again to see what Patsy would do next.

"Please rise," she said.

Everyone stood. Patsy set down her baton, and for long moments, an interlude I feel certain Patsy savored, she gazed out at the assembled crowd, according each attendee either a smile or a nod. At last, she picked up the gleaming silver trophy and held it high.

"I now declare the winners to be . . . Missy, Anna, and Pauly!"

The Stars of Tomorrow talent show produced one winning act. All the rest, in a sense, were losers. And some took it badly.

But the three young winners, thrust into the dazzling glare of instant fame, went from being toddling afterthoughts in the neighborhood mix to overnight celebrities.

Patsy swore she would never hold another talent show, but in its defense, *The Stars of Tomorrow* afforded those of us who will never dance on Broadway, sing at LaScala, or win an Olympic medal, a stage on which, for a few shining moments, we were this close to experiencing the stuff of dreams.

Meegan

the white box

Years ago, when I was in my twenties, I had a friend named Jeanne, an older woman who edited the articles I freelanced to newspapers and magazines. Jeanne was a plump, dimpled, abundantly freckled redhead with delicate hands and a laugh so hearty it gave her an air of jollity that belied a desert-dry wit.

Jeanne was fond of giving advice, and when I was expecting my first baby she ordered me to stop reading. "No newspapers. No magazines or books, either. Stop watching television. And don't go to the movies."

"What! Why?"

"The minute you get pregnant," she said, her tone knowing, for she had two boys at the time, "every TV show, every magazine story, and every newspaper article is about an expectant mother or newborn baby in some sort of peril or terrible condition. As soon as you have your perfectly fine baby, it stops . . . until the next time you get pregnant."

I continued to read, of course, and subjected myself to bouts of extraneous dread, given that the odds on my obstetrician being an ax murderer or me giving birth at sea in a hurricane were fairly long.

Had I thought of it, which I did not, I would have realized it is often something commonplace that puts a child at risk.

And *that* would have been most frightening of all.

Meegan's gone missing. Mrs. Mooney's worried sick.

I wouldn't much care if Meegan Mooney stays missing until the cows come home, but that's probably a sin if you say it out loud, so I don't. Anyways, me and Jane and a bunch of kids have been helping Matt and Mark Mooney look for their stupid little sister in the back yards while Mrs. Mooney tears the house apart. Meegan's only four, four going on five. She's got white-blond hair and the bluest eyes you've ever seen, and I think her mom's worried she got kidnapped.

If it was any other kid, I would've figured they probably just swiped a nickel from their mom's pocketbook and ran up to Snyder's Five & Dime to buy candy, but Meegan Mooney doesn't eat candy. Heck, Meegan hardly eats *anything*. Ever since last winter, the only food she eats is French fries.

Last fall the Mooneys' grandma and grandpa went on a trip to Ireland and France and at Christmas they gave all the Mooney boys, of which there's lots, thick cream-colored sweaters like the Irish people wear to go fishing in. Meegan got a fishing sweater, too, and also a blue skirt with a white French poodle on the front. Meegan looked pretty darn cute in that skirt, I'll tell you that. Meegan started wearing that skirt every day, and one day her mom brought home a picture book about France from the library, which Meegan read a kabillion times before it had to go back to the library. After that she stopped eating everything except French fries. I'm pretty sure Meegan wants to be French.

More kids are looking for Meegan now. Even some of the moms. I hear Mrs. Mooney on the telephone in her front hallway. She's calling Mr. Mooney. She tells him Meegan's lost, come home right now. Then she slams down the receiver, runs out to the front porch, and plops right down on the first step. I think she's crying.

Patsy Warfield and me decide to scrounge around in Mrs. Pearson's garden shed, thinking maybe Meegan got stuck in there. We're about halfway to Mrs. Pearson's when we hear somebody yelling, real loud:

"Gloria, come quick—it's Meegan!"

It's Mrs. Lofton! She's down at the beginning of Thistle Way, near the through-road. She's hollering the same thing over and over, "Come quick! Come quick!"

I'm kinda scared, cuz Mrs. Lofton never hollers.

Me and Patsy and the rest of the kids and the other moms and Mrs. Mooney run fast to where Thistle Way meets up with the through road.

Even before I get there, I see my Mom with Mrs. Lofton. They're pacing back and forth, squinting into the sun and pointing at something out where the through road connects up to the superhighway.

"Someone call the police!" Mrs. Lofton shouts. Patsy Warfield runs back home to tell her mom to call for help.

Mrs. Mooney gets to the through road and squints into the sun and her knees give out and she starts to kinda collapse. Mrs. Lofton and Mark catch her just in time. I squint into the sun to see what's so awful out on the superhighway, but I think I know.

Meegan.

She's sitting cross-legged in the grassy strip between the two lanes that zoom toward the city and the two lanes that zoom away from the city. It's almost dinnertime. All four lanes are streaming with cars and trucks.

Mrs. Mooney wobbles to her feet and starts to call out to Meegan. Quick as a wink, Mrs. Lofton claps a hand over her mouth to stop her.

"Don't, Gloria," she whispers. "You'll scare the child and she'll panic. She'll get up and try to run to you, across all this traffic. Stay calm. Wait for the police."

Mrs. Mooney lets out a little cry. It sounds more like a dry, gagging cough.

Patsy and Mrs. Warfield come running. They get to the crowd of moms and kids standing on the through road near the highway, and when Mrs. Warfield catches her breath she says the police are on their way. "It might be a minute or two," she says. Mrs. Mooney and the rest of the moms creep along the through road and we kids follow them up a low, grassy hill. Everybody stops when we get to the skinny strip of gravel that runs along the outside of the traffic lanes. I've never ever been this close to the superhighway. Even the older boys like Mike Mooney don't go up here, except on a dare. Jane's holding Charlie so tight he starts to whimper so I whisper for him to shut up and he does. Charlie's good that way.

The moms shuffle back and forth on the gravel watching Meegan and checking their wristwatches. Every time a car or truck zooms by, my hair blows straight back. The trucks sound like a hundred mix masters and a hundred vacuum cleaners all going at the same time.

Meegan hasn't moved so far. I squint into the sun again and notice a small white box on her lap. She reaches into it, pulls something apart with her fingers, and takes a little bite.

I tug on the back of Mom's blouse. "What's she doing?"

Mom just shakes her head and makes a strange sound, like her throat's all closed up cuz she's so scared.

"What is she eating?" Mrs. Lofton asks, softly. A couple of the moms shrug their shoulders up and down. Nobody takes their eyes off Meegan.

"A donut?" Matt says.

"No, a croissant," Mrs. Warfield says. "The box must have fallen off a bakery truck. She must have wandered out here and seen it and gone out there to get it."

Mark lets out a long whoosh of air. "Good God," he says, putting his arm around his mother's shoulder. Mrs. Mooney jerks off his arm, stands up real straight, and turns to face Mrs. Lofton and the rest of the mothers. Her eyes are huge and bulgy. She's sucked in her lips so far they're almost invisible. She doesn't even look like herself.

"Where are the damn police?" she hisses, glaring at poor Mrs. Lofton, as if it's Mrs. Lofton's fault that the police aren't here yet. Heck, it hasn't even been two seconds since Mrs. Warfield came running from her house.

I've never heard any of the moms say a curse word, except for Mrs. Henry and Mrs. Haverkamp. And I've sure never heard anybody hiss at Mrs. Lofton.

Mrs. Lofton tries to pat her on the back, but Mrs. Mooney just whirls around to face the highway again. It looks like she's gonna bolt across the lanes of traffic! Mark and another lady grab her just in time, cuz a big truck speeds past us, blaring his horn and blasting us all with a huge whoosh of swirling dust. More cars are racing past us now, too, right behind the truck, roaring up and then roaring away from the city. More cars and more. There's no good spaces in between the traffic for anybody to go get Meegan. Everybody stops staring at Meegan for a moment to glance at Mrs. Mooney. She's covering her eyes with her hands. Tears are sliding down through her fingers, all down her cheeks.

All of a sudden Matt groans. "Oh, no."

We all turn to look. Meegan must have seen her mother, cuz she's getting up. Now she's on her feet, waving the little white box at Mrs. Mooney!

A station wagon and a milk truck zoom toward us, going side by side, kicking up pebbles and grit just a few feet from where we're standing. I blink three times and rub my eyes. As soon as they pass us, three more cars speed toward us. I look way down the highway, but there's cars and trucks coming for as far as I can see. Meegan loses her grip on the white box and it flies into the air. Everybody watches it sail over the stream of traffic. It twirls in a circle three times and then drifts down to the pavement. A car races past and misses the box by inches. A couple of the moms say "Ahh," like they're relieved. Now the box is flying in the air again, floating over more cars going like the blazes. I look down the highway—in the distance, I see two trucks roaring toward us. One is kinda small. The other one is humongous, a long silver tube with the word "Texaco" painted on the side.

The little white box is spinning along the pavement, not far from Meegan. "Please God," I hear Mrs. Mooney say.

The trucks zoom toward us going a mile a minute. Right ahead of them, the white box rises up and smacks the big truck's pointy front bumper. It sticks there a second, then flies off and lands in between the two lanes. It's all smushed now. Another humongous truck blasts past us with another tornado of wind and grit, but I keep my eyes open to watch. Six big tires run right over Meegan's little box and the truck streaks away. The box isn't white anymore. It's flat and filthy, tattered to shreds.

Mrs. Mooney starts to wail. Across the highway lanes, Meegan is shouting something. It looks like she's saying hello, but we can't hear her cuz of the roar of the traffic. She's getting mad. We're not waving back to her and she's mad. Oh, no she's starting to take baby steps toward the highway lane! One step. Another. She pauses, waves again, and frowns at us.

Mrs. Mooney and all the rest of us fling out our arms straight, so Meegan will stop. Mrs. Lofton yells at the top of her lungs, "Stay there!"

I've never heard Mrs. Lofton yell. Heck, I didn't think she even *could*.

More cars and trucks are whistling between us and Meegan. If anything, the traffic is worse than when we got here just a couple of minutes ago. Mrs. Mooney bends forward, like she's gonna run through that traffic anyway. It takes Mark and three mothers to hold her back.

Meegan's inching forward again. Holy smokes, she's stepping right onto the gravel on her side of the pavement lanes.

Bang! Bang! BANG!

Everybody turns around to see who's banging on the low grassy hill behind us. It's Mrs. Zaldoni! She's banging her wood spoon on her big old pasta pot, just like she does every night to call Luca and Antony home for dinner. What the heck?

Mrs. Zaldoni's pretty gold-darn fat, and she's got short legs, but she climbs that hill in no time. With the next couple of bangs, she's right behind us, but she's not stopping. With two more bangs she's marching right across the gravel toward the highway lanes.

Two moms step aside to let her through. Nobody says a word. Down the highway, a pickup truck and a station wagon are speeding toward us. Behind them is a really, really big truck and two motorcycles. Behind them is a Greyhound bus. Mrs. Zaldoni's gonna get squished flat!

I scrinch closed my eyes and then peek them open again.

Bam!

Bam-Bam-BAM!

Mrs. Zaldoni whacks the pot real fast and real loud. The station wagon slows down a little and moves behind the pickup truck. They whiz past us in the far lane. Lucky for her. The really big truck can't stop, can't do anything but honk its horn like crazy, but the motorcycles swerve way over to our side of the pavement, spraying us with gravel as they pass by. Whew. At least Mrs. Zaldoni isn't killed. Yet.

All of us let out our breaths, which we didn't even realize we were holding.

Mrs. Zaldoni gets to the other side a split second before the Greyhound bus zooms past us in the far lane, the lane closest to her and Meegan. When I open my eyes again, I see the hem of her big black skirt fluttering. In front of me, Mrs. Mooney's on her knees. Mom and Mrs. Lofton are bending over her.

Mrs. Zaldoni sets the pasta pot down on the grass. She scoops up Meegan and plops her on her hip, which makes a good seat cuz it's real puffy. She dips down, picks up the pot and spoon, and wraps both arms around Meegan, tight. Finally, banging that old pot like crazy, she just waltzes right back across the highway to us. Three cars screech to a stop, but they don't hit Mrs. Zaldoni and Meegan.

Mrs. Mooney lets out a little cry that sounds like a puppy yipping. She scrambles to her feet and grabs Meegan and kisses her all over. Everybody cheers and cheers. Mrs. Zaldoni traipses down the grassy hill toward the through road. In the distance, I hear a bunch of sirens. The police cars must be on their way. It seemed like everything happened in slow motion, but I guess it was really fast.

Anyways, all the way back to Thistle Way, the moms and kids make a parade behind Mrs. Mooney and Meegan, and at the front of the parade is Mrs. Zaldoni, beating on that big old pot.

Over the years, I've tried to hold at bay my unrealistic fears for my children's safety, and I'm pretty sure I found the middle ground between smothering vigilance and blasé complacence. But it's impossible to safeguard a son or daughter every minute, hour, day, and year of their childhood. We bring our babies into a capricious world and sometimes, for some of them, things do not go well. They grab the handle of a boiling pot or reach out to pet a sick, stray dog. They climb, slip, and take a nasty fall. They manage to uncap a prescription bottle and snack on its contents. They toddle off and roam into the onrush of traffic, into a neighbor's swimming pool, into the path of someone who snatches them up and does them no good. No good at all. For a long while, perhaps ever after, the parents carry in their anguished hearts the absolute certainty that they are to blame. After all, hadn't they turned their attention elsewhere, just that once? Chatted on the telephone, finished a grocery list, left the kitchen door ajar, the upstairs window open, the gate unlatched, the car in gear. It was only a moment, but still, they tell themselves, over and over, still. . . .

And the rest of us, witness to the pity of the thing, draw our little ones close, enfold them in safety until they squirm from our chastened arms and run off, to get on with the serious business of growing up.

Of course, when something terrible befalls a little boy or girl it is the rare, rare exception. Most children get along just fine. I know that.

But it happens.

Which is why shouts of terror across a quiet suburban neighborhood ignite the sizzle of dread every mother keeps, banked and tamped, at the core of her. And why deciding to have a child is an act of courage, a profession of faith, hope, and boundless love.

Benny

the bugle

Benny Herman had always been chubby. The Mooney boys claimed Benny polished off three desserts each and every night, a feat much discussed but never independently verified. It was plain to see, however, that meals clung to the boy's frame like overstuffed pillows.

In late June that year, a few short weeks before the big Thistle Way Talent Show, Benny decided to take up the bugle. Each evening at seven o'clock, he would raise his bedroom window and perch on its sill, an amazement we kids gathered to watch. He'd plant one leg indoors, for stability, and let his other leg dangle fifteen feet above his mother's rose bushes. After squeezing through the opening, he'd lean out, point his bugle toward the street, and blow.

What came from that horn were sharps and flats and bleating goat noises, sounds that rarely coalesced into anything any of us could identify. Neighbors out for an evening stroll rolled their eyes and tried to guess whether Benny's current tune was "Boogie Woogie Bugle Boy" or "Here Comes the Bride" or something else entirely. I once heard Mrs. Henry call up to Benny and ask if his parents had bothered to provide him with sheet music or lessons.

What Benny's evening recitals lacked in proficiency, they made up for in volume. That horn was louder than the incessant buzzing of the cicadas. Much louder than the whirr-whirr of push-mowers crisscrossing Thistle Way's shaggy lawns. Even louder than the ice cream truck.

The Greeleys grumbled that Benny's horn playing so aggravated Bullet, their dog, that he chased his tail until he was hopelessly wrapped up in his chain. Mrs. Pearson told Mrs. Daily that during Benny's rehearsals, her bird, Jenkins, fell into stupefied silence, which, she said, was worrisome. Our little Charlie developed prickly heat, a condition my mother connected to the aggravation of Benny Herman's bugle playing.

At some point each night, Benny stopped, momentarily, in order to swab the sweat from his neck. In that interlude, Jane and I would look at each other and ask, "Is he done? Do you think he's finished yet?"

Not a chance. After a brief break, Benny would move on to scales that were simultaneously flat and sharp.

Everyone, it seemed, had something to say about Benny's horn playing. My sister said it came out in a key yet to be invented. My father said that the sound reminded him of a moose he once heard giving birth. My mother said it furnished us all with a preview of Purgatory.

If I get desperate, I could spend a night or two at Benny's house, maybe. Nah.

Benny's performance at the talent show set teeth on edge. Afterward, I watched him shuffle home; he looked forlorn. Mike Mooney walked partway with him and then came back and announced that Benny had sworn never to play a bugle again.

That night, as twilight faded to lavender dusk, a group of us kids stood outside the Hermans' house, waiting to see what would happen. Benny raised his bedroom window and sat on its sill, forking chunks of coconut cake into his mouth. Next door, Jenkins was tweeting merrily in his cage. Across the street, Bullet rolled belly-up in the grass, opened his mouth, and yawned. I recall that the ice cream truck came, attracted an appreciative crowd, dispensed its treats, and left, swirling moths, mosquitoes, and lightning bugs in its wake. My mother popped Charlie in the kitchen sink for a cool rinse-off, dusted him with powder, and let him run around naked a few minutes before settling him on her lap for a bedtime story.

Evening wore on. We watched as Benny finished his cake and crawled back inside. In the calm that followed, a few of us applauded. Then a few more. And then more. The light in his room winked off, the window went dark. The show was over.

I think about that now and am ashamed. Surely Benny must have first assumed we were clapping because we wanted him to take up the horn again, and then, to his chagrin, realized we were applauding the sweet sound of silence.

the Zaldoni Boys

the trattoria

The old Italian section of St. Louis is called the Hill, and on that old hill, the name Zaldoni was—and still is—spoken with a good deal of reverence. As with many families of Sicilian origin, every Zaldoni was expected to participate in the family business. Absolute loyalty might or might not be rewarded with steady movement up an ever-changing hierarchy, but in any case, loyalty was demanded. Family expectations might have loosened somewhat, but in the mid-1950s, a Zaldoni who broke away to start a rival business did so at his own risk, which was why everyone on Thistle Way was shocked, but not surprised, to wake up on the Monday morning after Patsy Warfield's talent show to find the Zaldonis had moved out, lock, stock, and barrel. They vanished without a trace.

Every Christmas Eve, we drive all the way down to the cathedral for Mass. A cathedral is gobs bigger than a regular church, and Christmas Eve Mass is way, way longer than regular Sunday Mass. There's tons of priests on the altar, and they all want to recite the important prayers, and in the middle of the whole thing, they line up behind Archbishop Ritter and do a procession around the inside of the church, and one of them swings a gold container of incense on a long chain, which makes the whole place smell burnt.

The best part is during the sermon cuz parents let their older kids take their younger kids up to look at the statues of Mary and Joseph and Baby Jesus and camels and stuff in a real manger that somebody built in the church. But at the end of Mass—just when the priests and Archbishop Ritter finally get to the last prayer and Archbishop Ritter wishes everybody a Holy Christmas and you have to pee something awful and your petticoat is scratching you like crazy and Charlie and the other little kids are bawling—right then, the danged choir cranks up to sing every verse of "Joy to the World."

Last Christmas Eve, after we finally got out of the cathedral and after my legs froze to death walking to our car, we drove down Lindell Boulevard and looked at all the pretty mansions, and after a while, we got to my grandpa's department store. The store was closed by that time, but the window displays were all lit up.

My grandpa's store has the best window displays. Last winter, they had a fairy tale theme with Hansel and Gretel, Robin Hood, Goldilocks, the Three Blind Mice, Rapunzel with her long hair, and Red Riding Hood and the Big Bad Wolf. They were all puppets that moved by themselves.

Pretty soon, we got too starving and freezing to keep looking at the Christmas windows, so we piled back in the car. Dad turned the heater on full blast all the way to the Hill, where we always go on Christmas Eve for a big spaghetti dinner.

We usually would go to Angelo's, but Dad forgot to make a reservation till too late, and Angelo's couldn't squeeze us in. The man at Angelo's told Dad to try Osteria la Siciliana. So Dad called Osteria la Siciliana, and they said they could squeeze us in at seven o'clock. When we got there, it was jammed. If the choir back at the cathedral had chopped off a couple of verses of "Joy to the World," we could have beat the crowd. Sheesh. We stood around in the lobby with a kabillion people, who all had on damp winter coats that smelled like basement closets and lasagna.

A pretty waitress finally led us to a table. Dad ordered two double Old Fashioneds (one for him and one for Mom) and kiddie cocktails for Jane, me, and Charlie. Jane spooned out her red cherry, like she does every year, and popped it in her mouth. I gave mine to Charlie, and he gobbled it up. Mom didn't care that there was cherry juice dribbling down Charlie's chin cuz she always brings a cute bib for him with a reindeer or a gingerbread boy on it.

After Charlie finished the cherry, it was still a long time till we got food, so Mom gave him the candy cane that was part of the flower arrangement in the middle of the table. It was a real candy cane, not plastic or anything. I'd have loved to taste that candy cane, I'll tell you that, but Mom said I had to preserve my appetite. Then Dad got out his big old camera and took a picture of Charlie cuz he looked so cute in his little round collar Christmas shirt and reindeer bib and red sticky goo all over his face, and Jane gave me one of her smarty-pants looks, and I picked up Jane's spoon and licked it while she wasn't looking, and then Dad put down the camera and said, "Girls, that's enough."

At Angelo's, me and Jane liked to turn around in our chairs and look at the pictures of dead people on the walls. We would make up funny names for them, like Rita Ravioli and Luigi Linguini. There's pictures of old dead people at Osteria la Siciliana too, but Jane said she was too old for such a baby game, and she just sat still being all polite.

I remember the first stuff we got to eat, even before the tossed salad with house dressing—it was toasted ravioli. Toasted ravioli is crispy, puffy little squares stuffed with meat and cheese. They burn the roof of your mouth, but I never care cuz I'm always starving to death. Also, they're delicious.

My sister, Jane, is the only person in the world who doesn't like toasted ravioli. Jane's a picky eater, and when she doesn't want to eat something, she wails bloody murder. One day last winter Miss Finch, Jane's teacher, tried to force her to eat the snack, which was carrot sticks. My sister hates carrot sticks even more than she hates toasted ravioli. When she wailed bloody murder, Miss Finch made her go stand in the corner.

Then the recess bell clanged, and the whole class lined up and went out to the playground. I guess Miss Finch thought Jane would follow them, but she didn't. She walked home. Mom woke up Charlie and plunked him and Jane in the car and drove to Immaculate Heart of Mary and bawled out Miss Finch something good. Pretty soon all the kids in school were asking me if our mother is nutso, which we didn't appreciate, I'll tell you that. My sister Jane's a pain in the neck.

Anyways, last Christmas Eve, Dad ordered three plates of toasted ravioli, and guess who brought them to our table? Luca and Antony Zaldoni! The Zaldoni boys looked real embarrassed too, cuz they knew we were staring at the tuxedos they had on and the white aprons that came all the way down to their shoes. Jane and me just about died laughing till

Mom gave us her I'm-gonna-kill-you-girls look, and we clammed up.

After Luca and Antony went back to the kitchen, Dad leaned over to Mom and whispered, "Those kids were Zaldonis, right? Do you think the Zaldonis in our neighborhood own this place?"

"I didn't think they were a restaurant family," Mom whispered back. "I always thought they were hooked up with the you-know-what."

That's what Mom says when she doesn't want to say the word. When Dad doesn't want to say the word, he uses pig Latin. Jane says she's figured out pig Latin, and for fifty cents, she'll tell me how to do it. I'm saving up my money.

"Honey, shhh, look!" Dad tilted his head toward the bar.

Mom and Jane and I looked too. Luca and Antony's father was lugging a bin of dirty glasses back to the kitchen. "They might be family here," Dad said, "but they're sure not the owners."

Right about then I got up to go to the bathroom, but I got lost trying to find it, and I wandered into a back hall. Wood boxes filled with lettuce and tomatoes were stacked along the walls. A mean old lady was back there bawling out the Zaldoni boys' mother. Luca's mom was crying, but I couldn't understand what the mean old lady was saying cuz it wasn't English.

There was a bunch of cannoli crumbled up on the floor, so I figured Luca's mom got in trouble cuz she dropped them. Cannoli look like cardboard tubes when the toilet paper runs out except they're smaller and filled with sweet creamy stuff, and they're a dessert. The mean old lady yelled some more, and Luca's mother got down on her knees and made kind of a hammock out of her apron and gathered five cannoli in the hammock that weren't cracked, but the mean old lady yelled again and swatted the apron and even the good cannoli got broken to pieces. Then a girl came out of the ladies' room, and it was my turn.

It's a few days after Patsy's big show, early morning, the start of another blazing hot summer day.

Just about everybody who lives on Thistle Way is standing in the street in front of the Zaldonis' empty house, except Mrs. Haverkamp. Mrs. Haverkamp doesn't wake up till late afternoon, when Mrs. Pearson rings her school bell. Anyways, I'm pretty sure the neighbors who are here are all wondering what happened to the Zaldonis and all their furniture.

Detective Greeley walks up the Zaldonis' driveway and knocks on the front door. Everybody watches. The door pushes open on its own, so Detective Greeley walks right into Luca and Antony Zaldoni's house. Holy cow!

Marty Throckmorten's dad hitches up his trousers and says, "Let's just see what's going on here."

Mr. Throckmorten always acts like he's the most important person in the world. I heard Dad tell Mom that Mr. Throckmorten's got a superiority complex, which I didn't quite get. Anyways, Mr. Throckmorten walks up the drive and waltzes into the Zaldonis' house, too. Detective Greeley is a policeman for the City of Brentwood, so he can go in anyplace he wants without getting permission, even if he isn't wearing his uniform with the shiny silver badge, which he isn't. Detective Greeley's wearing striped pajamas!

"Must've been on the late shift again," Dad says to Mom.

Pretty soon we see Mr. Throckmorten back at the door, shrugging his shoulders up and down. "They're gone all right. 'Goners,' I should say."

Everybody starts talking at the same time.

"—put the finger on him. . . . "

"—heard he was the triggerman for . . ."

"—bunch o' hoods, that's what they were."

"—mixed up with . . . "

Dad steps in front of the crowd and makes the time-out hand signal. Everybody except Mrs. Henry shuts up. I'm glad Dad got dressed for work before he went outside to get the morning newspaper; he looks important.

"Any of you ever been to Osteria la Siciliana?" Dad says.

Nobody says anything until Mrs. Henry pipes up, "What's that got to do with the price of tea in China?"

"Everything," Dad says. "Nello Zaldoni wasn't in the Mafia. He wasn't involved in the rackets, and he wasn't a triggerman. For God's sake, the guy was a glorified busboy!"

Benny Herman's dad snorts. "I heard he was one of Buster Wortman's boys."

"You heard wrong, Saul," Dad says, talking soft. People get really quiet and lean forward to hear. Dad makes a church steeple with his fingers and presses them against his lips, thinking.

"I'll tell you a little story. Every Christmas Eve, I take the family down to the Hill for dinner after Mass. Best Italian food this side of the Bay of

Naples. Most of you know that. You've made the drive down to Angelo's for mostacolli. You've bought bread at Amighetti's."

Lots of people nod.

"We usually go to Angelo's," Dad says. "But last Christmas Eve, we tried Osteria la Siciliana. Fantastic toasted ravioli, by the way."

"So?" Mr. Throckmorten says. "When are you gonna get to the part about these thugs, Mitchell?"

I'm thinking Mr. Throckmorten doesn't like Dad doing all the talking. He pulls Mr. Henry aside, and the two of them start grumbling, saying Thistle Way was supposed to be a safe neighborhood. Pretty soon, more people are grumbling.

Right then, Detective Greeley walks out of the Zaldonis' front door and down the driveway. "Pipe down, everybody," he says. "Paul Mitchell's a regular guy. Let him say his piece."

"Thanks, Joe," Dad says. "Anyway, Osteria La Siciliana is owned by Sal Zaldoni—Salvatore, the old man. Last Christmas was the first time I'd been there, but I gather Sal holds forth at the restaurant every night. It wasn't hard to see he's the owner of the place; I watched him checking on the bartenders and cooks, signaling the waitresses that a water glass needed ice or a napkin was on the floor. And the old guy made a point to stop at every table, introduce himself, and ask if the people were being well taken care of. It's authentic, I'll tell you that."

Mrs. Henry blows a stream of cigarette smoke sideways out of her mouth and says, "Plenty of restaurants front for the Mob. I'll bet the place has a real busy back room. Nello and Marianna are probably filthy rich."

"I don't think so," Dad says. "Not filthy and not rich. Let me explain: the old man, Sal, gets to our table and introduces himself. Thick accent. I told him we live near a family I assumed were his relatives, Nello and Marianna, in Brentwood. Old Sal gets a sour look on his face and turns to the next table. Just like that." Dad snaps his fingers.

"Where are you going with this, Mitchell?" Mr. Throckmorten calls out.

Dad ignores him.

"A couple of minutes later, Luca and Antony come out of the kitchen with our hors d'oeuvres. The boys worked there as junior waiters, I guess. You should have seen them, decked out in tuxedos and long white aprons. Meanwhile, their father's carrying bin after metal bin filled with dirty glasses from the bar to the kitchen. And their mother's in a back hall getting chewed out for spilling a couple of cannoli."

"What's your point?" Lt. Lofton says. "We can't stand out here all day."

Dad takes a deep breath. "Salvatore Zaldoni came back to our table and asked me to step outside with him a moment. I thought maybe the old man felt guilty for leaving so abruptly. Anyway, I'm standing on the sidewalk in front of the restaurant, freezing my tush off, when Sal launches into this long story about his family. I think the old guy had had a few nips from the red wine jug. He says he's got five sons and Nello— the one who moved out to Thistle Way with his wife and two boys—he's the youngest. He says all the other sons and their wives and their kids live on the Hill and work at the restaurant. He says they're all happy to have jobs in the family's restaurant, all except Nello and Marianna. He tells me Nello asked him for fifteen thousand dollars as seed money so he and Marianna could open their own restaurant in Clayton. They want to call it Nello's Trattoria. They want Sal's blessing, and his money.

"At that point, Sal blows up. I'm out on a city sidewalk on Christmas Eve, half frozen, with my whole family and a hot meal waiting inside, and I can't shut the guy up. He's in a full-blown rage.

"'A two-bit trattoria in Clayton with a Zaldoni name on it!' the old man shouts, and he throws up his hands in disgust.

"I get Sal somewhat calmed down, and he tells me he struck a bargain with Nello. The deal was that for six months, Nello and Marianna and the boys would work the lowest jobs at the restaurant. Then if they still wanted to open a trattoria in Clayton, Sal would consider giving them the money and his blessing. But there was a catch. As soon as they got the money and started construction, Nello and Marianna and the two boys had to move back to the Hill.

"Back in the restaurant, I'm just digging into my lasagna when Sal comes up to the table and taps my shoulder. He looks sheepish, embarrassed or something. I think he was mortified to have confided so much of the family's business to me. He kept saying, 'This no like a true Sicilian.' At first, I thought he meant Nello leaving the Hill, but then I realized he meant spilling the family's dirty laundry to a complete stranger."

Dad stops talking. Mom and me and Jane and Charlie walk up to the front of the crowd and stand next to Dad. Everybody's quiet. I'm thinking they're waiting to hear more about the Zaldonis getting the worst jobs. For a couple of minutes, it seems like everybody's forgotten the

Zaldonis' empty house.

"I think what we've all seen here is something special and wonderful," Mom says. "When Nello and Marianna moved to Thistle Way a couple of years ago, can you imagine how it must have broken Sal's heart? And when they told him about their dream to open a trattoria in Clayton, it probably was like a kick in the stomach for the old man. So what does Sal do? He does what good fathers do: he tests their will. He gives them the worst jobs at the Osteria, and if they stick it out for six months, they get his blessing and his cash . . . maybe."

"Maybe?" Mr. Throckmorten says.

"Right," Dad says, nodding at Mom. "If you remember, Sal said he would *consider* giving them the cash and his blessing. Consider."

"So the old man welshed, is that what you're saying?"

"Bear with me." Dad continues. "Every Saturday morning, Maddy and I and the kids drive to Clayton to get a deep butter coffee cake from Pfeiffer's. It's our little outing. Yesterday morning, we were on Clayton Road, just passing Bemiston, when we saw a sign that said, 'Coming Soon! Nello's Trattoria!'"

"Then Nello and Marianna welshed," Mr. Throckmorten said, sounding like a know-it-all. "They got the money for the new place, but they never moved back to the Hill."

Dad dug his hands in his jacket pocket and blew out a puff of air. "I wouldn't say welshed, exactly. Luca and Antony are a handful, you all know that. A parent's first duty is to his children. Nello and Marianna probably thought another move would be hard on the kids."

"Two days ago," Mom says, "we all saw the whole extended Zaldoni family troop in to Thistle Way to watch Luca and Antony in the talent show. And we now know Luca tried to threaten Patsy Warfield into declaring them the winners. The morning of the show, Luca must have told his father they're a sure-fire bet to win a silver trophy. Nello invites his parents and his brothers to the show so they can see for themselves that Luca and Antony are doing much better here in Brentwood than they ever did when they lived on the Hill."

"But it backfired," Mr. Throckmorten said. "The kids blew it."

"It backfired," Dad repeats. "The boys fouled up. Nello and Marianna marched them back to the stage to make amends, but the damage was done. They didn't win, didn't even come close. That must have embarrassed old Sal, sitting there stone-faced and smoldering like Vesuvius."

"So where are they now?" Mrs. Henry says. "Where'd they go in such an all-fire hurry?"

Dad doesn't answer her directly.

"Last night, about 3:30 a.m., I heard a commotion," Dad says. "I looked out the front window to see what was going on. It was dark, but I saw a truck cruise around the circle slowly. Now, you can't see the Zaldonis' house from our place, but I followed the tail lights, and I'm pretty sure the truck turned into Zaldoni's driveway."

"What kind of a truck?" Detective Greeley said.

"A pickup truck. On the side, big red and green letters spelled out *Osteria la Siciliana*."

"What gives?" Lt. Lofton asks.

"Sal, the old man, struck me as a guy with a short fuse. I'm pretty sure that when he saw his two grandsons roughhousing at the talent show, he was furious. After all, he'd paid the money for the Trattoria. He'd kept up his end of the bargain. But Nello and Marianna were dragging their feet about moving back to the Hill. So Sal sent his older sons in the truck to pack up and move their kid brother back to the Hill. Nello, Marianna, and the boys aren't on their way to Sicily. My guess is they were taken straight down to Daggett Avenue."

Everybody starts laughing and talking at the same time. Mom hugs Dad. Jane and I do too. Charlie holds out his little dimpled arms for a hug, but he's still gooey with oatmeal, so Jane and me sorta back off.

Detective Greeley steps to the front of the crowd and cups his hands around his mouth. "All right, the fun's over. Everybody go back home now."

All the neighbors do what he says, even though Detective Greeley looks pretty gol-darn stupid. First of all, he's wearing his pajamas. And second of all, the pajamas have little firecrackers printed all over them.

Sicily is renowned for its stunning geography, sumptuous cuisine, delicious wine, and picturesque villages. And the Mafia.

For every famous Sicilian painter, poet, Nobel Prize winning dramatist, sculptor, composer, architect, mathematician, physicist, and philosopher whose name eludes us, there is a Sicilian mobster whose name does not.

Lucky Luciano. Frank Scalice. Carlo Gambino.

The presumptive identity of Sicilians is a disservice to men like Sal Zaldoni. Men who left their homeland and sailed to America with what they could pack in a small valise, a spare shirt, a few old daguerreotypes, and a recipe for slow-simmered pasta sauce. Who came with what they carried in their hearts, a zest for life. With what filled their souls, abiding faith. With what they knew beyond a doubt, that family helps family. Men who believe that these are the sum of life's treasures, no more, no less.

After weeks in the belly of a ship, men like Sal took to the rocking decks and leaned into the rails. Holding doe-eyed babies fast in their arms, beaming at wives who beamed back, they turned their gaze to the spectacle of Lady Liberty, to the torch she raises heavenward, and breathed air tinged with salt, air laced with boundless opportunity.

Rainer

the hideout

As I recall, the child-rearing model of the 1950s was predicated on absolutes: Parents knew best. Allowance was a reward for chores completed. Bad behavior brought swift and sure punishment. And in neighborhoods like mine, children were responsible for finding their way home when a triangle pinged, a ship's bell tinged, or a cowbell clanged.

Until then, however, we roamed unfettered, as far as we wished, as far as we dared, and then some. Parents didn't hover, counting our every breath. There was no need. The dangers that lurked in cities' dim tenements and soulless alleys could not possibly reach Thistle Way. A house in the Elysian suburbs inoculated children against the perversions and perdition of the city.

Or so it was presumed.

It's lucky the Niesen kids are rich, cuz they sure do have weird names.

Gregor's the oldest. His whole name is Gregor Wilhelm Niesen. Gregor's in the same grade as my sister, and Jane's had a crush on him for an age and a half. Her diary's got all this stuff in it about how blue Gregor's eyes are and how in summer, his hair gets blond streaks in it cuz he's on the swim team at Old Warson. Blah, blah, blah.

I looked in her diary a while ago, and here's what she wrote:

140

It's only the middle of June, but Gregor's already got knots of muscula-ture across his shoulders and an exemplary tan.

Every time Dad hears Jane gushing about the Niesens and Old Warson Country Club, he says "la-dee-dah," and he reminds her that Grandma and Grandpa Reinhardt belong to two fancy clubs. Every year, right before Christmas, they have a big family party at the Missouri Athletic Club, and in summer, Grandma Reinhardt takes me and Jane and Mom to lunch at Topping Ridge Country Club, which is just as good as Old Warson, I'll tell you that. We used to get to swim at Topping Ridge before lunch with Grandma, but for the last couple of years, Mom hasn't let us swim any-where, not even at Topping Ridge, because of polio. I keep telling Mom that the Niesen kids are on Old Warson's swim team and they go in the pool every danged day, but all Mom says is "maybe next year, honey."

Anyways, at the beginning of summer, Gregor got a ten-speed English racer bike. It wasn't even his birthday or anything. That English racer is the skinniest bike I ever saw. The first day, Gregor showed off how light the bike was by picking it up with one hand. Then he rode all around Thistle Way, and pretty soon, boys were lining up on the Niesens' drive-way for turns on Gregor's new bike, which Gregor was selling for a dime for a five-minute ride. First, though, Gregor had to teach every kid who wanted a ride how to work the gears.

Gregor's allowance is a whopper, five dollars a week, but he still likes to think up ways to make more money. Rainer says that for thirty cents, his brother will show you how to sneak into the Brentwood Theater and see a movie for free. For thirty-five cents, Gregor will keep Mr. Snyder busy at the back of his store while you filch all the candy you want. And for fifty cents, Gregor will show you how to whistle real loud through your fingers and how to hold your finger over an open bottle of Vess so that when you shake it, the soda squirts out in the exact direction you want it to go.

Gregor's darn popular and getting richer by the minute this summer.

Rainer is Gregor's younger brother. His whole name is Rainer Welf Niesen. Rainer's in my grade at Immaculate Heart of Mary.

Gregor and Rainer have a little sister. Her whole name is Elsbeth Potthoff Niesen. She's not even in kindergarten yet, so I don't think she knows she's got a dopey name.

The Niesens are almost as rich as the people who live in Warwick Knoll.

In summer, Rainer and Gregor wear polo shirts with little alligators on them and Sperry Top Siders with no socks, and they get blond streaks in their hair from the sun and the swimming pool water. The whole danged Niesen family just about lives at Old Warson. Mr. and Mrs. Niesen play a ton of golf, and they've got a special lifeguard out there who watches Elsbeth and the other little kids in the baby pool.

Rainer used to be my third best friend after Davey Lofton and Melinda Potter. Except now Melinda doesn't count since she hates me and she moved away, so I'm making Rainer my second best friend. It's a rule of mine: if a person hates me, I move the next person up on my best friend list.

Most all the girls in our class have a crush on Rainer, just like the girls in Jane's class have a crush on Gregor. One day last spring, Connie Wertz told me that Melinda was jealous cuz Rainer broke a piece off his Clark bar and gave it to me. Melinda Potter being jealous of me felt pretty darn good, I'll tell you that, but Rainer and me aren't boyfriend-girlfriend or anything. We're just pals.

Way back in June, when I ran away from home, I decided not to go to Rainer's and my special place, the one nobody knows about. I was worried Rainer might show Mom and Dad where our secret fort was, but that was stupid cuz Rainer and me always keep each other's secrets. Like when we went to the Clayton High Halloween House last fall, and I was so scared, I wet my pants. Rainer just said, "Everybody does that sometimes." And like when I told Rainer that me and Melinda Potter played the mean bathroom trick on Connie Wertz. All Rainer said was, "Yeah, I've done that trick too."

Rainer told me he sometimes picks his nose and eats the buggers, and I told Rainer I sometimes still suck my thumb, and neither one of us even laughed. He didn't snitch on me, and I didn't snitch on him. Him and me always tell each other stuff we don't want anybody else to know. Heck, we don't even have to pinky swear.

When Rainer's not at his country club, me and him like to watch TV together. Right after the Warfields added a Florida room onto their house, the Niesens added a better Florida room onto *their* house. The Niesens' Florida room has lots of rattan furniture and fake palm trees and stuff. Best of all, it's got a color TV set. At my house, there's just a stupid black-and-white TV. Mom and Dad hate television so much that one time, for a whole week, they stuck our TV set up in this little storage room behind the bedroom where me and Jane and Charlie sleep. The roof slopes down so you can't stand up in there, and it's freezing cold in winter and smothering hot in summer. Also, there's spiders. And no good furniture. Heck, when me and Jane want to watch *I Love Lucy* or *The Honeymooners*, we have to drag blankets and pillows off our beds.

Rainer and me have a kabillion favorite shows, most of all the *Mickey Mouse Club*. Rainer likes *Spin and Marty* the best. I like Anything-Can-Happen Day. We both like *This Is Your Life* and *Father Knows Best*. We love it when Buddy gets chewed out by his dad.

I'm starting to run out of families to spend the night with, but I've been putting off asking if I can stay over at the Niesens'. I'm thinking it might be weird to sleep in the same room with Rainer, and I sure don't want to get stuck sleeping with Elsbeth. There's only one bed in Elsbeth's room, and Rainer says his little sister still wets the bed at night.

There's still almost a whole month of summer vacation left, and I don't want Mom to figure out I'm running out of new families to try out. I guess I could sleep in the Niesens' Florida room. There's a couch in there. Heck, it's probably tons more comfortable than the moldy old davenport I had to sleep on at Susan and Sharon White's house. Actually, spending a night in that Florida room might be kinda fun, like going to a beach of something. I'll go ask Rainer if I can stay over.

"Sure," Rainer says when I ask if I can sleep over. "How about tonight? Mom and Dad are playing golf at Old Warson, and after that, there's some sorta dinner dance out there, so they won't care. And Gregor'll be here."

While I'm packing my red plaid suitcase for the umpteenth time, I hear Mom on the phone with Grandma Reinhardt. Mom's telling her the dog days of summer seem to have come early this year.

"Wouldn't you know?" Mom sighs. "I really don't need to be any more uncomfortable right now."

Then Grandma says something, and Mom says, "I've been praying for rain."

After lunch, I lug my suitcase over to Rainer's house. He just plops it on the sofa in the Florida room, so I still don't know where I'm gonna sleep. I hope it's the Florida room. That'd be great. I could watch TV until the test pattern comes on.

Rainer's got a new box of colored chalk, so we go outside and sit at the bottom of the driveway and make pictures on the street. Rainer says he feels like he's sitting on a skillet. I say it feels like I'm sitting right on the stove burner, and we both laugh.

I stand up and holler, "I wish polio would go to H-E-double toothpicks!"

After we stop laughing, Rainer draws a cowboy on a horse on the street. I tell him his horse looks like a goat, and we laugh some more. I draw an Indian princess, and he tells me she looks pretty, like Princess Summer Fall Winter Spring. Rainer's like that—always saying nice things.

One time, Jane told me Rainer has a compliant personality. I told Jane I didn't know what that meant. Jane said it means docile, and I said that didn't help, and then Jane yelled, "He's sweet!" and stalked off.

Anyways, next, Rainer draws a pirate, and I draw a Hawaiian princess in a hula skirt. Then we scrooch down a ways, and Rainer draws an airplane pilot and I draw a stewardess. After that, the chalk is down to stubs, and we're starting to scrape our knuckles on the street, so we stop.

"Wanna go up to Snyder's?" Rainer says. "I've got money."

Rainer's always got money. One time, he showed me the fifty-dollar bill he got just for making his First Holy Communion.

Up at the Five & Dime, I buy a pack of Hostess Cupcakes, and Rainer buys Chuckles and a Dreamsicle. We take the treats outside and sit on the grass in front of the store. I give Rainer one of my cupcakes, and he gives me most of the Chuckles, which I'm not exactly too keen on ever since I ate all those candied orange wedges at Mrs. Pearson's house. Rainer takes back a couple of Chuckles and lets me lick the creamy filling out of his cupcake, which was really nice cuz everybody knows the filling's the best part.

After I eat my cupcake and four Chuckles and Rainer's creamy filling, I'm a little sick to my stomach. Rainer says it's because it's so gol-blasted hot.

"Hey Rainer, wanna run under the sprinkler?"

"Nah. Let's go down to the creek."

First, we go to the Niesens' garage, and Rainer gets his bamboo fishing pole. Then he gets a can of soup from the pantry. He cranks open the can and pours the soup into the dog dish, and in two seconds, the Niesens' golden retriever is up off the floor and slurping up chicken noodle soup. Next, we go across the street and dig up some worms from Mrs. Dietrich's iris garden. Some lumpy iris roots come up, too; even though they're a little beat up, we stick them back in the ground again. They'll be okay. We drop the worms into the soup can and watch them wriggle.

There's still some yellow globs of soup in the can, so it's kinda sickening.

The creek has a concrete bottom and sides, but it's shallow enough to just step right down and stand on the bottom. Dad calls it a culvert, but I say it's a creek. It's been so many days since it rained that the water is just a trickle and all the green fuzzy slime is dried up, which is fine by me. I brought along an empty Hellmann's mayonnaise jar, but the water's so shallow, there's hardly any tadpoles to catch, and none of them have leg buds.

On the far side of the creek is the sledding hill, the one I walked up to the top of when I ran away from home. The whole hill is spotted with Queen Anne's lace. Also dandelions, the yellow kind and the white wishy kind. There's no trees or bushes, so when it snows, the kids from Thistle Way drag sleds and saucers and toboggans to the top and slide down. After a while, the snow gets packed down, and we go so fast, we have to stick our feet out and dig our heels into the snow or else we would get to the bottom and plop right down into the creek. Once, Mark Mooney went so fast on his saucer that he zoomed down the hill and flew right over the creek and landed on the other side.

A whole bunch of bees are flying around the flowers on the hill, which is why Mom says Jane can't go to the hill except in winter. Jane's allergic to bees, which we found out when Jane and me spent the night at our rich cousins' mansion. That was a month ago, at the very, very bad part of summer vacation. Jane got stung by a bee and almost died. And while everybody was running around in the garden trying to get Jane to breathe again, that's when our older cousin Carolyn got up on a chair inside the house to swat a different stupid bee and lost her balance and whacked her head on the window and fell and died.

I don't like to remember that day.

Rainer and me are sitting at the edge of the creek, swinging our feet and trying to splash the water with our toes. Rainer sticks a worm on his fishing hook, and I look away cuz there's a good chance I'll throw up a bunch of Chuckles if I watch a worm covered with chicken noodle slime get stuck to death on Rainer's fish hook.

"There's no fish in the creek," I say. "Just tadpoles."

"Sure there are!" Rainer jumps down into the creek. "Come see."

The water's brownish and feels kinda good even though it's warm cuz the concrete's so hot to stand on. I'm getting a little woozy staring at the sparks of sunshine flashing on the surface of the water.

It's quiet at the creek today. It's so quiet that when a bullfrog croaks somewhere in the reeds that grow down the creek a ways, I can hear him plain as day. Down a ways is where the creek stops having concrete and starts having mud sides and a mud bottom. There's cattails and reeds along that part of the creek. Weeping willow trees hang over the water. Rainer says the creek goes all through Warwick Knoll and then follows some railroad tracks a while and then goes into a big sewer pipe under the highway. I've never gone that far.

Rainer slaps the back of his neck, and we look at his hand to see if there's a squashed bug. There is. Also a smear of blood. Rainer waves his bloody hand next to my face, and I scream and stumble backwards and plop butt-down in the disgusting water.

"Wet pants! Wet pants!" Rainer chants, which is not like Rainer at all, but I guess he can't be nice all the time. Nobody can.

I climb out and scrunch my eyes so Rainer can't see I'm starting to cry.

"Aw, sorry, Grace. I shouldn't have said that. Go home and get some dry clothes on. Then meet me at our hideout. If I'm not there, just come over to my house. Mom left us Swanson pot pies for dinner."

The whole way home, creek water squishes in my Keds.

Last summer, Rainer and me found the perfect place for our secret hideout. We were exploring one day, thrashing through thick bushes and real high grass along where the creek starts to have muddy sides. We came across a big flat rock that sticks out over the creek a little ways. There's bushes and stringy weeping willow branches all around the flat rock, so nobody can see in. Right away, we claim the spot as our secret hideout and pinky swear to never tell anybody where it is. We go there a lot together cuz it's shady and nobody can find us. Last week, Rainer brought his brother's BB gun to the hideout and shot it off twice into the air, and nobody came to yell at us so we figured nobody even heard. There's hardly any kids in Warwick Knoll, just a lot of old people like Mrs. Krieger, and old people never go outside in the dog days of summer.

When I get home, the first thing I smell is gol-durn dinner. Creamed chipped beef on mashed potatoes—yuck. I'm even gladder to be spending the night at the Niesens' house cuz I get to have a Swanson chicken pot pie, which Mom never buys. I change into dry clothes, but there's nothing I can do about my soggy Keds, and the only other shoes I have are my church shoes and the saddle shoes I wear to school. I shove my feet into the saddle shoes, but they're really pinchy. I'm thinking that's because I didn't put on socks, and my feet still have creek water between the toes and lots of popped tar bubbles on the bottoms.

Right when I'm all set to walk out the door, Mom makes me and Jane fold all the clean laundry and haul it upstairs and put everything in the right drawers. Jane makes perfect little balls out of each pair of her clean socks and perfect little triangles out of all her underpants. Then she stacks the towels and washrags so all the edges are a perfect line. Jane drives me nuts. I just want to get done and get back to the hideout, so I combine Charlie's pajamas, undershirts, and socks with Dad's tee shirts and socks and stuff everything back in the laundry hamper, which would've worked out fine except that Jane squealed, and Mom made me yank everything out and do it right. Sheesh.

As soon as the stupid laundry's done, I walk all the way to the hideout, but Rainer isn't there. Back at the Niesens', I let myself in the back door and check to see if my suitcase is still in the Florida room. Gregor's on the rattan sofa with Elsbeth, watching TV, and my suitcase is just lying on the floor. I've been packing and unpacking that dang suitcase all summer, lugging it all around Thistle Way. I've kept my end of the bargain with Mom, but I'm sure sick and tired of sleeping over at other people's houses, I'll tell you that.

"Rainer's holed up in his room," Gregor tells me. "Go on up, Grace. I'll let you know when the pot pies are done."

Rainer's bedroom door is closed. I knock, but he doesn't answer. I open the door a crack and peek in; Rainer's laying face down on his bed, and he's bawling. Something's really wrong.

I sit on the twin bed opposite Rainer's bed and wait to see if he's gonna stop crying. Finally, I figure I'd better say something.

"Hi, Rainer."

No answer.

"What's wrong?"

Rainer turns over and flips an arm across his eyes. He's still crying and snuffling, but not as hard. I watch him a while, waiting for him to tell me what's wrong. But all Rainer's doing is crying, so I try to guess what happened. I'm thinking he couldn't have gotten a spanking cuz his parents are still at Old Warson and Gregor isn't exactly the kind of older brother to give spankings. His knees look a little scratched up, but I don't see lots of blood so he couldn't have fallen out of a tree or crashed a bike. Maybe somebody stole his piggy bank with all that money in it.

"Grace," he says, all croaky, "before you got here, did you go to the hideout?"

"Yeah."

"Did you see a kinda trampy guy there?" He lowers his arm and stares at me, hard.

"Nu-uh. Nobody was there."

Rainer gets a faraway look, like when on real hot days, we stare off in the distance so we can see the air get wavy.

"When I got to the hideout, there was this old guy sitting on our rock," Rainer says, looking away again. "He said he was glad I came along. He asked if I wanted to finish his cigarette, so I sat on the edge of the rock, and he gave it to me."

"You smoked a cigarette?"

"It didn't have a filter, so I got bits of tobacco on my tongue. And the smoke was so strong, it made me cough. When I finally stopped coughing, the man says, 'You ever hopped a moving train, kid?' When I said no, the man said he's hard of hearing, so I should come closer."

"Did you?"

"Yeah. Then he starts telling me this great story about riding trains across prairies and watching buffalo stampedes. He said he and his buddies ride all over the place free in empty boxcars. He said they swipe apples and pears and corn and stuff from farms along the way. They hop out of the train while it's still moving, swipe the food, and run like blazes to get back in. He said sometimes they have to pull a buddy back up into the boxcar, and once, a buddy got halfway up and fell, and the train wheels sliced him in two, like a cucumber."

"Ick! That's awful!"

"He said at night, they cook pork and beans over campfires, and if they don't want to get back on the train, it's okay. They sleep on blankets under the stars. He said sometimes they hear wolves howling, but they aren't scared cuz they all have knives hidden in their boots."

Rainer has sorta stopped crying. I think telling me all that stuff about buffalo stampedes and campfires and wolves kinda took his mind off whatever bad thing is making him cry. At least for a minute or two. But his face is still blotchy. He still looks miserable, but I can't figure out why. He's quiet for a few minutes, just laying on his back on the bed, and I wonder if we're gonna go down and get those pot pies, but then he starts talking about the old man again.

"His shirt and pants were dirty, and his zipper wasn't zipped all the way. I could see he wasn't wearing any . . . "

Rainer lets out a long, jaggedy sigh and tucks his hands under the small of his back. He still won't look at me, just stares at the ceiling.

"The man starts another story. Him and his buddies are in the Rocky Mountains. They're standing in this river, right near some rapids, and the water's ice cold even though it's summer. One guy pulls this trout out of the water with his bare hands, and they all think they're gonna have this great dinner, but they turn around and there's a huge black bear on the riverbank staring at them. The guy throws the trout to the bear, and the bear catches it in his mouth."

"Did the bear go away?"

"No. Yes. I don't know!" Rainer starts crying again. I figure I better not ask him any more questions.

"Sorry, Rainer."

"So later that night, they hear scratching outside their tent, and—"

"Wait. Are they sleeping in a tent or in the boxcar?"

All of a sudden, Rainer looks right at me and says, "I'm just a kid. A stupid kid! What did I know?"

Rainer folds his arms across his chest and fists his hands under his armpits. Then he looks away again.

"The man's stories were so good, I asked him to tell another one. 'Come sit right next to me, and I will,' he says. So I scrooch next to him, and he starts telling about him and his buddies wrangling wild ponies in Texas. But pretty soon, there's something about the man that's making me nervous. I try to crawl a little away from him, but he puts his hands around my waist and pulls me back. He keeps saying it's hot, it's so hot, aren't I hot? He says one buddy is real good with horses. He says when the buddy slips a metal bit into a little pony's mouth and slips the bridle over the pony's head, his buddy can do anything he wants with the little pony."

I can't look at Rainer anymore. My heart's thumping like when somebody is telling a ghost story, and you know something bad is gonna happen, but you don't know what.

"The man wouldn't let me go." Rainer starts crying again. "He put one hand over my mouth, so I couldn't yell. He pulled down my shorts, and his hands were dirty, and . . . "

Rainer scrunches his eyes shut. His lips are straight white lines.

"He let you go, right?" I say. "You got your shorts back up and ran away, right?"

Gregor is calling up the stairs to us. Dinner's ready.

"The man was big, Grace, and really strong." Rainer's voice is flat. He curls up in a ball, facing away from me.

I'm crying too now. I'm thinking the mean man made Rainer drink disgusting creek water, or spitted on him, or maybe even went pee on him.

I turn sideways so I don't have to look at Rainer all curled up on the other bed. I can still hear him, though. He's telling me what the man did, but I don't want to hear, so I start humming. I still kinda hear Rainer, but his voice is high and thin now, like his throat's closing up, like he's begging.

"Rainer! Grace! Your pot pies are turning to glue!"

It's Gregor. Rainer and me just stare at each other until I figure one of us has to either say something or do something, so I do a little game I play with Charlie sometimes that always makes him laugh. I put my hands together and turn my fingers to the inside so they're hidden, and then I say, "This is the church, this is the steeple, open the doors, and here's all the people."

Rainer doesn't seem to hear. He doesn't even seem to see me do the church and the steeple game. He's got a kinda glassy look to his eyes, and he's talking about the man again, about what happened back at the hideout.

The bedroom windows are open. I watch a breeze puff the curtains. I watch the Kit-Cat clock on the wall roll its eyes back and forth, back and forth. Rainer's Erector Set is scattered across the rug, so I get down on the floor and count the pieces: twenty-eight. I count the pieces of Pez on the bedside table: seven. I count the money on Rainer's desk: three quarters, a dime, a penny, and four green plastic mills—eighty-six cents, plus the mills. Rainer's still talking, but I can't hear him cuz I'm counting the number of times the Kit-Cat wags its tail, and I have to count the Pez again to make sure I counted them right the first time, and I have to count backwards from a hundred.

I count back to sixty-three and stop. Rainer's quiet now, watching me. His eyes look sad.

I hear Mom ringing our cowbell. Next will be Lt. Lofton's ship bell and Mr. Mooney's referee whistle, which sounds a lot like Detective Greeley's police whistle, but their kids can tell the difference. Then the Dailey's hand bells and Mrs. Finnegan's tin whistle and Mrs. Warfield's triangle ... just like every night. Just like always.

By the time Rainer and me go down to the kitchen, our pot pies are cold.

As an adult, as a parent myself now, I am wincing as I remember this, for it surely was not my finest hour.

Although I did not fully understand what had happened to Rainer and although I could barely imagine it, I chose to shut out my friend's terrible revelation and in so doing, insulate myself from his pain. How crushed he must have been.

I found out later from Rainer that he finally told his brother what happened, and Gregor told their parents. At first, Mr. and Mrs. Niesen asked Rainer if he'd made up the whole story. Then they accused him of embellishing what surely was a minor incident. When Rainer held firm, they questioned him closely about what he may or may not have done to egg the man on.

That evening, Mrs. Niesen drew a warm bath for her son and stood just outside the bathroom door. Rainer told me that he'd heard his father pacing the hallway and his mother softly crying.

The Niesens did not go to the police. They did not have Rainer examined by a physician or counseled by a therapist. They told the boy to forget it ever happened and to not tell a soul. At the time, in some circles, it was a common method of handling such things. I suspect the Niesens feared that, should the news leak out, it would not only marginalize their child but also cast a shadow on the entire family. At the club, the once popular Niesens would be whispered about and, far worse, excluded. For a husband and wife whose sense of self-worth and whose very identity were anchored to an exclusive country club, that could not be allowed to happen. And so, they circled the wagons.

That day, I failed Rainer too. I did not march downstairs and tell Gregor that his little brother had been brutally molested. I didn't run home and tell my parents. I didn't tell Jane. I didn't walk across the circle and report it to Detective Greeley. I didn't ring the convent doorbell and confide in Sister Josephina. I didn't say a single word to anyone.

To this day, I am ashamed.

the Haverkamps

the planets

My father used to say the Haverkamps had gone to the dogs. My mother used to say truer words were never spoken.

In the summer of 1956, I was eight, going on nine. So was Janice Haverkamp. Although she and I attended different schools, and although the Haverkamps were the scourge of the neighborhood, I counted Janice as one of my pals. That said, my friendship with Janice was predicated on a single rule that was enforced on my end and understood on hers: we played at my house or on the circle, never at her house. I'd heard a thing or two about the Haverkamp place.

Anyway, it was my rule, and I broke it just once. I have the scars to prove it.

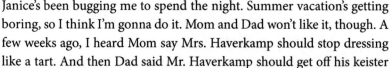

Janice's been bugging me to spend the night. Summer vacation's getting boring, so I think I'm gonna do it. Mom and Dad won't like it, though. A few weeks ago, I heard Mom say Mrs. Haverkamp should stop dressing like a tart. And then Dad said Mr. Haverkamp should get off his keister and get a real job instead of loafing around that lab of his while his kids do anything they please.

Heck, the Haverkamp kids doing anything they please is what makes them fun.

Besides, I've gotta come up with places on Thistle Way to sleep over at, and the list is getting kinda short. There's the Mooneys. Nah, too many boys and not enough girls.

There's the Greeleys. Heck no. Their dog's a maniac. He already bit the mailman, the milkman, and the Vegetable Man.

There's Benny Herman, but I already decided about him. No way.

Bradley Backer? Nope. Bradley's got whooping cough.

Marty Throckmorten and Tommy Stieger are in my class at school, but they might think it's weird if I ask to spend the night.

There's Jean Marie Walsh and June Marie Walsh. It wouldn't kill me . . . well, it might kill me. They're dopes.

That leaves the Haverkamps.

There's lots of Haverkamps, but it's not too tough to keep them all straight.

There's Mr. and Mrs. Haverkamp, of course. Their names are Diane and Frank.

I've only seen Mrs. Haverkamp a few times, and I've almost never seen Mr. and Mrs. Haverkamp together.

A while back, I heard my mom and Mrs. Lofton talking while they hung out laundry. They were talking about Mr. and Mrs. Haverkamp.

"I've always thought Diane wanted more out of life than life sent her way," Mom said.

"More of everything," Mrs. Lofton called over the fence, "except children."

"Even after five kids, though, she's still kept her figure," Mom said, which made Mrs. Lofton sigh. I think that's cuz Mrs. Lofton's kinda, well, kinda chubby.

"I heard she's working up at that Hi-Ball Lounge now. You know the place, the dive bar up in Wellston. I heard the drinks there are lighter fluid and the bathrooms are so awful you don't dare go near them."

"A torch song singer at the Hi-Ball Lounge," Mom said. "Diane's forever pining away for a more fascinating life, and looking in all the wrong places."

"I've seen bruises on Diane's arms and legs," Mrs. Lofton said. "I think Frank beats her."

Mom pinned a couple more damp towels to the line. "Did you know Frank and Diane first met at the Velvet Freeze in Clayton? Frank was majoring in chemistry at Washington University. One of my sorority sisters knew him. Back then, lots of us would get together at Velvet Freeze.

Diane wasn't part of our crowd, though. She was just a good-looking girl making chocolate malteds."

Mom paused a minute and added, "Frank was handsome, you know, before the worry lines and the coke-bottle glasses."

Mrs. Lofton took three clothespins out of her mouth and walked over to the fence. "Diane must have thought Frank came from money."

"But he didn't," Mom said. "He was on a full-ride scholarship. I know for a fact that they'd only been dating a few months when Diane managed to get herself pregnant."

That's mostly all I know about Mr. and Mrs. Haverkamp, except that he has a chemistry lab and he's nice, and I don't think he beats up Mrs. Haverkamp. I don't think that at all.

Anyways, the Haverkamp kids are Curt, Janice, Pete, Joey, and little Anna. All of them are boney-skinny with kinda pointy noses and freckles all over their cheeks. Also, their hair is all choppy cuz they never get to go to a beauty shop or barber shop, so Curt cuts the kids' hair with

his mom's manicure scissors. Back when the Zaldoni boys lived on Thistle Way, they always laughed about that, but the Haverkamp kids don't care what anybody says, which is good cuz people say a lot about the Haverkamps.

People also say a lot about the Haverkamps' house.

At the beginning of summer, the house went from being what my mom called a nothing-special Dutch colonial to being what my dad called an eyesore. That's partly because Mr. Haverkamp was trying to invent ultra-violet paint, but he wound up with plain old violet paint, so he brought the paint home along with some brushes from Nutz & Boltz Hardware, and he let his kids slap purple paint all over the front door and shutters.

The kids were starting to paint the porch railings when Mrs. Haverkamp came outside, which she almost never does. It was late afternoon, but she was still in her nightgown, a yellow chiffon nightgown and high-heel bedroom slippers with fluffy little pom-poms. She walked out a ways, took a few puffs on her cigarette, and then slowly turned around to look at the house.

By then, lots of us neighborhood kids had gathered in the street to watch the Haverkamps slop purple paint on their house, and we all held our breaths to see what Mrs. Haverkamp would do. We expected her to get all mad and yell at her kids, but she didn't. She just smoked her cigarette down to a stub, dropped the butt on a dandelion, of which there are quite a few on the Haverkamp lawn, and went back inside the house. When she passed Anna, she ran her fingers through the little kid's stringy hair. Mike Mooney said it was the darndest thing he'd ever seen.

After the Haverkamp kids ran out of shutters and doors and porch railings to paint, things really got good. Half the kids in the neighborhood traipsed after them and watched while the Haverkamps snuck into a bunch of garages and swiped the license plates that were tacked to the walls. Then we all traipsed back to the Haverkamps' house and watched them paint the license plates violet and stick them onto their front walkway with special glue their dad made in his laboratory. It looked kinda like a footpath, only purple.

The next day, we all gathered outside the Haverkamp house again to see if anything interesting would happen, and it did. Janice lugged six big papier-mâché farm animals out the front door and one by one she lined them up on the front lawn. Curt tossed four long ropes over a big tree limb and then tied the ends of the ropes onto the handles of Anna's old bassinet. He plopped Anna in the bassinet and gave her a little push, and she swung back and forth like the rock-a-bye baby nursery rhyme. Then Mr. Haverkamp lugged out an old beat-up dollhouse and nailed it to the trunk of the tree on the opposite side of Anna's bassinet swing. He sprinkled birdseed in each little room of the dollhouse, and before we knew it, a pair of nuthatches came along and snatched some of the seeds out of the tiny parlor and stuck them into cracks in the tree bark.

That was about the time my dad started calling the Haverkamp house an eyesore.

"Come on in," Janice says when she opens the front door and sees me standing on the porch with my suitcase. She sounds all happy. Heck, I'm probably the first kid to ever ask for a sleepover at the Haverkamps' house.

Janice takes me by the hand, waltzes straight to the kitchen, and lifts a big butcher knife out of a drawer, which I'm thinking isn't good. Then she waltzes me to a bathroom and rifles through a bunch of junk under the sink until she finds a box of Band-Aids.

"Stick out your hand," she says.

It's a rule of mine to never stick out my hand when I'm in a bathroom with Janice Haverkamp if she has a butcher knife, but Janice just grabs my hand anyway and jabs the point of the knife into my thumb.

Sheesh! No wonder nobody wants to spend the night with Janice.

Right when I'm starting to cry and deciding to grab my red plaid suitcase and go home, Janice jabs the knife into her own thumb.

"Now," she says, "rub your thumb onto mine and repeat three times: 'We're blood sisters forever.'"

I don't exactly want to be blood sisters with a Haverkamp, but Janice is standing between me and the bathroom door, so I'm stuck. After we rub thumbs, Janice turns on the faucet and runs cold water over our hands, which feels good. I'm still worried, though. Sister Josephina told us that God made our fingerprints and our immortal souls just like snowflakes, no two alike. Now one of my fingerprints has a stupid jab mark on it, just like stupid Janice's. I hope God doesn't get our immortal souls mixed up.

After we put Band-Aids on our thumbs, Janice says, "We've got a bunch of new puppies. They're in the basement. Wanna see?"

The Haverkamps' basement is really dark. In the grayish light coming from a snowy TV screen, I see Janice's little brothers. They're sprawled on the linoleum floor, listening to a cartoon show. The picture's just fuzz, so they have to follow along by listening. They don't seem to mind. And they don't seem to mind the mess down here or the smell, which is gosh-awful. The place is a wreck. There's piles of dirty laundry all over the floor, plates and bowls with food crusted on them, broken lamps, chewed up shoes, and about a kabillion dogs. Some of the dogs are chewing on an old couch, yanking out the stuffing. Others are sniffing at the puddles of pee. A bunch of puppies are crawling all over Janice's little brothers, and a bunch more are sleeping on lumps of dirty towels.

"Say hello to our Chinese Foo dogs," Janice says. "The Chinese people say Foo dogs are good luck charms. My brother, Curt, he breeds the dogs down here and sells off the babies." She picks up a puppy and hands it to me. "Give it a kiss, Grace. It won't bite."

I take the dang Foo dog in my arms, but I can't figure out where to kiss it cuz its sharp little face is buried in black fur.

"How many dogs you got down here?" I say, giggling. A Foo dog is licking my ankle.

"Search me. All I know is they keep on coming!"

Suddenly, Janice turns to me and says, "I'm taking care of Bullet for the Greeleys. They pay me for it too. You can help, and I'll give you a share!"

What? Cripes!

The Greeleys live next door to the Haverkamps. Bullet's the killer

German Shepherd Detective Greeley keeps chained to a stake in the backyard during the day and chained to a stake in the front yard at night.

I'm pretty sure Janice doesn't get a regular allowance cuz during the school year when we walk up to Snyder's Five & Dime together, she borrows from me. In summer, though, she has money. Now I know why: each weekend in summer, when the Greeleys go to their cabin in the Ozarks, Detective Greeley pays Janice thirty cents to feed and water Bullet while they're gone. I wish I'd have known about her deal with the Greeleys before I decided to sleep over. One of my rules is I don't go near Bullet. It's pretty much everybody's rule, except for Detective Greeley.

Back upstairs in the kitchen, I watch Janice scoop dog food into a small sack. Paper napkins and Cheerios and potato chips and stuff are blowing all over cuz the window is open, and it's gotten windy outside. Beyond the screen door, I see dark clouds. Janice motions for me to follow her outside, which is not where I want to go. We tiptoe around some bushes between the Haverkamps' backyard and the Greeleys'. Bullet sees us! He scrambles to his feet and runs toward us until the chain yanks his neck.

Whew!

Janice shakes the paper sack. "Hear that, Bullet? It's lunch."

Bullet growls. His ears are flat back, and the hairs on the back of his neck are sticking straight up. Janice hands me the bag of dog food and inches forward. "Talk to him, Grace. He thinks you're the enemy."

A streak of lightning flashes. Bullet cowers, straightens up, and barks furiously.

"Grace Mitchell, you've gotta help me. I have to get this dog fed before it starts raining."

Janice murmurs soothing words and manages to get close enough to Bullet to grab hold of his collar. "Grace," she calls over her shoulder, "come here and dump the dog food in his bowl, quick."

Bullet's beady eyes are glaring at me. Dog spit is drooling from his pink and black gums. I just know he wants to eat me alive!

"Hurry, Grace! He's not gonna stay calm all day."

I make a run for the dog bowl, praying I'll be safe. Right when I get close, Bullet wriggles out of his collar . . . and charges at me.

"Halt!" Janice screams.

I freeze.

Bullet lunges. He plants his huge paws on my shoulders. His snout is inches from my face. I smell his stinky breath. My life is over!

I stumble backward and curl in a ball on the grass. I feel part of the dog collar digging into my cheek. I hear Janice yelling. I stay quiet as a mouse, hoping he'll go away. He doesn't. He sinks his jaggedy teeth into the soft skin right above my knee. Hot electric jangles of pain sizzle up and down my whole leg.

"Help!" I shout. "He won't let go!"

Janice pulls at Bullet's tail, shouting, "Halt! Halt!"

Right when I think I'm gonna die, I hear somebody running toward us. It's Curt! It's Janice's older brother!

"Git!" Curt shouts. He's carrying a broom, and he swats Bullet hard with the bristle end. Bullet lets go of my leg and slinks off toward the street.

Curt and Janice help me back to the kitchen. Curt grabs a paper napkin off the floor and soaks it with dish soap and water. Then he dabs two puncture marks on my leg, right behind my knee.

"Stop crying, Grace," Janice says. "It's just a scratch. You can still sleep over."

It's not a scratch. It's a gol-durn wolf bite!

Curt leaves the kitchen for a minute and comes back with a roll of gauze and a big bottle of rubbing alcohol and a tiny bottle of Mercurochrome. He patches me up pretty good and then he calls my mom and tells her what happened.

"Here," Curt says, handing me the telephone, "she wants to talk to you."

I wipe away the last of my tears and take the receiver. "Hi, Mom," I say. I'm surprised how steady my voice sounds. "I'm okay. And I still want to stay over with Janice."

Mom asks me a few more questions to make sure I'm not going to die. She says Dad's gonna have a talk with Detective Greeley about that dog of his, and that's that. Actually, I'd love to go home right this minute, but I'm worried that would cancel my deal with Mom and Dad, and I'm not gonna give up until the very end of summer.

After a while, the storm blows itself out. Curt keeps a lookout for Bullet, and when he sees the dog creep into the Greeleys' backyard and lay down next to the stake, he goes outside. Janice and me watch from the kitchen, and after Curt gets Bullet in the collar again, buckled a little tighter this time, I feel much better.

Janice and me get out a game of Parcheesi and set up the board on the living room rug. Her younger brothers, Joey and Pete, are banging out

"Chopsticks" on the piano. Little Anna is plinking the two top keys over and over. Curt comes back inside and starts strumming a guitar in the kitchen. Nobody seems to care about the racket. What a nutso house.

It's almost dinnertime when the Haverkamps' beat-up old Chevy pulls into the drive, and Janice's dad gets out. Janice's mom must've heard cuz she waltzes down the stairs, straight through the living room, and right out the front door. She pats Mr. Haverkamp on the shoulder and gets into the car. And then she drives off. I did not notice her fixing dinner before she left, which has me worried. I do notice she's wearing a slinky red dress and very high heels. I notice Mr. Haverkamp too. He stands a while on the purple license plate footpath, watching the car until it's completely out of sight.

Janice rolls the Parcheesi dice and then it's my turn again, like what happened is nothing unusual, like a mom in a slinky dress walking out the door at dinnertime is no big deal.

"Does your mom make dinner before she goes to work?" I ask.

"Nope."

"Doesn't your dad get mad?"

"My dad never gets mad. He's the best dad in the world. We're gonna be rich, just you wait and see. He's currently on the verge of a major breakthrough at his lab."

That'll be the day.

"Dad says a chemistry lab is a lot like life. He's even got this quote from Charles F. Kettering framed on a wall in his office."

"Who?"

"Kettering. He invented the stuff that makes air conditioners work. Lots of other stuff, too."

"What's the quote say?"

"One fails forward toward success."

Huh?

Mr. Haverkamp calls all the kids to the kitchen. I'm hoping he brought home a tuna casserole, but the only thing on the table is bowls, measuring cups, and some powdery stuff.

"Ladies and gentlemen," he says, "I present the latest and possibly greatest chemical concoction from Synergistic Labs."

Anna and the little boys applaud.

"Tonight," Mr. Haverkamp says, "we will mix two solutions together and come up with a modern marvel. Ready?"

Everybody nods.

"First, we make a four percent solution of polyvinyl alcohol, four grams in one hundred milliliters of water. See? It's like a gluey gel, right? Then we mix one part of the gluey gel with three parts of warm water."

Mr. Haverkamp holds up a glass beaker. I'm wishing it had a milkshake in it.

"Next, we stir in one teaspoon of zinc sulfide powder per sixteen teaspoons of warm water. Janice, would you add the water? Count carefully now."

Janice trickles sixteen teaspoons of warm water into a bowl. Mr. Haverkamp adds the zinc sulfide. "Now stir, Anna," he says. Anna stirs and stirs, but not all of the powder dissolves.

"That's okay," Mr. Haverkamp says. "It's not supposed to. See? The first solution is prepared. Now we make the second."

Mr. Haverkamp tells us this part is too dangerous for kids to do, even Curt. He tells us that he's gonna be using borax, which is boric acid, which comes from boron. He says borax can give you a skin rash, plus it contains a little bit of arsenic, which is poison and which can get inside of you right through the skin, so no kid should ever handle plain borax. Curt sort of smirks, like he thinks he can handle it okay. I'm expecting him to make some smart aleck crack, but he doesn't.

"We take four grams of borax and mix it with one hundred milliliters of warm water, see? We stir, stir, stir until the borax is dissolved. Now there might be some left at the bottom of the beaker, but that's okay. Next, we mix two tablespoons of our gel with two teaspoons of our borax solution, see? Voila! It's viscous!"

Just when I'm thinking, *It's what?*, Mr. Haverkamp says, "Kids, somebody tell Grace what viscous means."

"Dad told us it means gummy," Pete says.

Mr. Haverkamp scoops out a glob and plops it in Janice's hand. Then he pinches off a little bit and gives it to Anna. "Now, my girls, squish it like you'd knead bread dough. See? It won't hurt you, I promise."

Janice and Anna squeeze the gel-dough. It oozes between their fingers like clear Jell-O. Mr. Haverkamp breaks into a big smile and starts yakking a mile a minute.

"—or you can use polysaccharide guar gum along with some sodium tetraborate, or— "

He takes the gel from Janice and Anna and holds it up to the ceiling light. "This activates the phosphorescent glow," he says. "Now children, follow me!"

I'm more starving than I've ever been in my life, but I troop down the basement stairs after Janice and the rest of the Haverkamps. Mr. Haverkamp is holding a big blob of the gel stuff, which so far doesn't seem all that great.

"My dears," he says over his shoulder, "you ain't seen nothin' yet."

The basement and stairwell are pitch dark. I hear claws clicking on linoleum. Chinese Foo dogs must be prancing over to see what's going on. Sheesh.

At the bottom of the stairs, Mr. Haverkamp turns around and holds out his hands.

The glob is glowing! It's glittery and white, bright as the moon!

"Holy cow!" Janice and me shout. And then, "Jinx, you owe me a Coke."

"Keen-o, Dad," Curt says. "This one's got real potential."

The little boys and Anna hug their father's legs. Foo dogs scramble all over each another. Two puppies start a tug-of-war with a pair of striped pajama bottoms. Another puppy drags a damp towel around in circles. Nobody cares. All we can think about is the shimmery, shiny thing Mr. Haverkamp managed to make.

After everybody gets a chance to hold the glowing glob, Mr. Haverkamp says it's time for a celebration.

"Who wants a root beer float at Fitz's?"

Everybody shouts, "Me! Me!"

Then Curt whispers something to his father, and Mr. Haverkamp's smile fades. Curt whispers something again, something that sounds like "taxi."

Mr. Haverkamp looks at each of us and makes a kind of dry-sounding chuckle. "Kids, if we want root beer floats, we're gonna have to walk. You up for it?"

Everybody except Anna jumps up and down hollering "yes!" and "you betcha" and "no problem." Little Anna puckers her face, like she's about to cry. I'm pretty sure Anna can't walk that far. Curt sweeps her up in his arms and hands her over to Mr. Haverkamp, who twirls her onto his shoulders. Anna breaks into a huge smile.

Twenty minutes later, we're all settled at a picnic table outside of Fitz's Root Beer, slurping creamy root beer floats. I'm on cloud nine. It's the first time I've had a root beer float for dinner.

Mr. Haverkamp puffs out his skinny chest and tells us he can name all the secret ingredients in Fitz's special recipe.

"No way," Curt says.

"Okay, son, you're on. Let's see now . . . botanicals of sassafras root, vanilla bean, birch bark, anise . . . "

Janice peers into her glass, frowning. "Dad, you're kidding about the birch bark, right?"

"Not entirely," he says, smiling.

That night, Curt, Janice, and me stay up really late molding gobs of goo into planets. Mr. Haverkamp suggested we add Easter egg dye to make different colors. So we make Earth, Neptune, and Uranus blue; Saturn and Venus yellow; and the sun yellow with orange streaks. We make Jupiter the biggest and Pluto the littlest. Curt gets a roll of tape, and Janice brings clear glass dessert plates from a dining room cupboard.

"Go get your lanyard strips, Grace," she says. "I saw you had some when you unpacked your suitcase."

Upstairs, I peek under the Band-Aid at my thumb, the one Janice jabbed with a butcher knife. There's just a speck of blood on the bandage, and the throbbing's almost stopped. Next, I gently rub the gauze that's covering my dog bite. It still hurts, but not as much as before. I'm glad I didn't go skulking home this afternoon—I would've missed all the fun!

After I bring down a bunch of lanyard strips, which I do not know what we're gonna do with, I hear Anna start to wail in her crib. Mr. Haverkamp and Janice race up to see what's wrong.

"Anna's got a fever," Janice calls over her shoulder. "I'm gonna give her a baby aspirin, and Dad's gonna rock her back to sleep. We might be up there a little while." She sounds worried.

I'm pretty sure the Haverkamps don't have enough money to pay for a doctor visit, and there's no car to take Anna to the emergency room. Everybody's parents are so worried about their kids coming down with polio, but not everything's gonna turn out to be polio. Heck, Charlie got a fever and it turned into strep throat and then it turned into romantic fever, but he's okay now.

When she gets back to the kitchen, Janice looks up at the ceiling and breaks into a huge smile. While she was gone, Curt and me made slings out of the lanyard strips. Then Curt stood on a chair and stuck each sling to the ceiling with thick tape. Now the slings are dangling like parachute cords.

"Hand me up the sun," he tells Janice.

One by one, Janice passes up our goo planets, each on its own clear saucer. Curt sets them into the slings, making sure they're not tippy. We're just finishing when Mr. Haverkamp comes down and lets us know Anna's sleeping soundly. He puts an album on the record player in the living room, and music fills the house.

"It's Holst, Mom's favorite," Curt tells me.

"Holst—like a gun holster?" I say.

"Nah, the composer Gutav Holst. Each song is about a different planet. The one about Mars sounds like thunderbolts and war machines. Venus is the goddess of love and peace, so her music is pretty and ladylike with flutes and violins and an oboe. Mercury is fast cuz Mercury is a messenger, but Saturn is slow and steady. Just wait, Grace, you'll hear all of them. Dad likes to play Holst over and over."

Mr. Haverkamp stands in the kitchen doorway, admiring our project. "Why don't you kids make some comets and asteroids? Or make any kind of celestial body you can dream up. Who knows what may be out there?"

It's midnight by the time we get all our planets, comets, asteroids, and spaceships suspended from the ceiling. Mr. Haverkamp wakes up the two little boys. He carries Anna downstairs too, which I don't think is a good idea cuz usually it's a rule that sick kids are better off sleeping, but the Haverkamps don't really go by other people's rules. I guess he just didn't want her to miss whatever neat-o thing is gonna happen next. Anyways, he plunks Anna in Janice's arms, and then he goes into the living room and starts up the Holst music again.

"Curt," he says, "douse the lights."

The kitchen goes black, all except the sparkly planets and twinkly stars and silvery comets with streaking tails glowing over our heads. Oh, what a sight!

"Shazaam!" Janice shouts.

"Ooohhh," the little boys whisper.

"Dad, it's great!" Curt claps his father on the back. "You've really got something here."

Mr. Haverkamp rubs the stubble on his chin. "All it needs now is a name."

"Silly Putty," Janice says.

"Flupper," Curt says.

"Goo Gobs," one of the little boys shouts.

"Primordial Ooze?" Mr. Haverkamp says, and then we all start piping up with crazy names.

Foo Goo Gai Pan!

Space Sludge!

Ringy-Dingy Saturn!

Yucky Muck!

The Holst music is playing Jupiter, the happiest song of all. Me and the Haverkamps are laughing and making space monster noises and comet-schussing noises and laughing like crazy. And then Mrs. Haverkamp walks in.

Her mascara is smeared. One of her bra straps is down around her upper arm. She looks tired.

None of us says a word. We watch her light a cigarette and blow a stream of smoke out her nose. To me, she looks like a dragon.

"Diane!" Mr. Haverkamp says finally. "Take a look! Really something, eh? This stuff is going to hit the market and go nowhere but up."

He's beaming.

"The sky's the limit if we can just come up with a name for. . . "

Kettering would be proud, he goes on. The goo is going to bring in a fortune. They'll be swimming in dough, eat steak every night, drive a Cadillac! He'll buy her a mansion with a tennis court and swimming pool.

"Diane!" he shouts. "We haven't really hit on a name yet. What do you think? What would you call—"

We all hold our breaths, waiting to see what Mrs. Haverkamp will say about her good glass plates hanging from the ceiling. She walks around the kitchen table, lifting her finger to touch each of the plates, making the comets and asteroids sway. A couple of them clank together gently, but they don't break.

The kitchen's hot and crowded. The air smells like Foo dog and cigarette smoke. The Holst music is blaring.

I see a little bulge throbbing at Curt's jaw line, as if he's grinding his teeth. He turns his back to the table. Janice clenches her hands so hard, her knuckles are white. The little boys look miserable. Anna starts to whimper. Mrs. Haverkamp keeps jiggling the planets, and Mr. Haverkamp keeps twitching his fingers.

I close my eyes.

Eventually, Mrs. Haverkamp stops walking around the table. She plants her hands on her hips and gives each of us a hard stare.

This is gonna be ugly. I think I want to go home.

"If you want to be successful," she says, giving each of us a hard stare, "you've got to have courage, faith in yourself, and fortitude. And you can't follow the crowd; you have to stand out from the crowd."

We wait. I don't think anybody can figure out what she's talking about, even her husband.

"You're gonna think I'm crazy," she says, "but I'd give this stuff a name nobody expects and nobody can forget. I'd call it . . . Slop!"

None of us said a word. Then, all at once, all of us started cheering like crazy!

I'm having an awful time trying to fall asleep on this cot next to Janice's bed. I keep thinking about Chinese Foo dogs being good luck charms and killer German Shepherds being afraid of thunder, about drinking a root beer float for dinner, and holding a sparkly comet in my hands.

This was a strange day, all right. But the thing I'm gonna remember is what happened after Mrs. Haverkamp called our beautiful goo "Slop."

"That's it!" Mr. Haverkamp shouted. "Diane! It's perfect!"

Mrs. Haverkamp flicked her cigarette in the sink and held her arms wide. With two long steps, Mr. Haverkamp was holding her tight and swinging her around and around. When they stopped, they hugged for a really long time. And then they kissed.

Really kissed.

Cowabunga kissed!

Janice scooted the little boys upstairs. Curt was right behind, carrying Anna. They all turned around in time to see their mom and dad kiss, and they all heard what happened after that. I didn't know what to do, so I stayed where I was.

"Did you take your medicine?" Mr. Haverkamp asked her.

Mrs. Haverkamp tucked her chin and pulled a bunch of folded-up dollar bills from the top of her dress. She slipped them into his trouser pocket.

"For the mortgage, Frank."

"It's leukemia. It's nothing to fool around about. Look at you, covered with bruises. God knows what they think about that up at the nightclub."

"Medicine costs," she said with a smile so sad it caused Mr. Haverkamp's shoulders to slump even worse than they usually slump.

"I'll make the payment tomorrow," he told her. "If Slop takes off, we'll burn the mortgage. You'll have all the medicine you need, and no more leukemia bruises."

They stared all dreamy-eyed at each other for a minute, Janice's mom and dad, not saying anything. Then Mr. Haverkamp walked to the living room and put the record player needle on the prettiest Holst song, the Venus one with harp music. When he came back to her, Mrs. Haverkamp leaned toward him and whispered in his ear.

"Perfect," I heard her say. "Everything's perfect, Frank, just the way it is."

Anaïs Nin put it well, although either her syntax or her punctuation was a little wonky. I'm not sure which.

"We do not grow absolutely, chronologically," she wrote. "We grow sometimes in one dimension, and not in another, unevenly. . . . We are mature in one realm, childish in another."

My childhood excursions left more than a few lasting impressions, and some of them I could have done without. I still have a small scar on the pad of my thumb, and I still have two tiny puncture marks above my knee, reminders of my sleepover with the Haverkamps.

But the summer of 1956 was formative too. I was still a child, of course. Most of what I thought, said, and did was childlike. But that night, in the Haverkamps' starry kitchen, I experienced a glimmer of maturity. I came to realize that the inner workings of families are private occurrences, nuanced and layered and easily misunderstood by those assessing from a distance.

Thistle Way regarded Frank Haverkamp as a poor provider. It was true at the time. But that assessment failed to take into account the man's creative genius, his perseverance, his devotion to his wife and to his children. And theirs to him.

Neighbors looked down their noses at Diane Haverkamp too, she of the slinky dress and lounge singer hours. I doubt that any of them knew she willingly handed over every dollar she earned to her husband so that he—not she—could pay the mortgage and save face at the bank.

If the neighbors had bothered to leave their assumptions on the stoop and venture past the door, they would have seen things as they really were. They would have seen a young boy and girl with no expectation of receiving a weekly allowance motivated to earn their own spending money. Seen children who adored and respected their father. Seen a father who instructed his children as he entertained them. Seen alarm register on every face at the prospect of Anna, the baby, possibly getting sicker. The neighbors would have seen the older Haverkamp children carrying the younger ones up to bed, unbidden.

They would have seen a husband and wife, deep into their marriage, embrace in a star-spangled kitchen and kiss fully and lushly with mutual attraction and red-hot desire.

I walked home the following morning lost in thought, and by the time I'd unpacked my red plaid suitcase, I'd come to a conclusion: the opinions of the neighbors about the Haverkamps said more about the neighbors than they said about the Haverkamps.

I suppose it's a moot point. By the following summer, Slop had taken off. The family that was the scourge of the neighborhood suddenly had more money than anybody else on Thistle Way. Lots more.

The first thing Frank did was to make sure Diane got lifesaving medical treatments. The bruises disappeared, and she improved dramatically. The second thing Frank did was to have his kids make a "For Sale" sign and plant it in the front yard.

To the chagrin of everyone except the Haverkamps, the sign was enormous. And purple.

Cate

the queen

I wanted so many things that summer. I wanted to go to Camp Coureur des Bois and ride horses and braid lanyards. I wanted polio to go away, so I could go swimming again. I wanted a big brother and an Easy-Bake Oven and ankle socks with ruffles on the edges. I wanted to be a Charles of the Ritz beauty consultant, just like Cate Finnegan.

I idolized Cate. Everybody did. The girl was as beautiful as Grace Kelly. That's why I was over the moon at the prospect of spending a couple of nights at the Finnegans' and sharing a bedroom with Cate.

I arrived at her doorstep giddy with expectation and returned home two days later, pensive. In the interim, I discovered how it is, sometimes, for girls whose spectacular beauty brings spectacular popularity in school, girls like Cate. Accustomed to easy achievement and perpetual adulation, they slip into the expectation that good things come without putting forth effort or summoning an ounce of fortitude. And then, inevitably, they are extruded into the larger world, which is not so fawning. In that world, there are no prom queens, and title roles are not bestowed on ingénues of marginal talent, at least not on the chaste ones. In that world, the real world, spectacular beauty can be problematic, and moving on to a different boyfriend every week is not all it's cracked up to be.

Not by a long shot.

It's broiling hot. There's nothing to do. I'm just sitting around, watching flies buzz around our garbage. Wait! I hear kids out in the street. It sounds like they're popping tar bubbles. I'm gonna go out front and get in on the fun. I love popping tar bubbles, even though the bottoms of my feet stay splotched with tar all summer.

Yesterday, Mom had a bad headache. She made a telephone call to Dad at his office and told him she couldn't make dinner because St. Louis is too gol-durn hot to turn on the oven. Dad got home early and barbecued wieners.

"You watch," Jane told me. "Any day now Mom's gonna get creative with vanilla ice cream."

Jane was right. Last night, Mom made snowball ice cream sundaes that were almost as good as the ones at the Missouri Athletic Club. And tonight, she's making Frost on Fire, which is a scoop of vanilla ice cream plopped on a slice of cantaloupe.

I'm done staying at the Loftons'. Also the Whites'. I wound up spending one miserable night at the Whites' and came right back home. The White twins are spoiled brats. And besides, Mrs. White made me, Sharon, and Susan drudge a moldy old davenport up from the basement for me to sleep on. Sharon and Susan got to sleep on their nice matching beds, and I got a stinky davenport. That afternoon, I told Mrs. White about Frost on Fire being a good dessert, but she said Susan and Sharon don't like cantaloupe, and that was that. The dessert she made that night was stupid—all she did was sprinkle pecan nuts on top of banana coins. Heck, that's not a real dessert.

The next morning, I heard Mr. White tell Mrs. White he'd like his davenport back, thank you very much. And Mrs. White told me to keep my dirty clothes in my suitcase because she wasn't put on this earth to be Grace Mitchell's personal washerwoman. I got the impression I'd worn out my welcome already. Sheesh.

I'm thinking about staying at the Finnegans', but I don't know if it's going to work out. Their house is just about busting with freckle-faced Finnegans. I talked to Jane about it, and Jane said that's because they're Irish, but I don't know whether she meant that's the reason there's lots of freckles or that's the reason there's lots of Finnegans.

Cate and Bridget are the oldest of the eight kids. Below them are Patrick, Sean, Kevin, Brendan, Hugh, and Pauly. Bridget's a blast and a half. Last time she babysat us, she fixed ginger ale martinis with three cherries and taught us how to play gin rummy, which is a very adult card game, and she let Charlie stay up so late, he conked out cold on the living room sofa. Bridget didn't give two hoots what time Jane and me went to bed either, so we got to stay up and watch *The Tonight Show*. Bridget's fun, but her older sister, Cate, is the amazing Finnegan.

Cate is super duper beautiful. Spectacularly beautiful, Jane says. Cate's got long legs and creamy skin, but everybody says Cate Finnegan's hair is her crowning glory. Cate's hair is this pretty shade Jane calls strawberry blond, and she wears it in a pageboy. Even when St. Louis is practically drowning in humidity, Cate's hair stays sleek and silky all the way to her shoulders.

Bridget told us Cate doesn't go to school anymore, but back when she went to Brentwood High, she was homecoming queen twice, Winter Snow Ball queen twice, and prom queen three times. When the Drama Club held tryouts for their spring play, something stupid called *Hedda Gabler*, Cate got to play Hedda even though some of the parents who went to the play said Cate Finnegan's acting left a lot to be desired.

Bridget told us that guys at Brentwood High wanted to be home-coming king just for the chance to walk in with her sister. Bridget said Cate dated so many guys at Brentwood High that the kids called her the Queen of Momentary Boyfriends.

Cate and Bridget get a bedroom all to themselves. One time when Bridget was babysitting us, she took us to her house to show us her bedroom. There's two canopy beds, and they're so high that Bridget said she feels like the Princess and the Pea. There's a bulletin board covered with Brentwood High pennants, ticket stubs from Brentwood Theater movie shows, an autographed picture of Bobby Darin, and tons of dried-up corsages. Under a slanty part of the ceiling is a closet that's jam-packed with long and short dresses, tight skirts and pleated skirts, twinset sweaters, and a kabillion pairs of shoes.

Bridget told us every time another baby comes along, the whole family except her and Cate have to shift around their bedrooms, or at least their beds. When Mrs. Finnegan and the new baby come home from the hospital, the baby gets the white wicker bassinet next to Mrs. Finnegan's side of the bed. The next older Finnegan gets booted to a crib with drop-down sides next to Mr. Finnegan's side of the bed. The third youngest Finnegan moves to a day bed with side rails in the boys' room down the hall, and everybody else gets moved upwards too.

The Finnegan boys are in a Davy Crockett phase, which I guess their parents think is wholesome. Last winter when Bridget was babysitting Jane and me and Charlie, she told us her brothers got a ton of Davy Crockett stuff for Christmas: vinyl wallets with stitched seams, stage-coach play money, King of the Wild Frontier cereal bowls, and card-board puzzles that show Fess Parker with a old-time rifle. Bridget said her mom even sewed little army forts and teepee villages on plain brown bedspreads that she bought at the Woolworth's on Grand Avenue.

Mrs. Daily told my mom she won't go there because Woolworth's did a huge remodeling a few years ago and added new escalators and air con-ditioning, but they kept separate lunch counters for whites and coloreds. I like that Mrs. Daily said that cuz I'd want my friend Cherry from camp to sit next to me if we ever get to meet up again and go eat at the Wool-worth's lunch counter.

Pauly's the Finnegan who's the most gaga about Wild West stuff. Pauly always wears a hat these days on account of Luca Zaldoni telling him Irish kids' brains can leak out of their ears. Most times Pauly wears a whirlybird beanie, but sometimes he wears the snap-off hook to his winter jacket. On the mornings he wants to be Davy Crockett, he wears a coonskin cap, which doesn't exactly go with his little kid eyeglasses. Pauly's new glasses are thicker and rounder than before, and they hood around his ears so they don't fall off too easy. When Pauly rode his tri-cycle over his glasses at Patsy Warfield's variety show, Mrs. Finnegan marched home and sewed snaps onto a little elastic strap that's just the right length to go around the back of Pauly's head and snap onto his glasses. Pauly's ears kinda stick out worse than ever, but I think he's too little to notice. Pauly's almost as adorable as our Charlie.

About once a week, Pauly sneaks out of the house at the crack of dawn and roams around Thistle Way, pretending to be Davy Crocket. Every now and then, Mr. Henry or Lt. Lofton or Mr. Haverkamp or Detec-tive Greeley goes out in a bathrobe to get the morning paper and sees Pauly Finnegan traipsing around naked except for his cowboy boots, his little Y-front underpants, and the whirlybird beanie. Usually, he's trotting on an invisible horse. Mrs. Finnegan isn't the kind of mom who counts her children's every breath, I'll tell you that. On mornings Pauly goes missing, she gets out her tin whistle and whistles "Danny Boy" out the front door and then goes back to making breakfast for the rest of her kids. I think she figures if "Danny Boy" doesn't get Pauly to stop being Davey Crockett and come home, the smell of fried sausages will.

I'm giving the idea of staying at the Finnegans' some thought and popping the last of the tar bubbles when Jane comes running out with news. She got a letter from her friend, Lizzie, who's at Camp Coureur des Bois. Lizzie wrote that the camp's archery instructor woke up with a headache and a bad sore throat, and by flag-raising time, the girl's cheeks were all flushed. For the past couple of summers, sore throats and flushed cheeks have been real scary for parents. Lizzie's letter said that by lunchtime, the archery girl got taken to the camp infirmary cuz she also had a stiff neck, which sounds a lot like polio. The girl's parents rushed her to a hospital, and she isn't coming back to camp.

"So, Grace," Jane says, "Bridget Finnegan passed the counselor-in-training test, and she just got called up to be the new archery instructor."

Bridget's at camp. Bridget's bed is available!

I run inside, open my red plaid suitcase, and dump out the dirty clothes from staying over at Susan and Sharon White's stupid house. I kick the used-up clothes under my bed and pack the suitcase with clean clothes. Luckily, Mom washed my green shorts set—they're perfect. Irish people like the Finnegans always appreciate it when you wear green. My suitcase got a big scratch across the top from shoving it under Susan and Sharon White's stupid davenport couch, but I spit on my finger and rub the scratch, and it almost disappears.

Over at the Finnegans' house, Mrs. Finnegan tells me that one less child at her table makes her lonely, and with Bridget gone, she's happy to have me. I lug my suitcase up to Bridget and Cate's room, and then I go out to the backyard and play with some of the little Finnegans.

Cate Finnegan is in her early twenties. I'm eight, going on nine. So all afternoon, I'm wondering if me and Cate are gonna get along. Maybe she'll hate me cuz she misses Bridget; after all, the Finnegans are what Mom calls a close-knit family. Cate still lives at home even though she's done with school, and she works at Stix Baer & Fuller, which is sorta like my Grandpa Reinhardt's store, but the stuff at Stix isn't as expensive. Cate's also a Charles of the Ritz beauty consultant, which is pretty cool.

When Cate gets home from work, she's really nice about me staying over.

"I'm used to being surrounded by family, lots of family," she says. "I wouldn't know what to do with myself if Bridget's bed was empty for too long."

Whew. I feel better.

After dinner, I follow Cate up to her bedroom and keep quiet while she writes in her diary. When she finishes, she caps her fountain pen, locks the latch, and tucks the key under her pillow. She rubs swirls of cold cream into her cheeks and forehead and chin, and she sticks Tip Top Wave Clips in her hair. I heard my mom tell Mrs. Lofton that Cate Finnegan was born to be a beauty consultant and "that girl is so gorgeous that women spend a fortune on Charles of the Ritz products hoping to look just like her." Cate smooths a pink lotion all over her arms and legs and feet. When she's finished, she turns to me.

"Gracie, you've been so quiet, I forgot all about you."

"It's okay. I like watching you."

"Now, Gracie, how about I give you a little beauty treatment? Would you like that?"

Would I?! But right away, I'm kinda worried. I can't imagine how Cate's gonna get me beautified. First of all, I'm just a kid. Second of all, I'm ordinary-looking. I'm excited to have her try, though, I'll tell you that.

Cate snaps open the pretty little train case she takes to work each day. Inside, there's tons of small bottles and jars organized on folding trays and stuck in rows of elastic bands. Cate takes out a bunch of jars and brushes and shows me the proper way to custom-blend facial powder so that it is ideally matched to my skin tone. Then she shows me how to apply lipstick regardless of the shape or size of my lips. And then she teaches me the advantages of wearing eyeliner and false eyelashes on certain occasions and the disadvantages of wearing them on other occasions, like funerals.

When she finishes, she lets me look in the mirror. *Holy cow, I look grown up!*

"You're so pretty, Gracie," she says. "Would you like to try on some of my prom gowns? I kept them all."

This is the best night of my whole life.

Cate helps me into a beautiful long dress and a pair of high heels dyed to match it. I swish around the bedroom and wobble out to the hall. A couple of Finnegan boys start marching behind me, and Cate laughs and says they're my honor guard. I'm in heaven.

A little later, back in the bedroom, Cate hands me one of her year-books from Brentwood High and lets me read the notes her classmates, mostly boys, wrote in the margins. There's lots of hearts with Cate's initials inside them.

I love living at the Finnegans'. Getting a beauty lesson from Cate, trying on her prom dresses, and parading around the house in her high heels—wow, that was the chance of a lifetime! Also, it was kinda fun working Fess Parker jigsaw puzzles with the little boys and rocking the newest baby to sleep for his nap this afternoon. And Mrs. Finnegan's sure better than Susan and Sharon White's mom. Mrs. Finnegan's gonna make Frost on Fire for tomorrow's dessert.

On my second night at the Finnegans, I force myself to stay up till almost midnight, which is when Cate gets home from her date. When she finally comes into the bedroom, I'm thinking something's wrong, but I don't know what. The whole time she's writing in her diary, I stay quiet as a mouse. At last, she leans over to switch off the bedside lamp and notices me, and she gives a little start.

"Hi," I say. "I'm still here."

Cate smiles, but it doesn't seem like a happy smile. Her lips don't curve up at the corners; they just stretch in a straight line. She turns off the lamp. There's a sliver of a moon tonight, and it's shining just enough light for me to see tears on her cheeks.

"So, Gracie . . . " Her voice gets bright again, like she's forcing herself to cheer up. "Can I call you that? Some people don't like nicknames, and I wouldn't want to give you one if you didn't like it."

"You can call me anything you want."

"Gracie, then. Well, Gracie, I have a confession to make. My nickname in high school was the Queen of Momentary Boyfriends. Isn't that awful? But it was true then, and the sad thing is, well, it's still true."

She reaches on the bedside table and pulls a Kleenex out of the box. I think she's crying again.

"The boys in high school were all right, I guess," she says. "I just got bored with them sooner than they got bored with me. But lately, I don't know, my love life's been one flop after another."

I don't know what to say, so I just wait.

"Gracie, would you like to hear about some of my momentary boyfriends?"

"Sure."

"Okay, but there's lots," she says. "Some go back to my years at Brentwood High. One or two I met while I was in beauty school, and the latest ones I've dated in the last year or so, ever since I started as a beauty consultant. I gave each one a nickname. If I got a nickname I didn't especially like, then they can just get nicknames too, right?"

I don't answer. I don't dare breathe.

"Let's see. Okay, I'll start with New Testament Jake. He had the cutest dimple in his chin, just like Kirk Douglas. Jake was the quarterback of the St. Louis University High football team, but he wasn't all that popular. He didn't smoke or tell dirty jokes like the other guys. He didn't even like beer. We dated all throughout the fall of my senior year of high school, but right before Christmas, he told me he wouldn't be able to go out with me again until August."

"Were his parents moving away?"

"No. He was going to spend every weekend at some kind of religious youth retreat center out near Jeff City. Jake said his parents weren't too keen on him going there cuz it's Christian but not Catholic."

I don't quite get that, but I pretend to understand. "Did you break up with him because of him being Christian but not Catholic?"

"Not at all, but I wasn't going to wait around for football season to start up again. I told Jake our relationship had been heaven on earth but, like the Red Sea, it was time we parted."

I'm trying to figure out whether that was a joke or not, but Cate's already talking about the next momentary boyfriend. Now that my eyes have adjusted to the dark, I can see her better. She's got kind of a far-off look. I get the feeling she's talking to herself. She cups her hands under her chin and says, "Let's see. I think LuVelda Craig came next."

It's really late, but I want to stay up and hear about all of Cate's momentary boyfriends, so every time I yawn, I hide my mouth behind one of Bridget's pillows.

"Let's see," Cate says. "Craig. Small Town Craig. He was born and raised on a farm just outside of LuVelda, Iowa, and he didn't ever want to leave that farm. But his parents convinced him to go to college at Washington University. When I met him, he was in a decent fraternity, and he was working part-time at Stix. We met in the employee lounge.

"Craig was tall with sandy blond hair and dreamy brown eyes," she says. She's got a dreamy look to her eyes too. "And he talked incessantly about LuVelda."

"What did he say?"

"Well, he told me there's a little store, the Old Time General Store, where you can get a side of beef, a bushel basket of corn, a sack of dog food, you name it. The store sold ladies' face cream too—obviously nothing like Charles of the Ritz though."

"Is it like Reinhardt & Krug? That's my grandpa's store."

"Oh, Gracie, not really. Let's see, what else did he say about LuVelda? There's a beauty shop called Pearl's Curls and a barbershop called Rusty's Barber Pole. Oh, there's a little park in the middle of LuVelda with a historic jailhouse available for tours by appointment."

"That's weird."

"No kidding. What else? Oh, and the LuVelda Community Improvement Board posted a sign out on State Route 47."

"What does it say?"

"When You Get to LuVelda, Stay Put!"

Cate and me just about die laughing.

"Is he still in St. Louis?" I ask when I catch my breath.

"No way. He went back to LuVelda. The last I heard, he was the president of the LuVelda Community Improvement Board."

When we stop laughing, Cate tells me about Bottled-Up Bruce.

"All the guys in Bruce's family are hunters, and when they go hunting, they bring along a cooler filled with beer. One Saturday afternoon, Bruce called me from a phone booth at a gas station way out in the country. He was all excited because he shot a two-hundred-pound buck. He said the bullet went right through the heart."

"Ick!"

"Right. Anyway, he said he wanted me to see the dead deer, and they would stop at Thistle Way on their way home. Grace, it was horrible. Bruce and his uncles had roped the deer to the roof of the station wagon. The head and antlers were draped over one side, and the skinny legs were hanging down the other side. Blood was streaking down the windshield."

"Ick!"

Cate's next boyfriend was somebody named Peter the Miserable who painted the scenery for a theatre group that showed free plays in Tilles Park. The one after that was Tango Rick. He was a ballroom dance instructor. Maternal Mark was best friends with his mom. Tad Unhinged walked through a glass sliding door and had to have eighty-nine stitches, and then the next day, he got fired from his job, and the day after that, he backed his car into a fire hydrant, and then he had a nervous breakdown.

"Tad didn't bathe, at least not on a regular basis," Cate says.

"That's disgusting!" I say, pinching my nose. "Mom makes Jane and me take a bath every single night in summer and every other night in winter."

Underwear Joe was the next boyfriend Cate tells me about. She says his mom and dad live on Lindell Boulevard in a big mansion, and they have six cats and they don't wear any clothes when they're in their house.

"The cats?"

"No, silly, Joe's parents!"

At that, we just about die laughing. Then Cate gets serious again. "One night, I was at Joe's apartment, and I dropped my lipstick. It rolled under Joe's gun cabinet, and when I got down to look for it, I discovered something else Joe collected."

"Bullets?"

"Women's panties!"

Cate and me howl so loud, Mr. Finnegan pounds on the wall.

Then Cate gets all serious and says, "You know, Grace, I was queen of this and queen of that in high school, but the one title I didn't get was the title everybody on Thistle Way said I most deserved: Breck Girl."

It was right after graduation, Cate tells me. She sent a letter to the man who painted the advertising pictures of beautiful girls with great hair who use Breck shampoo.

"I sent him a picture of myself, but he never wrote back," she says, twirling a section of her hair between her fingers. "When the new issue of *Good Housekeeping* came out with the latest Breck Girl ad, I raced up to the newsstand in Clayton to buy a copy. When I got home and showed Mom, she said it was a travesty of justice."

"You should've been a Breck Girl," I say, and I really truly mean it.

"It's okay, Grace. I wasn't heartbroken."

We stay quiet a little while, thinking about how famous Cate could've been as a Breck Girl, and then she starts telling me about even more momentary boyfriends.

Funeral Home Rob. Rock 'n' Roll Andy. A guy named Broadsword Rory who Cate says is a semi-professional juggler.

"When Rory had too much to drink, he would light a bunch of charcoal in a Weber kettle—that's one of those newfangled barbecue grills—and then he'd lift the thing up and balance one of the legs on his chin."

Cate pauses a long while and then says, "I broke up with Globetrotting Steve just tonight."

"Are you sad?"

"Yes and no. Every few months, he'd call me from Japan or Peru or Iceland and ask me to meet him there," Cate says, pulling a pillow to her chest. "I sell makeup in a department store. World travel is definitely not the world I live in, or probably ever will. Besides, I was never the center of that guy's universe."

The bedroom's suddenly quiet. Cate's alarm clock says it's almost five-thirty in the morning. My eyes are swimmy, and I've never been up this late in my life, but I want to stay awake.

"You know," Cate says, "if I could only find a guy who was born and raised in America, who doesn't have a panty collection or a strange relationship with his mother, and whose parents *wear clothes*, or if I could let myself get past a guy's flaws and give us a chance to know one another, then I think I'd lose my nickname once and for all."

Cate gets up and stands at the window. I get up and stand beside her, looking out at Thistle Way. The sky is getting light. The houses all look kinda bluish-grayish. Detective Greeley is awake already. He opens the front door and bends to pick up the newspaper. Light from the Greeleys' front hall floods onto the stoop.

I hear a soft clicking noise. It's coming from below Cate's window. Cate and me lean out until our foreheads bulge the screen, but we don't see anything unusual.

Another noise! A squealing sound, like a door opening.

Cate puts her arm around my shoulder. I look up and see she's smiling now, a real smile this time.

"It's all right," she says. "It's just Pauly traipsing out to play Davy Crocket."

Perhaps I was merely a convenient sounding board for Cate that night, but I don't think so. She could so easily have resented a much younger visitor barging into her room, setting up housekeeping on her sister's bed. She could have resented the loss of privacy, which was a hard-won commodity in the Finnegan household. Instead, she was uncommonly gracious.

It's said there are two kinds of remorse: regret over having done something and regret over having not done enough.

At the end of that long night, I realized that even a prom queen, a homecoming queen, and a Snow Ball queen, even a spectacularly gorgeous Charles of the Ritz beauty consultant, could be burdened with both types of remorse.

I remember thinking about Cate Finnegan's serial romances throughout the following day. But change was afoot. The Eagans had come to Thistle Way. Soon my sweet childlike world would never be the same.

Mark and Sissy Eagan

the names

Amonth after the second-generation Zaldonis and all their worldly goods were summarily whisked back to the old Italian neighborhood, Mark and Sissy Eagan took up residence in the Zaldonis' empty house on Thistle Way.

From the beginning, the Eagan occupancy was beset with problems. They found the closets too small, the grassy yard too big, and the infamous St. Louis humidity too tropical for their tropical plants, which appeared to be in dire distress when they were finally extruded from the moving van. But for Mark and Sissy, the most perplexing issue was a persistent but not entirely unpleasant odor throughout the house. They scrubbed the walls with lemon juice. They washed the floors with Spic 'n Span and perfumed the rooms with Air Wick, to no avail. The place was infused with the smell of Bolognese sauce.

The Potters and the Zaldonis were gone, but all that summer, the old-timers of Thistle Way continued to refer to the two houses as the Potter place and the Zaldoni place. As for the Blairs and Eagans, they would forever be known as "the new people" and described with a degree of derision as "modern."

Me and Sally and a couple of Finnegans and Mooneys and Haverkamps are camped out on Sally's front lawn, watching the new people move into the Zaldonis' house. There's no kid stuff coming off the moving truck, so we figure the new people don't have kids.

I'm kinda worried. Thistle Way's getting awful sparse on kids, I'll tell you that.

Anyways, the new lady walks out the Zaldonis' front door, down the driveway, and across the street, aiming straight for us. The Haverkamps and some of the Finnegans scramble to their feet and run away, but me and Mark and Sally and Matt and Pauly Finnegan get up and sorta stand there, pretending to watch the movers. Heck, we're on Sally Daily's property; we've got a right to stare at a moving truck all we want.

The new lady's got a big straw purse with a starfish embroidered on it. When she gets across the street, she opens the purse and hands each of us a Zagnut bar. Then she starts yakking about how wonderful California is and how she and her hubby hated to move away from Los Angeles where all the movie stars live, except that Mark, who I guess is her hubby, got a job with Anheuser Busch. Rainer says moving from California to St. Louis is pretty stupid. I jab my elbow in his ribs, and he clams up.

Zagnut bars! They're my fifth favorite candy bar. I rip open the wrapper. The other kids do too.

I'm thinking the lady's gonna be ticked off about Matt saying they're stupid, but she just kinda chuckles and says, "Well, kid, you might be right. So far, Thistle Way looks a lot like Nowheresville."

"Whats-its-Ville?" Pauly Finnegan asks.

We all laugh at Pauly, but we stop real quick cuz Pauly's got red blotches all over his face. Dang! Pauly gobbled up half a Zagnut bar. Everybody knows Pauly Finnegan's allergic to coconut. Stupid new lady.

I grab Pauly by the hand and start lugging him home. Behind me, I hear the new lady. "Well, see ya, kids. And don't forget, it's not Mrs. Eagan. It's Sissy."

The sky's getting that blue-dark look, like it's gonna rain buckets any minute. A breeze picks up; it swishes the oak leaves overhead, even some of the biggest branches. The whirlybird on Pauly's beanie twirls like crazy. Mrs. Finnegan thanks me for bringing her little boy home. She says Pauly will be just fine, not to worry, the hives will go away in an hour or so. I offer to go to Snyder's and get a bottle of Galomine lotion, but Mrs. Finnegan just sorta chuckles and says, "It's Calamine lotion, dear, and I always keeps a bottle on hand."

"None of my other kids are allergic to anything," she adds, "and Pauly's allergic to everything."

I start to leave and then turn around.

"Pauly's special," I say.

"Oh, sweet pea," Mrs. Finnegan answers, "all of God's kids are special."

Some women are born to be mothers. Mrs. Finnegan was one of them.

I remember that when I got home late that afternoon, the air was oddly cool, as if the first hint of autumn had decided to waft into Missouri well before it should. My mother was in the kitchen. The almost chilly weather wouldn't last, she surely knew, and so it had inspired her to turn on the oven and fix a good hot meal. I peeked in the kitchen just in time to see her sprinkling crumbled potato chips onto her signature casserole: cubed ham, sliced onion and diced potatoes in a creamy cheese sauce. At the dinner table, she spooned steaming mounds of ham casserole onto our plates. I distinctly remember feeling a sense of calm come over me, an awareness that I was safe, I was being tended to. It occurred to me that I was in just the right place, if that makes any sense, in my chair with my sister on one side of me and my little brother opposite us, with our mother at one end of the table and our father at the other. Each time my mother handed another plate down the table, she smiled, and I knew we were loved.

Later that night, I remember asking her if it would be all right for me to call the Blairs and the Eagans by their first names.

"Yes," she said, surprising the daylights out of me. Then she added, "You may call the Blairs and the Eagans by their first names when you are thirty years old and they are sixty."

It was a dilemma. Mrs. Eagan had insisted I call her Sissy, and my mother had insisted I call the woman Mrs. Eagan. I resolved to steer clear of the Eagans. The Blairs too, for good measure.

Before long, however, the new people and their modern ways would teach me a hard lesson about avoidance as a means of problem solving: it doesn't always work.

the Dailys

the shank end

In St. Louis, the school a child attended—the grade school, and especially the high school—was the fixed prism through which all other St. Louisans viewed the adult ever after. That was true more than a half-century ago, and to some extent, it is still true.

Catholics sent their children to Catholic schools. Everybody else sent their children to public schools. In the late summer of 1956, I was getting ready to start fourth grade at Immaculate Heart of Mary. Sally was going into fourth grade at Thomas Hart Benton School. Student intermixing was not outright prohibited, but it was hardly encouraged. So it might seem unlikely that Sally and I would have been best friends. It wasn't. But to know that, I guess you had to know Sally, and her parents.

Sally was a happy little girl, even-tempered and conciliatory, a soft child, as rounded at the edges as Janice Haverkamp was pointy. Sally's eyes were sky blue and wide-set behind thick lashes. Her hair was the color of summer straw, blunt cut at the chin with straight-across bangs. A spritz of faded freckles dotted the bridge of her nose. She was an only child, indulged but unspoiled. She had a doll collection to die for, a palomino horse statue collection, a basement filled with toys and games (more than a few of which were "educational"), a backyard filled with play equipment, and a disposition inclined to share all of it.

Most importantly—and I realized this even at the young age of eight, going on nine—Sally had exemplary parents. Mr. Daily was the producer and creative director of children's programming at KMOX-TV. He was not a tall man, but a thatch of thick wavy hair gave the illusion of height. That and a bouncy stride offset the twin horizontals of a pronounced mustache and blousy trousers. Mrs. Daily maintained a clean and well-organized house without taking the concept to the extreme. She had taught kindergarten in South St. Louis until Sally was born, and I imagine she kept the normal clutter and chaos of the classroom in check too. After Sally started at Thomas Hart Benton, her mother took a part-time job at the South St. Louis School in the nurse's office. I once heard Mr. Daily say kids used to fake sore throats so that they could go to the nurse's office and get a pack of cherry LifeSavers. I dare say Mrs. Daily knew exactly what they were up to.

Even before my "deal" with my mother, I practically lived at the Daily house. One evening, as I took my normal place at their dinner table, Mrs. Daily remarked with a chuckle that she felt like my second mother. I misunderstood, thought I'd worn out my welcome, and began to cry. Mrs. Daily swept me into her arms and reassured me that she said that because she loved me. Sally ran to her bedroom and brought back one of her little horse statues and gave it to me. Mr. Daily said he was going to use his wood-burning kit to make a plaque with my name on it, and he'd hang it over his workbench in the garage so I'd know I was always welcome at their house. He actually made that plaque and hung it in the garage.

Mr. and Mrs. Daily were wonderful parents, and their benevolence extended to all the children of Thistle Way, not just me.

Sally was a kind and true friend.

Their house and everything about it was my idea of perfection, pure and simple.

Until one humid August night, when it wasn't.

It's Sunday. Rainer and me are sitting on the grass next to Rainer's driveway, waiting for something interesting to happen.

Dinner's over. Dessert's over. It's too late to start a new fort and too early to take a bath and get ready for bed. The cicadas are making that wee-wee noise again, like they always do after dinner, and the crickets are chirping like idiots out in the ivy surrounding the oak trees, and a dang mosquito keeps whining at my ear. All of which I could tolerate, except that Benny Herman gave his trumpet to one of the Finnegan kids, and now the Finnegan kid is sitting on his bedroom windowsill, half in and half out, trying to play Benny's gol-durn trumpet.

When I was walking out the front door to go over to Rainer's tonight, Dad looked up from the evening paper and said, "Grace, we are now officially in the shank end of summer. You and your friends will have to think extra hard to come up with ways to stay out of trouble."

Sitting beside Rainer, I swat a mosquito away from an old scab on my knee, wondering how there could be a shrink end of summer cuz you can't shrink summer cuz it's the same amount of time every year, June, July, and August, so nobody can shrink the end of summer or there'd be no August. I pick at the scab's flaky edges to see if the whole thing's ready to come off.

"Wish I had a dime."

"What for?" Rainer says. "Snyder's Store?"

"Nah. For a turn on Gregor's bike."

Gregor's standing a little ways away from us in his driveway. He's not paying any attention to me and Rainer, though, cuz he's busy making sure the kids taking turns on his bike don't take more turns than they paid for.

Down in the street, Mike Mooney zooms past us on his way around the circle. His head is way out front over the handlebars, and his feet are going like crazy pumping the pedals of Gregor Niesen's brand new English racing bike.

"Dummy," Rainer says, thonking his forehead. "Gregor won't let you ride it. For one, that bike's only a month old. For two, you're a girl. And for three, you're too little. Heck, you'd never reach the pedals."

Gregor's been raking in dimes ever since he got that bike. Ten cents for a ten-minute turn on the bike. Lots of guys on Thistle Way have been spending their whole allowance riding Gregor's bike.

"Wanna go to the creek?" I ask, moving on to a different scab.

"Nah."

Rainer's been a scaredy-cat ever since the bad thing happened. He won't go anywhere near the hideout. He won't go down to catch tadpoles at the creek. Now that I think about it, when Rainer's not at his country club, he's been sticking to just his own yard. Rainer isn't as much fun as he used to be, but it's too hot to go looking for somebody else to play with.

"Let's play spinning statues," he says.

Me and Rainer get up and start spinning each other around. With spinning statues, you're supposed to let the other kid go and see if they can stand up without moving, but Rainer and me just grab each others' wrists and spin together so we get dizzy on purpose and then fall down. We're on our fourth spin and fall when Mike Mooney comes speeding up the Niesens' driveway on Gregor's bike and skids to a stop.

"What the hell," Gregor yells, jumping out of the way. "Watch it, Mooney, will ya?"

Mike takes a gulp of air and says loud, "The Mosquito Man's coming!"

Finally. Something good.

The older boys take off like the blazes. I'm still dizzy, but I run too. You gotta be quick, or you'll miss the fun. At the bottom of the Niesens' driveway, I wave to Rainer to come, but he pretends to be all interested in the grass stains on his shorts. Usually, Rainer'd be one of the first kids to get to the Mosquito Man truck. I hope he forgets about the bad thing pretty soon and goes back to being good old Rainer.

I see the truck rumbling onto Thistle Way. You can tell it's the Mosquito Man because there's a big container on the back of the truck that looks like our hot water heater, only it's gray and it's laying sideways. The container spews out billows and billows of gray smoke that kills all the mosquitoes for a few days. Then they come back. Pretty soon, just about every kid on Thistle Way is running behind the truck, all of us skipping and jumping and twirling, pretending we're lost in the whitish grayish fog.

Mom comes out with her apron and rubber gloves still on from doing the dinner dishes and hollers, "Don't get too close." Then she goes back inside. No kid ever got into trouble for being too close. Heck, getting as close as you can is the whole point. That's where the smoke's the thickest.

I just love the smell of Mosquito Man smoke.

Sally Daily's the only kid whose parents won't let her run in the smoke. I don't know why; she's got just the best parents in the universe. Sally says her mom and dad think the smoke is poisonous, but that can't be true. Nobody keels over dead just by breathing Mosquito Man smoke.

The Mosquito Man goes all the way around the circle and then out to the through road. Me and a few other kids play in the fog till it's all gone. I sure wish Davey was back from the hospital. Davey used to love Mosquito Man nights.

Rainer's still sitting on the dumb old grass next to his driveway. He's no fun anymore either. Things sure have changed this summer. Anyways, now that the fog's almost all gone, I go sit with Rainer again.

"Wanna play some more spinning statues?" he says.

"Sure."

Rainer's yanking my arm out of the socket when we hear Sally Daily's garage door crank open.

Everybody knows what that means. Kickball!

In summer, there's three good things to do after dinner. Catching lightning bugs and pulling off the lighted part while it's glowing and then sticking it on your finger to make a diamond ring. Sucking all the cherry juice out of your snow cone while a whole bunch of kids are still sweltering in a long line at the ice cream truck window. And kickball.

Two or three times a week, Mr. Daily lugs a big canvas sack out to the street, and kids come running from all around Thistle Way. Mr. Dailey lets anybody play who wants to. The oldest ones are Mark Mooney, Curt Haverkamp, Jack Henry, and Gregor Niesen. The youngest kid is Pauly Finnegan.

Pauly has to go to bed early, so he comes to kickball in his footie pajamas. The only kid cuter than Pauly Finnegan is our Charlie, but Charlie gets his bath right after dinner, and then Dad rocks him in the old rocking chair from Grandma Reinhardt until he falls asleep, and Dad tries to get up without the rocking chair creaking and slowly, carefully, lays Charlie down in his crib, so Charlie's conked out for the night even before kickball starts. Maybe next year, Charlie can stay up long enough for the first couple of innings.

Anyways, at the beginning of each summer, Mrs. Daily makes a brand new home plate with an old pillowcase from the Goodwill store. She fills it with dried beans and straw and stuff, sews up the open end, and then sews a big gold star on it. First base is always red, second base is white, and third base is blue. They don't have stars; only home plate gets a star on it.

Mr. Daily always lets us kids set out the bases cuz we know exactly where they go. First base is three long steps past the fireplug in front of the Zaldonis' old house. Second base goes on top of the manhole cover in the middle of the street, way back after Patsy Warfield's house. Third base is in front of the "Slow, Children" sign next to Mrs. Pearson's driveway. Home plate is in the middle of the street, smack dab in front of the Dailys'.

Mr. Daily is always the pitcher, which I think is good cuz then there's no fights. He makes up the teams too. He makes sure both teams have kids who kick the ball a mile and kids who hardly ever get on base. Also, Mr. Daily never ever put Luca and Antony Zaldoni on the same team, which doesn't matter anymore since the Zaldonis moved back to the Hill.

Mr. Daily starts every game by flipping a coin, just like tonight.

"Blue Team, batter up!" he shouts.

Sally tugs her dad's shirtsleeve. "Dad," she whispers. "Pauly Finnegan's crying."

Everybody looks at Pauly. The first thing we notice is the elastic strap is broke, the strap that goes around the back of Pauly's head to hold his little round glasses on. Pauly's glasses are dangling from one of his sticky-outy ears, and he's bawling so hard that he tilts his face up to the sky, which makes his whirlybird beanie fall off, which makes him bawl even louder cuz he's afraid his brains are gonna leak out.

Mr. Daily crouches down next to Pauly and wipes off his tears and snot with a big white handkerchief. Patrick Finnegan and his brothers Sean, Kevin, Brendan, and Hugh all gather around to make Pauly feel better. Patrick picks up the beanie and plops it back on Pauly's head, which seems to help cuz Pauly stops bawling. Now he's just hiccoughing.

Mr. Daily fixes Pauly's eyeglasses strap and talks to him gently.

"Son," he says, "I'm going to roll the ball toward you, slow and smooth, and you just try your best to kick it back to me. You get three tries, remember? So if you kick the ball, run as fast as you can toward the fireplug. Okay?"

Pauly nods.

"Now," Mr. Daily goes on, "you're a very important person on the team. Can they count on you?"

Pauly puffs out his chest, all proud, and clomps over to home plate.

"Cowboy boots are good for kicking, son," Mr. Daily says, "but next time I recommend you put them on over your footie pajamas, not under."

Mr. Daily rolls the ball toward Pauly so slow and smooth, you'd think it was a raw egg, which is not unusual cuz he always asks each kicker how they want him to roll the ball. Most of the boys say "medium" and all the girls say "slow and smooth." Luca Zaldoni was the only kid to say "fast and rough." When it was Luca's turn, the outfielders always backed up a mile, but it didn't make any difference cuz Luca blasted the ball into the treetops and got a home run every time. That was the only good thing about being on Luca's team.

Mrs. Pearson is watching the game from her front porch like always.

She sits on a little chair made out of white painted metal with curlicue designs. Moths flit around her porch light, but she doesn't swat them away. She says the moths and mosquitoes don't get too close cuz she puts toilet water on her wrists. I wouldn't go near Mrs. Pearson either if she'd dunked her hands in toilet water. Sheesh.

We get eight innings done while it's still light enough out, but now the sky's kinda purplish-grayish.

Mr. Daily says, "That's all for tonight. Did anybody keep track of the score?"

Mr. Daily never keeps track of the score, which I like.

Mr. Daily is the best dad in the whole wide world. For example, for the last three years on the Saturday after Thanksgiving, he's put on a marionette show that's better than Patsy Warfield's circuses and melodramas. Sally makes cute invitations that look like tickets and drops them off at each house on Thistle Way that has kids.

Usually, the Dailys' basement is taken up by Sally's doll stuff and Mrs. Daily's sewing and laundry stuff and a big ping-pong table. On the day of the show, though, Mr. Daily shoves the ping-pong table against one of the basement walls, and Mrs. Daily folds all the clean clothes in a neat stack on top of the washing machine. Then she vacuums the big braided rug so the kids have a nice clean place to sit. Sally piles up her kabillion dolls on the ironing board so there's plenty of room, which is good cuz just about every kid in the neighborhood goes to Mr. Daily's marionette show.

I'd hate to think if the marionette show was in the Haverkamps' basement with all that dirty laundry and Foo dog poo!

Mr. Daily made the marionette theater a long time ago out of boards and plywood. Each year, he repaints the front to look like a castle or a forest or a candy house or whatever the new show is about.

Right before the show starts, Mrs. Daily greets everybody at the door and tells us to go down to the basement. Then she plays peppy songs on the living room piano while all the kids are getting settled downstairs, which we can hear cuz Mr. Daily made an intercom system all by himself and stuck it in right through the walls and floor of the house.

Anyways, Mr. Daily hides behind the marionette theater so we can't see him, cuz that would ruin the show. When Mrs. Daily starts to play real loud, Mr. Daily pulls a cord, and red velvet curtains on the marionette stage open. All us kids get as quiet as mice, and the first two marionettes come prancing onto the stage. Mr. Daily makes up the story and does all the voices and works the long strings attached to the marionettes' hands and feet so they move like real people.

The show last year was King Jeer. The main marionette was a king who goes cuckoo because he didn't want to be king anymore. He gave away his kingdom to his three daughters who said they loved him, but they really didn't. There was a court jester called Fool, too, and a couple of princes who married the king's daughters. Mr. Daily told us he didn't make up the story; he just adopted it from Shakespeare, which I didn't get because how can you adopt a story and besides, I think Shakespeare died in the Civil War.

At the end of the marionette show, all the kids stand up and clap and cheer except for Luca and Antony, who whistle real loud through their fingers. Ha ha, the dumb Zaldonis are gone now. Luca's never gonna kill our ears again after a marionette show, or sneak up behind me and Sally when we're playing dolls in the yard and clunk our heads together. Hard-ee-har-har-har, stupid Zaldonis.

When I'm at Sally's house, we always play dolls. If the weather's nice, Mrs. Daily brings an old flannel blanket out to the backyard and shakes it flat under a shade tree. Then me and Sally carry a bunch of her dolls out and arrange them on the blanket and make up tons of pretend things to do with them. Sometimes a doll gets a deadly illness or a broken leg. Sometimes a doll wets her pants, and we have to change all her clothes. We feed Cheerios to the dolls, and if they can't swallow them, then Sally and me eat the Cheerios. When the baby doll needs a nap, we sing lulla-bies to her. We love to make the dolls be teenagers and go out on dates with cool Brentwood High boys. Of all Sally's dolls, my favorites are the identical twin dolls with beautiful blonde hair that goes down past their waists. I fix their hair in ponytails and braids and buns and French twists. I'm not so good at French twists, but Sally says they look just fine.

When I stay at Sally's too long, Mom calls Mrs. Daily to see if I'm being a pest. Mrs. Daily always says I'm no trouble, and lots of times she asks Mom if I can stay for lunch or dinner, which I love. Mrs. Daily always makes Kraft Macaroni and Cheese with cut-up hot dogs and orange Jell-O with marshmallows. It's the best dinner ever. I've been to Sally's house to play so many times Mrs. Daily says she feels like my second mother, which I think she likes.

Sally comes to my house sometimes too. One time, me and Sally wanted to take a bubble bath, but Mom was out of liquid dish soap so we sprinkled Bab-O in the tub. That's what Odetta uses to scrub out the sink and toilet and bathtub. Me and Sally turned on the water full blast, and the Bab-O foamed up almost as good as Ivory dish soap. Sally and me splashed around a long time singing "Bab-O in the bathtub!" at the top of our lungs, even though the suds went away pretty fast.

By the time Mom came up to check on us, our skin was all prickly and our whole legs and bottoms looked sunburnt. Mom saw the can of Bab-O and burst out crying, which I didn't quite get since it was me and Sally scratching ourselves to smithereens. Anyways, Mom got out the big jar of cold cream she keeps under the skirt of her dressing table and slathered up me and Sally. After that, we stopped itching, but our pajamas stuck to our legs all night.

At the beginning of the summer, I made a list of all the families I wanted to stay with, even though I already knew which family is the best in the world. The Dailys. They're a kabillion times better than any other family on Thistle Way. Saving the Dailys for last meant I got to sleep over at the Finnegans', Loftons', Potters', Henrys', and lots of other houses first, which kept up my deal with Mom and was mostly fun except for the bad ones like Missy Henry.

It's almost dark. The kickball game's over. Before I drudge home, I ask Sally if I can sleep over. She was kinda waiting for that. I told her at the beginning of summer about my deal with Mom, and I told her I wanted to save her for last. I'm just gonna love living with the Dailys.

For the few days, I savored the prospect of joining the Daily household. After all, Mr. Daily was the perfect dad. Mrs. Daily was the perfect mom. Sally was the perfect friend. Every aspect of the Dailys' house contributed to their flawless existence in my mind. The piano. The stereo. The ingenious speaker system. The sleek sofa with its flat throw pillows. The modern appliances in avocado green. The curvy breakfast bar with little boomerang designs on the Formica.

Sally did not wear hand-me-downs. Sally did not get Cuddle Bun for Christmas when she asked for Hollywood Bride, and she certainly did not want for home entertainment. There was that epic doll collection, for starters. Her palomino statue collection. The swing set, slide, sandbox, and Tyrolean-style playhouse with geraniums in the window boxes out back. It was like Playland over there.

Even now, decades later, I am still under the happy delusion that the Daily family came as close to the ideal as it gets. But I relinquished the notion that their house was picture-perfect one humid August night in the summer of 1956, when I opened a bedroom door and saw what no child should.

Theresa

the dream

I was in Walgreens this morning with a list a mile long—Kleenex, shampoo and conditioner, Jergens lotion, Mentos for my purse, another thumb drive for my laptop, the usual. Instead, I found myself standing in the greeting card aisle. Of course. The sympathy cards.

Charlie.

How many sympathy cards have I read this week? Too many.

I moved down the aisle, to the birthday cards. The funny ones didn't hit me right, and the sappy ones were just too . . . sappy. Every day of my life, and every day of theirs, I have loved each of my brothers and sisters with the visceral, complex, and enduring template of love shared by siblings the world over. I don't need a store-bought card to remind me of that. One card intrigued me, though. I plucked it from the rack. On the cover was a vintage 1950s photo of two sisters sticking out their tongues at one another. I opened the card, expecting a pithy message. There wasn't one, just a photo of the same little girls, fast asleep in a small bed, wrapped in each other's arms.

There were times when we were kids that I wanted to wring my sister Jane's neck. Well, that was then. Now, we phone each other every Tuesday and talk for an hour. There's almost nothing we don't share, including memories of our childhood on Thistle Way. Jane's the only person I can talk with about our sister Theresa.

Yes, there was another little Mitchell.

She was almost one year older than me. Her birthday was six days before mine, but our parents always made sure Theresa and I had our own birthday celebration, separate from one another. How I wish they hadn't, just once, just the year Theresa substituted a dream for a birthday wish.

I know stuff, secret stuff only our family knows, the kinda stuff you can't tell anybody cuz if Luca Zaldoni or the Mooney boys heard about it they'd laugh our whole family off the face of the earth.

Like the time I got a brand new finger paint kit for Christmas and Mom let me make a picture around the inside of the bath tub. I painted a real cute picture of a boat sailing on waves—with fish too. After my bath was over, I got in my pajamas, dumped all the finger paint jars back in their box and put the box under my bed, all except the jar of blue, which I could only find the cap for.

My little brother Charlie likes to crawl around a lot and we figure he must've been crawling in the bathroom the next day and found that jar of blue finger paint stuck behind the toilet or something. Charlie probably thought it was blueberry pudding, cuz he ate every last dang drop of paint in the jar. He didn't get sick or anything, which was good. But for two whole days Charlie woke up with bright blue poop in his diapers, which I'm positive the Zaldonis and Mooneys would keel over laughing about, if they knew.

The next secret of our family is about the pony rides. One Saturday morning two summers ago Mom and Dad took all of us to the pony rides on Brentwood Boulevard. That was the time our washing machine broke down and the repairman hadn't come yet and everybody was running out of clean clothes. Right before we left for the pony rides, I found Theresa rooting around in the drawer where I keep my underwear and undershirts and socks. She was stealing my last pair of clean underpants! I yanked them out of her greedy hands, stuck out my tongue at her, and put them on over the sorta clean underpants I was already wearing. Theresa started to cry, but she stutters so much Mom and Dad couldn't figure out what was wrong so they just crammed us all in the car and drove to the pony rides. When the pony ride man lifted Theresa up onto a horse, the hem of her skirt flew up and everybody in the whole wide world saw my sister's bare naked bottom! Mom let out a little cry. I won't even tell you what Dad said, but he reached out his arms for Theresa, got her off that horse, and plunked her back down on the ground. Quick as a wink, Mom passed Charlie over to Dad and waltzed Theresa back to the car. Jane and me were glad about it, I'll tell you that. Theresa sat in the car with Mom and cried the whole time Jane and me were enjoying our pony ride.

The third secret is that our Mom's the meanest mom in the whole world. Every single gol-dang school night last year she checked my spelling homework and made me do over all the words I got wrong. And when I ripped Jane's new white nightgown, Mom didn't fix the tear, she just handed me a needle and thread and said, "Make sure the stitches are small so they don't show on the good side." But the meanest thing about our Mom is that she used to poison us to death. I think any Mom who feeds her kids chicken livers fried in bacon fat with plain old white rice and boiled lima beans ought to be put in jail.

The last time Mom made her poison dinner was a while back. Jane pushed her plate away and said, "*Death at the Dinner Table*, a true crime story by Madeleine Mitchell." Mom cut Jane a look and Jane clammed up. Dad was holding his napkin over his mouth, trying to hide a big fat smile. Mom cut him a look and he clammed up, too. Mom stopped making her poison dinners a long time ago, and I'm happy to say they didn't kill any of us. That's because the only real poison-y part was the chicken livers, and each of us had figured out a way to trick Mom into thinking we'd eaten them (which we didn't).

It's Jane's job to answer the front hall telephone during dinner and politely say that none of the Mitchells can come to the phone right now, would the person please call back later. If the person can't call back, Jane's supposed to write down a message with the pencil and paper Mom keeps by the phone. On poison dinner nights, right before all the neighborhood bells rang, Jane used to tell her friend Lizzie to call our number four times between six o'clock and six-thirty. By the time Jane got done answering the telephone and pretending to take messages, dinner was over.

Theresa didn't get to answer the telephone, but she had a darn good way to get out of eating those chicken livers. It was sneaky, but I figured it out by watching her real close. Every time Theresa took a bite of liver, she'd take a quick swig of milk. I could see Theresa swallow the milk, but for a while I couldn't figure out why the milk glass never got drained down to the bottom. Then one night it hit me: Theresa was spitting chunks of liver into her milk glass! Wow, I didn't think she was that smart.

As for me, I am an expert gagger. Dad has what he calls "a low tolerance for gagging," so as soon as Mom would hand me my plate, I'd pop a chunk of liver in my mouth, hold my nose, chew twice, and start gagging. Bluh. Blugh. BLUGH! It worked like a charm. After the third gag, Dad would wad up his napkin, throw it down on the floor, and say, "Up to your room, little girl. You're going to bed without supper." I think that was Dad's way of getting me out of eating liver, cuz Dad hates liver, too.

Dad would get out of eating them by cutting off a greasy blob and then holding his fork low, down by his side, while he was telling Mom what a wonderful meal she'd prepared. Our dog, Penny, always plunked herself under Dad's chair at dinnertime. Penny just loved liver, so on poison dinner nights Penny got as much as she wanted.

Charlie had the best way of all. He took one look at the little cut-up bits of liver and lima beans Mom sprinkled on the tray of his high chair, held out his arm straight, and swiped the tray clean as a whistle—swoosh! Mom got all exasperated, but Penny was there snip-snap to clean up the mess on the floor, and Charlie's so cute nobody can stay mad at him for long. Pretty soon, Charlie was opening wide for spoonfuls of Gerber mashed bananas, which he loved.

Sheesh, who wouldn't love Gerber mashed bananas on Mom's poison dinner nights?

The biggest secret in our family was about Theresa.

First of all, the thing to remember is that Theresa stuttered. Bad. Which is why she almost never talked. It's also why she never played with the kids on Thistle Way, cuz most of the time when you play with kids, you've gotta talk, and Theresa didn't want to get laughed at. After school and on weekends and during summer vacations, Theresa hung around the house playing with her doll and helping Mom. The only kid Theresa would play with once in a while was Mary Lofton, cuz Mary's so nice she never laughed when Theresa stuttered (which was a lot).

Mom and Dad took Theresa to a kabillion doctors. They had a bunch of meetings with her teachers and her Brownie Scout troop leaders, too. They even took her to a lady in Maplewood who gave acting lessons to kids. Nothing worked. Theresa still stuttered like crazy.

The only thing that sorta worked was the morning when Mrs. Daily called mom and said she had an idea, could Mom send Theresa over for a while? It was October, two years ago in October. I remember cuz Theresa's and my birthdays were coming up. Mrs. Daily sat Theresa on the piano bench in the Daily's living room. Then Mrs. Daily sat down beside her and started playing "Happy Birthday."

"Sing along with me, dear," Mrs. Daily whispered.

Theresa sang the whole song without hardly stuttering at all! Me and Sally came running in from the breezeway to watch, cuz we'd never heard Theresa's voice make so many words in a row like that. It was something!

That afternoon, Mom said I should come up with a birthday present, even a small one, for my sister, cuz Theresa had already gotten me a present for my birthday. *Sheesh*. So I emptied my piggy bank, walked to Snyder's Five & Dime, and bought two Milky Way bars, one for me and one for Theresa's birthday present. When I got home, Mom said one candy bar wasn't enough of a present for Theresa but two of them might just do. She made me give her both of the candy bars, which I was sorta mad about. She said she'd put them away some place safe, so I wouldn't eat them before Theresa's birthday. I should've eaten my candy bar on the way home from Snyder's. What was I thinking?

The day before Theresa's birthday, she and Jane and me walked home from Immaculate Heart of Mary, like always. Mom made us a snack, like always, and told Jane to sit at the dining room table to do her homework. I was too little back then to have homework and Theresa didn't have any homework either. Mom doesn't like kids lollygagging around the house after school, so she told Theresa and me to push little Charlie twice around the circle in his baby buggy. I was starving to death for one of those Milky Way bars, but Mom had hid them pretty gol-darn good. I didn't have any allowance left to go to Snyder's with but I knew Theresa had two nickels in her Tinkerbell wallet, and her Tinkerbell wallet was right there, half sticking out of her jacket pocket.

"Hey, Theresa, wanna go up to Snyder's after we get done with Charlie's walk?"

"S-s-sure."

"Lend me a nickel, will ya?"

"S-s-s . . ."

Sha-zaam! All I had to do was push Charlie real fast around the circle a couple of times, drop him off at home, and drag Theresa up to Snyder's. I could practically taste that Milky Way bar.

One problem: Theresa kept stooping down right in front of the baby buggy, collecting acorns. Theresa was nutso on making little acorn-people.

"Let's go, Theresa! Lickety-split," I said, giving the buggy a shove. "Lickety-split, right Theresa?"

"L-l-li- li-lic . . . "

"Say it, Theresa!" I hollered. "C'mon, get up and say it lickety-split!"

"L-l-l . . ."

"Say it! Say it!"

Theresa stopped right in the middle of the street and sucked in her lips, trying to say lickety-split.

I tapped my foot a couple of times like my Mom does when she says we've just about used up her last ounce of patience. Then I yanked the buggy sideways, turned it around, and headed back home. I gotta say, Charlie looked a little startled.

Jane's class had just started to learn long division, and she was still at the table when I lugged Charlie inside and plopped him on the dining room rug. Jane loved reading class, especially reading for comprehension, but she hated arithmetic. Her homework paper was all smudged with eraser marks.

"Hey, Jane, guess what Theresa's trying to say—"

"Shut up, I'm busy."

"Lickety-split! Isn't that a riot and a half?"

"No. Lickety-split isn't funny," Jane said. Then she added, "But lickety-*spit* is!"

By the time Theresa wandered into the house with her pockets bulging with acorns, Jane and me were shouting "lickety *spit*" and laughing our heads off.

That night, Dad came up to our bedroom, like always, to read us a bedtime story. Dad always read four pages of a longer book. He'd been reading *The Wizard of Oz* for a while now and we were finally at the part when Dorothy clicks her magic shoes together three times and all of her wishes come true, and she and Toto get to go back to Kansas.

After that, Mom came up to hear our prayers, like always. Every night Jane says the Our Father and I say the Now I Lay Me Down to Sleep. Theresa got to pray the Hail Mary silently to herself. Mom always gives us a little religion talk before we start praying, and that night she told us her favorite prayer is Remembo-arry, something like that. She said if you pray it real hard, Mary way up in heaven hears you and maybe makes your prayers come true.

"Is it magic?" I asked.

"Not quite. Now go to sleep, girls."

Before I fell asleep, I heard Theresa trying to say the "m" in "magic."

The next morning, the morning of her birthday, Theresa told me about a dream she'd had. She was excited, so she stuttered lots more than usual, but I figured out what the heck she was saying. She'd dreamed that Mary Lofton had spit on her arm, and Theresa had clicked her heels together three times and licked the spit off. Then voila! Theresa could talk perfectly normal.

I told her it was just a dream. I told her licking somebody else's spit was the ickiest thing I ever heard of.

"Besides," I said, "it won't work. Don't do it."

Theresa just smiled and walked away.

A few minutes later, I saw her climbing over the crossed board fence, the one between our yard and the Lofton's.

On the day of her birthday, Theresa got the two candy bars from me and a little blanket from Jane for her Ginny doll. Grandpa Reinhardt gave her a card with dollar bills inside that added up to her age, plus one dollar to grow on. Grandma Reinhardt gave her a dotted Swiss party dress from Reinhardt & Krug. It was just our family for the birthday party cuz Theresa didn't have any good friends. Mary Lofton was pretty much Theresa's only friend, and not really that close of a friend, and besides, by then Mary was too sick to come over. Mom baked a coconut layer cake and stuck candles in it, but before we got to eat it, Dad told everybody to come out front a minute, so we all traipsed out to the drive-way. Dad opened the trunk of his car and pulled out a brand new two-wheel bike, and held the handle bars while Theresa tried sitting on it. She didn't go anywhere, though, which was probably a good idea, cuz the bike was kinda big and her feet didn't touch the ground. The best part of all was when Theresa blew out all the candles on her cake and sang "Happy Birthday" along with the rest of us. She didn't stutter once. She was so happy!

After the birthday party, Theresa got a fever. Mom and Dad just thought she had the flu. Dr. Welton came over and took a long time upstairs with Theresa. He said he thought it was the flu, too, but he told Mom to watch Theresa carefully. "Watch the rest of the children, too," he said, "and call me right away if anything changes." Mom and Dad moved Theresa into their bedroom so the rest of us wouldn't get the flu. Mom made Jell-O and Campbell's chicken soup, but Theresa didn't eat much and she didn't get better. By the next day, she had a bad headache, and by a couple of days after that, she couldn't even sit up in bed. Heck, she couldn't even pee. Dad came home from work and Dr. Welton came over again and then Mom and Dad hugged each other and talked in real low voices. I peeked in their bedroom and saw Theresa wasn't breathing too good. She was drooling, too. An ambulance came with the siren blaring and when it left for the hospital with Theresa and Mom inside, Dad followed right behind it. Dad backed his car down the driveway so fast the tires squealed and left black marks on the concrete.

Theresa didn't get better in the hospital. She didn't have the flu, either. She had polio.

Poliovirus.
Extremely contagious.
Compromises the nervous system.
Can affect the muscles required for breathing.
Can cause lifelong paralysis.
Can cause death.
Lives in an infected person's throat and intestines.
Invades the brain and spinal cord.
Spreads through contact with the feces of an infected person and through droplets from a sneeze or cough.
Can spread to others immediately before and one to two weeks after an infected person develops symptoms.
Of 100 people infected, four to eight experience flu-like symptoms that go away on their own.
Fewer than 1 in 100 will become paralyzed.
Among children paralyzed by polio, 1 in 100 will die.
Ninety-nine out of 100 children who get all the recommended doses of the polio vaccine are protected against infection.

That's from the US Department of Health and Human Services, Centers for Disease Control and Prevention. You can take it as gospel.

The first polio vaccine, pioneered by Dr. Jonas Salk, was licensed in

April of 1955, six months after our Theresa died. By then, polio had taken its full measure on Thistle Way. It sat Mary Lofton in a wheelchair and consigned her to leg braces for years thereafter. It squeezed the living breath from our Theresa. And then it moved on, to some other dear child in some other house on another lane in another city. A hundred houses in a hundred cities. More.

The disease struck Theresa so swiftly and ravaged her so brutally that we could hardly comprehend what had happened. On the day we laid her to rest, we functioned only marginally, crushed to the core. I don't know how my parents survived. Truly, I don't.

But I know how I did: I tried to block out all memory of Theresa. I reasoned that if she had never lived, then she had never died. As a coping mechanism, I quickly learned that avoidance is only marginally successful.

At the funeral parlor, everyone who knew and loved Theresa tried to piece together how she became infected with the virus. Was it that school field trip when she followed a sneezing classmate into the city's signature art museum, each child palming the massive doors, anxious to see the mummy in the great marbled foyer? Or the day Mom took us to the zoo in Forest Park and Theresa used the public lavatory and bent her little face to an outdoor drinking fountain? Or that afternoon at our grandfather's department store when she glided up a crowded escalator, running her fingers along the black rubber handrail and stayed for an ice cream sundae in the tea room? What invisible trace of evil doomed our Theresa? What did she touch for a fleeting instant that a hundred others had touched, with impunity?

All that afternoon, I was riddled with guilt. I kept thinking that if Theresa and I had shared a single birthday celebration, then it might have been six days later, on my birthday. By then everyone would have known that Mary Lofton was in the hospital and Mary Lofton was the only "Mary" that Theresa would have ever, ever asked to do something as improbable as spitting on her arm. Anyway, at the funeral home and for a few hours thereafter, I kept the secret. I told no one that Theresa had licked Mary's saliva, a child who was highly contagious with polio. I told no one that she did it because I happened to want a candy bar that day, and that I happened to think up a tongue-twisting phrase to tease her. Told no one that Jane and I happened to share a joke that day, for once, and teased our sister all over again. Told no one that our father happened to be reading *The Wizard of Oz* that night, that our mother happened to explain the *Memorare* that night, and that Theresa's sweet, vulnerable, hopeful mind had reassembled all those elements into a cure for her debilitating affliction.

Even as a child barely seven years old, I understood that breaking my silence about how we had fueled Theresa's dream—a dream that led to her death—would shred to tatters each broken heart in our family. So, in the hours of my sister's wake, I stood well back of her small white casket, and I kept the secret.

By late that afternoon, I couldn't stand it any longer. I walked next door and poured out the story to Mrs. Lofton and the Lieutenant. When at last I stopped sobbing and fell silent, Mrs. Lofton looked down at me, bewildered.

But Grace, she said, *that couldn't have happened. We took Mary to the hospital on the night before your sister's birthday, and she's been there ever since.*

I fairly melted with relief, so self-absorbed I barely noticed how haggard Mrs. Lofton looked, how pinched and drawn her rounded features had become. I realize now that when Theresa died, the Loftons must truly have feared for their own child's life. To my chagrin, I don't remember even asking them how Mary was doing. What I do remember, clearly, is that the Lieutenant lifted me up and carried me all the way to our front porch. Dad answered the door and the two men stood awkwardly on the stoop a while, heads low. They talked about baseball, the weather, the latest street repairs out on Brentwood Boulevard, how the grass had stopped growing for the season.

No bells rang at dinnertime that night. There was no need. In sober houses around the circle, the children of Thistle Way played quietly indoors with one another. Mothers hovered. Fathers kept watch.

When it was time to lower his flag, Lt. Lofton did so with military precision and then chimed his nautical bell, slow as a dirge. Ting . . . ting . . . ting . . . ting.

In twos and threes, neighbors drifted out to the street and stood in small clots under a sky fading from orange to violet. Stars hid and winked behind sheeting clouds.

Our family joined the Niesens, the Mooneys, the Henrys. Dad and Grandpa Reinhardt stood on either side of Mom, holding her. Jane and I laced our arms around one another. Mrs. Pearson stood behind me.

She cupped my cheek in her paper-dry palm, and when I turned to look up at her, she tucked a lemon drop into my hand. Grandma Reinhardt wrapped Charlie in a light blanket and clasped him to her. Around the circle, women hugged. Men dug their hands deep into their pockets and stared at the pavement. Other than an occasional breeze rustling in the canopy of oak leaves overhead, there was no sound, none at all, save for the silent echo of that slow ting-ting.

Then, across the way, the Zaldoni's kitchen screen door creaked open and slapped closed. Through a gap in the yards, we saw Mrs. Zaldoni walk down her driveway, and heard her solemnly tap a wood spoon on her pasta pot. The Warfield's porch lamp winked on, and a moment later Mrs. Warfield appeared in a pool of golden downlight. She held up her silvery triangle and plinked a series of high, sweet notes, keeping time with Mrs. Zaldoni's dirge-like backbeat.

In the gloaming, Mrs. Potter swayed her leather strap of jingle bells like a clock pendulum, and for once they did not sound merry, not merry at all. Mrs. Finnegan sang "Danny Boy" with tears in her eyes and, after she finished, Detective Greeley walked the circle, whistling a melancholy tune. Bullet loped along at his heel. The Dailys set up their hand bells on small tray-tables at the edge of the pavement, tugged on white cotton gloves, and rang "Lullaby and Good Night."

Odetta had come to us that morning, though it was not her day to clean. Without a word, with none spoken to her and none needed, she simply walked in and set to work straightening up the house and doing a mountain of laundry. In the afternoon she baked an apple pie, boiled corn on the cob, and mashed Idaho potatoes. She cut up a whole chicken, dipped the parts in milk, dredged them in flour, and fried them in a cast iron skillet. We had no appetite.

In the waning light, at the close of a grievous day, Odetta left the last of the dishes to dry on the rack, untied her apron, and walked toward the bus stop. On her way, she raised her rich, strong voice and gifted us with "Amazing Grace," an evensong to soothe the souls of Thistle Way.

When Jane and I went upstairs to our room, we saw that Odetta had been there, too. She had laid out our school uniforms at the foot of our beds, a signal that tomorrow we must somehow pick up and go on.

And she had set a small candle in an empty jelly jar and placed it on the table next to Theresa's bed. The window was open a crack, and the cool night air flickered the flame.

the Neighbors

the party

I live among people who are strangers to me. My home sits way back from the street, on a manicured lawn measured by the acre. Unlike the Thistle Way of my youth, Brindlecone Estates is a neighborhood in name only, for the neighbors do not seem to know one another enough to speak of. Not even to speak to.

My husband and I and our daughters moved out to Brindlecone Estates a year ago, and yet we still do not know the names of our next-door neighbors, not to mention the neighbors who live across the street. I see cars come and go, the BMWs and Mercedes SUVs, but I see little of the people who own them. I'm guessing they're professionals with demanding careers and arduous commutes, with killer schedules neatly plotted on iPads.

I presume that at least some of them have children, though I've seen no bikes or trikes, no inflatable swimming pools or chalk drawings in the street. I guess the kids growing up on Brindlecone are as schedule-bound as their parents without a moment in their day, their week, their year, their entire childhood for unsupervised outdoor play, as if catching tadpoles in a mayonnaise jar or building a fort out by the fence line would somehow imperil them.

It could be worse. I could have neighbors who park rusty sedans on cement blocks or who store ancient fishing boats in the front yard. I could live across the street from people who regard lawn mowing as a biennial chore. I could have neighbors whose tone-deaf son forms a garage band. Whose daughter sunbathes topless. Whose dog bays at the moon.

I could have neighbors who breed ferrets in outdoor cages, keep bees, sell term life insurance, leave Christmas lights up until Memorial Day, or leave trash cans out unto perpetuity.

I could have neighbors like the Blairs and the Eagans. In fact, long ago, I did.

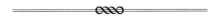

I told my pal Sally Daily at the beginning of the summer about my deal with Mom. I told her I'd save her house for last cuz I just knew it would be the best. Sally said she understood, and she didn't mind waiting.

Now, finally, it's my turn at the best house on Thistle Way!

"Bring your stuff over on Saturday," Sally says when I tell her I'm ready for my sleepover. "My mom and dad are having a cocktail party that night. Dad made a slideshow out of their vacation pictures; he and Mom invited all the neighbors over for cocktails and to see the show."

"Cool beans."

"We're having tons of good food too. Fondue, chipped beef rolls, shrimp cocktails, and little bitty wieners on toothpicks," she said. "You can help me pass the trays. It'll be fun."

Sally's the nicest girl in the whole world.

Mr. and Mrs. Daily got to go on a vacation to Europe last spring, all expenses paid. Dad said it was one of the perks of producing a television program on KMOX that won a big award. I asked him if the Dailys are rich, and Dad said, "Yes, but not in monetary terms," which I didn't quite get.

Finally, it's Saturday! I lug my suitcase over to the Dailys' house. I'm counting on this being the last time I have to haul that plaid suitcase around Thistle Way. It's getting kinda beat up, and I'm sick of packing and unpacking it.

Sally and her mom are spearing little squares of yellow cheese with toothpicks and sticking them onto the outside of a whole entire pineapple. Those cheese squares are sure making a neat-o spiral design. Sally and me get to eat all the cubes that break. We stick around to watch Sally's mom peel the shells off a bunch of cooked shrimp and cut the icky line of black stuff out of each one. Sally says that's the poo.

The kitchen's hot and it stinks like shrimp, so Sally and me go out to the living room. Mr. Daily's sorting through a big stack of phonograph records, picking the ones he wants to play during his slideshow.

"Grace," Mrs. Daily calls from the kitchen, "did your mother remind you to pack a good dress?"

"Yep. My good shoes and socks too. I'm all set, Mrs. Daily. I even took a bath before I came over."

Mr. Daily glances up from the stack of record albums. "That was thoughtful of you, Grace."

I hear Mrs. Daily chuckle.

Mr. Daily's got about a kabillion records. In fact, the whole Daily family is nuts-o about music. Mrs. Daily plays the piano really good. She can play with both hands at the same time, and her fingers never get jumbled up. Sally's kinda musical too. Not musical like Benny Herman's bugle playing, thank goodness. And not musical like Mrs. Haverkamp's torch song singing, very, very thank goodness. Sally just likes to play records. At the beginning of the summer, she started her own record collection, and it's gotten lots bigger already. Every Saturday, her father drives her to the Record Bar in Clayton, and Sally gets to pick out a new single. Pretty soon, her record collection's gonna be as good as her doll collection and her palomino horse collection. I wish I had a collection of something like dolls or palomino horse statues. All I've got is a bunch of baseball cards, and the Mooneys traded me out of all the good ones, which I didn't know were good ones at the time.

"How about this one, Dad?" Sally says. It's "Be-Bop-A-Lula."

"That's a good number, honey," Mr. Daily says, "but it's maybe too good. The music should never dominate the party, only set the mood. Here, girls, take a look at these."

He hands me and Sally a few album covers. I look at the one titled "A Pretty Girl Is Like a Melody."

"I know that one," I say, showing them the album. "My dad sings it to my mom all the time."

Mr. Daily winks at Sally and says, all whispery like it's a secret, "I'm going to put on the song that the band at the Casa Loma Ballroom was playing when your mother and I went out on our anniversary. Let's see if she remembers, okay?"

He looks through the big stack of records and picks out "Some

206

Enchanted Evening." Mrs. Daily comes right out from the kitchen, and they dance around the living room. They dance pretty darn good too, even though Mrs. Daily's got on rubber gloves that smell like shrimp.

At the bottom of the stack is a record with a funny name, "Begin the Beguine." Mr. Daily says all the guests will know that one. Then he puts on "Java Jive" by the Ink Spots, and we all do a crazy rock 'n' roll dance together.

After looking at the records, we help Mrs. Daily line up a bunch of glasses and liquor bottles on the dining room table and fill little bowls with maraschino cherries, stuffed olives, and teeny-tiny white onions. Next, Sally and me fill two wood bowls with mixed nuts and put them on the coffee table. Mrs. Daily tapes a sign at the start of their back hall, the one that goes to the bedrooms.

This Area Closed. Please Use Powder Room by the Front Door.

The first guests knock on the door at exactly five o'clock, and pretty soon, the house is jam-packed. Everybody got spiffed up for the occasion, that's for sure.

Mrs. Greeley's got on a polka-dot dress with spaghetti straps, and Detective Greeley doesn't even look like Detective Greeley cuz he's wearing a regular shirt and a skinny tie instead of his police uniform. Mrs. Pearson is prettier than I've ever seen her. She's got on a pink flowered dress with a wide collar and a sparkly brooch. She gives Sally a small dish filled with Hershey's Kisses.

"You and Grace take one each," she tells Sally, "and give the rest to your mother."

Somebody hands her a cocktail, but she just sits in a chair in the corner and holds the glass in her lap. Pretty soon I notice the paper napkin around the glass is all soggy, and after a while, I see she's sorta nodding off, but she looks happy.

Lots of people are standing in little groups, yakking about Governor Donnelly and Mayor Tucker and the Cardinals and stuff. Everybody looks like movie stars almost. Mrs. Haverkamp has on the sparkly red dress she wears to sing torch songs. I'm pretty sure that's her only good dress. Mrs. Lofton's got on a beautiful goldenish-colored dress with a really wide skirt made out of netting. The belt's black and wide and so tight that Mrs. Lofton's middle bubbles over the top of it. She takes a sip of Coca Cola and tells my mom she bought the dress right out of the window at Reinhardt & Krug. I hear her whisper to Mom that she's got on a new Jamaica-length girdle that melts away unwanted inches. Mom says she notices Mrs. Lofton's looking slimmer and has a new hairdo too, short and swept up with cute bangs. Mom tells Mrs. Lofton she looks just like Audrey Hepburn in *Sabrina*. Mrs. Lofton says that'll be the day, but I think she liked hearing what Mom said.

I pass around a plate of little wieners; over the noise of the crowd, I hear Mr. and Mrs. Niesen telling everybody they came to the party straight from the country club.

Mrs. Niesen's yellow sundress sure shows off her suntan. She tells Mrs. Warfield the dress is a Claire McCardell, which must be kinda bragging cuz Mrs. Warfield says, "Ooh."

Mr. Niesen's got on a pink shirt and pink seersucker slacks and penny loafers with no socks. He asks Mr. Daily if he knows how to make something called a stinger, and Mr. Daily says, "Why don't you show me?"

Mr. Daily puts the music from *South Pacific* on the record player. When "Some Enchanted Evening" comes on, I look to see if Mom and Dad can hear it cuz it's one of their favorite songs. My mom's the most beautiful lady at the party. She's tall and tan and not fat at all, except for a little pooch around the front of her waist. She's got real long legs and only a couple of gray hairs. She could've gone to my grandpa's department store and gotten a real expensive dress for free, but instead she sewed the dress she's wearing from a Butterick pattern and used pretty turquoise-colored silk she got at Welek's Fabrics. The dress is sleeveless and fits her snug but not tight.

"It's going to be a sheath dress," Mom told me when she was in the dining room last week, bent over the big table, pinning the tissue paper pattern to the pretty material.

A she-dress? Of course it's a she-dress; boys don't wear dresses.

Anyways, this morning, Mom went to the bank in Clayton and got her good pearls out of the safety-posit box. Mom picked out a new blazer and slacks for Dad at Grandpa Reinhardt's department store. Mom always says when she buys ready-made clothes, they're gonna come from the department store her grandfather started a kabillion years ago. Heck, maybe it was her great-grandfather. I'm not sure. Some old guy. Anyways, when Dad saw the Reinhardt & Krug packages, he grumbled about getting expensive clothes for free, but Mom gave him a look so he clammed up. Later, when he got dressed for the Dailys' party, I caught him staring in the mirror and smiling.

Right when I'm thinking if one more neighbor squeezes into the Dailys' front rooms, the house is gonna explode, the Blairs and the Eagans walk in, without even knocking. Mr. and Mrs. Blair moved into Melinda Potter's old house after Melinda's dad died in the flooded sewer. And Mr. and Mrs. Eagan moved into the Zaldonis' house after the Zaldonis disappeared one night with all their furniture.

Everybody stops talking and stares at the new neighbors. Mrs. Blair slips out of a long mink coat, which she must have been sweating to death in, and twirls around so all the other guests can admire her.

"Peacock blue and a dipping neckline," Mrs. Warfield whispers to herself. "Devastating!"

"Oh my," Mrs. Lofton says.

Mrs. Eagan's dress is black and lacey, and it looks like there's only just her skin underneath, which you could pretty much almost see through to.

"And clouds of perfume followed them into the room," Mr. Haverkamp says, staring into his cocktail glass.

Sally starts passing the shrimp cocktail again, and Mrs. Daily starts making more martinis and Mr. Daily puts a Johnny Mathis record on the record player, and people start talking again, all at the same time.

"Tom Collins for the ladies," Mr. Eagan calls over the heads of people, "and screwdrivers for Ted and me." Then he says real loud, like he's talking to the whole party, "Who doesn't like a good, stiff screw . . . driver!"

Mr. and Mrs. Blair just about split a gut laughing, but Davey Lofton's parents and some of the other guests kinda turn away. I don't exactly know what's so funny about a screwdriver, but something's not right. If Mr. and Mrs. Blair thought it such a funny thing to say, why aren't the Greeleys and the Loftons and the Walshes laughing too? Heck, it's like they're not even looking at the Blairs on purpose.

After that, the Blairs and the Eagans stick together, drinking their cocktails and watching Mr. Daily fiddle with his slide projector. Benny Herman's dad offers to take over at the bar, so Mrs. Daily can go around introducing the new people to everybody else. Sally and me follow her cuz it's easier to hand out cheese cubes and chipped beef rolls that way.

Mr. Blair rattles the ice in his glass at me, which I took to be a signal that he wants me to get him another cocktail. Mrs. Blair waves her empty glass in the air too. Mrs. Daily comes over with fresh drinks and tells Mrs. Blair that her dress is quite striking. Mrs. Blair says it's called a wiggle dress.

"This thing is so tight at the knees, you have to wiggle into and out of it," Mrs. Blair says. She's drunk two cocktails already, and she's kinda mushing her words together.

Missy Henry's mom jabs Missy's dad in the ribs cuz he's staring so hard. "Sorry, dear," she says. "Not your type. That's the kind of woman who wears a peignoir to bed. You're used to a woman who wears cold cream to bed."

Mr. Eagan looks at Mrs. Blair and says, real loud, "Give us a demonstration, Lou! Wiggle out of that dress!"

Right then, Mr. Daily scratches the needle all the way across a record album, and "Papa Loves Mambo" turns into a long, loud screech.

"Attention, everybody," Mr. Daily says. "The bar will be closed for the next thirty minutes. Find a seat wherever you can, and I'll start the slideshow."

The Blairs and the Eagans look kinda put out, but Mrs. Daily seems relieved.

Everybody scrambles to find seats, of which there aren't enough. Sally and me giggle when Mrs. Haverkamp has to sit on the carpet in her slinky dress. Mrs. Lofton takes a seat on the floor too, and her skirt poofs out around her like a golden mushroom. Mr. Daily adjusts the movie screen and tells the people in front that they'll have to move back a bit, which jams everybody up even more, but nobody seems to mind.

Mrs. Daily turns out the lights. Mr. Daily turns up the record machine, and we hear "The Happy Wanderer" and then a peppy version of "Rule, Britannia!" The slideshow goes to pictures of England, and Mr. Daily tells everybody about a clock called Big Ben and the queen's house, which is called Buckingham Palace. The next country is France, and there's a ka-billion pictures of the Eiffel Tower and the Archery Triumph and people drinking coffee at teeny-tiny tables on a sidewalk. There's three slides of Mrs. Daily in front of a bakery window and four slides of an artist drawing a picture of a river with a big church in the background. The music's changed to a lady singing a sad song in French.

Mrs. Pearson leans over and whispers, "It's Edith Piaf, the Sparrow." I think she must be wrong. It's a French lady, not a bird.

Next, the slideshow goes to Switzerland and the Alps mountains. Most people are watching, but Mr. Henry gets up and helps himself to another bottle of Budweiser from a cooler underneath the dining room table, and Mrs. Haverkamp gets up and stands in a corner, smoking and looking bored. Somebody else gets up to use the bathroom by the front door. Then there's lots and lots of slides of Rome and the Coliseum and the ancient Forum, which is mostly just broken buildings and lots of rocks. Now the song is "Three Coins in a Fountain."

Some more people get up to get fresh cocktails and little pieces of food which Mrs. Daily called "ordovers." It's getting dark outside, so we can see the slideshow even better. The pictures are in Portugal now, with lots of swirly ceramic tiles. When it gets to Madrid, I've kinda lost track of who's watching the show and who's walking around. And I have to pee.

Somebody's still hogging the powder room by the front door, so I go look for the other bathroom, the one back by the bedrooms. Mrs. Daily doesn't want the party guests back there, but I figure it's okay cuz I'm spending the night.

All the lights are turned off, so I feel my way along the short hall. The doors to the bedrooms and the bathroom are all closed, and I'm kinda mixed up about which is which. I open one door, but it's Mr. and Mrs. Daily's bedroom. Another door leads to Sally's bedroom. One of these dang doors has to be the bathroom! I open another door and peek inside. It's the guest bedroom, but it's not empty like it should be. The Blairs and the Eagans are in there.

The Blairs and the Eagans are flopping around on the twin beds in the Dailys' guest room!

It's a rule of mine to never stare at the neighbors when they're on other people's beds, but tonight, I stare anyways.

Mrs. Blair is wiggling around in her stupid wiggle dress. Mr. Eagan's shirt is all untucked. Besides, Mrs. Blair is flopping around on one of the twin beds with Mr. Eagan—not her husband! And Mrs. Eagan is flopping around on the other bed with Mr. Blair, which is backwards. And they're all moaning, "Ahh, ahh."

Holy cow, they're all starting to take off more of their clothes! If this was a TV show, Mom'd make me turn it off, I'll tell you that.

After a minute or two, I close the door as quietly as I can.

I think I'm gonna throw up.

The slideshow is still in Spain. I hear Missy Henry's dad shout, "Olé! Olé!"

All I want to do is go home and curl up in my own bed. I'll think of something to tell Sally tomorrow, but for now, I just want to get out of here.

I let myself out the back door and cut through the yards, running like the blazes for home. I'm crying really hard, so hard that I trip on the bricks that outline Mrs. Dietrich's iris garden. I fall down hard, and both my scabs from last week scrape off. Now my knees are all stingy and bleedy, and there's grass stains on my good church dress and something else bad too: when I was in Sally Daily's hall peeking into the guest bedroom, I kinda wet my pants, which I haven't done since last Halloween when Rainer talked me into going through the Clayton High haunted house with him.

Back at home, I crawl into the hall closet under the stairs. Jane's up in our room, changing Charlie's diaper. After that, she'll put him in a clean undershirt and rock him to sleep. After that, she'll go watch TV. Then I'll sneak upstairs. She won't even know I'm back.

My plan works like a charm.

The hall closet is dark and stuffy. Also, it smells like dust. That's because Odetta stores our brooms and the big vacuum cleaner in here. There's no chair or anything, so I turn the mop bucket upside down and sit on that. I'm kinda enswarmed by old winter coats and scarves and boots, which Mom stores in here and which don't smell too good either. I wish Jane would hurry up and get out of our bedroom. My knees are stinging, and my underpants are sticking to me. Also, they kinda smell. I don't feel like throwing up anymore, but I sure feel like crying.

I start to think about what the new neighbors were doing, but I'm pretty sure Sister Josephina would tell me it's a venial sin to think about that on purpose, so I start on the alphabet and think of something to eat that begins with each letter.

Let's see. A is for apple pie. B is for deep butter coffee cake from the Lake Forest Bakery. That's a B, right? Bakery?

Jane finally comes down and turns the TV on. I sneak upstairs and get ready for bed, still going through the alphabet.

I'm all the way to X, which is giving me trouble cuz I don't think you can eat X-rays, when I hear the front door open, which means Mom and Dad are home. I'm in bed with my nightgown on and my knees bandaged and even my teeth brushed. It's hotter than all get-out tonight, but I have the covers all the way up to my chin anyways.

"There you are," Mom sighs. She peels off the covers except the top sheet. Then she sits on the edge of the bed and waits for me to tell her why I left. I hear an ambulance siren outside, somewhere far away. It's the only noise in the whole world.

"Sally's confused, Grace," Mom says. "Don't you think you owe all of us an explanation?"

I feel bad about hurting Sally's feelings, but I can't tell anybody why I snuck out. First of all, I don't want to say in words what I saw. Second of all, if I tell Mom, then she'll tell Dad, and then Mom and Dad will tell Mr. and Mrs. Daily. And maybe the Dailys will yell at the Blairs and the Eagans, and before long, everybody on Thistle Way will know the horrible thing that happened at Sally's house, and nobody will want to go there ever again or be friends with the Dailys. If that happens, Sally will feel a whole lot worse than she does now.

"I got a stomachache. I was gonna throw up." I cross my fingers so it doesn't count as a lie. "I didn't want to throw up all over the cocktail party, so I just came home."

I gag a couple of times for good measure. I'm a good gagger.

Mom crinkles her eyebrows and lays a hand across my forehead. "Honey, how much did you eat at the party?"

"Not much," I say, curling up in Mom's lap. Boy oh boy, do I want to suck my thumb right now, but I'm too big.

Mom's buying the throw-up excuse. I can tell. She eases me off her lap and shoots me her out-with-it-Grace look. "What did you eat, Grace?"

I do a pretty good double gag and then gulp hard. "Five cocktail wieners, nine Hershey's Kisses . . . "

"And?"

"And eleven and a half shrimps."

Over the years, I've had neighbors whom I would gladly give back to the dogs. But I would not then, in that summer of 1956, and I would not now, in the full of my life, swap my family for someone else's. Not for all the tea in China.

I am still almost reverential about those Dailys, though. Mr. Daily was an imaginative, energetic, and involved father. Mrs. Daily was an exemplary mother, a vivacious wife, and a model homemaker who managed a part-time job in an era when women who did not need to work outside the home for financial reasons felt little desire or social pressure to do so. And Sally was a doll (no pun intended), the rare childhood friend who was bestowed with abundance and thought nothing of sharing all she had.

At the beginning of my summertime travels, I fully expected to wind up a permanent member of the Daily household. I regarded Sally and her parents as the ideal family, their house the perfect environment in which to relocate myself for ultimate happiness. I had been gravitating away from that opinion as the summer wore on, and I knew it for sure on the night of the Dailys' party. Not because the Dailys themselves were besmirched by the clandestine goings-on behind their backs (although in my mind, their guest bedroom sure was). But because when I crawled into my own bed that night, when I glanced over at Charlie sleeping like a lamb in his crib, smelled the lingering scent of sugar cookies Jane had baked earlier that night, and heard my mother and father's footsteps on the front stoop, which was a sound as familiar to me as my own heartbeat, I knew that the perfect family for me was my own.

As for those Blairs and the Eagans, the less said, the better.

Odetta

the heat

By happenstance, our cleaning lady had the given name of a woman whom *The New York Times* described posthumously as the "imperious queen of African-American music."

Odetta.

Unlike the famous Odetta Holmes, Odetta Jones did not study the operatic voice and was not invited to join the national touring company of a Broadway show. Our Odetta did not perform at swanky nightclubs in New York City and San Francisco, she did not appear on television with Harry Belafonte, and she did not thrill Carnegie Hall audiences who paid top dollar to hear a black woman's soulful songs bearing witness to generations of heartache in the Deep South.

Odetta Jones did not expect roses and applause when she sang, and she did not get them. How could she? Odetta Jones belted out "The Battle Hymn of the Republic" kneeling on our bathroom floor, scrubbing away a week's worth of grime, her old bristle brush swishing like a metronome. Our Odetta sang "Amazing Grace" standing on her tiptoes, vinegar rag in hand, wiping dust from four dozen delicate crystal spears that dangled below our dining room chandelier. Our Odetta hummed "The House of the Rising Sun" through drifts of steam rising off her late afternoon ironing board, hummed so mournfully that you would swear she had given up her purity in just such a place. Whether that was so, I'll never know, for I knew nothing of houses that were "the ruin of many a poor girl" during that clammy summer of 1956.

Odetta Jones was long on natural-born talent and short on God-given patience. So although Jane and I and our pals were often within earshot of her soul-stirring music, we knew to steer clear of whatever room she was singing in while cleaning.

Odetta was a man-sized woman, thick through the middle and haunchy. Her teeth were flashing white bricks behind lips painted an unholy shade of scarlet. She kept a flyswatter within reach at all times and wielded it with stunning speed and deadeye accuracy, scattering me and my sister and our pals like swished-at gnats on the few times we were fool enough to wander into her breathing space.

It is, in hindsight, incalculable how much we owe to Odetta Jones.

Summer vacation's almost over, which is good cuz it's boring, boring, BORING!

Odetta's here to clean again. Every other week, Odetta takes a bus from where she lives—which I've never been to—to the bus stop in front of Snyder's Five & Dime. She and the Niesens' maid walk to Thistle Way from there.

Odetta never knocks. She just comes right in the kitchen door. She used to not even say hello or anything, but lately she's been asking Mom, "Mizz Mitchell, how we doin' today?" right away. That's how Odetta talks, in a real deep voice, which I would like if the rest of Odetta wasn't so darn scary.

Mom always says "fine" even if she isn't so fine, which she hasn't been lately. Dad's been making us breakfast, and Grandma Reinhardt keeps coming over with dinners boxed up at Topping Ridge Country Club. Grandma keeps telling Mom she looks peaked, and each time she says that, Jane gets all worried looking. I asked Jane what peaked means, but she just told me to stop being such a baby and grow up.

Anyways, Odetta and Mom always stand in the kitchen for a few minutes, leaning against the counter and drinking coffee and talking. Mom always asks how Odetta's boy is getting along, and Odetta always says, "He's a might better now." Then Mom says, "Please let him know I asked after him," and Odetta says, "Melvin will take kindly to that." Then Odetta takes her big carpetbag purse into the powder room and changes into her uniform.

The Niesens are the only other family on Thistle Way that's got a maid besides us, and Odetta's got a plainer uniform than Rainer's maid. Mrs. Niesen bought the uniform for her maid; it's black and shiny and it's got a collar made out of lace. Dad says the Niesens put on airs, which is another thing I don't quite get cuz how can anybody wear air. Hey, I'm a poet and I don't even know it!

Anyways, Odetta's uniform is pale-ish blue with a white collar and cuffs. She must starch that uniform to smithereens cuz no matter how many times I see her kneel down, stand up, and stoop over, it never gets wrinkled. Also it kinda crackles when she walks. Her shoes are brown and clunky, and on the side of each shoe, she cut a little round opening. I asked her about that once.

"Them?" she said. "Them's bunion contentment holes."

I know what bunions are. Grandma Reinhardt told me. Odetta's bunions are bigger than Grandma's, though. Heck, Odetta's bunions are bigger than onions. Hey, now I'm a two-time poet for "wear air" and for "bunion onion." That kinda makes me smile. But if I say anything, I'll get a swat for sure.

We've had Odetta for ages. Jane told me that when I was born, Grandpa Reinhardt told Grandma Reinhardt to find out from her lady friends at Topping Ridge Country Club if they knew of a maid that needed work. Jane told me that when Grandma heard about a woman named Odetta who was a hard worker and who needed extra money cuz her little boy got polio and has to go through life in a wheelchair, Grandpa said, "Get the woman over there. I'll pay the bills."

My dad isn't too happy about Grandpa paying for Odetta, but Mom says Odetta's a blessing.

Anyways, a long time ago, I asked Odetta why maids wear uniforms. I had to stand on the far side of the dining room table cuz a kid can never get in Odetta's breathing space.

"Cain't wear street clothes to do cleanin' in," she answered.

"Why not?"

Odetta glanced over each of her shoulders to see if anybody else was near enough to hear, but they weren't.

"Why not?" I asked again.

"You a big whop of a nuisance, chile," she said, folding her arms across her chest. She puffed out her lower lip till I could see the pink inside, and said, "White ladies make their maids wear a uniform so nobody'll confuse us with company, I reckon. What they don't know is we don't mind wearin' a uniform, don't mind at all."

"Why?"

"Chile, no colored maid wants to go home with white people's dirt on they clothes. Don't y'all know that?"

"Why?"

That's when Odetta picked up her flyswatter and chased me around the dining room table. Zing! Man oh man, that fly swatter left a red mark on the back of my leg that lasted till lunchtime.

The first thing Odetta does after her cup of coffee with Mom is fill a 7-Up bottle with water and put a little sprinkling cap on the top. Then she takes each piece of clean laundry out of the big wicker basket and sprinkles them good. Then she rolls up each piece like you roll a towel when you're going swimming, which we still can't do cuz of dumb old polio. Anyways, Odetta says clothes need most of the day to relax their wrinkles, which I don't get cuz how can wrinkles be nervous?

Odetta has a particular way of cleaning. She scours the upstairs bathroom first and the downstairs powder room next and then for the rest of the day, she kinda smells like Bab-O. After we finish lunch, Odetta gets to eat her lunch. Mom always gives Odetta leftovers from last night's dinner warmed up in the oven. Sometimes, it's dumb old hash. Other times, it's a chicken leg and mashed potatoes or ham and baked beans. Odetta always says, "Thank you, Mizz Mitchell, that was real tasty."

Once I asked Mom why she always gives Odetta our leftovers.

"Odetta appreciates a good, solid meal at lunchtime," she said. I'm not so sure that's true. I think Mom just wants to get rid of the leftovers.

Lately, Mom's been going upstairs after lunch and taking a nap with Charlie, which is good cuz now I don't have to sneak when I run off to the Dailys' house to play dolls with Sally. While Mom's conked out, Odetta vacuums and dusts the downstairs and mops the kitchen floor.

Sometimes, Mom puts out the gravy boat and a couple of trays along with the bottle of silver polish, which is a signal she wants Odetta to do that too. Odetta clomps around the kitchen extra hard, but she never says no. Once, Mom asked Odetta to wash the insides of the windows with vinegar water and dry them with crumpled up newspapers. That was the day that Jane had Lizzie over and I had Davey Lofton over, and Odetta was so gol-durn feisty that all four of us got swatted.

When Davey got home, his mom noticed the red mark on his leg, and she called Mom. Mom said, "I'm so sorry. It won't happen again," but she never yelled at Odetta. I think Mom's a little afraid of Odetta, which is exactly how Jane and me are, I'll tell you that.

In the late afternoon, Odetta puts up the ironing board in the dining room, right by the bay window, and for the next hour, the only sound in the house is the hiss and thud of Odetta's iron. One time, Odetta told me she likes to iron by the window so she can listen to the sun.

"The sun doesn't talk," I said.

Odetta bent to plug the cord into a wall socket. "It do, too. That sunball talk to me jes' about every afternoon."

I wanted to know what the sun says, but asking Odetta too many questions is risky. I took a deep breath and got ready to bolt. Then I piped up and asked, "What does the sun say?"

For once, Odetta acted like she was really considering one of my questions. She started on one of Charlie's baby pants and ran the iron along the straps. Steam rose up and stuck to her forehead, and she started to sing.

I don't mind workin', Captain, from sun to sun.
But I want my money, Captain, when payday come.

When she finished ironing Charlie's little things, she looked sideways at me, surprised I was still there. She reached into the basket for a rolled-up blouse. "The sun say goodbye."

I must've gotten one of my google-eyed looks, cuz Odetta laughed so hard I could see all the way to the way back of her mouth.

"You listen real hard, girl," Odetta told me. "Every day about this time, you gonna hear that ole sunball say, 'So long, St. Louie. See ya tomorrow, bright an' early!'"

I was still sitting by the dining room window waiting for the sun to say something when Dad got home from work and asked what the heck I was doing. When I told him, Dad said Odetta was pulling my leg.

Then I was even more confused. Odetta swats, but she's never yanked my leg.

Anyways, Odetta's got a system for ironing. First, she does Charlie's little sun suits. Then she does all the shorts, then the pants and skirts and blouses, and Dad's white shirts last of all. She shakes out each shirt and gives it a look over to make sure the sprinkling got all the wrinkles good and relaxed. Then she lays the shirt on the ironing board and glides the hot iron across all the parts. At the end, she slides it onto a hanger.

One day last spring, Dad got home from work early. Odetta was still ironing, and Mom was gathering up Dad's winter sports jackets and suits to take to the dry cleaners. Dad uses the little closet in our upstairs hall cuz Mom's clothes take up their whole bedroom closet. All of a sudden, Mom hollered, "Paul!"

Dad and me came running cuz ordinarily Mom doesn't holler at Dad. When we got to the closet, Mom shoved one of his white shirts at him and poked him in the chest with her pointing finger.

Holy cow, Mom looks furious.

"What's this?" Mom said. Her voice was all hushed, and she was staring squinty-eyed at Dad.

"Madeleine . . . Maddy, honey . . . I have no idea what you're talking about."

"Mister, you'd better have a good explanation."

Dad looked stumped. "Explanation for what? What's wrong, Maddy?"

"Just you look at this shirt."

Mom folded her arms tight across her chest and tap-tapped her foot. Dad uncrumpled the shirt and held it out in front of him. On the collar was a bright reddish stain in the shape of lips. Mom started rifling through the rest of the shirts, throwing each one out of the closet. Pretty soon, Dad was standing in the middle of a bunch of shirts with wire hangers poking out.

Every shirt had a lipstick stain on the collar.

Dad backed away. "Maddy, I have no idea how that got there!"

Mom picked up one of Dad's wingtip shoes and threw it at him. The heel conked Dad on the forehead, which Mom didn't see cuz by then, she was storming into their bedroom and slamming the door so hard that the picture of the Blessed Virgin Mary out in the hall went all crooked.

Then everything went to H-E-double-L in a hand basket, as Grandma Reinhardt would say.

Charlie started bawling to beat the band. Jane smacked a record on her new record player and cranked up the volume so that Elvis was belting out "Don't Be Cruel." Downstairs, Odetta slapped the old ironing board together and shoved it in the closet under the stairs and started up one of her heartache songs.

Don't let the sun catch you lying,
Lying at my front door.
Mama's gonna tell you something,
Baby, you made her sore.

It was hard to think with all that racket going on, but I was sure Dad wouldn't let anybody but Mom kiss him on the shirt collar, which I never saw Mom do. Heck, I've only seen my mom wear lipstick about six times, and it's never as red as the lipstick on those shirts, I'll tell you that.

That was last spring. Dad brought home a bouquet of daffodils, but Mom stayed mad at him for two whole days. She didn't even talk at dinner except to ask for salt.

The next time Odetta came to clean again it was the Thursday before Easter, and Easter was also April Fool's Day. Mom always lays out Jane's and my church clothes at the foot of our beds on the night before Easter so that we wake up and know exactly what to wear. But last Easter, Mom laid out a bunch of old cleaning rags instead of our church clothes. When I woke up, I got a feeling like there were worms in my stomach just by thinking that I'd have to wear old rags to Easter Sunday church. I woke up Jane, and she told me I was a dope. She said those rags were just Mom's April Fool's Day trick on us, which I didn't think was such a funny trick.

Anyways, on the cleaning day before Easter, Odetta scrubbed and vacuumed and mopped, like always. Late in the afternoon, she put up the ironing board in the dining room, like always. I crouched underneath the dining room table. I was pretending to play hide and seek with Charlie, but I was really waiting to hear the sun say goodbye to Odetta. Every so often, I peeked out from under the tablecloth, and that's when I figured out the lipstick problem.

Before Odetta starts the ironing, she takes her "personal rejuvenation break." Most times, she sits in the kitchen or on the patio and flips through one of her movie magazines. But that day last spring, right before Easter Sunday, she went into the little bathroom by the back door and when she came out, she looked different, somewhat beautified. I must've stared at her pretty hard cuz she told me that she'd gone shopping at Kresge's and bought a tube of Hazel Bishop lipstick.

"Saleslady said it's new formula. Extra long lastin'," Odetta said. "Now git, 'afore I swat y'all good."

Odetta started her ironing, and I went back to hiding under the dining room table, which was sorta goofy cuz Charlie had stopped playing hide-and-seek and crawled into the kitchen looking for Cheerios on the floor. Anyways, I noticed that each time Odetta finished one of Dad's shirts and lifted it up, she held the collar between her lips while she slid a hanger up the shirt from the bottom. That's how the lipstick stains got on Dad's collars! Odetta didn't even notice; she just hung the hanger over the dining room curtain rod and went right on to the next shirt.

When I told Mom and Dad, we all had a good laugh. Mom said she'd have a word with Odetta, and Dad said "No, honey, I'll do it," and then they got all lovey-dovey and went into their bedroom and closed the door behind them, real soft.

After that, Dad's shirts didn't have lipstick on them anymore. Which is good, cuz Mom and Dad are getting along swell again. Better than swell. Jane told me she saw them making moony eyes at each other. I don't know what that means, but it sounds good.

For most of the summer, Mom hasn't been feeling too perky. Jane and me are worried she's coming down with polio. First of all, Mom's taking naps, which she hasn't done since before Charlie was born. And second of all, Grandma Reinhardt keeps saying, "Madeleine, I know a thing or two about this, so sit down and get off your feet." And third of all, Dad's doing a gol-darn lot of the cooking these days, which isn't as tasty as Mom's cooking, I'll tell you that.

If you ask me, Mom would feel better if she lost a little weight. She's getting kinda chunky through the middle.

Anyways, Dad went to Sears and bought two fans for the downstairs and a window air conditioner for his and Mom's bedroom. He says the bedroom door has to stay closed so all the cold air doesn't get out. August has been so hot that last week, Dad moved Charlie's crib into the their room with the air conditioning, and yesterday, Mom told Jane and me to bring our sleeping bags and pillows in there too.

I just love sleeping in Mom and Dad's room. It's kinda like having a slumber party with everybody you love. Besides, Dad cranks the air conditioner up so much that we all need blankets, except Mom. She says she's cool as a cucumber with just a sheet over her.

Odetta's singing while she wipes down the baseboards. She's already sung "Jack o' Diamonds" and "Muleskinner Blues." Now she's singing "Shame and Scandal." I like that one the best, even though Odetta says it's sad.

Woe, misery
Shame and scandal in the family
Woe, misery

I'm bored. Watching Odetta's no fun. Summer's almost over, there's nothing good to do, I've stayed over at just about every house on Thistle Way, and I'm worrying about fourth grade. First of all, I'm gonna miss Sister Josephina like crazy. And second of all, when I ask Jane about fourth grade, she says it's lots harder than third.

"In fourth grade, you have to write with pens, not pencils," she says, "and you have to do big, long theme papers for homework."

I start to cry, and Jane puts her arm around my shoulder, which she almost never does, and tells me Sister Patrick Louise is okay.

"Every Friday afternoon, she gives you a spelling bee with funny words she makes up," Jane says, "and she gives out a Pez each time a kid spells a word right."

"That sounds good."

"It's really fun. Once, I got the word plinkadoodle. I asked Sister Patrick Louise for the definition, and she said it's a poodle that plinks instead of barks!"

Jane and me have a good laugh about that. I'm starting to feel better already.

"Yeah, and once, Mike Mooney got the word fartsenshar."

"What!"

"Sister Patrick Louise said it's a chair with a hole in the seat to let the gas out!"

Jane and me just about die laughing. Odetta stops ironing and smiles at us, which kinda has me worried again cuz Odetta's never smiled at us before.

"Jane, let's go in the dining room and play Monopoly. Odetta's ironing, so the big fan's going full blast in there."

"All the Monopoly money's gonna blow around," Jane says.

"Nah. We can stick the money halfway under the board."

"Mom got a whole bag of those big brown potatoes from the Vegetable Man. We can put a potato on top of each deed card."

"He's not the Vegetable Man. His name is Dezso and he's Lovari."

Mom and Charlie are taking an extra long nap today. Heck, if I was them, I'd stay asleep forever cuz they're in the air-conditioned bedroom. Charlie's probably cool as a gol-dang cucumber.

Odetta's got the fan on full blast, but it's just blowing around the smelting hot air. Every time she thumps the iron down, she gets a blast of steam in her face. Her pretty blue uniform's all dark and wet under her arms and down the middle of her back. Sweat's trickling down from her hair too. It must be getting in her eyes cuz she's squinting and blinking a lot, and the white part of her eyes is all red and veiny-ish.

Jane's buying her first house when Odetta smacks down the iron especially hard. She digs in the wicker basket and takes out one of Dad's big white handkerchiefs. Jane and me stop playing and watch to see what Odetta's gonna do. She twirls the handkerchief till it looks like a fat rope and ties it around her forehead, and then she bends down so her face is right in front of the fan. A couple of drops of Odetta's sweat blow onto the Monopoly board, but Jane and me just shrug our shoulders up and down. We've kinda stopped playing cuz it's too gol-durn hot to worry about whether we can afford Park Place or collect all four railroads. For the next few minutes, we just take turns shaking the dice and tossing them on the board.

Odetta gets finished cooling off her sweat and goes into the kitchen, which she usually doesn't do in the middle of ironing. She must've seen that huge sack of potatoes and figured Mom's planning on having potatoes for dinner, and by now, she must be figuring Mom isn't gonna get up from her nap in time to get potatoes cooked all the way through. Jane and me stand at the door to the kitchen and watch to see what Odetta's gonna do. First, she turns on the oven. Then she rinses off six big potatoes, pricks them with a fork, and sticks them in the oven.

"Great," Jane says, "now the house is gonna get even hotter."

Odetta's done in the kitchen for now. After she starts ironing again, me and Jane go sit at the dining room table again. Jane crosses her arms and lays her head down on the table. I throw the dice a couple more times and snap up Ventnor Avenue and the Waterworks for free. I think Jane's corked off cuz she doesn't yell at me for cheating. She doesn't even lift her head up when the fourth stair step creaks.

The third and fourth steps from the bottom of our stairway always creak when somebody is going up or down. Lots of times I don't even notice the creaking cuz it's just one of the regular sounds of our house, like the slapping sound our Venetian blinds make when you pull the cord real fast. And like the sound of the upstairs toilet running and the sound the washing machine makes when Mom stuffs it with too many towels. Ka-thunk ka-thunk put-put-put . . . sigh.

There's a big opening between the front hall and the dining room, but you can't see the stairs when you're in the dining room cuz they're a little ways off to one side of the front hall. I figure that creaking noise means Mom's finally coming down to start dinner. I check my Cinderella wristwatch. Holy cow, Mom and Charlie slept a long time! It's almost five o'clock.

I know I heard that fourth step creak. Odetta must've heard it too. But the third step still hasn't creaked. Mom must've stopped. Why would she do that?

Odetta puts down her iron. I stop shaking the dice. A big hairy fly with a bluish-greenish belly zooms around the chandelier and lands on one of the bay window panes. Odetta takes her fly swatter and holds it real still, right behind the fly.

Smack! That fly is history.

"Hurray!" I shout.

I'm thinking Odetta's gonna get a scrap of newspaper from the kitchen to wipe the fly guts off the window, but she doesn't. She does something I would've never expected: she turns off the fan.

Now it's really, really quiet. It's so quiet, I can still sorta hear the fan going even though it's off. There's no steam hissing out of the holes in the iron. No crows caw-cawing outside either. Cicadas should be whee-wh-eeing, but they're not. Out in the big old oak trees, squirrels should be chattering. Birds should be tweeting too. Come to think of it, why hasn't Mrs. Pearson clanged her school bell? Why hasn't Lt. Lofton rung his ship's bell?

And how come there's no lawn mowers put-putting outside? Somebody's dad is always mowing their lawn right before dinnertime, but not tonight.

I listen for the icebox motor, but it isn't even humming.

Our upstairs toilet has been making a trickling sound all week, but it isn't making a sound.

And by now, that third step from the bottom should be creaking.

Everything feels strange all of a sudden, like the air is prickling my skin.

Mom should be down the stairs by now, in the dining room seeing how much ironing Odetta has left to do, and saying, "Girls, put the game away. Jane, come help me peel some potatoes. Grace, set the table."

I toss the dice, and they bonk Jane's hotel off Connecticut Avenue. The clacketing sound is as loud as the time I threw pennies in the clothes washer. Odetta cuts me a look. I take it to mean "if-y'all-throw-those-dice-again-I'm-gonna-kill-y'all." She stands up real straight and turns her head, listening for the third step. I stand up and listen too.

Nothing.

Odetta walks around to the front of the ironing board. "Mizz Mitchell," she says, "you all right out there?"

"I, uh . . . "

It's Mom. Her voice is so wispy, it barely sounds like Mom.

Everything gets chopped up into parts, and each part takes scads longer than it should.

I stand up. The chair tips over behind me. My heart's racing, and there's a loud noise whee-wheeing in my ears, like the sound when I rollerskate on the driveway.

Odetta starts to run to the front hall. She stumbles over the cord to the iron. The iron clunks to the floor, but she doesn't even stop to pick it up, she just keeps running.

I'm right behind Odetta. My feet are as heavy as bricks. I glug down a big gulp of air, but it feels all pasty.

I hear Mom sigh. No. More like a long breath that stops fast. Like "ugh." Like yesterday when Mom was lugging heavy grocery bags from the car to the kitchen, and the grocery boy packed them way too full of cans, and Mom pulled a bag out of the trunk and put it down right on the driveway and said, "Ugh." That's the sound.

Odetta spins around the corner of the opening. I'm one step behind. Finally, I see Mom! She's pale and trembling and hanging onto the banister.

Her knees buckle. She loses her grip. Starts to sink.

Mom's gonna faint, and I can't get there in time. Mom's gonna fall. She's gonna fall from the fourth step and land flat on her face!

I open my mouth to scream. No sound. My throat's all strangly closed.

Odetta plants her feet at the bottom of the stairs. She leans toward Mom and stretches out her arms.

Mom falls. Her arms flap like she's trying to grab hold of the air. Her knees bend more. Her feet are behind her now, and her shoes are barely touching the stair steps. Her mouth is loose and open. Her eyes are scrunched shut.

Odetta moves up. Now she's got one foot on the floor and the other foot on the first step. She leans way up toward Mom, and catches her! Mom's head flops over Odetta's shoulder.

I let out a huge whoosh of air. My insides go all saggy. I plop down and sit cross-legged on the front hall rug.

Odetta picks up Mom like she's as light as one of Sally Daily's dolls. She carries her all the way upstairs and lays Mom down on the bed in the big bedroom. I'm right behind.

"Don't worry," Mom says in a woozy voice. "I don't want to be a bother."

Odetta is worrying. I can tell. She's looking at the air conditioner and scowling something awful.

Man oh man, it sure is hot and stuffy in here.

Charlie's standing in his crib and bawling his eyes out cuz he's hot and his diapers are all wet and smelly and everybody's ignoring him. Jane comes running in to Mom and Dad's bedroom now, asking a kabillion times what happened. I lift Charlie out of his crib and dump him on Jane so they'll both shut up. Then I sit on the edge of Mama's bed and pat her hand while Odetta telephones Dad at work.

"She'll be fine, Mr. Mitchell. Jes got up offa that bed too fast, I reckon. Forehead felt hot, though. That new air conditioner of yours must be on the fritz."

As soon as Dad gets home, he calls Dr. Welton. He's our family doctor. Dr. Welton lives in a big house in Warwick Knoll, right behind the Niesens, so he just comes out his back door, cuts through the backyards, and walks right into our house.

Dr. Welton's got silverish hair and pale blue eyes that crinkle at the edges when he smiles. His breath always smells minty, which I like. One time when Mom suspected my rash was something more than a rash, something like measles or chicken pox, she called Dr. Welton's office, and on his way home, he came by to check on me. He snapped open his black case and took out some shiny doctor instruments that looked scary, but when he looked in my ears and nose and throat, it didn't hurt at all. Afterward, he gave me a cherry sucker with one of those looped handles.

"No, Paul," Dr. Welton tells Dad, "your air conditioner's not on the fritz. While I was examining her, Maddy told me she turns it off during the day to save electricity."

"What?!"

"You know as well as I do that she shouldn't, in her condition. Make sure it stays on, and make sure she stays in the bedroom another day or two," Dr. Welton says. "No housework either. Odetta and your girls can do what needs to be done."

"I'll do that. Lowell, thanks for running over on short notice."

Everything settles down, but nothing's exactly back to normal. For one, Odetta is staying to fix our dinner, which she never does. And for two, we're having baked potatoes, sliced peaches, and scrambled eggs for dinner, which we never have. After we finish, Dad takes a tray up to Mom and tells Jane and me to take Charlie into the living room and do little kid puzzles with him, so Odetta can eat her scrambled eggs and peaches in peace. Odetta always eats by herself. She says she likes it that way. After a while, Jane and me hear Odetta singing while she washes the dinner dishes.

> *He's got everybody here in His hands,*
> *He's got everybody there in His hands,*
> *He's got everybody everywhere in His hands,*
> *He's got the whole world in His hands.*

From that day on, Odetta was not our "maid" anymore. Mom started referring to her as our "cleaning lady," a title that made Mrs. Henry arch one over-plucked brow. And my father immediately vaulted Odetta to "household assistant."

What's more, he took to picking her up in the morning and dropping her off in the late afternoon at the St. Louis County Courthouse so that she would only have to change buses once. There was an envelope too. A creamy envelope with the Reinhardt & Krug department store logo on the flap. It was sealed, but I was pretty sure back then and I am confident now that it contained a substantial amount of cash.

At the time, these seemed like monumental changes in the structure of our relationship with Odetta, but I was glad. She had saved my mother from a nasty tumble, which could have been serious, even critical, for Mom and fatal for the child within her. After my cousin Carolyn Reinhardt fell to her death earlier that summer, a fall her unborn child did not survive either, we all were keenly aware of the danger a fall presents to a pregnant woman.

I thought Odetta an ill-tempered, impatient woman. But in hindsight, she was probably just an exhausted woman with a disabled son at her home and a full day of physical labor to get done at ours. A good, swift swat at children who got in her "breathing space" was the surest way to stay on task. And now that I think about it, I wonder if Odetta calibrated those swats so that they stung only a minute or two. Well, most of the time anyway.

Odetta Jones had been part of our household since I was born. She was one of the many constants in my life back on Thistle Way. Everything about her was familiar, and if she wasn't a member of our family per se, she surely was a member of our household.

I sometimes think of my life as a leaf floating on the surface of a stream, rushing the shallows, drifting deeper lengths, snagging on a fallen branch here and there, swirling the occasional eddies, but bobbing along, moving ever forward. It's a journey, one in which there are no absolute constants. I learned that on a stultifying August evening in 1956, a few hours after Odetta stretched out her arms and saved my mother.

It was the last day of the world, as I knew it.

the Mitchells

the end and the beginning

W e must accept finite disappointment, but never lose infinite hope."

Martin Luther King, Jr. said that, a man who left behind a legacy of towering faith, abiding hope, and unbounded love.

"Living is strife and torment, disappointment and love and sacrifice, golden sunsets and black storms." That was Sir Laurence Olivier, a sublimely hyperbolic Shakespearian actor.

"If we will be quiet and ready enough, we shall find compensation in every disappointment." And that was Henry David Thoreau, poet, author, philosopher, abolitionist, naturalist, surveyor, historian, and transcendentalist, a man who, we can assume, flicked off disappointments as if they were gnats.

Disappointment is one of those universal, timeless emotions. Haven't we all experienced that sickening, sinking feeling when we discover things haven't gone, or won't go, as we expected? As we planned or prepared for, as we hoped?

At the tail end of August 1956, I would come face-to-face with the biggest surprise of that long summer of awakening, and it was a supreme disappointment. Ironically, Thoreau would have been disappointed in me, for I was neither quiet about it nor ready for it.

I was furious.

By the time Dad comes downstairs again, it's pitch dark outside except for lightning bugs, porch lights, and the stars. Jane and me are sitting on the patio, looking for the Big Dipper. Odetta's finishing up the dishes. She calls out the kitchen window that we shouldn't bother looking for the moon cuz it's in its last quarter, so it won't come say hello to St. Louis until midnight. Odetta's moons talk, just like her suns.

After Odetta dries and puts away the last of the dishes, Dad drives her all the way home cuz she missed her last bus. Also cuz she saved Mom from falling. By the time he gets back, Jane and me are watching "The Phil Silvers Show," and Charlie's conked out on the floor.

"Girls," Dad says, "would you come to the big bedroom a minute? Bring Charlie and put him in his crib, and then Mom and I want to talk to you."

I'm pretty worried Mom and Dad are gonna yell at us for not giving Charlie his bath. I'm thinking we won't get allowance this week, or we'll have to polish all the good silver stuff tomorrow or crawl around on the scalding hot patio pulling weeds out of the cracks between the stupid bricks.

The worry must show on my face, Jane's too, cuz the first thing Dad says when we get to the big bedroom is, "Girls, you didn't do anything wrong. You're not being punished."

Jane and me give each other a look that means "whew, close call."

"Mother and I want you to know there's nothing wrong with her that a day or two in air-conditioning won't fix," Dad goes on. "Pregnant ladies feel the heat more than the rest of us."

Wait! Pregnant ladies? Mom's pregnant? Again?

Dad's still talking. "And with a new little one coming right around Thanksgiving time, we're going to need more space, don't you think?"

I sure do. Usually, me and Jane and Charlie are all squished into one bedroom. And all of us fight over the bathroom every morning.

"Are we gonna add on a bedroom?" Jane says, all hopeful.

"And another bathroom?" I chime in. "And a Florida Room?"

"We could do that. . . . " Dad says.

I don't have a good feeling about this, so I scale back my plan for making our house bigger.

"We just need one more bedroom, Dad. Jane and me can have the new bedroom, and Charlie and the Thanksgiving baby can have the old one. And we promise never to fight over the bathroom. Right, Jane?"

Jane gives me a look that means "what the heck." I don't think she's noticed Mom and Dad are kinda frowning and not saying anything right now. Jane always says I'm as dense as a rock, but right now, I'm thinking Jane's as dense as a denser rock.

Dad draws Jane and me into his arms and gives us a big hug, which normally would be good, but tonight, I'm thinking it means something bad's coming. I wish we could stand here like this forever, but stupid Jane stands up and glares at Dad.

Finally, Dad says, "Jane, Grace, I admire you for coming up with suggestions so quickly, but adding on rooms to this house isn't realistic. Mom and I talked all this over weeks ago. We know how much you both love it here, but—"

"But what?" I wriggle free and glare at Dad.

Jane balls her fists and turns her back.

Dad stands up, digs his hands in his trouser pockets, and lets out a big breath. He looks at Mom, and she nods back at him.

"We need much more space," Dad says, "and the size addition we'd have to put on this house doesn't make sense financially."

"Why not?" I'm yelling now, crying and yelling. "Why can't we just make more bedrooms and stay here?"

"We looked at lots of neighborhoods," Dad says, running his fingers through his hair. "The house your mother and I bought is in a brand new neighborhood in Chesterfield. It's only about twenty minutes from here."

I clamp my hands over my ears and look at Mom, pleading. Maybe Mom can make Dad stop talking about stupid Chesterfield. But Mom's not saying a word, even though her eyes are filled with tears.

I throw myself on the floor, wailing. "You're killing me!"

"That's enough!" Dad says, quiet but firm. "The decision was made weeks ago."

"Grace, Jane, come here, will you?" Mom says.

Jane's in a corner of the bedroom, facing the wall. She doesn't move, but I crawl onto the bed and curl up next to Mom. I stick my thumb in my mouth, which I haven't done since kindergarten, except for the day I ran away from home and fell asleep in the flower meadow. Mom takes my thumb out of my mouth and strokes my hair and pretty soon, I stop hiccough-crying.

"The moving truck is coming on Saturday," Mom says.

I bolt up. "What!"

"I know it's a shock," Mom says. "But you and Jane are going to be going to St. Peter's now, and school starts in three weeks. Dad and I agreed it would be best for both of you to start out on the first day with the rest of the kids."

"Before you know it, you'll have a whole bunch of new friends," Dad says. His voice is all bright and peppy.

I want to kick him in the shin.

I don't want new friends. I've got plenty of good friends right here. The kids at Immaculate Heart of Mary and the kids on Thistle Way, they've been my friends forever. We're used to each other. We know stuff about each other, stuff nobody else knows. Like Davey Lofton being nutso about spying on Mrs. Krieger, so if I live in stupid Chesterfield, who's gonna keep Davey from building another secret tunnel after he gets back from the rehab center, which he's been at most of the whole summer? Like I know the bad thing that happened to Rainer at the hideout, so if I go to stupid St. Peter's for school, then who's gonna cheer like crazy when Rainer finally gets the courage to leave his front yard again? Like I know Mrs. Haverkamp sings torch songs so that Mr. Haverkamp can pay the mortgage. And Dezso lives in a nice house on Hickory Street, not in a gypsy tent, so who's gonna stop Mrs. Henry from saying bad things about him? I know Cate Finnegan wants a forever boyfriend, not a bunch of momentary boyfriends. I know Patsy Warfield won't ever take a bribe and won't ever be scared of a threat, not even a Mooney bribe and not even a Zaldoni threat. I know it made Mrs. Pearson sad to think nobody would keep her memories so she gave them to me, and I've got tucked them away safe and sound under my mattress. What if the movers lose Mrs. Pearson's memories? Ack!

"Grace," Mom says. "Grace, stop brooding and listen to me. Your dad and I made this decision with your best interests in mind, the best interests of all our family."

"What's so best about it for me?"

"That's enough, Grace," Dad says, all snappish. "It's been a long day. Girls, it's time to get ready for bed."

Jane and me stomp out of the room as hard as we can. Jane stomps to the bathroom and slams the door. I stomp to our bedroom, slam the door, flop down on the bed, and cry my eyes out.

How could Mom and Dad be so mean? They're usually the best parents in the whole world. Heck, they're better than Mr. Haverkamp who lets his kids eat root beer floats for dinner and stay up till midnight. Better than Rainer Niesen's parents who practically live at their country club and can't even see there's something really wrong with Rainer. My dad's tons better than Detective Greeley who keeps a mean, biting dog on a chain all the time and wears stupid-looking pajamas. And Lt. Lofton who gives Davey spankings with a folded-over belt. My dad is miles better than Missy Henry's father who drinks beers in the morning, and my mom's way, way better than Missy's mother who locks her little girl outside in a pen while she takes a bubble bath with Frank Sinatra music. And the new people, the Blairs and the Eagans, I won't even say what they do even if I talk silently to myself.

After a while, I stop crying, but I'm still too mad at Mom and Dad to fall asleep.

Gol-durn Thanksgiving baby.

I'm not going to Chesterfield, I'll tell you that.

I'm gonna run away from home and this time, I'm going way far. Past the creek and the sledding hill and even the hideout. I'm gonna go to a faraway woods where nobody'll find me, not even the police. I'll pack all my clothes in my suitcase and some bread and peanut butter and marsh-mallows and stuff.

I lie on my back and close my eyes. Then I close them tighter. I blink a couple of times and close them tight as I can.

I can't fall asleep. Something's prickling at my mind. I keep thinking about living in the woods. First of all, where would I go to the bathroom? Second of all, what happens if a tornado comes? And third of all, how do I get my allowance? I have to figure all that out before Saturday.

I turn over on my stomach and try to go to sleep. I hear Mom tiptoe into the room. I scrunch my eyes tighter but leave a little slit open so I can see what Mom's doing. She pulls up the sheet so it covers Jane's shoulders, and then she runs her fingers through Jane's hair. Jane's got naturally wavy hair, just like Mom. Then Mom comes over and kisses me on the forehead, which I like.

Before she leaves, she puts something at the far end of my bed. I wait till I know she's gone and then I sit up to see what she left. It's my Brownie Scout sash. Mom's the leader of Jane's Girl Scout troop, and she's also the leader of my Brownie troop. She helped me with all my Try-It badges last year: painting, sewing, and first aid. Mom's the best Brownie leader ever. She sews on badges so you can't even see the stitches. My mom's prettier than any of the other moms. She doesn't wallow in front of the television all day either. She shows us how to make home-baked cakes and cookies and she takes us to parks and to the zoo and the library and to tour the Anheuser Busch brewery and once, she even took us to tour a sewerage treatment plant.

A little while later, Dad comes in the bedroom. I'm still awake and not scrunching my eyes, so he knows I'm awake.

Dad sits on the edge of my bed. "It's late, sweetheart."

"I know. I can't sleep."

Dad pretends to think a little and then says, "Oh, that's the problem. Grace, you are afflicted with Can't Get to Sleep Disease. Let me see . . . yes, I believe I have a cure for that."

I start to giggle. It's what Dad always says when he comes up to sing me and Jane to sleep. He always sings the same songs, "The Yellow Rose of Texas" and the one that begins with "From The Halls of Montezuma." Dad says they're the only songs he knows the words to, but that's a fib. Sometimes, after the dishes are done, Dad dances Mom around the kitchen, and they both sing "Tea for Two."

"Dad?"

"What is it, Grace?"

"When the Thanksgiving baby's born, are you gonna take me and Jane out to dinner?"

"Sure I will. You know the story."

I do. Jane and me make Dad tell the story all the time. I ask him to tell it now.

"The day Jane was born," he says, "I was so lonely with Mom and the baby in the hospital that I went out to dinner all by myself at the Cheshire Inn, which is a fancy restaurant. I brought along a red rose and had the waiter put it in a vase on the table. Then, the day you were born, I took Jane out to dinner at the Cheshire Inn. Jane sat in a high chair and ate mashed potatoes and ice cream, and I had the restaurant people put two white roses in a vase on the table.

"Then, the day Theresa was born, I took Jane out to dinner at the Cheshire Inn. Jane sat in a high chair and ate mashed potatoes and ice cream, and I had the restaurant people put two white roses in a vase on the table."

"And me?" I know the answer already, but I always ask it when Dad tells the story.

"And when you were born, I took Theresa and Jane to Cheshire, didn't I? And what color were the roses?

"Pink. You got three pink roses."

"Right. And Charlie got four yellow roses. So what should we have for the Thanksgiving baby, Grace?"

"Five roses, all different colors!"

"Like a cornucopia, right?"

"A corn-o what-ee-ya?"

Dad hugs me a long time and then tiptoes out and closes the door. He thinks I'm finally asleep, but I'm not. I keep going over in my mind whether to go live in the woods or go to Chesterfield. If I run away and live in the woods, I wouldn't see Mom or Dad or Jane and Charlie ever again. Cripes, I wouldn't even get to see the Thanksgiving baby.

I guess I'm gonna have to pack my red plaid suitcase one more time.

I turn over on my side and bunch up the pillow. Then I turn over on my back and throw the pillow on the floor and think some more. I kick off the twisted sheet and go stand at the window. All up and down the street, the porch lights look like gold dots. The moon is shining over the treetops. From here, I can see almost every house on Thistle Way. Lt. Lofton's lowered his American flag, like always. The Henrys' garbage cans are overflowing with bottles, like always. Gregor Niesen left his English racing bike out again. Benny Herman's bedroom window has a screen on it now. One of the purple license plates came off the Haverkamps' stepping stone path, but it looks like all the papier-mâché farm animals are still there. Bullet is sound asleep in the Greeleys' front yard, chained to a sign that says, "Beware of Bullet."

I'm gonna remember this. I'm gonna remember every single thing about this summer my whole life. Thistle Way isn't the perfect place for a kid to grow up, I'll tell you that.

But it's close.

For a long while that night, I stared at a splash of stars beyond the treetops. The air was thick, another August evening loath to forsake its heat. I heard the oak plank floor at the bottom of the stairs creak as it swelled, hardwood bending to dauntless Missouri humidity. Below me, trellised roses drooped under the weight of softball-sized flower heads. Along the circle, sedans bedecked with chrome and fins sat silent on driveways, reserving garages for bikes, baby carriages, push mowers, paint can towers, and cardboard boxes that held military uniforms and medals in boxes labeled with places of indelible conflict.

Normandy.

Tarawa.

Eventually, I knew, Thistle Way's canopy of oak boughs would turn color. Breezes with a hint of frost would release leaves by the hundreds, by the thousands and more, from their spindly moorings and send them twirling to the ground in knee-high layers. Mothers would make casseroles and apple pies spiced with cinnamon. Dads would take down screens and put up storm windows, coil garden hoses, and oil the chains they would struggle to fit around car tires, come the first snowfall. Kickball games in front of the Daily house would recess for the season and then, before long, the ice-skating rink behind the Mooney house would take shape. Rooflines would glow with fat holiday lights. Snow would drift over sleeping gladioli beds, pillow on fireplugs, cling to twiggy lilac bushes, and transform sagging telephone wires into silken skeins. Easter would bring the first ravishing whiff of thawed earth and, not long after, wimpled nuns would release their eager charges again for summer vacation. Mrs. Daily would sit at a Singer sewing machine embellished with golden scrollwork and stitch new kickball bases. Patsy Warfield would hold auditions for another theatrical extravaganza. Mr. Snyder would provision his Five & Dime with ample quantities of Popsicles.

I knew these things with absolute certainty, though I would never again experience them, for my family did, indeed, move to Chesterfield.

We live in the flashing immediacy of real time, relegating each moment to remembrance the instant it's over. But memories are as capricious and insubstantial as fog coiling over a jagged cliff. They exist only where we carry them, in the corrugations of the mind, the wellings of the heart, the recesses of the soul. They are our truth, ours alone.

A life is a complex thing. First-person accounts of it are purely subjective. And so I am left to wonder this:

Have I rewritten the script of my childhood as some arcadian fantasy, soft at the edges, bathed in golden light with just a hint of a shadow here and there? Or was it really like that, the summer of 1956, the summer I was eight, going on nine?

epilogue

As you see, I eventually put my recollections in writing. It's just a personal memoir, a fat file folder tucked away in a drawer. But I hope someday my children find it and read it.

There's a bit more to the story, of course. The people I once knew didn't just vanish at the end of that summer. But there are close to one hundred of them in this memoir, if you count Cate Finnegan's momentary boyfriends (and who wouldn't?). I can't give an update on each one, but I know what happened to some of them.

Me, for instance.

Late that August, I packed my red plaid suitcase for the last time. Having lived all my short life in Brentwood, an established, inner-tier suburb of St. Louis, I went kicking and screaming to Chesterfield, where, at the time, I found an alarming absence of kids. My parents had bought a newly built five-bedroom house out where exurban St. Louis County bumped up against rural Missouri, a line of demarcation as cultural as it was geographic. Jane and I didn't need fancy explanations for that; the three-strand barbed wire fence at the back of our lot illustrated the point quite well. For almost a year, our house was a pin-dot of civilization surrounded by woods, meadows, and farmland making a valiant, if futile, attempt to stave off creeping exurbia.

On the first morning in Chesterfield, I sat on our new brick stoop and stared disconsolately at our new front yard, which was still a swathe of sun-baked dirt freckled with stones. Uprooted from everything known, disoriented and discontented, I was writing postcards to my old class-mates at Immaculate Heart of Mary when Jane called out to me.

"Come, quick! I found a creek at the bottom of the hill. There are baby ducks, and I saw a beaver!"

I skittered feet-first alongside Jane down the sharp, grassy drop where our property fell away to the south. A beaver, now that was something.

And so it began. For as long as the warm weather lasted, Jane and I, even little Charlie splashed in the clear-running stream, squealing as small, slithery things glided between our ankles. We searched the shoals for arrowheads and carried them home in cupped hands. We had picnics with bologna sandwiches in a field and tamped winding trails in its tas-seled grass. We built forts in thickets and made plans for a tree house in a nearby hardwood grove. One afternoon, I glimpsed a red fox who eyed me with indignation and pranced away. Dad brought a puppy home for his heartsick daughters. He built a fenced run for the little dog, but more than once, our new pet dug his way out and loped to the back door, reeking of skunk.

Jane and I made friends with the kids who lived in an old farmhouse beyond the barbed-wire fence that marked the farthest reaches of our lot. These were wary, temporary alliances formed by means of shy invi-tation. Their barn cat had a new litter, did we want to see? Their mother was putting up peaches in Mason jars, did we want to watch? In the eve-nings, our dad changed into Bermuda shorts and barbecued hamburgers on a Weber grill; their dad dressed in clip-strap dungarees and plowed a field that had been in the family for generations.

In September, just as school started, a fleet of bulldozers rumbled into the subdivision, and by the following summer, we had half a dozen neighbors. Then came more houses, speed limit signs, tennis courts, and a deep-water neighborhood pool. We kids stayed up late, spying on twi-light pool parties at which adults toppled fully clothed into the water, cocktail glasses in hand. It was the '60s, and like before, a couple of our neighbors were what my parents called "fast."

The farmer sold his land. Soon, architects, builders, and landscapers were walking his corduroyed fields. In the '70s, the line between exurban and rural was in full retreat. Forts and tree houses built by kids trans-planted from Brentwood, kids reveling in the novelty of Outer Mongolia, vanished altogether.

By then, my sister and I had picked a hundred thousand rocks out of our yard, and the lawn was lush. Our mother tended roses in raised beds. Our father spent whole Saturdays on his riding mower. The three-strand barbed wire fence was gone, replaced by arbor vitae from a commercial nursery. The Thanksgiving baby, Peter, had arrived on the day after Thanksgiving, 1956, and was in nursery school. There was a new baby in the crib. My parents had named her Hope, and she was a towhead, like Charlie.

I made friends in Chesterfield, of course. And later, at St. Joseph's Academy, I formed bonds that last to this day.

In my junior year at Northwestern University, I met Kent Stone, a sandy-haired business major with heart-melting eyes. He was independent-minded, but funny and kind. He admired my love of writing, encouraged my ambition, and treated me like a princess, all of which I liked. We married soon after he finished grad school, and then we moved back to St. Louis. Kent went to work at McGraw-Hill. I wrote freelance articles for *The Globe-Democrat*, *The Post Dispatch*, and *St. Louisan Magazine*. In time, the Reinhardt money flowed down the family tree; Kent and I bought our first house and started filling it with babies—first Emily, then Leslie, and finally Ann.

My father passed away in 2004. Two years later, Mother died. In the eulogies, I spoke about the remarkable way my parents dealt with an eight-year-old who ran away to find a better family.

"Paul and Madeleine Mitchell were not perfect," I said. "Nobody is. But I'll tell you this—they were the very best of parents."

Which is God's honest truth.

My sweet brother Charlie majored in sociology at Michigan and went on to get a master of social work degree. In the '70s, he organized a network of food pantries in Detroit. In the '80s and '90s, Charlie and his wife, Samantha, headed up a community organization that offered free debt reduction and credit card management counseling. After 9/11, he and Sam started a successful statewide campaign to provide personal computers and Skype services to the families of Detroit-area national guardsmen called up for duty overseas.

Later, with the auto industry in crisis and Michigan's unemployment rate on its way to 15.2 percent, Charlie and Sam opened a storefront recruitment office in one of the many Detroit neighborhoods on the steep downslide. In the first two months, they found temporary jobs for 66 downsized factory workers.

Jane, me, Theresa, Charlie, Peter, and Hope eventually inherited money through our mother—trickle-down Reinhardt money. By family consensus, Theresa's portion was donated to the March of Dimes. Charlie and Sam use their share of the windfall to subsidize their nonprofit work. They lived simply by choice—no car, no fancy trips. In the end, they were making do in a small apartment over the recruitment office. They said they always wanted kids, but they never got around to having them. The years slipped by, and then it was too late.

It was amazing that Charlie lived as long as he did, given his damaged heart. He and Samantha were almost sixty when tragedy struck. It was a time of life when people settled into a comfortable and predictable routine. Each weekday, they woke up early, grabbed two small cartons of Greek yogurt, and went downstairs to the recruitment office. Last Friday, like always, Samantha turned on the lights, unlocked the front door, and fired up their laptops. Meanwhile, Charlie made coffee in a small alcove in the back.

Police reconstructed what happened in the next few seconds: The front door opened. A man walked in. Charlie heard a pop and whirled around in time to see his wife slip to the floor.

According to the police report, Charlie would have recognized the guy. According to papers found at the office, four days earlier, the man had walked in off the street, looking for work. Charlie had interviewed him, noted his sketchy employment history and contact information, and promised to try and find something. In his notes, Charlie had written, "Creepy. Possible nutcase."

Each morning after that, the man was waiting on the sidewalk for Sam to unlock the door. Charlie's notes indicate the man acted agitated and appeared to be simmering with undefined rage. Although Charlie scoured the files for something suitable, he probably knew there was nothing for a guy like that.

The man shot Samantha through the heart. Then he put three bullets into our dear Charlie. According to the coroner's report, they died in seconds, died before the coffee finished brewing.

We laid them both to rest at Calvary Cemetery, beside Mom and Dad and Theresa.

As I said, I am grieved to the bone.

Samantha's family held a memorial service in Sam's hometown, Ann Arbor. After the funeral and burial in St. Louis, we had a reception at Topping Ridge Country Club, the lovely old golf club in Southwest St. Louis County where, once upon a time, my grandparents were founding members. My parents had their wedding reception at Topping Ridge. The band wore matching monogrammed tuxedoes. The guests did the cha-cha around the ballroom. My wedding reception was at Topping Ridge too. The band wore polyester jumpsuits and played a gosh-awful rendition of "Hey, Jude" that went on for ten minutes.

Kent and I keep up the family membership there, though we don't use the club much. Charlie wasn't a country club kind of guy either, but as children, we all loved going to Topping Ridge after new vaccine eased fears of polio. At the far end of the huge tiled pool was a snack bar with a sliding window screen. Charlie would stand with his chin to the counter and order three grilled hot dogs slathered with mustard and pickle relish, then pout his little lower lip when Mom told him he'd have to stay out of the water for a half hour. In the late afternoon, we would change into our best clothes for dinner with Grandma and Grandpa Reinhardt in the main dining room. The bartender always dropped an extra maraschino cherry into Charlie's kiddie cocktail.

The funeral reception took place on a beautiful June evening. At first, we mingled with the guests on the terrace, talking about Charlie and Sam and looking out at a velvet sweep of fairway that fell away beyond the pool deck. The club manager had lowered the flag to half-mast and had reserved the main dining room for us. The staff had laid out the club's heirloom silver and placed ivory candles in cut-glass hurricanes on each table.

My siblings had asked me to say a few words. When everyone was seated, I stood and ruffled my notes. The dining room fell silent.

"Time is an enigma," I began. "It's elastic and misty and willful. It lingers, indolent, and then rushes headlong. It lurches, as uncertain as the breaths of a fevered child. It marks the hours, as steady as the beat of a watchful mother's heart.

"In the droplet of time during which my brother and his wife took their leave of this world and made their way to the next, four thousand new stars winked in the heavens, a hundred thousand waves broke on caramel shores, violinists paused with bows aloft, blossoms in the East bent to the sun, lovers in the West kissed in the moonlight, and infants around the world closed petal eyelids and drifted off, to sleep the sleep of angels.

"A second, an instant, an hour, a decade. Who calibrates a lifetime? Who says this one has lasted overlong or that one was snatched away too soon? A worthy life may be of any duration. A life fully lived is not counted by the year, but by the moment.

"When we were little, Charlie slept with Jane and Theresa and me in a room with deep closets for games of hide and seek, with fairytale wallpaper for sweet dreams, and with Venetian blinds that angled up and down, admitting the world in even doses. We thought nothing of sharing a hairbrush, a toothbrush, a cup of blueberries. In many ways, we three were one. Everything I wore was something Jane had outgrown. I stepped into shoes that were conformed to the planes and knobs of their feet. I shrugged into tartan plaid coats and velvet leggings that retained the innocent scent of them. And Charlie? We bathed and fed him, read to him, swung him on swings, dawdled with him in a two-ring backyard pool. We dressed him in sailor suits and buckle-strap sandals, in soft cotton undershirts and teddy bear pajamas. Each night, back on Thistle Way, Charlie perfumed our bedroom with the aroma of Johnson's Baby Powder. We fell asleep to the lullaby of his baby breaths.

"After school, in those early years, Jane and I walked home together, she and Lizzie a little ahead and me a little behind. Charlie would stand at the living room window waiting for us, palms pressed against the glass. The moment we were in sight, he would bounce up and down, spread his starfish fingers, and wave, as ecstatic to see us as we were to see him.

"As a teen, Charlie had a crush on Cher. Later, he graduated to Italian opera. Once a year or so, he took a train to Manhattan, splurged on a room at a fine hotel, and bought tickets to the New York Ballet. He played cutthroat Scrabble, and he usually beat me, the stinker. At age fifty, he was determined to work his way through *The New York Times* list of 100 greatest books ever written, a list that included works by Flaubert and Chekhov, Plato and Proust, George Eliot, Mark Twain, and Shakespeare. It took him five years; he emerged triumphant. Charlie baked strawberry rhubarb pies in spring and batches of thumbprint cookies at Christmastime, and he gave them all away. Though his heart struggled with every beat, his goodness knew no limits.

"Once upon a time, I had a brother named Charlie. I have him still, held fast in remembrance. And yet my comfort this day is hard fought, for my brother, the little boy at the window, is beyond reach now. Well, he is at peace. There's solace in that and in the memories of him that reside in the deepest wellings of my heart.

"One week ago, a morning star awoke from slumber behind ribbons of cloud, shook loose from a pearly sky, and drifted to Earth, to an austere office on a grim city block and hovered there, heaven-sent, bathing my brother Charlie and his wife, Samantha, in pure, golden light."

My sister Jane graduated from William and Mary at the top of her class, and soon thereafter she married Rob—Robert Clarkson Brookings—a great guy who had just finished up at Princeton and was on his way to the US diplomatic corps. Over the years, Jane and Rob lived in Paris, Brussels, Copenhagen, Lisbon, and Seville. With each new posting, Jane mastered a new language. A few years ago, they retired to Denver, Rob's hometown. Jane is president of a suburban garden club, a book club, and an investment club. Rob volunteers in the library of one of Denver's charter schools. Their children and grandchildren all live in Colorado. Every Christmas, they celebrate the holiday at their mountain lodge.

My brother Peter, the so-called Thanksgiving Baby, arrived on the day after Thanksgiving, 1956. Peter and his wife, Katie, are dermatologists in Portland, Oregon. They never tire of hearing the old Thistle Way stories. The third and last Mitchell kid, Hope, was a towhead, like Charlie. And like Charlie, Hope is extremely good-hearted. Although she never knew Theresa, she has always had a keen sense of our sister's short life and tragic death. For the past twenty years, Hope has lived in St. Louis and worked at the headquarters of Post-Polio Health International helping enhance the lives and increase the independence of polio survivors and home ventilator users.

My friendship with Sally Daily did not survive the distance between Brentwood and Chesterfield, but years later, we bumped into one another quite by accident.

It was summer. Sally was majoring in nursing at the University of Missouri-Columbia, getting a killer course out of the way before the fall semester. I was a full-time student at Northwestern, but I was taking an easy elective at Mizzou, mostly so I could spend part of the summer at the off-campus apartment of my adventuresome cousin, Conrad Reinhardt.

Sally was rushing to a lecture on health assessment and pathophysiology. I was hanging around the quadrangle, deciding whether to cut my "Twilight of the Sioux" class again. We crossed paths, stopped, and did one of those comedic double takes. We exchanged a generic greeting, promised to get together, and never did.

A few years ago, though, during one of my nostalgia drives around Thistle Way, I saw Sally's mother in front of the Dailys' house. She was extracting catalogs from her mailbox, shaking her head as if bemused to think that J. Crew and Anthropologie had pinned their hopes on an order from an octogenarian.

I pulled up to the curb. She bladed a hand over her brow and squinted into the sun.

"Grace? Is it Grace Mitchell?"

We sat on her breezeway, sipping lemonade. I said I should be plunked on a blanket in the yard, surrounded by dolls, and we laughed.

"Mr. Daily?" I asked, treading lightly.

"Heart. It was fast. He didn't suffer."

"He was a fine man, a terrific father."

"Oh, I know," she said, "as was yours."

And then, with a little prodding, she told me what she knew about the old neighborhood people, and about Sally.

"Sally calls twice a week," she said. "She and Jeff live in Georgia now. They want me to come live with them, but I just can't fathom leaving Thistle Way."

I wrote my address on a scrap of paper and asked her to pass it along. At Christmas, I got a card and snapshot from Sally. There was my old friend with the same sweet, open face, standing beside a guy I took to be her husband. They were wearing khaki shorts and serious hiking boots. In the background, tall pines marched up a steep, rocky rise.

According to a note on the Christmas card, Sally and her husband lived at the foothills of the Blue Ridge Mountains. There's a stone fireplace in the living room, she wrote, and a patchwork quilt on every bed.

On a cold but clear day eighteen months after his terrible accident, Davey Lofton had improved enough to come home for a visit. He begged his mother to drive him out to Chesterfield to see me, and she did so. He brought his baseball cards along. We carried our cards outside and tossed them one by one against the garage wall, just as we'd done on Thistle Way. After a while, he unzipped his backpack and pulled out a small bank. It was made of cheap tin and shaped to resemble a pirate's treasure chest. I watched, curious, as he fished in the pocket of his jeans and pinched out a soupspoon. We knelt beside a forsythia bush in the yard, a thicket of dry, rangey shoots. With effort, Davey managed to dig a hole in the partly frozen soil. When the hole was deep enough, he asked if I would bury my cards with his.

"Why?"

"Cuz I'm making The First Ever Super Duper Baseball Card Time Capsule."

I didn't have much in the way of a baseball card collection; the Mooneys had taken care of that. But Davey did. He added his cards to mine, and we tucked them in the little chest. Then we buried it among the forsythia roots. Afterward, we sat back on our heels and pinky swore to return in fifty years, dig up the bank, sell the collection, and split the money fifty-fifty. It was generous of him; he had put his best cards in the ground.

We said goodbye late that afternoon. Davey held up his pinky finger as a reminder and whispered, "We'll be rich someday." It would have been true too, had the cards lasted underground; my friend's collection included two Mickey Mantles, three Roger Marises, a Willie Mays, and six Stan Musials.

That was the last time I saw Davey Lofton. I've always wondered what became of him.

A month after we moved to Chesterfield, my mother spotted a familiar name among the newspaper obituaries. *Sylvia Pearson.* She had passed away in her sleep and was laid to rest between the two loves of her life, Cliff Phillips and Lloyd Pearson.

According to Mrs. Daily, Patsy Warfield graduated from the Yale School of Drama, doffed her cap and gown, and boarded a train to New York, where she landed a starter job at CBS-TV. She rose steadily up the ranks. A few years ago, *Time* magazine's television critic noted Pat Warfield was one of the first network insiders to recognize the massive appeal of reality shows.

Luca and Antony Zaldoni's father died of wounds suffered in a 1977 car bombing. News accounts quoted police as saying the grisly attack that killed Nello Zaldoni was part of an ongoing spate of violence by warring organized crime factions.

The Globe-Democrat ran an in-depth story the Sunday following the attack. Reporters traced the origins of the Mafia in St. Louis back to its beginnings and gave a detailed account of the tragic death of Nello Zaldoni, "one of the most beloved restaurateurs in St. Louis."

According to the story, on the day Nello Zaldoni died, two mob thugs had enjoyed a hearty lunch at Osteria la Siciliana. After the men paid the bill and walked out, Nello noticed they had left their doggie bags on the table. Nello trotted out to the parking lot with the sacks, hoping to catch the men before they drove off.

"It was the last thing he ever did," a source close to the investigation was quoted as saying. "Zaldoni passed these little bags of cannoli through the open car window right as the driver turned the key in the ignition and BOOM! The first cops on the scene said they couldn't tell what was ricotta cheese and what was brains."

After Nello's death, Osteria la Siciliana passed to his two sons. It's a stretch to think of Luca Zaldoni making the rounds of tables each night, schmoozing the clientele, but I get a kick out of envisioning him sneaking up behind two customers dining on toasted ravioli and then smacking their heads together, like he did to Sally and me when we were kids.

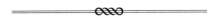

The day my mother stonewalled my request to invite Cherry, my Camp Coureur des Bois friend, to spend the night, I moped and pouted until I was quite sure it was doing no good. Then I took my case to a higher authority.

Dear Abby,

I made friends at camp with a girl named Cherry. Everybody at camp thought Cherry was mean, but she was just poor. I want to invite Cherry to my house, but my mom won't let me. Cherry's a Negro, and we're white. What can I do?

Love,

Grace Mitchell (faithful reader)

I waited two months for a reply. When it came, I tore open the envelope and pulled out the single sheet of cream-colored stationery. At the top was a black-and-white photograph of Abby.

Dear Reader,

Thank you for faithfully reading my newspaper column. As you know, newspapers across America publish "Dear Abby" for helpful advice about the everyday problems of readers like you.

I advise you to obey your parents until you are old enough to make all of life's many decisions for yourself.

Sincerely,

Abigail Van Buren

Pruitt-Igoe, where Cherry once lived, declined and decayed. At three o'clock in the afternoon on March 16, 1972, the first of the thirty-three Pruitt-Igoe towers was demolished with a controlled implosion. The last block of buildings went down in 1976. During the years of demolition, the US Department of Housing and Urban Development relocated some of the tenants. Others scattered. They went to live with relatives. They flopped, sick and tired and penniless, at homeless shelters. They eked out a hard living on the streets.

I like to think Cherry survived the traumas of her childhood. If anybody could leave the misery, danger, and decay of Pruitt-Igoe behind and forge a decent life, it was my skinny, stubborn, belligerent friend from Camp Coureur des Bois.

After giving birth to four boys, Mr. and Mrs. Mooney produced two girls and another boy. Each popped out with a thatch of blond hair and ice-blue eyes.

I saw various Mooney kids now and then at football games and school dances. Eventually, I lost track of them, but Google didn't. I did a search the other day and learned Mark is a part-owner of a Preakness-winning race horse, now gone to stud. The horse, that is. Matt Mooney is a statistician for ESPN. Mike is a freelance writer who travels the world covering bicycle races. Mason, an Evans Scholar, is the golf pro at Old Warson Country Club in St. Louis. Molly and Meegan Mooney coach Olympic-bound speed skaters at a huge indoor rink in Milwaukee.

In her later years, I occasionally took my mother to the Missouri Botanical Garden. I would push her wheelchair along the trails meandering through the garden's themed plantings. Before heading home, we always stopped at the gift shop, and it was there that I learned what had become of Mortimer, the youngest Mooney. A collection of birdhouses had caught my mother's eye, whimsical wooden things that resembled castles with crenellated turrets. They were remarkably intricate, the work of a master. On each was a small card printed in script:

Castles in the Sky, handcrafted by Mortimer Mooney

I tried to track down Missy Henry and finally got a lead through a people-finder search engine.

It seems that in the fall of 1956, the Henrys drove their daughter to a mental institution in Iowa. According to Wikipedia, when the place first opened in 1855, it was called a lunatic asylum. In the 1890s, the name was modernized to Hospital for the Insane. The main building and grounds were designed to be an idyllic refuge for 250 patients from well-to-do families. After sixty years of gradual overcrowding, it had deteriorated substantially. By the time Missy arrived, it was a gritty custodial facility for two thousand patients who were subjected to treatments that included hydro-immersion and electric shock therapy.

There is scant reason to hope that a Down syndrome child's medical issues would be addressed at such a place. I assume Missy Henry survived into her teens, at the very latest.

Frank Haverkamp's Slop did not take the country by storm. Undaunted, he returned to Synergistic Enterprises and, by the following year, perfected a new miracle product: Glimmer. With little money for a marketing campaign, Frank took out a domino-sized classified ad in *The*

Globe-Democrat. He wrote the advertising copy himself.

Amazing new silver polish! One squirt and tarnish trickles away!

Frank failed to mention the name of the product, the price, and where Glimmer might be purchased.

It was early autumn 1957, according to Mrs. Daily's recollection. Perfectionist housewives were planning their upcoming holiday meals with lavish spreads that would showcase the bone china and sterling silver they had received on their wedding days. Glimmer's time had come.

Frank and his son Curt filled the back of the old Chevy wagon with cartons of Glimmer and made the rounds of St. Louis corner grocers. Shopkeepers agreed to take a bottle or two, period. With a dozen cartons to spare, Frank and Curt branched out to ma-and-pa grocers in cities from Hannibal to Arnold with no better luck.

When they got to Festus, Curt spotted a big variety store and told his father to pull over. Curt sprinted into the store and returned to the car with a spool of silver ribbon, a packet of white sticky labels, and six bottles of Revlon nail polish. At a drinking fountain in town, he emptied the little bottles and rinsed them clean. He filled them with a few drops of Glimmer and attached each little sample bottle with silver ribbon to a regular-sized bottle of Glimmer. He stuck the white labels to the large bottles and carefully printed the following suggestion:

This holiday season, give a girlfriend a little Glimmer.

Housewives couldn't buy the cleverly packaged Glimmer fast enough. Stores in Illinois, Arkansas, and Kansas began placing large orders for Glimmer. A national home products company in Racine offered a substantial sum for the patent. A very substantial sum.

The Haverkamps decamped to Ladue, Missouri. Frank took up golf. Curt bought a Thunderbird. Janice enrolled at Mary Institute, the city's most exclusive girls' school, and went on to study art in Paris. In her last few years, Diane took to wearing ballet flats and Lily Pulitzer sheath dresses, her nights singing torch songs up in Wellston forgotten.

Upon the death of Silvia Pearson, the Haverkamp kids adopted her parakeet, Jenkins. Curt rigged up the bird's cage so that it dangled from a beam in the Haverkamp basement, suspended above legions of inquisitive Foo dogs. Not surprisingly, Jenkins suffered ongoing paroxysms of nervousness and perished within the month. The Haverkamps repurposed his cage as a lawn ornament.

Susan and Sharon White spent their entire Disneyland vacation in a hotel room, laid low by chicken pox.

Bullet, Detective Greeley's dog, slipped out of his collar one evening in the summer of 1958 and followed the Mosquito Man's truck all the way to the St. Louis County Maintenance Depot. For the next two weeks, the Mosquito Man allowed Bullet to accompany him on his appointed rounds. The dog was in heaven, Mrs. Daily said, lolling his head out the truck's open window, holding his mouth wide to the delicious breeze. Detective Greeley was mowing his lawn one evening when the truck lumbered around Thistle Way. He spotted his dog, of course, and trotted after the truck, inhaling mists of fog and whistling for Bullet. The dog glanced back once, Mrs. Daily recalled, and looked quickly away. Bullet had weighed a life in chains against a life on the road, and had chosen the latter.

I assume Bullet and the Mosquito Man continued to course suburban byways in happy companionship, dispersing clouds of insecticide into air. It was fruitless, of course; it's impossible to vanquish a population of insects when each individual is capable of maturing from egg to larva to pupa to egg-laying adult in four days.

Our move to Chesterfield signaled the end of Odetta's cleaning days with the Mitchell family; her commute would have been impossible. My grandfather immediately employed her as a ladies room attendant at his flagship department store where she quietly passed out linen hand towels. The dimes she collected in a porcelain saucer supplemented her salary. Occasionally, a customer needed part of a hemline stitched up or a wind-mussed hairdo repaired, and Odetta must have somehow carried this out. Although I remember her many domestic skills well, I do not recall that Odetta Jones was adept at fine hand sewing or versed in the art of coiffure. Two years after she was installed at Reinhardt & Krug, her son took a turn for the worse and required constant home care, and my grandfather quietly arranged for Odetta to retire from Reinhardt & Krug with a lifetime pension generous enough for her and her boy to live out their lives in respectable comfort.

I saw Benny Herman again. It was years after I'd moved from Thistle Way, and it was in an unlikely place: Calvary Cemetery. The spring afternoon smelled of damp earth and fresh-cut grass. Shafts of sunlight fell wan on obelisks and marble angels. Kent and I and our three girls were at graveside services for a friend of Kent's whose car skidded off a rainy road and slammed into a tree. When the priest was almost finished with his remarks, a bugler blew the first notes of "Taps." He was only a short distance away, for across a small rise, another burial was winding up. The man with the bugle was scruffy, I noted, frowning. Hair down to his shoulders, faded jeans frayed at the heel, and strands of colored beads.

I squinted into the late-day sun and realized it was Benny. Benny Herman. Of all people.

I tried to connect the dots between the chubby boy who had blasted sour notes from his bedroom window on Thistle Way to the lanky musician playing "Taps" with precision and patience and gorgeous tenderness.

Afterward, Benny chatted with the mourners a few minutes and then walked over to our small group. He had recognized me as well. I introduced him to Kent and our daughters, Emily, Leslie, and Ann, and for a while, time melted away as we chatted about the old days on Thistle Way, the kickball games and marionette shows, the sledding hill and pilgrimages to Snyder's Five & Dime.

I dared not mention the talent show, but he did and was good enough to laugh about it. I told him the backstory about the Mooneys and the White twins and the Zaldoni brothers who had tried to rig the results. He said he wasn't surprised, but giving trophies to the three little kids was the best of all outcomes.

I told Benny about going to St. Joe's and then on to Northwestern. He said he'd majored in history at Tufts and later, on a whim, studied at the Berklee College of Music. He played sax there, then trombone, and then took up the bugle again. Small gigs at Boston brew pubs led to a stint with a jazz band and a recording contract. When the album took off, he moved to New Orleans, found ready work, and a measure of fame. He and his wife live in a restored historic house on Burgundy Street in the Quarter.

"Funerals are different down there. More festive, lots of brass. I've played horn at more than my share of them." He gestured at the group a ways off. "That guy, the one who passed, he was one of my favorite instructors at Berklee. He always said if and when, he wanted me to blow a horn over his grave."

Benny turned to my daughters. "Any of you know the words to 'Taps'?"

They nodded, a little uncertain. They were still girls, children.

He took a scrap of paper and a pencil from his jacket pocket, scribbled something, and handed it to my youngest daughter, Ann. "Here's the version I like. Want to sing it?"

There was a long pause and then she pointed to the bugle and said, "Will you help?"

"You start. I'll pick it up after."

Ann's a shy girl, uncomfortable in the limelight. But to my surprise, she studied the paper closely, as if considering Benny's request. We waited for what seemed like forever, but at last, she started to sing. Her childlike voice wavered; the words were nearly inaudible. After a few lines, she faltered and stopped.

Kent groaned.

I wanted to say something, anything, to get past the awkward moment, but Benny made a small motion with his hand, a gesture I took to mean that I should wait. He nodded at Emily and Leslie. The older girls twined their arms around their sister's waist.

Ann brought up the scrap of paper so her sisters could see it. As they skimmed the words Benny had written, a breeze scented with lilac fluttered the page. Time stopped. The world went cool and utterly soundless.

For a long moment, my girls were silent, gathering themselves. Kent and I held our breaths.

Then, in unison, as if they were a choir of three, they raised their voices and sang in pitch-perfect harmony.

I closed my eyes to the timeless anthem, took in its lilting melody, its soothing words.

For golden moments, the sweet sound of children rang out across manicured grounds of remembrance, pure and clear as a bell.

Then good night, peaceful night,
Till the light of the dawn shineth bright
God is near, do not fear—friend, good night.

author's note

This is a work of fiction, although I have tried my best to make it not seem so.

To varying degrees, each writer draws on his or her perceptions and experiences, as did I when writing *Going on Nine*. Yes, I grew up in a suburb of St. Louis. And yes, I was blessed with the gift of loving and able parents, and further blessed with robust health. Yes, I played with kids in my neighborhood, collected tadpoles in mayonnaise jars, sledded snowy hills, braided lanyards at camp, and, yes, it's true, I once "borrowed" my mother's diamond engagement ring. But *Going on Nine* is not about me and it's not the true story of anyone I know or knew. It's about an era as fabled as it was flawed, an era in which one child's serial encampments and her thoughtful remembrances years later underscore this timeless truth:

Families and friendships are nuanced in ways imperceptible to the fixed regard of outsiders.

Catherine Underhill Fitzpatrick
Summer, 2013

discussion guide

1. Grace Mitchell is meant to embody many of the aspects of a child of eight (going on nine). Give examples from the story that illustrate her personal strengths and her weaknesses.

2. *Going on Nine* is told from two perspectives: the adult Grace looking back on the summer of 1956, and the child Grace experiencing it. What are the advantages and disadvantages of this dual-timeline format? In what ways would the story have been different if it were told only from the child's viewpoint?

3. Except for three chapters, the entire story takes place on Thistle Way, a quiet neighborhood in a suburb of St. Louis. Why do you think the author chose this location?

4. *Going on Nine* is imbued with a sense of time. The Fifties is a fabled era in the communal memory, but one that, in reality, was as flawed as any other. Give examples from the story that illustrate this.

5. A key to the structure of the novel is Grace's deal with her parents, setting up her summer-long travels around her neighborhood. In the context of the time and of Thistle Way, what do you think about her parent's decision? In today's world, would responsible parents offer the same deal to their eight-year-old child?

6. At the beginning of the summer, Grace yearns to live with a family that's "better" than her own. Give examples of how the Mitchells are, in fact, a pretty terrific family.

7. Each stop along Grace's journey is a story unto itself, peopled with characters in turning-point situations. Which character or family did you find most memorable and why? Which characters or families does Grace discover are different from how the neighbors of Thistle Way perceive them?

8. Several chapters deal with sensitive and even tragic events. How do think these events affected the story, which is essentially sweet and nostalgic?

9. In the end, Grace comes to realize that the place she belongs—the place she wants to be—is with her own wonderful family. In a coming-of-age novel, we more or less expect this. What revelations in the Epilogue did you not expect?

10. At age eight (going on nine) Grace had mastered the art of making excuses for her behavior. In several instances, the adult Grace acknowledges that, ruefully. "It was not my finest hour," she says at one point. Did *Going on Nine* bring back remembrances of your own childhood? Does the long lens of time afford a clearer view about that period of your life?

11. Many novelists draw on their personal observances and experiences in developing plots and characters. In the Author's Note, Catherine Underhill Fitzpatrick mentions that a few aspects of Grace's life seem to track with her own childhood. What are the risks in writing a novel that reads like a memoir? How is this different from writing an autobiography? A biography?

notes

Historical information about St. Louis in Chapter Three can be found in the following places:

"1950 US Census," United States Census Bureau, http://www.census. gov/prod/www/decennial.html

US Bureau of the Census. *Census of the Population, 1950. Census Tract Statistics. St. Louis, Missouri, and Adjacent Area.* http:// www.worldcat.org/title/united-states-census-of-population-1950- census-tract-statistics-st-louis-missouri-and-adjacent-area-selected- population-and-housing-characteristics/oclc/39780380.

Living Places. "Hickory Street District," http://www.livingplaces.com/ MO/Independent_Cities/St_Louis_City/Hickory_Street_District. html.

The *Angel of God* prayer in Chapter Four, and other prayers to and about angels can be found at Catholic Online: http://www.catholic.org/saints/ angels/angelprayer.php.

An excerpt from Chapter Six, "Cherry," appeared in the 2013 Black and White Anthology (Outrider Press, 2013) and is available by emailing outriderpress@sbcglobal.net.

An excerpt from Chapter Eight appeared under the title "Sunshine Time" in the 2012 Black and White Anthology (Outrider Press, 2012) and is available at www.amazon.com or by emailing outriderpress@sb- cglobal.net.

Portions of Chapter Ten were written by the author as part of an unpublished eulogy for her sister, Mary Pamela Underhill Orzechowski (1948-2009).

Facts in Chapter Ten about rheumatic fever and polio, and other information about these afflictions, can be found at www.mayoclinic.com and at www.webmd.com.

An adapted and condensed version of Chapter Twelve appeared under the title "Taps" in the second quarter 2013 edition of allthingsgirl.com.

The quote in Chapter Fifteen by Anais Nin can be found at http://www.goodreads.com/quotes/64155-we-do-not-grow-absolutely-chronologically-we-grow-sometimes-in.

"Labor Blues," mentioned in Chapter Twenty, was recorded by Tom Dickson in Memphis, Tennessee, in 1928. More information about "Labor Blues" and Dickson's music can be found at http://www.early-blues.com/WorryBlues.htm.

Background about the song "He's Got the Whole World in His Hands," mentioned in Chapter Twenty, can be found in *The Book of World Famous Music, Classical, Popular and Folk* (Dover Publications, Fifth Edition, 1912).

The history of the mountain ballad "House of the Rising Sun," mentioned in Chapter Twenty, is documented in *Chasing the Rising Sun The Journey of an American Song* (Simon & Schuster, 2007) by Ted Anthony.

Quotes in Chapter Twenty-One by Martin Luther King, Jr., Sir Laurence Olivier, Henry David Thoreau can be found, among other places, at www.brainyquote.com.

acknowledgements

I would like to thank the following people who encouraged, assisted, and supported me in this project, many of whom were around long before the gestation and birth of *Going on Nine*:

Dennis John Fitzpatrick, my husband, the love of my life.

Claire Fitzpatrick Gould and Margaret Ann Fitzpatrick, my beloved daughters, and Daniel E. Gould, my wonderful son-in-law.

Lillian Leslie Gould, my first grandchild, who, in the wee hours after she was fed, dried, swaddled, and rocked in my arms, went all floppy and pensive as I hummed "Oh, Shenandoah," and beguiled me.

Jenny Lewis, my cousin, the younger sister I never had, who is ever a phone call away—a heartbeat away.

Karla Linn Merrifield, poet, adventuress, and brilliant editor, who lugged an early draft of *Going on Nine* from a cabin in Canada to the headwaters of the Amazon River deep in Peru, making it better every step of the way.

Shellie Blumenfield, my dear friend, who, on bleak winter afternoons in Wisconsin, brewed herbal tea and sat, enthralled, as I read aloud.

Colleen McCarrier, Mary Ann Dowd Sussman, Kathleen McElligott, and Mary Jo Goodwin, who reviewed early drafts and offered commentary that proved invaluable.

Whitney Scott, president of the Chicago-based TallGrass Writers Guild, who as both mentor and friend has gifted me with unwavering support and opportunity.

My late sister, Pamela, who encouraged me to take up writing and, in

260

so doing, set the course of my life. And my brothers, Bob, Tom, Ken, and James, who still refer to me by my childhood nickname, Cath, which I like. Sorta.

Mary Ann Martin Graf and Karen K. Marshall, who throw the fizziest publish parties ever.

Kathleen Arenz, Anne Metz, Annie Regenfuss, Pattie Welek Hall, Stephen Perepeluk, Wendy Randall, members of the Mequon-Thiensville Newcomers Book Club, and members of The Dinner Group and of The Play Group, who hold front-row seats in my cheering section.

LaVerne Sanford and the late Shirley Gore, good and true St. Louis women and singers of hymns, whose years of service and dedication to my family will not be forgotten.

Steve Aspacher, who has yearned for this novel since the moment he turned the final page of my first novel, *A Matter of Happenstance*, and whose smile at a Chicago back door was ever a welcome sight.

Maggie Wickes, whose insightful editing buffed the manuscript's tattered edges with a gentle hand, and whose patience with an author who tinkers knows no bounds.

And last but certainly not least, Familius Publishers Michele and Christopher Robbins, who went way out on a limb to bring this sweet story to the world. Thank you, for the courage of your convictions.

about the author

Catherine Underhill Fitzpatrick grew up in the 1950s and 1960s in suburban St. Louis. She is the second of six children. She, like many children her age, enjoyed summer vacations unscheduled and unfettered. After graduating from the University of Missouri School of Journalism, she worked as a metro daily newspaper feature writer in Hannibal, St. Louis, and Milwaukee.

In September of 2001, Catherine was in Manhattan to cover New York Fashion Week. At first word of the terrorist attacks, she rushed to Ground Zero and filed award-winning eyewitness reports. An account of her reportage that day appears in *Running Toward Danger*. A front page of the newspaper edition containing one of her 9-11 dispatches is among those memorialized in Washington DC's Newseum. Her book-length account of her harrowing experiences that week has been accessioned into the State Historical Society of Missouri archives.

Catherine's articles, stories, and essays have appeared in The *Vocabula Review*, *Prick of the Spindle*, *Sew News*, *Fan Story*, *Yesterday's Magazette*, *Reminisce Magazine*, in three Outrider Press anthologies, and *Lessons from My Parents*.

Her debut novel, *A Matter of Happenstance*, is a four-generation family saga that explores the power of personal character over coincidence. Like *Going on Nine*, it is set in St. Louis.

Catherine is a board member of the Chicago-area TallGrass Writers Guild. She and her husband, Dennis, have two daughters. Their first grandchild, Lillian Leslie Gould, was born in June 2013. Catherine and Dennis divide their time between Chicago and Bonita Springs, Florida.

about familius

Welcome to a place where mothers are celebrated, not compared. Where heart is at the center of our families, and family at the center of our homes. Where boo boos are still kissed, cake beaters are still licked, and mistakes are still okay. Welcome to a place where books—and family—are beautiful. Familius: a book publisher dedicated to helping families be happy.

Visit Our Website: www.familius.com

Our website is a different kind of place. Get inspired, read articles, discover books, watch videos, connect with our family experts, download books and apps and audiobooks, and along the way, discover how values and happy family life go together.

Join Our Family

There are lots of ways to connect with us! Subscribe to our newsletters at www.familius.com to receive uplifting daily inspiration, essays from our Pater Familius, a free ebook every month, and the first word on special discounts and Familius news.

Become an Expert

Familius authors and other established writers interested in helping families be happy are invited to join our family and contribute online content. If you have something important to say on the family, join our expert community by applying at:

www.familius.com/apply-to-become-a-familius-expert

Get Bulk Discounts

If you feel a few friends and family might benefit from what you've read, let us know and we'll be happy to provide you with quantity discounts. Simply email us at specialorders@familius.com.

Website: www.familius.com

Facebook: www.facebook.com/paterfamilius

Twitter: @familiustalk, @paterfamilius1

Pinterest: www.pinterest.com/familius

The most important work

you ever do will be within the

walls of your own home.

CPSIA information can be obtained at www.ICGtesting.com
Printed in the USA
BVOW09s0446260214

R5658300001B/R56583PG345906BVX1B/1/P